THE SPELL OF THE RHBU

◆◇◆◇◆◇◆◇◆◇◆◇◆◇◆◇◆◇◆◇◆◇◆◇◆◇◆

Leifr slammed the door behind Raudbjorn and himself. He was in the hall where the mummified dead hung as trophies from the rafters, he saw.

Then, with a final murderous crash and triumphant roar, the pursuing Dokkalfar smashed through the door and charged into the hall. Raudbjorn gave a resounding bellow of defiance, and Leifr shook the imitation sword and opened his mouth to echo the cry. But the words that came from his mouth startled him.

"Komast Undan!"

At the Rhbu words, one of the dead heroes plummeted down, wheeling his sword around his head. Overhead there was a sound of wires snapping, and more dead heroes dropped down to join the fight against the Dokkalfar.

Leifr pointed to the unguarded northwest door, and Raudbjorn reluctantly followed.

By Elizabeth H. Boyer
Published by Ballantine Books:

THE
DRAGON'S CARBUNCLE

Elizabeth H. Boyer

A Del Rey Book

BALLANTINE BOOKS • NEW YORK

A Del Rey Book
Published by Ballantine Books

Copyright © 1990 by Elizabeth H. Boyer

Library of Congress Catalog Card Number: 90-92910

ISBN 0-345-35459-1

Manufactured in the United States of America

First Edition: June 1990

Cover Art by Greg Hildebrandt

Some Hints on Pronunciation

✦✦✦✦✦✦✦✦✦✦✦✦✦✦✦✦✦✦✦✦✦✦✦✦✦✦

Scipling and Alfar words sometimes look forbidding, but most are easy to pronounce, if a few simple rules are observed.

The consonants are mostly like those in English. G is always hard, as in Get or Go. The biggest difference is that J is always pronounced like English Y, as in Yes or midYear. Final -R (as in FridmundR or JolfR) is equivalent to -ER in undER or offER. HL and HR are sounds not found in English. Try sounding H while saying L or R; if you find that difficult, simply skip the H—Sciplings would understand.

Vowels are like those in Italian or Latin generally. A as in bAth or fAther; E as in wEt or wEigh; I as in sIt or machIne; O as in Obey or nOte; U like OO in bOOk or dOOm. AI as in AIsle; EI as in nEIghbor or wEIght; AU like OU in OUt or hOUse. Y is always a vowel and should be pronounced like I above. (The sound in Old Norse was slightly different, but the I sound is close enough.)

Longer words are usually combinations of shorter ones; thus "Thorljotsson" is simply "Thorljot's son" run together without the apostrophe.

Of course, none of this is mandatory in reading the story; any pronunciation that works for the reader is the right one!

Chapter 1

✧✧✧✧✧✧✧✧✧✧✧✧✧✧✧✧✧✧✧✧✧✧✧✧✧✧✧✧✧✧✧✧✧✧✧

Leifr blew a warm cloud of breath on his frost-numbed fingers and slithered to another spying spot behind a snow-rimed skarp. Early spring in this realm was cold and unpredictable, with days of lingering cold as the winter begrudged its gradual yielding to spring. The cold and the reek of the settlement below were not enough to make Leifr forget how hungry he was. The smell reminded him of Gotiskolker's rendering pot on its worst-smelling days, with the bones and hides of dead trolls burbling over a low fire. Djofullhol smelled as if at least half its occupants were avid scavengers and renderers of unsavory things. A sullen cloud of dingy smoke overhung the settlement, rising from squalid huts and the campfires of the indigent clustering around in an encrustation of tents and hovels.

Behind him, Raudbjorn sniffed hopefully, testing the edge of his halberd for sharpness, as if he intended to overwhelm some-one's cooking fire by force, if necessary, to silence the hollow growling in his vast, unprovisioned belly. Starkad waited in the cleft of the ravine below, keeping the horses and the troll-hounds quiet and out of view. Their larger purpose in following Djofull to earth in his own den to retrieve Sorkvir's ashes was tempo-rarily obscured by their preemptive need for nourishment.

Ten days of ill-prepared travel had finally brought them to Djofullhol. Djofull and his fylgjur-wolves could travel through a host of lesser evils with impunity, but three travelers with limited magical skills seemed to draw trolls to the attack, and bands of ragged, desperate scavengers lay in wait for unwary travelers. Perhaps Djofull had alerted them or, perhaps in his passing, he laid traps for those who followed. Crossing running water saved the travelers several times, but usually at the ex-

1

pense of losing Djofull's trail for hours, or sometimes several days. Twice the fylgjur-wolves doubled back on them, but having learned how *Endalaus Daudi* so drastically and permanently reduced their ranks, the wolves were content to menace without directly attacking, while Djofull traveled on ahead. The land itself seemed to have turned against them, denying much natural foraging for food.

A small, untidy settlement had gathered piecemeal around the base of an ancient hill fort. Crowded between the walls of the earthworks, a morass of huts and squalor had formed that rivaled the Thieves' Market of Ulfskrittinn for atmosphere. By day the inhabitants, who could not tolerate light, kept themselves muffled or masked and lurked in the shadows of the overhanging walls. Those day-farers who dwelt by choice or mischance in Djofull's shadow warily plied their trades in the narrow unsavory alleyways of the settlement. Leifr selected their target, a hut standing by itself, away from the protection of Djofullhol. What attracted his eye most were the three scrawny sheep tethered near the door.

Raudbjorn eyed the dispirited creatures, and his tongue rasped his lips. His eyes glittered through narrow slits as he drew his knife from its sheath.

"Raudbjorn get sheep," he rumbled. "Cut throats, not a sound. Raudbjorn quiet, like shadow of death."

Leifr considered the hut a moment and the advancing gloom of twilight. If they waited much longer, the night-farers would be out in full force, too numerous and dangerous for the three of them to challenge. He nodded his head, and Raudbjorn glided away, astonishingly silent for a creature of such vast bulk. Accustomed as he was to Raudbjorn's peculiar and usually silent society, Leifr thought to himself with a wry smile that he was glad that he was not Raudbjorn's prey. Raudbjorn was the most amiable of fellows, even while he was thinking of cutting a throat or cleaving a skull, but Leifr knew from past experience how zealously Raudbjorn dogged the trail of his enemies, intent upon the hunt and inevitable kill.

Shortly Raudbjorn was back with two sheep slung over his shoulders. Retreating to the opposite side of a shallow skerry, where no evil being would dare cross the running water, they built a fire and feasted upon charred, half-raw mutton. The flavor of the tough, stringy meat, dripping with grease, was enhanced by charring and the greatest sauce of all, which was hunger.

They finished their feast about midnight, wiped the grease off their hands, and looked over their weapons before mounting their horses for the short ride to Djofullhol. Mounted and cloaked and hooded, no one would be able to tell them from the nightfarers who now busily and brazenly thronged the settlement. Itinerant warriors and bounty hunters strolled up and down in search of business or pleasure, both of which probably involved killing; the usual tradespeople and carts hawked their wares and fought off the thieves. Travelers, wanderers, outlaws, beggars, all turned and suspiciously scrutinized the three horsemen riding through their midst, but since no overt threat was evident, they allowed the strangers to pass through without challenge.

The path to the fortress wound between the walls of the hill fort ditches, designed originally to confound attackers who got past the outer gate. Now most of the ways were clogged by fallen debris from the earthworks, or the miserable huts of those who hung tenuously upon the fringes of Djofull's favor. The way was marked with rows of stones and posts set up as pointers. On both sides of the rutted road, between the hovels, grew masses of dark foliage where large white blooms perfumed the night air.

"Flowers were the last thing I expected to find here," Leifr muttered, distaste in his tone. Scavengers and beggars and thieves eyed him predatorially, and the scent of the flowers was mixed with a hundred unpleasant stenches that rivaled even the smell of Gotiskolker's rendering pot.

"Those are grofblomur," Starkad said, pleased to be the source of some useful information. "They only bloom where dead men nourish the soil. Or so the old wives say. Now I daresay they don't smell as sweet to you."

Leifr eyed the grofblomur with distaste and retorted, "If that were true, most of Skarpsey would be buried with these flowers. Particularly this place."

Rounding the fifth turn in the path, they came into view of the main hall, its lights lowering sullenly in the silvery twilight.

A tremendous ruin formed the bulk of the fortress, a ruin mainly roofless and crumbling, like a noble skull now harboring only worms and maggots.

Leifr and Starkad crouched to watch the Dokkalfar coming in and out, going about their business as day-farers would in the daytime. There seemed to be no guards lurking around, which was another puzzling circumstance. Vaguely uneasy, Leifr watched the shadowy scene before him, striving to think of a plan of attack, but the sickly sweet smell of the grave flowers seemed to be cloying his wits.

Starkad nudged him. "We could ride right up to the door," he whispered in a voice that shook with excitement. "I never dreamed it would be this easy. Djofull must be lazy and over-confident."

"Or he knows no one in their right senses would dare walk into his fortress," Leifr said.

"Come on, here's our chance!" Silently Leifr pointed to a file of perhaps a dozen horsemen entering the main portal. Joining their number was an easy matter, and, after receiving a sharp poke in the back from Starkad, Leifr remembered to lower his head and adopt a wary, hunched posture to match those around him. His eyes hastily scanned his surroundings, but even such a cursory scrutiny was sufficient to impress him with the grandeur of Djofullhol. Inside the main portal was a courtyard open to the sky a hundred feet above, with galleries and stairways climbing the cliffs on all sides. Red lights winked through small openings, as if dozens of eyes peered down upon the minute scuttlings of the Dokkalfar going in and out. The courtyard shadows were alive with lurking forms that resolved themselves into knots of Dokkalfar hurrying back and forth with silent purpose. Others crouched indistinct against the walls, with an occasional red flicker of a watchful eye that filled Leifr with unease. Off to one side and down a cavernous tunnel came the smells and sounds of stabled horses. Ahead lay a massive flight of stairs, with a balustrade formed to resemble dragons and snakes and runes. At the top of the stairs stood a pair of towering doors covered with beaten copper that gleamed in the light of the torches held by two bearers. From within came the sounds of drinking and feasting and merrymaking, sounds that reminded Leifr of the hardships he had endured since leaving Dallir.

"Djofull seems to have set himself up well here," Starkad observed, echoing Leifr's thoughts. "Wizards aren't usually able to profit so grandly by their powers."

"Perhaps there was a benefactor once," Leifr replied, thinking of Ulfskrittinn, "and Djofull killed him and changed the name of the place. Those who harbor wizards often come to a bad end, it seems."

"I hope that doesn't apply to Thurid and us," Starkad answered nervously.

A ragged thrall scuttled forward officiously, taking hold of Jolfr's rein and making impatient motions for them to dismount. The noises the wretch uttered were meaningless, until Leifr realized that the fellow's tongue had been removed at some point in his career. Since his only objective seemed to be the harmless stabling of their horses, Leifr dismounted and permitted the thrall to lead the horses away. The troll-hounds, Kraftig, Frimodig, and Farlig, clung to Leifr's heels, whining uneasily and gazing up at him hopefully with their golden eyes.

"No, you must stay and protect the horses," he said to them. Their tails drooped in dismay, but they obediently trotted after the horses and the hostler. Uneasily Leifr made note of where the beasts were taken, in case a hasty retrieval became necessary.

Other travelers were leaving their horses and entering the main hall, without glancing at the new arrivals, as if strangers were a matter of course in Djofullhol. Deciding quickly to play the part completely, Leifr led the way up the stairs to the hall, where he supposed the three of them would be quickly lost among the merrymakers.

Inside, he found all as he had suspected. The hall was brightly lit by Dokkalfar standards, which meant a dull red glow that would hurt nobody's eyes nor wither unprotected skin. The long table and benches in the center of the room were crowded with the figures of men feasting and drinking in a happy uproar of voices lifted in bantering shouts and song, nearly drowning the music of the harper in the corner. The guests were not all Dokkalfar, Leifr was surprised to see, as he recognized the garb of

Ljosalfar and dwarfs and burly Norskur among their number.

"I hadn't suspected Djofull of keeping such a hospitable board," Starkad whispered. "Another sign he's going soft."

As they crept along the shadowy wall, no one seemed to notice them. Starkad pointed toward a doorway leading into the interior of the fortress. A subdued light filtered into the dark hallway beyond, emanating from a room at the far end, where a massive door stood partially ajar, as if left open by accident. The corridor was unpopulated and dusty underfoot. On either side gaped empty doorways, like black maws, smelling of dank earth and rot.

Leifr crept nearer, flattened himself against the wall, and risked a glance into the room. From that much he could tell it was uninhabited and was a workroom of some evil sort. A low fire burning on the hearth provided the light. Bottles, flasks, and crocks lined the walls on cluttered, dusty shelves, where unfamiliar plant fibers were stuffed in untidy handfuls wherever they would stay. Near the hearth stood a large caldron of water. Small cages held little animals such as rats and squirrels and rabbits. Charred bones on the hearth indicated that their fate was not to be a kindly one, although their entrails might possibly tell a clever diviner the shape of the future.

In the center of the room stood a battered table with no object on it save a small pouch. Starkad drew a hissing breath.

"The ashes!" he whispered. "This is going to be easy!"

Leifr reached out to clamp a restraining hand upon his arm, but he glided out of reach.

"Starkad! Don't be a fool! It's a trap!" he cried. "Can't you see this has all been too easy?"

Leifr seized him just as his hands closed upon the bag—closed upon it and passed through. The illusion exploded in their faces, and the ensuing thunderbolt flung both of them backward into Raudbjorn, who collapsed with a grunt. Leifr leaped to his feet, smelling the dank smell of ice magic in the roiling clouds of dust and mist filling the room. His face and hands were rimed with frost crystals, so deadly cold that it took his breath away until he could brush them off his flesh. Starkad sprawled on the ground, pale and stunned, gasping for breath. Raudbjorn lurched to his feet. Dragging Starkad's dead weight after him, he plunged toward the hallway, pushing Leifr ahead, still half deaf from the explosion and gasping in the icy air.

Revived by both the fresher air in the passageway and the warning shouts of approaching Dokkalfar, Leifr led their desperate dash into the main hall, hoping to plead for the protection offered to all wayfaring guests of whatever persuasion. The great outer doors into the courtyard were even then swinging shut, closing with a thunderous crash that echoed throughout the hall. Leifr halted, dismayed, then he turned his attention to the other guests. Gazing around at the scene before him, he stood frozen by amazement and horror.

Instead of the merry roisterers crowding around the tables and benches, the jolly assembly was now silent—silent as only death can be silent. One and all, they dangled in midair, suspended from the roof beams by wires in lifelike poses, still clutching their weapons as they must have done moments before their deaths. Now they were dried and stuffed trophies of Djofull's conquests. The jolly scene of eating, drinking, and singing was only another of Djofull's illusions.

Leifr wheeled around toward the only escape. The doorway was already blocked by a wall of Dokkalfar, helmed with dark metal, their ornaments fashioned into shapes of bats and skulls and spiders, and their broadaxes and swords gleaming with recent honings.

Leifr took a step forward, unsheathing his sword, and Raudbjorn also crowded forward with his halberd cocked in readiness at a murderous angle behind his ear. The eight or nine Dokkalfar also surged forward with a bloodthirsty growl, hoisting their savage weapons. For a long moment, the two sides measured each other, evaluating the certain losses in the coming conflict.

From their rear a voice rebuked them, and the Dokkalfar slunk aside to allow the speaker to pass. It was Djofull in his chair, being borne along by two Norskur almost as large as Raudbjorn and rather more slack in expression. They put down the chair and Djofull reached for his staff and rose to his feet.

"Scipling, you have the rare gift for enlisting against hopeless causes," he greeted Leifr. "I knew I could trust you faithfully to sniff out my footsteps to Djofullhol, where I could deal with you most competently. When one travels, one must leave behind so many needful implements and facilities."

"We'll fight for what we've come for," Leifr replied grimly. "We want those ashes you stole."

Djofull shook his head. "And you knowing that all I need do is summon an influence to crush the life out of you, as I nearly did at Fangelsi?" He raised his single living hand, which now sported a black hole burned through to the bone. "But for this distraction, I would have done so. The weakness of flesh that we both share saved you then, but what will save you now, Scipling?"

"Only this," Leifr replied, raising his sword. "Who wishes to be the first to taste everlasting death?"

The warriors shifted forward a pace, thirsting for the opportunity to wreak some havoc. Djofull raised his hand, halting them. He gestured to include the entire dusty hall and its macabre decorations swinging gracefully above.

"Slaughter and mayhem are not my way. You've seen my old friends. I've preserved them the way I remember them best, fighting for their lives. In vain, I might add." His eyes glowed with the pride of his accomplishment. "My friends," he continued in the same dry, congenial tone, "there is no hope for your escape. Surely you wish to be remembered by future generations in your present youthful strength. I can do nothing with the heaps of scraps left by these slaughterers."

His good hand sketched an airy gesture toward the Dokkalfar, who grinned at the compliment. Leifr was stepping forward with an angry retort on his lips, but Djofull's gesture cast a filmy substance into the air over their heads. It settled like cobwebs, feeling light and sticky on Leifr's hands and face, but as he pawed at it, the fibers instantly thickened to the meshes of a heavy net. Raudbjorn roared with fury, thrashing around until he was too entangled to do anything but fall over, drawing Leifr and Starkad helplessly after him in a tangled cursing heap. The more they struggled, the tighter and heavier the net became, until no one could move a hand or a foot. Raudbjorn continued his rumbling, ferocious snarling, like a captured bear.

Djofull motioned to the captain of his guards, who divested

the captives of their weapons, reaching through the net as if it did not exist for him.

"Now we have nearly all the tokens in the game." Djofull chuckled, making a summoning gesture. "When I get Heldur's blue orb, I shall be at last content."

"You'll never get it away from the Wizards' Guild," Leifr grunted, relaxing the struggles that did nothing except to tighten Djofull's meshes.

"With Sorkvir's aid I shall. Not to mention Gedvondur's hand, now restored to my rightful possession."

A tapestry was thrown aside and Svanlaug stepped into view, holding Gedvondur in a net of the same manufacture as Djofull's, while Gedvondur struggled angrily like a spider in a web. Gedvondur threw up clouds of emotions as a smoke screen, visiting waves of fear upon the attending Dokkalfar, a fit of rage, and even a fit of laughter, which Djofull contemptuously waved away.

"I have him, Meistari," Svanlaug said with a treacherous smile, coming forward to deliver Gedvondur to Djofull, who held him up a moment like a fisherman examining a particularly fine fish.

"Come, Gedvondur!" Djofull said impatiently. "Enough of this frivolity! You know you're nothing without me."

Gedvondur answered with a rude gesture. Djofull dropped him into a carved box and fastened the lid securely.

"Thank you," he said to Svanlaug. "We'll wait until he cools down before trying to reason with him."

"Is there any sense in keeping these others alive?" Svanlaug inquired pleasantly. "Without their weapons, they're not worth much. I daresay Sorkvir, when you've restored him, would like to see the Scipling once more, and this Villimadur who deserted him. It could be more amusing than stuffing them for the main hall."

Djofull tapped one finger on the arm of his chair and chuckled darkly. "Bloodthirsty, are you? It might be amusing to save them awhile yet. I would like to see their faces when Sorkvir stands before them, restored to all his former power and more besides."

"I look forward with awe to standing in the presence of such a great one," Svanlaug said reverently. "Though it is more inspiring to be here as acolyte with his master in power. You, who know the secrets for returning him from Hel, are surely greater than even one who has seen Hela and learned her secrets."

Djofull waved one hand in dismissal of her praise, but his eyes glowed with pride. "It is I who am Master now," he said arrogantly. "It was I who killed him the first time and brought him back from Hel, so it is I who have the greater power now." He tapped on the lid of Gedvondur's box, eliciting an angry scuffling and scratching from within. "And now I have more power at my disposal. The powers of the Ljosalfar themselves shall be mine to use against them. Ritari," he snapped to the captain of the guards, "bring the prisoners to the pit."

The three captives were dragged from the Hall of Dead Warriors and into the dark passage beyond, with Raudbjorn still snarling horrible threats and biting at the net with his teeth. Leifr was able to observe that it was toward Djofull's laboratory they were being hauled. Slippery stone steps led downward, plummeting almost as low as Leifr's spirits. Their descent ended at the edge of a dark pit, where a clammy breath bespoke a long drop to destruction below. Two of the guards seized Leifr, one on each side, and dragged him forward. He put up a fierce battle despite the stricture of the net, but they succeeded in forcing him over the edge. Scarcely enough time passed for him to come to grips with the idea that he was surely going to die, when he landed on his back in soft sand with a breathtaking wallop. Cursing the Dokkalfar gave him a great deal of satisfaction, augmented by deep relief to discover that he was still alive. The net had vanished without a trace. As he was marveling at its disappearance, Raudbjorn came down, still spewing furious roars of rage, and Leifr took care not to be where the thief-taker landed. Starkad followed swiftly, amid a hail of rocks and earth. He sat up in the sand, feeling for broken bones.

"Now we're having an adventure," he said, a little breathlessly. "You're right, it's not meant to be fun."

The Dokkalfar leaned over the edge above with their torches and jeered at their prisoners awhile before shambling away with a sinister rattling of the bone and teeth trophies adorning their vestments. The captives were left completely in the dark. Still snarling threats, Raudbjorn clawed his way around the pit. Leifr followed cautiously, groping along the wall, which was rock oozing with slime and the sort of nasty fungus that grows without light and glows softly in the dark.

"What happened to the nets? Where are you, Leifr?" Starkad demanded. "Leifr, you're not leaving me here!"

"Hush, Starkad! Can't you see there's noplace to go?"

"I can't see anything," Starkad retorted, "but I don't think this is an ordinary hole in the ground. I feel influences all around us."

Just as Leifr thought he had surely made his way completely around his dungeon, Raudbjorn tripped over something under his feet, scattering brittle pieces. Cautiously Leifr stooped and felt around, discerning an array of curiously shaped sticks and rags. When his searching fingers encountered a round hard globe with holes in it, he leaped back with a shuddering yell of revulsion.

"A skeleton!" Hastily he recited the words and made the gestures for warding off evil draugar. He'd had no idea he was plundering around among the bones of a skeleton, but he had a very clear idea of the penalties for such rude desecration of the resting places of the dead.

Raudbjorn groaned and removed himself to the farthest extreme of the dungeon away from the bones and sat down with a weary sigh, like that of a tired horse. He made no sound of reproach, but Leifr was tortured by remorse for leading them into such a situation. He paced back and forth, ten paces each way, gazing up at the circle of flickering light above and racking his brains.

"This isn't quite right," Starkad muttered several times. "There's something wrong with this place."

Leifr snapped, "The worst thing about it is that we're inside it and we want out. What could be more natural?"

"Those nets," Starkad went on. "They vanished. Real nets would not have disappeared. Djofull is using mind-magic on us. I wouldn't be surprised if this pit was illusion, something we've been forced to believe. A trick like this could easily fool a person with little or no magical experience. I have little, and you and Raudbjorn have none.''

Leifr snorted. ''Real or not real, it's doing the job, isn't it? We're inside and can't get out. I can't believe this is nothing but my own imagination.''

''It's not. It's Djofull's, perhaps, and we're trapped in it, because we don't know how to get out. Like the nets. When the need for them was gone, Djofull made them disappear. I'll wager that we're not in a pit at all.''

Leifr felt the oozing walls and tried to peer through the darkness. His eyes were adjusting somewhat, and enough faint light from above trickled down that he was barely able to discern Starkad in the center of the pit, as a dark lump of shadow.

''This seems real enough to me,'' he grunted.

''It is real enough, and that's why we're trapped here.''

''So how do we get out of it? Tell it we don't believe in it anymore? I can't see that working.''

''No, we need a counterspell.''

''Fine. All we need is a counterspell. Are you a wizard? I'm certainly not, and neither is Raudbjorn.''

''What about that carbuncle you carry? The one Djofull doesn't dare touch?''

Leifr clutched the carbuncle and felt an answering warmth. ''I can't work that sort of magic,'' he said uneasily.

''You won't be able to do anything after you're dead,'' Starkad pointed out. ''You don't know how lucky you are to have a carbuncle like that given to you by its former owner. I've got only a grain of magic myself, so I'll never amount to much as a magician. But you could, Leifr. Hogni says that stone is the size of a bird's egg. Hogni says it's lucky to get one the size of a pea. What he wouldn't give for a carbuncle the size of that one.''

''I wish he had it, and I wish he were here instead of me,'' Leifr answered gloomily. ''I don't dare put that stone underneath my skin. Who knows what it would do to a Scipling?''

''Could it be worse than what Sorkvir will do?'' Starkad asked. ''You and that carbuncle destroyed him once. He's not going to forgive that very easily.''

Starkad's words hung in the darkness a long time as Leifr pondered the risks. At last he felt for the small knife he wore in his belt as his primary eating tool. The Dokkalfar hadn't bothered to take away such a toothpick; had he tried to menace anyone with it, they would only laugh at such a weapon in the hands of a warrior. He touched it against the flesh of his forearm experimentally, then hastily thrust it back into his belt pouch.

"A Scipling has no need of borrowed courage," he said harshly. "I'll take my chances with my own wits and strength a long time before I resort to Fridmarr's help."

He tried to avoid the nagging worry that, by making such a decision, he was asking for serious consequences. He could almost hear Fridmarr's impatient, know-it-all voice saying as much. Several times he removed his knife, considering where he would insert the carbuncle, but each time his nerve quickly failed him. The rest of the night must have passed and perhaps the next day, all without incident save three bombardments of stale black bread from above, and a wooden flask of water. Not once did the cold reality of the pit falter. Surely Starkad was wrong.

Starkad's suspicions, however, came to awful fruition the next day, when the walls of the pit suddenly shimmered and dissolved around the captives, while Raudbjorn was in the midst of a nap and Leifr was again contemplating Fridmarr's carbuncle. It sparkled warningly, giving him a tingle of danger as the pit disappeared. Raudbjorn awoke with a snort, and they found themselves standing in Djofull's laboratory, confronting Djofull himself, who sat in a chair formed of human bones and knobbed with skulls. Behind him stood Svanlaug in a haughty pose, eyeing the captives with a contemptuous smile.

"I hope you're enjoying your visit thus far," Djofull said with an evil leer. "I fear the most pleasant part is over, however. It's time we began our dealings. You're come at just the right moment. I'm in need of volunteers to help restore Sorkvir to life, and my acolyte Svanlaug has convinced me that you have powers that I shall find useful. Using a Scipling will be a novel approach, but, I hope, an effective one."

"There is nothing I have to offer you," Leifr snarled, after exchanging a furious glower with Svanlaug. "If you believe Svanlaug, you believe a lying, selfish traitor."

"You needn't offer," Djofull replied. "I shall take what I require, whether you offer it or not."

Chapter 2

❖❖❖❖❖❖❖❖❖❖❖❖❖❖❖❖❖❖❖❖❖❖❖❖❖❖❖❖❖❖

A five-pointed star was marked in the tile of the floor, with a pillar at each point and an altar-shaped stone in the center. A smoldering fire in a brazier burned in the center, and five other braziers waited at the points, laden with heaps of strong-smelling herbs. The entire scene filled Leifr with superstitious uneasiness, making his flesh crawl as he sensed the lurking of an influence of such evil power that his own powers of resistance withered into puny tatters of spreading fear. Two Dokkalfar dragged Leifr toward the Pentacle at Djofull's direction and tied him securely to one of the pillars, facing the center. They brought out Starkad next, then Raudbjorn, flexing his muscles and huffing furiously. It required four of them to haul him where Djofull commanded, and they tied each leg separately to the pillar and bound his wrists together tightly behind it. Even then he growled and strained with menacing creaking sounds from the ropes and the pillar.

Two dark-cloaked Dokkalfar with staffs took the other two positions on the points of the Pentacle, and Djofull led the sixth to the center stone, an individual who appeared raddled by the scars of many battles and was as unwholesome in appearance as Djofull himself. Leifr recognized the signs of dangerous tampering with unknown substances and spells, which left their marks on the person foolish enough to seek the forbidden knowledge. The third Dokkalfar lay down upon the altar, half hidden in the pungent smoke that arose from the brazier. Leifr guessed that the three Dokkalfar were acolytes or assistants to Djofull, judging by the calm and knowing manner in which they took their positions with no show of resistance.

Djofull surveyed the scene as his victims and assistants took

15

their positions. Then he lit the fires at the points of the Pentacle, lighting the one behind Leifr last.

"You are privileged to be part of the finest ritual ever perfected by the powers of necromancy," he said with cold pride. "A greater privilege than a Scipling deserves, but the working of this enchantment requires life forces, and by using the three of you I endanger three less Dokkalfar. The last time I brought Sorkvir back from Hel, the goddess required four other lives in exchange."

"So you intend to murder us," Leifr said.

"Something can't be taken from Hela without giving more in return," Djofull answered. "There's nothing more powerful than the ritual releasing of a life force. If you are lucky, I will spare you for the last, so you can stand face to face with Sorkvir again. Last time was very difficult. I admit, using four lives was shoddy work on my part. But one never knows how this spell will progress, once it is started. One life or ten lives for Sorkvir—the price must be paid."

"I'd rather die fighting for my life, instead of expiring like a goat with its throat cut," Leifr snarled, testing the tightness of his bonds and finding them tighter for the testing.

"A pity. You should have known not to throw your lot in with scavengers and maladroit wizards. The day you met Fridmarr was the day your doom began to gather."

Djofull next beckoned for the small casket containing Gedvondur's hand, and Svanlaug brought it forward. He made some signs and opened it warily, lifting out Gedvondur, still netted like a fish and struggling furiously.

"Come now, that's not necessary," Djofull said. "What power you lend me won't have to be taken from your friends, if you value them as such."

He sketched a small star on the floor and placed Gedvondur's hand at the center, where it crouched resentfully. Djofull then knelt within the star to work his spell, rolling carven rune sticks back and forth on the earth, repeating the words that would summon Sorkvir from death's realm. Djofull's acolytes stood firm in the gusts of influences that buffeted the chamber, driving the smoke in all directions. It burned and blinded Leifr's eyes with its awful reek, which made him feel drugged and ill. Djofull's chanting rang insistently in his ears with its senseless cadence drawing at him with unmistakable power. The flames in the braziers leaped higher, but the radiation from them was deathly cold, and their color was the deadly pale hue of Hel's realm. Such a cold and menacing presence filled the chamber that Leifr almost feared to breathe, lest he betray his life to the watchful and jealous entity that had been summoned.

"Hela, goddess of the dead, ruler of Hel! I have summoned you!" Djofull cried out in a sudden loud voice.

The smoke and the pale fire swirled, combining in the misty shape of a woman hovering over the central altar. Her hair hung long and lank, and her face was a cruel death mask, with sunken dark pits for eyes.

"I have come to bargain with you for Sorkvir," Djofull continued. "Take what lives you wish for recompense."

The smoke and flames hissed menacingly, and from the hissing came the words "You bargain too often, Djofull. Let me keep what is rightfully mine. I was promised all creatures slain by the sword of Endless Death."

"I have the power from the Dokkur Lavardur," Djofull replied. "You must yield up to me what I demand. Give back Sorkvir and take these lesser lives."

"It is not enough," Hela sneered, turning away and dissolving into mist and darkness.

Djofull reached for a sack with its mouth bound and unwrapped the binding.

"I have for you a particular gift, goddess," he called. "See if this feeds your power."

He drew a small creature from the bag, a gray-furred cat. In his other hand he held a short sharp knife.

Leifr's heart stood still a moment, then he roared, "Ljosa! Stop! Don't kill that cat!" He lunged against his bindings, ignoring the pain of the tightening knots, feeling the thongs stretching in protest. The pillar itself rocked slightly on its base.

The Hel flames surged, and Hela's face reappeared, with eyes glowing venomously. Djofull gripped the struggling cat with both hands, receiving some vigorous clawmarks in the process, as he tried to bring his knife into play.

With a bound, Gedvondur's hand climbed up his robe like a

scuttling spider, and Djofull was forced to free one hand in order to fend Gedvondur away from his throat.

As he was struggling and cursing, the ashes of Sorkvir in the small brazier suddenly rose in a dusty column, turning this way and that like an inquisitive snake. Djofull ceased his endeavors with the cat and crouched motionless as the column of ash glided stealthily from the brazier. With one hand raised in a fending-off gesture, he rebuffed the ashes when they drifted toward him, impelling them instead toward the central altar. With the same hand Djofull motioned for stillness, and Leifr halted his straining and swearing. Even Gedvondur froze, his fingers clutching Djofull's shoulder.

With shrinking horror, Leifr watched as the ashes hovered a moment over the face of the man lying there in drugged stupor. Then the ashes funneled themselves into the mouth and nose of the helpless victim, who started to resist Sorkvir's invasion by thrashing and choking, but Djofull's assistants glided forward warily and pinned him down by the arms and legs. The struggles soon weakened as the ashes diminished in the brazier. The assistants stepped back expectantly when the last of the ashes had vanished into their captive. Abruptly the pale Hel flames vanished, and the powerful swirling of influences left the chamber in sudden stillness.

Djofull hastily stuffed the cat into the bag and tied the neck shut. He grabbed Gedvondur and dropped him back into his box. Cautiously he approached the central altar.

"Sorkvir!" he ordered. "Awaken! Arise! Hela has freed you once again."

The body on the altar stirred, and a hand reached out experimentally, touching the stone, the coarse wool of the cloak, and the wood of Djofull's staff. Slowly he sat up, facing Leifr, who had no doubt that the creature now inhabiting that flesh was none other than Sorkvir. The revenant flexed his hands and felt his face and tentatively put his feet to the floor and stood up. When the creature spoke, his convictions were confirmed. It was the voice of Sorkvir who said, "Old Ostjorn? Is this the best you could do for me, Djofull?"

"I've never brought you back to life from nothing but ashes," Djofull replied testily. "You've always left me something to work with before, shreds and bones I could put together, at least. You shouldn't complain at starting over in a relatively new body. It's an opportunity no one else gets. I suppose you would have preferred the Scipling, but I thought it was dangerous enough using another Dokkalfar. Not enough is known about Sciplings, and he's still got that carbuncle of Fridmarr's about him.''

Sorkvir's eyes bored into Leifr and his voice throbbed with the menace of the bear form he had once taken. "It will take more than Fridmarr's carbuncle to protect you now, Scipling. You will wish you had died in that battle in the hall of the grindstone.''

"If the Norns decide to cut the thread of my life now, then I can do nothing about it,'' Leifr replied. "But perhaps that time is not now, and you can do nothing about it, either.''

"Much has been lost because of you,'' Sorkvir sneered, his new face already settling into the old evil lines. "Not merely Gliru-hals and the Pentacle. The Ljosalfar have lost their fear and respect for the name of Sorkvir. They will be punished heavily because of your interference, Scipling. I doubt your friends will remember you kindly after I am done scourging their land.''

"It remains to be seen, does it not?'' Leifr answered.

Svanlaug glided forward, obtruding herself into Sorkvir's notice. He turned sharply to stare at her, then at Djofull.

"Who is this woman?'' he demanded. "I've no use for Hela's acolytes, and you'd better not have either. She played no part in my restoration, did she?''

"I am Svanlaug and no acolyte of anyone's, save perhaps Djofull himself,'' she answered. "It was the desire of my heart to speak to you when you were restored, and to plead my cause to you.''

"I've no use for your causes,'' Sorkvir retorted furiously. "Djofull! You haven't explained why this woman is here and not as a captive. We never allowed anyone from the outside to see our work and know our secrets. I could accuse you of treason, Djofull!''

"Do it then, and see where it gets you. No one else knows how to bring you back from Hel. Svanlaug has been useful in bringing these captives to us. With that Rhbu sword in our possession, we can destroy the last three Rhbus. The oldest one who calls himself Malasteinn sharpens that sword. We can use it to summon him, and once we've got him, Gullskeggi and the other one won't be long in following. Do you not relish the thought of a world where Rhbu magic no longer exists? If the Wizards' Guild only knew what they were rejecting by calling Thurid into their Inquisition. Now I've got *Endalaus Daudi*, and we'll use it to get rid of the last of the Rhbus.''

Sorkvir shook his head and took a few impatient steps, rather awkwardly in an unaccustomed body. ''I took that sword from Bodmarr, and I consider it mine. I don't intend to use it for your purposes, especially if they've been put into your ear by that Dokkalfar witch. You'd do better to worry about that wizard Thurid. He's got enough of the knowledge to make himself into a Rhbu one day, if we don't stop him.''

''The Wizards' Guild is taking care of Thurid. He's too deviant for their rules.''

Sorkvir uttered a snort of mirth. ''Clever of them. But you're foolish to leave his destruction to them. We ought to go after him and the Inquisitors and make sure of the result we want, rather than haring off in search of the Rhbus. We haven't been able to find them before. Don't think to conceal the issue, Djofull. I don't trust this woman. She's come here to steal knowledge.''

''Indeed, I did not,'' Svanlaug protested. ''I came upon these brigands while they were stealing your ashes from Djofull's emissaries. I pretended to assist these thieves, with the intention of leading them into your hands. Have I not been successful? Am I not a Dokkalfar?''

Sorkvir turned away from her abruptly without answering her directly. ''I don't trust her. Get rid of her, Djofull. Then let's go after the Inquisitors before they get too far on their way with Thurid's destruction at the Guildhall.''

''As long as this fortress bears my name, I'll decide which of our guests to kill and which to save,'' Djofull replied coldly. ''Perhaps you've lost some of your nerve on this last trip to Hel. Hela wasn't very willing to let you go, and might not have, but for the Scipling and the cat fylgja. His rage quite appeased her taste for living spirit and emotion. The dead she takes are of no real use to her, once they are dead. It was Svanlaug who told me who the cat fylgja really is. Hroaldsdottir, who helped destroy you at Hjaldrshol.''

Leifr spared Svanlaug a deadly stare, which she pretended to ignore.

''A treacherous snake,'' Sorkvir observed with contempt. ''If she deceives them, she will deceive us—as she has already deceived you with her blandishments.''

''I am not deceived,'' Djofull retorted. ''She is too small and weak to deceive me for long. Save your wrath for your enemies the Ljosalfar and these enemies here before you. I've never known you to take such a hasty and ill-conceived dislike to someone before, old friend. She has brought that Rhbu sword into our hands.''

''Don't call me your old friend,'' Sorkvir snarled. ''That sword should be destroyed before it causes further mischief. Hela was angry at sending me back, when she had been promised all that the Rhbu sword touches. Even the Dokkur Lavardur can't break promises to Hela.''

''It was a Rhbu promise, when they made that sword,'' Djofull retorted. ''We're not obliged to uphold it, if we have the way for getting around it.''

''You don't know Hela as I do,'' Sorkvir answered bitterly, turning to stalk away, still lurching in the unaccustomed body. He glanced sideways at Leifr. ''You I'll deal with later. Don't think that I've forgotten a single one of your offenses against me.''

When he was gone, Leifr said to Svanlaug, ''You failed to impress him, witch. All your lying and posing was in vain, it seems. You're going to be thrown out on your own again. We should have left you to die when we found you.''

Svanlaug tossed her head arrogantly. ''He may change his mind when he sees what good fortune I shall bring to Djofull, with the aid of that sword of yours. The destruction of the last three Rhbu wizards is only one of my schemes.''

''You seem to have forgotten your brother rather quickly,'' Leifr said acidly. ''You told me once that all you wanted was revenge for his death upon his killers—Djofull and Sorkvir.''

Svanlaug blanched slightly, but she held her head up proudly, her eyes flashing. "Revenge won't bring him back," she said somewhat unsteadily. "He was unwise in angering the great ones against him. My way is to ally myself where the greatest strength lies, and my purposes will be realized in a roundabout manner."

Djofull eyed Svanlaug with a glinting stare. "I've killed your brother, have I? What did he do to deserve my personal enmity?"

"He was Reidur Rekjasson," Svanlaug replied in a stiff tone. "One of those who thought to oppose you in the matter of sharing some of your knowledge with the lesser magicians. He imagined himself to be a promising rival to you one day. But it was not meant to happen."

"Indeed it was not. I remember him. He needn't have died, if he had only been more reasonable when I made requests of him. Are you certain you bear me no grudge?"

"Certain," Svanlaug answered steadily. "His ways and my ways are very different. I seek to buy knowledge, as a reward for being useful to your cause. This Rhbu sword will be the instrument that brings the last of the Rhbus into your hands, or I will suffer the consequences myself."

"You're either very foolhardy, or very brave," Djofull mused, his eyes still hooded. "You are staking your life on whatever plan you have in mind. It will go well for you only as long as you suit my purposes. I only hope that Sorkvir soon comes to share my opinion about the sword."

Svanlaug nodded toward the prisoners. "What about these?"

"There's no use for them. They will be destroyed."

"I daresay Sorkvir will not agree. They could be used as bait in a trap for Thurid and the Inquisitors."

"Bah on the Inquisitors! They'll have nothing when the Rhbus and their insidious knowledge are gone." He scowled sourly in the direction Sorkvir had taken, then turned his scowl upon Leifr. "There's no sense in enraging Sorkvir any further by killing them now. Take them back to the pit," he commanded his acolytes, starting to stalk away. Glancing at Svanlaug, he said, "You'd better stay out of his sight. Your presence here is almost more trouble than it's worth."

It was a comment that afforded Leifr some satisfaction as he sat in the clammy pit, musing upon what he had witnessed. Starkad was shaken, but he recovered quickly, and Raudbjorn still simmered and growled at the notion that Djofull would have killed them all in exchange for Sorkvir. Leifr thought about Ljosa and suffered, wondering what Djofull intended to do with her. After his ordeal, his strength felt sapped, as if something vital had been taken from him in Hela's Pentacle, and it was a bitter thought to think that his fiery human emotion had caused Hela to release Sorkvir. At least their lives had been spared, except for the unfortunate Ostjorn, who would have been better off peacefully dead than to be the bodily vehicle for the unhallowed essence of Sorkvir.

Mistrusting Djofull perhaps, Sorkvir ordered the three prisoners moved to different quarters, adjacent to the chamber he used for his laboratory. There were more cages of small hapless beasts here, awaiting an uncertain fate, and the prisoners were put into heavily barred cells that represented the largest of these cages.

Djofull was enraged by this apparent lack of trust, and the two wizards frequently quarreled ferociously, but Sorkvir had put wards on the door against Djofull. What the prisoners heard was the crackling of contrary spells outside and the voices of the wizards reviling each other.

Sorkvir was in too black a humor even to taunt Leifr with his predicament; he appeared only briefly, always radiating cold fury, to snatch some substances hastily from his shelves or from hooks on the walls. His new body seemed to require certain adjustments or preservatives. Several times he drank down large quantities of some vile-looking dark fluid, then he examined his fingers and flexed them, waggling his knee and elbow joints experimentally. Ostjorn had been a sallow, cadaverous-looking individual with a sharp-pointed black beard, and Sorkvir's invasion had done nothing to improve his appearance. His facial skin had drawn tight, like that of a corpse, and the color was deathly pale. Sorkvir implanted his collection of carbuncles, carving various seams around his face and arms, wounds that oozed no blood except the black fluid. Some of the carbuncles created what appeared to be blackened, burned splotches under the skin.

Not many days passed before Sorkvir seemed to be satisfied with himself and turned his attention to other matters, of which Leifr was the foremost. Without betraying his secret intentions to him, Sorkvir was preparing a course of action with Leifr as a reluctant participant.

"We are going on a journey, you and I," Sorkvir informed him through the bars. "You've always wanted to see the Wizards' Guildhall, I daresay. This will be your opportunity—your last opportunity to do anything, if you don't obey my instructions exactly."

"Do you believe you can force me to betray Thurid?" Leifr asked disdainfully. "You'd do better to try deceiving him yourself."

"You should be quite willing, when you see the stakes I have in mind." He lifted a cage from the floor and set it on the table. Through its bars a gray cat peered out wildly, thrusting out a paw in futile rage to claw at the cage.

"Do what I ask, and I'll restore her true form."

"For what purpose? You don't intend to let us live."

"Now that I have the sword, do I need to kill you? What harm can a Scipling and a Ljosalfar woman do to me without an extraordinary weapon?"

"What harm would it do you to kill us? Or do you expect me to believe you've suddenly turned benevolent? It won't work, Sorkvir. I won't believe anything you say."

"A good answer. The one I expected. You might have pretended to believe me, to see where it would have got you. Nothing is more blunt and forthright than a Scipling. Or stupid, whichever word you prefer."

"What's your next plan, since that one failed?"

"I shall point out to you that Thurid will have a fighting chance to save his powers, if you help me get him away from the Wizards' Guild. It's something we both want, do we not? Neither of us can do it alone."

Leifr was forced to consider. "But you want to destroy him, before he becomes a Rhbu himself. I won't save him just to bring him into a trap of your making."

"Then the Fire Wizards will destroy him. If you bring him to me, there's a chance that he will defeat me. What chance does he have against the Fire Wizards?''

"He will at least survive, and possibly come out as good as any of them. You want to kill him, completely."

"It makes no difference if they allow him to be nothing but a mediocre Fire Wizard. The Guild is full of them. It's the Rhbu wizard that can challenge me and possibly win."

"Then let the Guild destroy the only wizard than can defeat you. It makes no sense to bring him out."

"True, I could do that. But perhaps those Fire Wizards will learn something from him. His Rhbu magic could pollute the lot of them, and I'd have over a hundred Rhbu wizards instead of just one. Which way do you want to gamble with Thurid's life, Scipling?"

Leifr had no ready answer, and Sorkvir laughed harshly. He patted Ljosa's cage, and her paw shot out with razor claws, etching four black trails across his hand, which he did not seem to feel.

"If you say you'll obey me, Scipling, I'll restore the girl at once. I have no grudge against her."

"But you do against me," Leifr said. "Whatever the outcome of this venture, I'll lose, unless Thurid is able to destroy you. I doubt if I'll get a second chance at you with *Endalaus Daudi*."

"No, you won't. Your fate will be in Thurid's hands. And you have that carbuncle of Fridmarr's yet. You have a chance of escaping, Scipling. Not a very good chance, and I'll do everything I can to keep that chance very small. I want Thurid from the Guild, and I'm willing to run the risks involved in dealing with him and you."

"And if I do nothing—" Leifr stopped to ponder.

"Then Thurid will be destroyed, and you will die. I won't turn you loose and I can't keep you in a cage indefinitely. I'd put you in some enchantment that would last a thousand years or so, if there were any cosmic penalties for destroying Sciplings, but we can kill you as if you were no more important than rats. I prefer the direct way out. I'll simply kill you and be done with it. I will if I can, in any case."

Leifr chuckled darkly, shaking his head in wonderment. "This must be a hoax. What do you plan to do with Starkad and Raud-bjorn?''

"I don't need them and neither do you. They die."

"Then I refuse. We will all die together."

Sorkvir shrugged. "Very well, if that's the way you wish it. I once thought that Sciplings weren't so faint-hearted, after our dispute over the Pentacle." He turned on his heel and strode out of the chamber with a sinuous rustle of his long cloak.

Raudbjorn grunted and gave his door a shake. The two Bat guards leaped forward and thrust their spears through the bars menacingly. One was snapped off in a swipe from Raudbjorn's great paw, and the other Dokkalfar withdrew his hurriedly. After snarling some suitable threats to salve their dignity, they re-treated nervously to their post by the door.

Starkad watched it all with admiration. "It was clever of you not to agree to his bargain," he said to Leifr. "Too much ea-gerness would only make him think he's got the upper hand of us. He won't give up this easily."

Leifr hoped Starkad was right. He waited for Sorkvir's return with gnawing uneasiness, which he managed to conceal when Sorkvir finally returned and busied himself preparing some con-coction over a low fire.

Abruptly Sorkvir turned and approached Leifr's cell. "We shall leave tomorrow," he said, then added as a negligent after-thought, "and you may take those other two with you. Thurid might become suspicious if they aren't there. It would be like you to tell him I killed them, so now you can't betray me with that small treachery."

"That's only a minor consideration. What is Thurid going to think when I appear without the Rhbu sword?"

"A copy has been made. One that you are forbidden to raise against me, in case that was your next thought."

"Ljosa was my next thought. I have consented to your plan, now show me you intend to keep your word."

Sorkvir removed the hissing cat from the cage, garnering a few more scratches, and passed his hand above her until she ceased her angry struggles and lay limp in his grasp, sound asleep. Then he placed the cat on a low platform and covered her with a cloth marked with cryptic symbols. Next he scratched a circle around her on the ground and a smaller circle around a small stone altar laden with the familiar staring stones marked with spiral designs. He sprinkled some dust around from a small pouch and wrote in runic inside the circles with the end of his staff. The letters glowed with a slimy gleam, and as he worked an evil smell became stronger in the chamber. As he took his place in the small circle, mist was beginning to ooze from the ground, buffeted about restlessly by the invading influences. Then Sorkvir beckoned commandingly with one hand, and the door of the cage burst open with a protesting screech, and Leifr found himself walking forward like an unwilling puppet under Sorkvir's control. When he crossed the circle surrounding Ljosa, he was halted with his feet upon a certain symbol.

Sorkvir turned the stones, speaking to the forces he summoned in words that made no sense to Leifr, rebuking them once when they gusted too near the circle, giving him a glimpse of a strange form of mingled beast and human character swirling within the mist and gazing at him curiously. With a sinister gleam of white fangs it vanished, leaving Leifr with the uneasy conviction that Ljosa restored by such means was a dangerous incursion into the forbidden territory of Dokkalfar magic.

The cavern darkened, and the two candles on the table burned low and their flames turned purple, as if half smothered. Sorkvir's voice chanted hypnotically as he ran his hands over the spirals of the staring stones. The cloth covering Ljosa's cat fylgja twitched and fluttered, and Leifr kept his eyes upon it as it gradually swelled as a form took place beneath it. Evidently not satisfied, Sorkvir rebuffed the powers and the form there vanished, returning to the slight lump that was the cat. Suspicious and alarmed, Leifr tried to call out, but found his throat paralyzed and his limbs weak and heavy, as if in a nightmare. He sank to his knees, unable to will himself to keep his balance. Again he sensed that strength was being taken from him, and there was nothing he could do about it.

When the sense of oppression was almost more than he could endure and still draw a labored breath, an icy current rippled through the room, setting up vibrations of opposition as conflicting powers clashed. With a tearing sound like thunder, an ice-cold deluge of rain and hail suddenly burst over the large circle, which left Leifr gasping, but his strength was restored and Sork-vir's hold upon him had vanished. Warily he stood up and turned in his tracks to look at Ljosa.

She lay on the platform, dressed as if for her funeral in a fine embroidered gown girdled with gold chains and fastened at the shoulders with gold brooches. A rich blue cloak was folded around her, as if for a journey, and on her feet were high boots made of sealskin, trimmed with soft white fur and gold buckles and strips of embroidery from ankle to knee. The tools and equipment for traveling surrounded her: bridles, weapons, provisions in baskets, and much more.

With his heart stilled with dread, Leifr moved toward her, scarcely able to believe what his eyes were seeing. Tentatively he touched the bare flesh of one marble-white arm, so completely expecting the stiff coldness of death that the sensation of warmth that greeted his touch startled him. He touched her cheek lightly and felt the soft breath of the sleeper.

"She lives," Sorkvir's harsh voice said behind him, with an undertone of sly amusement. "As I promised, I have restored her to her true form."

Leifr whirled around, reaching instinctively for the sword that wasn't at his hip. "But she's asleep! You brought back her body, but not her!" He moved forward warily, wondering how close Sorkvir would let him get.

Sorkvir smiled thinly, his eyes smoldering as he measured his opponent. A warning flicker halted Leifr beyond arm's reach.

"What did you expect, Scipling? Hroaldsdottir restored whole, so you could take her and abandon Thurid to his fate, perhaps? Stranger things have been done for the sake of a woman."

"The form without the essence is not Ljosa," Leifr said angrily. "Do you think I'll be fooled by such a simple trick? You won't bring her back to life once I fulfill my part of the bargain. There's nothing to bind you to your word."

Sorkvir pulled a small blue vial from the tail of his sleeve and uncorked its gold stopper beneath Ljosa's nose. She inhaled more deeply and sighed, raising one hand weakly. Sorkvir took the bottle away, stoppered it, and tossed it negligently to Leifr.

"She will remain like this until you have fulfilled your contract. When it is finished, for good or for ill, you can return to claim her, using this. Her life essence is in that bottle. Uncork it under her nose and life will return to her in a few moments. Of course, if you don't survive, she'll sleep here forever. Now go back to your cage until the horses are brought. At dawn you depart.''

Leifr tried to resist, but Sorkvir's will drove him back into the cell. But not without effort, Leifr observed with small satisfaction. The wizard glared at him rigidly, holding him in thrall, until the bolt had slid into place.

Chapter 3

Leifr knew that dawn was approaching when Dokkalfar hostlers brought three horses into the passageway outside the chamber—Starkad's gray, Raudbjorn's big hairy-footed beast, and faithful old Jolfr. Kraftig, Frimodig, and Farlig skulked around the horses' heels, snarling and bristling in wary protest of this unwarranted handling of their masters' property. The hostlers kept their eyes upon the hounds with no little fear evident, as if they had discovered the hounds' protective tendencies firsthand.

Sorkvir glided into the room and opened the doors of the cages to release his prisoners. As they stepped forth, a knock sounded at the door. Sorkvir considered a moment, then nodded at the guard to open it. Svanlaug in a long dark cloak unmuffled herself and motioned for the door to be closed behind her. To Leifr's astonishment, she went down on her knees at Sorkvir's feet.

"Sorkvir, I have come to beg a boon. You can't refuse to hear me, since I have asked for the protection of the powers that you serve."

Sorkvir stared down at her balefully a moment. "Then speak, witch. I am forced to listen, but whether I act or not is my choice. What is the boon you ask?"

"I crave vengeance for my brother and my father, and I can't rest until I have obtained it," she replied, her eyes blazing. "I want the life of your master Djofull."

Sorkvir snorted. "I knew you were treacherous. I tried to warn him, the fool. Are you now seeking to exchange one tool for a superior one?" He nodded to his prisoners. "You deceived them only to make use of them, and now do you think I am so easily fooled?"

31

"No," Svanlaug replied. "But you are not satisfied with being Djofull's pawn any longer. You're stronger than he is, with your knowledge from the realm of the dead. You must free yourself of Djofull first, and the only way to do that is by killing him. I beg only to assist you, to be the hand that holds the weapon."

Sorkvir regarded her with an intense stare. "Are you that brave, that thirsty for revenge?"

"Yes, I am," Svanlaug replied.

Sorkvir turned and strode slowly up and down the length of the room as he considered. Svanlaug and Leifr exchanged a coldly hostile stare.

"I shall remember what you have said," Sorkvir said at last. "Now begone. You'll know if I require you."

She rose and backed away, her expression momentarily illuminated by a sly smile before she turned and vanished into the corridor.

Leifr looked narrowly at Sorkvir, who answered his unasked question. "Djofull must die, if he insists upon standing in the way of my plans. But that need be no concern of yours, Scipling. You'll do well to remember, however, that I will not hesitate to kill anyone who fails to obey me. Don't think to escape me. You are day-farers, and you will travel safer then. But you needn't think you can deceive me. Every day leads to night. If you don't appear where I command you, our agreement is broken and Hroaldsdottir will die. I have ways of traveling that far exceed a lumbering horse. Your first destination is Steinveggur-dahl." He passed Leifr a vellum map made on sheepskin, with the valley Steinveggur marked in red. It looked like a day's journeying, and that only if no wrong turns were taken and no horses fell lame.

"What if we're late?" Starkad spoke up presumptuously.

Sorkvir turned a withering glare upon him, and Starkad looked abashed.

"You won't be late," Sorkvir said to Leifr, disdaining to speak to such a lowly object as Starkad. "You won't want me to come hunting you. The penalties will be severe."

Sorkvir raised his hand, palm downward, fingers extended stiffly, and Leifr felt a vicious pain shoot through his skull. He gasped and staggered back a step, momentarily blinded. Sorkvir chuckled without mirth and revealed a small pouch in the palm of his hand. "All that from a single lock of your hair, Scipling, and that was just a small sample of what I can do. I can make you blind, insane, drunk, or any of a dozen interesting maladies. I urge you to remember the being we knew as Gotiskolker whenever you happen to think about trying to outwit me."

"I'll remember all right," Leifr growled.

Another Dokkalfar appeared in the doorway carrying Raudbjorn's halberd and a sword that looked like *Endalaus Daudi*. Raudbjorn received his halberd with a suspicious grunt and began looking it over from top to bottom, testing its edge, which had been crudely dulled, and darting a murderous look at Sorkvir.

Sorkvir weighed the copy of Leifr's sword in his hands.

"This is Dvergar-made. Use it with caution."

Leifr hung it at his belt, his head still ringing from the effects of Sorkvir's demonstration of control over him. He was filled with misgivings and loath to leave Ljosa so helpless. As a cat, she had defended herself well, but who would protect her now in her sleeping state?

"Remember. Steinveggur-dahl by tonight."

"We'll be there," Leifr said shortly.

From the door, still standing slightly ajar after Svanlaug's departure, came a rusty cackle. The heavy door suddenly burst open with a crash against the wall behind it and Djofull stepped into the room in an icy gust of disturbed wind as the wards crackled and dissolved. He clutched a tall staff with a large knob with Gedvondur's hand perched atop it like an ornament. The shaft of the staff nearest the knob gleamed with a slimy substance that Gedvondur seemed loath to touch. Behind Djofull's billowing cloak lurked Svanlaug, her narrow face pale and vulpine.

"Treachery, Sorkvir, so early in the game?" Djofull's eyes gleamed with malevolence, belying his silky tone. "I have tolerated your ill humors and destructive whims, and I've permitted you to think that you have some degree of autonomy, but if you think to release these prisoners without my permission, you've gone too far down the road to rebellion. You know that I can control you if I wish, and it seems that now I must, if I am to preserve my plans to destroy the Rhbus. You are my creation, Sorkvir, and from now on you will be my slave."

Sorkvir uttered a harsh bark of mirth. "Nay, Djofull, you lost that advantage long ago. I have Hela's knowledge, a great deal of it, thanks to your repeated experiments."

"But I have her knowledge also, which you imparted to me, so I am the master with both the servant and the skills. Do not rely upon your arrogance too heavily, Sorkvir."

"Do you think I have always given you all I learned?" Sorkvir inquired in a voice like the hiss of a snake. "Did you trust me so completely that you didn't think that one day I'd turn against you when my knowledge was complete, and my skills more powerful than yours?"

Djofull snorted and tapped the staff upon the ground. "That day has not yet arrived, Sorkvir. Do you suppose that there are not things that I have kept hidden from you?"

"I have long known you feared my strength—and with good cause. One of us must perish now. There is no road back to the old days, when we were content in deceiving one another quietly."

"I'm not eager to destroy you so hastily," Djofull answered. "I still have uses for you—particularly if there is indeed knowledge that you have basely withheld from me and that I am entitled to possess. I don't fear you. I wisely took precautions some time ago, when I sensed a certain degree of resentment on your part. Personal wards will keep you off, Sorkvir, or you'll suffer some nasty consequences if you lift a hand against me in violence or in spell. Then there's the matter of some twenty fine warriors sworn to defend me and my holding."

"They can do nothing with their crude weapons that would destroy me," Sorkvir answered with disdain. "You have made me into the most dread species of draugar. I can think, reason, and plot independently from my creator, and I am invincible to death. Destroy this body, and I have the power to take another. It was your mistake to allow me to retain the will of a living being."

"So I see," Djofull answered coldly. "But I can rectify that. Only one will between us, and that will is mine."

"It is too late. You've been deceived for the last time. You were weak to trust the wrong persons too far, and too often."

Svanlaug stepped forward, her hands hidden in her cloak. "Indeed, you should have been more suspicious, as you were when Reidar approached you." She bared the weapon then, a short dark sword. Clutching it with both hands, she rushed at Djofull before he could raise a hand to stop her and buried the blade in his midsection.

"That was for Reidar," she said, as he staggered backward. "And for my father."

Djofull sank into a chair, his life fast draining out from his wound. "It is of no consequence," he said hoarsely, his teeth bared in a death's-head grimace. "You have won no lasting victory."

"Very poorly done," Sorkvir snapped. "He's got strength enough for one last spell. Finish him off, woman!"

Svanlaug swayed on her feet, the fire of revenge that had sustained her so long suddenly vanquished. Djofull struggled to lift his staff, his lips forming a spell. In the shadows near the door one of the thrall hostlers suddenly scuttled from his hiding place, bolting into the corridor. Djofull sagged then, his last energy spent, his last words trailing away faintly. "Sorkvir, you haven't done away with me yet, nor are you free of this fortress. Beware—of shattering—illusions."

The life left him sitting upright and staring vacantly past his assassins. Sorkvir strode to the doorway and looked out, snarling "We've not much time, if that thrall ran away to spread the news. Scipling, mount up and get away from Djofullhol. This place is not going to be healthy much longer."

Gedvondur suddenly made a wild flying leap from the knob of the staff, landing on Svanlaug's shoulder. He gripped there as she flinched with instinctive revulsion, then scuttled down her arm to clutch her wrist.

"There's another killing to be done before we're finished here!" Gedvondur's voice boomed powerfully from Svanlaug's mouth. Her hand seized the sword and jerked it free from Djofull's body, and she turned toward Sorkvir, her eyes blazing with Gedvondur's fury. "I haven't been avenged yet, and the loss of Sorkvir would be doing the world a favor!"

"Gedvondur!" Sorkvir swore. "Another of Djofull's experiments gone frightfully wrong!"

The short sword in Svanlaug's hand blazed with unnatural light, and Sorkvir laughed harshly as he edged toward the door. "You'll destroy your medium very quickly, Gedvondur. She's a mere Dokkalfar, you recall. You'll melt her if you attempt any spell!" With a swirl of his cloak, he dived into the passage. Leifr glimpsed him raising one hand warningly, as if to dart another searing bolt into his head, but it was only a potent reminder. "Steinveggurdahl, Scipling! Remember!" Then he was gone.

Svanlaug turned toward Leifr. "You weren't much help!" Gedvondur's voice snapped.

"I can't touch him with this!" Leifr slapped the imitation sword in exasperation. "We can't get near him, and I don't know what damage we could do if we could! We're bound to follow his orders."

Raudbjorn shook his head and moaned, "Wizard duels not for Raudbjorn."

Starkad unfroze from his wary crouch somewhat behind Leifr and Raudbjorn and laughed incredulously, slapping himself all over and raising clouds of dust. "I'm still alive and in one piece," he declared, "and we've faced both Djofull and Sorkvir. What luck! I never expected to get out of there so easily! Are we really going to get away with this? And rich besides." He delved into his pockets, hauling up two handfuls of the precious gems. To his surprise, they were nothing but the common field stones that composed at least half of Skarpsey's harsh soil.

"I might have known nothing would be as it seemed," Starkad said darkly, heaving an unhappy sigh as he emptied his pockets of a large number of rocks.

Far away down the corridor came distant sounds of tumult: battle cries and the clash of sword on shield. Underlying the familiar sounds were undefinable rumbles and muffled explosions that made the earth quiver underfoot.

Svanlaug crossed the interval to the door in jerky strides. After a quick survey of the situation, Gedvondur's voice called, "We've got to get out of here fast! Djofull's men are fighting, and the glamour spells he's woven are coming apart! The whole structure might come down around our ears if we don't hurry!"

"We've got to save Ljosa!" Leifr replied. "And my sword is hidden here somewhere!"

Svanlaug's head shook vigorously. "Then we'd better hurry. I don't know how much time we have!"

"Where do we look?" Leifr demanded. "We know nothing about this hive! She could be anywhere!"

"There's a room in the northwest tunnel that Sorkvir had heavily warded and guarded. Ljosa is in there. Follow me!" Gedvondur commanded. "I know this place like the back of my own hand! You there!" Svanlaug's hand shot out and retrieved a cowering stableboy from the shadows. "Take these horses back to the stableyard and wait for us there, unless you want your liver pulled out and eaten before your eyes. I will come looking for you if you're not there."

Nodding frantically, the lad grabbed the horses' reins and turned them back toward the stableyard.

Svanlaug led the way down the corridor, with Gedvondur gripping her wrist. Small bands of Dokkalfar were skirmishing through the tunnels, with curses, clashes of metal, and occasional shouts. One struggling group suddenly recognized the strangers gliding past in the dark as Djofull's former prisoners. Their immediate hostilities suddenly forgotten, both factions united in a bellowing charge after them. Raudbjorn lumbered in the rear, falling back to exchange a few blows as a delaying tactic.

The number of their pursuers increased as the warring factions of Dokkalfar united in the common cause of capturing the prisoners. Yelling and clashing their shields and swords, they pursued their quarry into the main hall, where Leifr and Raudbjorn slammed shut the great doors and barred them. Altogether too swiftly, the Dokkalfar fetched a battering ram and commenced smashing their way through. Escape and freedom beckoned temptingly through the unguarded front doors into the courtyard.

Leifr crouched behind a bulwark of overturned tables and gazed around uneasily at the dangling corpses. "Well? How do we get to the northwest tunnel now?" he asked between crashes of the battering ram.

"We'll have to clear out this tunnel," Gedvondur's voice barked. "You've still got the Dvergar sword, haven't you? And Raudbjorn?"

Raudbjorn uttered a grating affirmative and gripped his halberd with an anticipatory grin.

"What's beyond there?" Starkad pointed to a passage leading off the main hall to another part of the fortress.

"Djofull's end of the fortress, the southeast tunnel," Gedvondur replied. "I've got some business to attend to there before the Dokkalfar wreck his chambers."

"We're going to get Ljosa first," Leifr said grimly. "Nobody is going to have any other business to attend to besides fighting when those Dokkalfar break through. Gedvondur, you'd better be ready to work some significant magic on them when they knock it down."

A particularly vicious, splintering crash riveted their attention as the doors began to give way. Raudbjorn rose to his feet, scything his halberd expectantly, while Leifr and Starkad took up positions slightly behind his range of destruction. Looking around for Svanlaug, Leifr saw no sign of her. Suspiciously he peered toward the southeast tunnel and glimpsed a dark shadow dashing past a guttering sconce.

"Svanlaug! Gedvondur!" Leifr roared furiously.

"Hold them off! I'll be back!" Gedvondur's voice replied.

"A likely story," Leifr grunted. "If ever there was a pair out to feather their own nests, it's those two!"

With a final murderous crash and a triumphant roar, the Dokkalfar smashed through the door and charged into the hall, half drunken with the heedless abandon of an imminent slaughter. Raudbjorn bared his teeth and took a step forward, responding with a bellow of defiance. Leifr followed his example, raising the useless imitation of *Endalaus Daudi* and echoing Raudbjorn's battle cry with a yell of his own. The words that came out of his mouth startled him, searing his throat as if he had belched flame.

"Komast Undan!"

The words, shouted forth with all his might, sent a current of wind rushing around the room, disturbing the lifeless trophies hanging from the beams and carrying echoes of Leifr's shout down both tunnels from one end of the fortress to the other.

The Dokkalfar warriors halted their disorderly rush and hastily made signs to ward off the noxious influence of the words.

All their eyes were fastened upon Leifr, their hairy lips curled in furious snarls. Leifr's eyes were fully upon his would-be assassins, so he only glimpsed something large plummeting down from the shadowy rafters to land with a clatter behind the Dokkalfar. The rearmost whirled around and found themselves facing one of the dead heroes, who stood on his feet wheeling his sword around his head, shrieking a windy battle cry, hollow eye sockets blazing with a blue light, fleshless cheeks split in a maniacal grin.

The Dokkalfar surged back as one body from this apparition that had taken possession of the doorway, blocking their retreat. Overhead there was a sound like the buzzing of angry bees and the sharp twang of wires snapping. Three more dead heroes dropped down in the hall, equally warlike and similarly bent upon revenge.

The leader of the Dokkalfar, his rank designated by tassels of wolf fur and wolf teeth and claws, made a contemptuous gesture with his sword, snarling "They're nothing but old bones and dust! It's only an illusion!"

With a feathery whistle, an arrow from above found its mark in his thigh, eliciting a very genuine roar of pain and rage. He lunged forward to slash at the nearest apparition warrior with a fiery clashing of steel. More warriors cut their mooring lines and dropped down to join the fight, and arrows flew from the advantage of the rafters.

Leifr barely restrained Raudbjorn from joining in, pointing to the northwest door, now unguarded. Disappointed, Raudbjorn lowered his halberd and followed Leifr down the passageway toward Sorkvir's region of the fortress. Doors had been smashed through by the ransacking warriors, and the rooms beyond were in flames. Between, the tunnels were lightless. Cursing the smoke and the darkness, Leifr clawed along the wall with agonizing slowness. Then Starkad surged ahead of him, pointing out the way down the unfamiliar tunnel. "She's here! I know she is!" he insisted, his eyes blazing like cat's eyes in the dark. Grabbing Leifr's arm, he dashed some of Hogni's eyedrops in his eyes so he could see. Raudbjorn plowed along behind, completely blind, stumbling over rocks underfoot, guided by his own great faith and the sounds of scuffling and swearing ahead of him.

At last they reached a wooden door; it was locked from the outside. A small watch fire still smoldered, but the guard who had been posted had fled or hastened to his demise somewhere in the bloody and disputed tunnels of Djofullhol.

"No wards," Starkad said, passing his hands over the door. "Sorkvir abandoned her to whatever fate befell."

Raudbjorn shouldered open the door and they plunged inside, swords drawn, blinking in the light. The room was comfortably appointed, and Ljosa lay on a couch against one wall. An ancient Dokkalfar woman looked up from her spinning wheel in amazement at the three scowling apparitions bursting into her quarters. She swiftly shifted forms to that of a skinny hare and bolted out of the room between their feet into the corridor.

Leifr crossed the room in three quick strides, pulling the blue vial from his belt pouch. After uncorking it, he held it beneath her nostrils and watched as a gray vapor was inhaled with increasingly deep breaths. Ljosa stirred restlessly and opened her eyes, gazing at him for a long moment before full recognition dawned in their depths.

"Leifr! Where am I?" she murmured in a bemused voice, and she threw her arms around his neck as a frightened child would do.

"Djofullhol. Sorkvir brought you back. Djofull is dead. There's nothing to be afraid of now; we're going to take you out of here. Don't be frightened. The tunnel outside this room is full of smoke and there's a fire and other strange things, but nothing is going to harm you now that I've found you!"

She was too weak to stand and clung to his neck with frightened desperation as he carried her into the tunnel. Guided by the light of fire at the other end, Leifr hurried as fast as he could with his burden, which was a slow trot. Raudbjorn stopped him with one heavy hand on his shoulder and gently took her from his arms. From then on they went much faster. Starkad trotted warily in the lead, taking them unfailingly back to the great hall where they had last seen Svanlaug and Gedvondur.

The battle was still going on inside, with clashing of metal on metal, shouts, shrieks, and a tumult of bodies careering around in death struggles. Leifr edged open the door a crack and peered in. Most of the Dokkalfar in the fortress were cornered in one end of the hall, facing a formidable army of Ljosalfar and Norskur warriors, the former dead trophies that had hung from the rafters. A few still swung from their wires, using their aerial advantage to good effect to slash at their enemies below. Now they moved forward, swinging their weapons and radiating a blue gleam from within that rendered their preserved hides almost transparent. The air surrounding them crackled with sparks, lending the dark hall a lurid flickering light.

"Djofull's rooms are on the other side," Starkad said, his eyes glowing with Alfar power, his young voice strong and sure. "Svanlaug and Gedvondur are there."

Leifr led a charge across the hall behind the dead warriors, who had accounted well for themselves already by taking a heavy toll of Dokkalfar, some of whom lay melting, shrinking, and sizzling horribly. Plunging into the tunnel beyond the hall, they found it filled with choking smoke, roiling from the far end where Djofull's laboratory appeared to be in flames. Leifr wavered a moment, torn between the easy retreat through the doors into the the courtyard and the fiery, smoke-filled passage that led toward Djofull's end of the fortress. Drawing a deep breath of relatively clean air, he raced toward the fire, followed by Raudbjorn and Starkad.

The scene that greeted his eyes was nearly as bizarre as the dead warriors swinging from their wires in murderous attack. Svanlaug, her back to Leifr, was ransacking the room, flinging away bundles of herbs, tearing open jars and pots and boxes and baskets, and dropping them in wild disregard. The animals from the cages scuttled hither and thither like mad things in their terror.

"Gedvondur!" Leifr roared, and Svanlaug whirled like a startled cat to face him, her eyes wild and her hair flailing in the waves of heat. Her hand came up in a defensive gesture, and Leifr saw that it was Gedvondur's hand meshed in hers. Svanlaug was drained of all color and her eyes stared, unblinking. A ragged gash in her forearm was soaking her side with blood. From the way she reeled on her feet, Leifr suddenly wondered if she was still alive in Gedvondur's grasp.

"*Endalaus Daudi* is there!" Svanlaug pointed to a carved

chest brutally broken open. The sword lay atop a pile of glittering loot that made Starkad swoop forward hungrily. Leifr seized the sword, and Starkad stuffed several handfuls of the gold and gems into his pockets and pouches.

"We've got to get out of here!" Leifr yelled over the bellow of the flames that were absorbing more of Djofull's possessions.

"You go! I've got more business to attend to!" Gedvondur replied. "My ashes are here somewhere! I've got to find them!"

"Gedvondur!" Leifr protested. "Svanlaug can't stand much more of this!"

"Get out while you can!" Gedvondur snarled, flinging up his hand in a repelling gesture. "This is no longer your affair, Leifr! Get out!"

A powerful wave shoved Leifr backward toward the door, blinding him with a gust of hot, acrid wind.

Leifr led the retreat through the Heroes' Hall, where the dead heroes were finishing up the bloody battle with the Dokkalfar. Some of the heroes were too damaged to fight, collapsed in ragged heaps that resembled nothing human. Ljosa gasped and moaned, as if gripped in a terrible nightmare, burying her face in Raudbjorn's mantle between reassuring glimpses of Leifr striding along beside her.

They crossed the courtyard to the stable, where furtive Dokkalfar scuttled out of their way, with only thoughts of self-preservation in mind. Most of the stalls were empty, but a trumpeting neigh from Jolfr at the far end guided them to their horses. Urged on by the dull explosions coming from the bowels of the fortress, they mounted their horses and emerged from the stableyard at a full gallop. Smoke boiled from the entrance to the Hall of Dead Heroes, and rocks clattered down from the highest pinnacles. The day had darkened ominously, and a late snowstorm added icy teeth to the restless wind. As they hurried through the earthworks, the grofblomur in the gloom on all sides of them began to stir and rattle. The horses snorted and shied, their eyes ringed with white. A host of skeletal hands reached from the shadows, clawing and grasping. The large white blooms were empty skulls waving on fragile stalks, waist-high to a man on horseback.

"Draugar!" Starkad shouted as his horse reared with a squeal of terror.

Leifr unsheathed *Endalaus Daudi*. Its strange metal gleamed as he raised it and swung it at the sea of bare skulls swirling around him. His first stroke clipped off several skeletal arms; his next bit into the dusty skulls with glaring eyes and trailing wisps of hair. Fragments of bone and dust and rotting rags exploded on contact, falling into moldering heaps.

Behind him, Raudbjorn scythed at the grofblomur with his halberd one-handed, balancing Ljosa against his shoulder, guiding his war steed with his knees. Ljosa lolled helplessly, insensible in Raudbjorn's grasp. Fingerbones scrabbled with their claws around her throat, tangled in her hair, gripping Raudbjorn's arms and legs as he kicked them away. Merely breaking apart their bodies scarcely slowed them down. The pieces lying on the ground jiggled and danced wildly, like a netful of fish cast up on the beach. Leifr charged into their midst to reach Raudbjorn and defend his back as they retreated. Raudbjorn hewed at them manfully, using his halberd one-handed to mow them down like dried corn stalks, and Leifr followed close behind him, with Starkad bringing up the rear.

As they galloped through the fetid streets of the settlement in the earthworks, they had to dodge around cartloads of people and possessions fleeing the doom of Djofullhol, fighting and clawing for the right of way, barely getting out of the path of the charging horses. To slow down would be to become mired in the maze of carts and wagons and old women with huge bundles on their backs.

Leifr rode away from Djofullhol more shaken than he cared to admit, with a feeling of impending doom driving him. Halfway across the side of a fell, perhaps two miles from Djofullhol, their horses stumbled and lurched when the earth suddenly swelled beneath them in a passing wave that dislodged rocks and ice from the glaciers above and sent them crashing downhill in clouds of flying dust and spray. Starkad led the rush toward a rugged black skarp that would offer them protection from above. Ljosa cried out in terror and cowered in Raudbjorn's arms as a mighty berg struck their skarp and exploded around them.

Holding their terrified horses with difficulty, they turned to look back. Djofullhol stood wreathed in a cloud of eerie flame, overhung by roiling black clouds that crackled with lightning. The towers dissolved in a cloud of rising dust, melting away even while Leifr gazed. A shuddering explosion shook the earth. When the dust cleared, the high, crumbling walls no longer stood jagged against the sky, and the dust rolled away in great, slow-moving clouds.

In numb silence they stared. Djofullhol was nothing but a heap of fallen stone. Gedvondur's fury and Svanlaug's vengeance had combined in supreme destructive power. Whether they were still alive, Leifr could not guess.

"Djofull warned Sorkvir about shattering illusions," Starkad said. "This was a powerful one."

Raudbjorn removed his helmet and shoved some flowers and leafy twigs into its devices, as a sign of mourning for fallen comrades. Leifr questioned the propriety or necessity of mourning for a severed hand from a dead wizard, and he was still not certain where Svanlaug's loyalties had rested, even after she had killed Djofull.

"Well, why are we standing here, staring at nothing like bullocks?" Leifr snapped, suddenly impatient and angry. "We've delayed ourselves too long already. I doubt if we'll make it to Steinveggur-dahl by nightfall. What's done is done, and there's no yesterday and no tomorrow unless we live through today."

"What about Ljosa?" Starkad asked. "Sorkvir's going to know something went amiss if we show up with her. He's not going to like having his plans interfered with."

"What do I care for his plans?" Leifr snapped. "If we hadn't gone back for her, she'd be dead now, and then he'd have no hold over me except that hairlock spell."

"Is she all right?" Starkad inquired worriedly.

"A little weak, that's all," Raudbjorn replied as Ljosa's head lolled against his shoulder. "I don't wonder, considering what she's been through. She'll be herself soon, I'm certain."

Chapter 4

◈◈◈◈◈◈◈◈◈◈◈◈◈◈◈◈◈◈◈◈◈◈◈◈◈◈◈◈

They reached Steinveggur-dahl in the pale twilight hours after sundown and set up camp in a protected spot across a small lake from the ruins that had given the valley its name. The walls were made of stone, rising high in roofless towers and walls open to the sky. Empty windows stared out upon the bleak landscape. The ditch around the fortress was still filled with water, and doubtless the rotting bones and rusting weapons of the defenders and attackers of the breached walls.

Starkad gazed at the fortress, his eyes shining with dreams and childhood legends. "This hill fort belonged to the Rhbus, I'll wager," he said, awe in his tone. "No one else has the power to raise stone walls like that. They say it's magic rather than mortar that holds those ruins together after all this time."

"I could use a little Rhbu magic now," Leifr said grimly as he knelt, looking at the sleeping Ljosa. She seemed to be slipping farther into whatever spell still held her. He had tried holding the vial under her nose again, but with no result. "She's not completely restored. Sorkvir must have held back something of her life essence. She can't spend the rest of her life sleeping— or as a cat."

"You'll find out when Sorkvir gets here," Starkad said uneasily. "He's not going to be pleased we went back for Ljosa, even if we did save her life."

"He'll have the real *Endalaus Daudi* to argue with, if he doesn't like it," Leifr replied.

"Sorkvir's not going to be pleased about that, either," Starkad muttered.

Leifr put *Endalaus Daudi* into his sheath and rolled some rocks on Sorkvir's imitation of the sword to hide it from view.

45

"Isn't there a hiding spell you could put on it?" he asked. "Thurid told me about spells that make your mind refuse to think about certain objects."

"I can do simple hiding spells," Starkad answered, "but nothing subtle enough to fool Sorkvir. Any spell of mine would be like waving a flag over it."

Leifr waited restlessly throughout the night for Sorkvir to approach. While Raudbjorn stood guard, he tried to sleep, but all he could see was the fire, Djofull dead in his chair, and Svanlaug's pale rigid face. Agonized doubts about Ljosa's condition tore through him, making inaction impossible. He rose and looked at Ljosa sleeping, her face shimmering with shadow and moonlight, sometimes the face of a woman, sometimes the face of a cat. He paced restlessly, fingering the power ring Vidskipti had given him and considering the name he had twice spoken with such spectacular results. He wanted to speak it again for Ljosa's sake, but, try as he might, he couldn't summon the name to his memory. Gloomily he assumed it was a signal that such usage was not proper, possibly even dangerous for Ljosa. With the wretched, helpless feeling that he wasn't much good in the Alfar realm, he joined Raudbjorn at his outpost overlooking their camp.

Raudbjorn greeted him with a companionable grunt and a slight nod. His head jutted forward, cocked to listen, and his good eye scanned the darkness, which was slowly fading to the long predawn twilight. From Raudbjorn's stance, Leifr knew the thief-taker's suspicions had been aroused by something in the shrouded landscape. The troll-hounds growled softly in their chests, too preoccupied to greet Leifr with more than perfunctory thumps of their tails.

"Sorkvir," Leifr whispered, his chest tightening with apprehension.

Raudbjorn shook his head. "Too many horses," he replied in a throaty growl. "Not Sorkvir."

Leifr awakened Starkad and they swiftly saddled the horses in preparation for a strategic retreat. The twilight was still deep in the surrounding fells and scarps, filling the low valleys with heavy shadow. Raudbjorn silently pointed, indicating four intruders who were taking positions around the mouth of the valley, moving toward their camp, with two on each side.

"Shouldn't we run while we can?" Starkad asked nervously, gripping his sword hilt.

"Only four," Raudbjorn replied reprovingly. "Shameful to run from four!"

When the first two of the strangers appeared, they rode forward harmlessly with their weapons all sheathed, holding up their hands in peaceable gestures to show they had no evil intent. Raudbjorn growled suspiciously under his breath and planted his feet wide apart, grounding the butt of his halberd with a warning thunk. Its newly sharpened edge gleamed like an evil sickle moon.

"Halloo-ah!" one of the strangers called. "We mean you no harm. We're just passing along the same road as you."

"You're making rather an early start, aren't you?" Leifr answered gruffly. "Or is it a late arrival for night-farers? Come forward and identify yourselves."

The riders approached until Raudbjorn grunted and picked up his halberd. They were roughly clad in greasy furs and pelts stitched crudely together over breeches and tunics that had long since taken on the hue of dirt and grease and, no doubt, dried blood. On their heads they wore battered helmets of disparate origin, which trailed locks of hair, taken as trophies of vanquished foes, most probably from the slain possessors of the helmets and shields. Their beards were stringy, their faces narrow and predatory, in spite of ingratiating grins. For travelers whose purposes were allegedly peaceful, they were armed to the teeth with longbows slung at their backs, two swords each, axes, lances, and knives in abundance.

"I am Nagli, and this is my son Modga," the oldest said with elaborate courtesy, still grinning wolfishly. Modga regarded the strangers sullenly and licked his lips.

"Thief-takers!" Raudbjorn rumbled, taking a step forward with a murderous flourish of his halberd.

"Are you following us?" Leifr demanded, half drawing his sword.

Nagli spread out his hands as if inviting sympathy. "It's a

lowly trade, but one that needs doing. Surely you could expect little else, after what you have done.''

"Word must travel fast," Leifr replied. "We don't even know ourselves what we're accused of.''

Nagli chuckled and winked one eye. "There's never a thief nor a killer that will freely admit what he's done. I've never yet slit a throat that wasn't protesting its innocence until the last moment. Let me say only that someone attacked Djofullhol yesterday and secretly murdered the wizard Djofull. Now I must say that the Dokkalfar are very understanding of killers and the need for murdering one's enemies, and we've devised a system of payment for our killings. You go and kill your man, then pay the weregild; it's that simple—unless you fail to declare your deed, as a brave man does. There's no advantage to secret murder, when so much of it is done openly. You ought to have announced that you were willing to pay what Djofull's relatives demand, instead of trying to slide away from your debt. Now they're after your blood.''

"Blood is as good as anything else, if you have no gold," Leifr answered. "It was Djofull who committed the first offense, by sending Sorkvir to Solvorfirth. Then he came after Sorkvir's ashes with armed men and took them from me by force. What else can he expect but retribution? I had to salvage what honor I could from the situation. Whoever killed Djofull had a reasonable right to do so.''

"Many people have that right," Nagli said agreeably, baring even more of his wolfish yellow teeth. "But you—or whoever killed him—forgot to follow the accepted protocol for murders. Now the matter will fall into the hands of thief-takers. Djofull's brothers and kin have pointed to you as the killer, if you are the Scipling Leifr Thorljotsson, lately of Solvorfirth, North Quarter. You can come back peaceably, or I'll take back just your head and save you the trouble of making the journey yourself.'' He laughed hoarsely at his own joke, and Modga continued to stare at Leifr like a hungry weasel, baring his teeth in a slight snarl.

Raudbjorn raised his halberd and stepped forward, his features contorted in a grimace of professional hatred.

"Thief-taker already here," he said venomously, his eye shifting between father and son. "Raudbjorn. Called Villimadur. Savage!'' He ground his teeth and shook his head until teeth and claws in his braided topknot rattled.

Nagli and Modga exchanged a wary glance. Raudbjorn's bulk would have made three good-size Dokkalfar.

"Be off with you,'' Leifr commanded, knowing the longer they delayed the closer the other two were getting to their backs. "I didn't murder Djofull in secret, although I'm not afraid to say I might have done the same myself. If you know what's wise for you, you won't keep following me.''

"How big reward?'' Raudbjorn inquired curiously, as an afterthought.

Nagli leaned forward in his saddle, his eyes shining with deadly cunning. "A thousand marks in silver, twenty in gold, ten horses, and twenty pieces of red cloth. It could be shared three ways.''

"Five ways, you mean,'' Leifr said, cocking his head toward the opposite side of the valley. "Two more sons, I suppose?''

Nagli grinned and licked his lips again. "Ovild and Lygari. Not much gets past them. Modga here is a mere infant compared to them, although he's plenty bad himself.''

Raudbjorn snorted with profound disdain. "Sheep ticks. Little worms. Raudbjorn's lice meaner than Dokkalfar thief-takers. Get out or lie and rot, gagnslaus!''

"Who do you call useless?'' Nagli demanded, his insincere grin vanishing into a sullen snarl. His eyes narrowed to mean little slits.

"You, gagnslaus,'' Raudbjorn said, swinging his halberd menacingly, with a creaking of his body armor as his muscles flexed.

Nagli and Modga backed away, drawing their weapons. Leifr drew *Endalaus Daudi*, which set up a sinister singing as if it anticipated more blood. Behind them, Starkad whistled warningly when the other Naglissons came riding leisurely into view. Gradually the thief-takers encircled their prey, pinning them in the clearing beside the lake, an excellent location for a battle.

The other two Naglissons were grinners like their father, and they also licked their lips and wiped their mouths on their knuckles in nervous anticipation. Lean and scrawny and ragged, they circled like vicious hounds around a stag at bay.

Nagli raised his hand, signaling for attack, and two of his sons set spurs to their horses and came charging down the fell with wild exultant whoops. Suddenly a sharp crack of thunder arrested them in midleap, sending their horses tumbling tail over ears as if they had hit a trip-rope. The Naglissons leaped off nimbly, diving for the shelter of a scarp as a hail of ice-bolts came screaming down from the top of the fell. Nagli and Modga gaped up at the dark figure on horseback rearing and dancing against the roiling dark clouds, then turned their horses and flogged away in graceless retreat, followed by exploding ice-bolts. Lygari and Ovild dodged from rock to rock in pursuit of their departing parent and sibling, ducking ferocious blasts of ice. As one of them passed nearby, Raudbjorn couldn't help making a savage lunge at him, slicing the air with his halberd a split second after the Dokkalfar vanished.

Leifr and Starkad peered out warily when the blasts ceased, and the Naglissons were seen galloping away into the fells.

"Sorkvir," Leifr said, feeling a tightening inside his skull, threatening a repeat of the pain the wizard wielded at the flick of a hand. He stepped out of his hiding place to meet Sorkvir as he rode down the fell, holding his staff to one side, still trailing a cloud of mist.

Sorkvir halted at an unfriendly distance, surveying Leifr suspiciously. Leifr signaled to Raudbjorn, who reluctantly lowered his halberd's head to the ground with a regretful clank.

Sorkvir urged his horse nearer, a black beast without a white hair, with long slender legs and small hooves and a small fierce head tossing against the bit. The horse edged around Leifr crabwise, as if sensing its rider's caution.

"I should blast the three of you on the spot and be done with you," Sorkvir said in a deadly tone, raising his smoking staff as if to suit deed to word. "But I couldn't let those filthy thief-takers do the job I intend to finish."

"It'll take more than those back-stabbing thief-takers to kill us," Leifr retorted. "Did you send them to Steinveggur-dahl, knowing we'd be here waiting for you?"

"They weren't sent by me. I do my own killing with far less trouble. Speaking of killing, it was rash of you to do what you did. Djofull was no friend, but he was an equal." Raising his hand, he drove Leifr backward with a searing blast that made his ears ring.

"You're wrong," Leifr gasped. "We didn't plot to kill Djofull. You and Svanlaug were the ones plotting against him, you in your greed for power and she with her burning for revenge."

"But if she hadn't killed him, you would have spoken those cursed Rhbu words and he would have died just as surely. You and that witch had it planned between you. Djofull and I have quarreled frequently with much bitterness, but I never intended that he should die. His last prophecy was correct. He said I would rue the day I trusted a Scipling as a factor. And to think this all came about because of a mere girl, a dead chieftain's daughter!"

"With your vast knowledge of the realm of dead souls, you should be able to restore him," Leifr replied in a tone that mocked in spite of himself. "If I hadn't gone to find Ljosa, she'd be dead now, buried in Djofullhol, and you'd have no hold over me."

"I should have removed her at once, knowing what dangerous thoughts would likely enter your Scipling head. But even I never suspected this audacity of you. How can you expect to live after this?"

"I've done nothing to deserve death. I was merely regaining my stolen property. It was the hand of Gedvondur that set those dead heroes to life, not mine. You know I have no such skill."

"Gedvondur." The name was spoken as an anathema. "With you as his embodiment."

"No, it was Svanlaug, the Dokkalfar witch you distrusted. I suppose they're both buried under the remains of Djofullhol. Gedvondur was searching for his ashes."

Sorkvir laughed coldly, without humor. "He didn't find them, that much I know. I hope he's buried. I would have destroyed him long ago. Djofull was a greedy fool in his seeking for power. Well, he's gone now, whoever it was that did it for him." His eyes rested upon Leifr balefully, with another fiery flicker that paralyzed Leifr's sword arm with numbness.

"What have you withheld from Ljosa?" Leifr went on. "She's not herself yet, as you promised she would be."

"You know by now that Hroaldsdottir is not all that she once was. I held back a portion of her essence, in case something of this nature happened."

"You would have cheated me even if I had defeated you," Leifr accused bitterly, taking a step forward, his hand touching his sword hilt.

"Yes," Sorkvir said with a hiss. "I'll strike at you in any way I can, whether I live or perish."

"I'll do the same, in spite of your hairlock," Leifr continued with ill-advised temper. "We're not completely at your mercy, Sorkvir. We can defeat you again."

"You're willing to test me?" Sorkvir uttered a harsh laugh, directing some of the wafting mist at Leifr. It smelled of open barrows and death, chilling him to the bone with such a sensation of hopeless horror that drawing his next breath seemed futile. His heart labored in the grip of Sorkvir's power, and his legs would hardly hold him. "You see, Scipling, I could put a stop to you at the blink of an eye—fragile mortal that you are. I have tasted death seven times, but you will pass Hela's bridge but once. I'm going to take Hroaldsdottir."

"No! I'll fight you for her!" Leifr summoned the will from somewhere to stagger forward desperately as Sorkvir moved toward Ljosa's sleeping form.

Sorkvir held up another vial, black with a gold stopper. "This is what will bring her completely back, as she once was. I'll leave this with you, in case you do defeat me. You are stretching my limited patience terribly thin, Scipling. I've never made such concessions before to any living creature. If you live, and if you deliver Thurid into my hands, you can find her in safekeeping at Hringurhol, the hill fort of the Dokkur Lavardur."

"Not good enough!" Leifr snarled. "You're not going to take her away again! She stays with me until the final battle!"

Raudbjorn rumbled anxiously and laid one hand restrainingly on Leifr's shoulder. Angrily Leifr shrugged it off and surged forward.

"Be still!" Sorkvir warned. "You push me nearer to the edge with every word!" He pointed suddenly at Starkad. "You, Alfar! Bring me the girl!"

"Starkad, if you touch her, I'll kill you!" Leifr roared in pain and fury, staggering against Sorkvir's rebuffing power. Raud-bjorn gripped him by the arms.

"You're playing traitor, too, Raudbjorn?" he growled, strug-gling with all his fury to get loose, wanting nothing more than to get his hands upon his sword.

Grunting when Leifr managed to bury an elbow in his ribs, Raudbjorn wrapped him in a powerful bear hug, pinning his arms down. Starkad looked at Sorkvir in awe a moment, then slowly knelt beside Ljosa to lift her up in his arms, passing her to Sorkvir to carry on his saddle before him. Her long pale hair fluttered over his black-clad arm as he reined his horse around. Lifting his hand in sardonic salute, he rode away with a flapping of his cloak, giving the momentary impression that man and horse were taking wing. His last words were "Be at the next point on your map tomorrow night if you wish to continue liv-ing."

Leifr watched until Sorkvir vanished in a cloud of swirling mist, his rage gradually slumping into despair. By the time he could breathe normally instead of gasping in fury, Sorkvir was gone, and he found Starkad half supporting him on one side and Raudbjorn on the other, with tears rolling down his mournful countenance. With one hand he patted at Leifr's back as gently as he could, unable to summon words to speak.

"We had to let her go," Starkad said unsteadily. He held up the black vial. "At least we've got this now. He would have killed us all, Leifr. We're sorry we had to go against you, but there was no other way."

Drained of his berserk rage, Leifr waved away Starkad's sup-port and Raudbjorn's anguished consternation. "I'm all right," he said with forced steadiness. "The horses are saddled and it's nearly daylight. Let's get moving before Nagli finds his courage and comes back to look for us. He's not going to give up that reward without some persuasion." He turned to Starkad and looked at him searchingly, trying to detect signs of fear in the youth. "You ought to go home while you can. If you go on, you may never see Fangelsi and Ermingerd again. This isn't your quarrel. You've seen how easy it is to die when you run afoul of wizards."

Starkad shook his head, setting his jaw in determination, although he looked a little pale at the mention of Ermingerd. ''I won't go,'' he said fiercely; then he added in an anxious tone, ''You won't try to force me to go, will you, Leifr?''

Leifr shook his head with a faint quirk of a smile. ''No, I won't force you. We can use your sword arm for better things than shearing sheep. Besides, it's rather too late for you to go back now. You've already been branded as a murderer by those thief-takers. You wouldn't want to lead them to Fangelsi.''

In the days to come, Leifr again learned the bitter meaning of being a hunted, driven man. Endlessly he scanned the harsh landscape for signs of the following Naglissons, glimpsing a distant wisp of smoke or dust, or often the sight of four horsemen silhouetted against the sky. The Naglissons swaddled their faces and traveled by day with impunity, and menaced as well by night, waiting for an opportunity when they were certain Sorkvir wouldn't come to the defense of his pawns.

''They're vultures,'' Leifr snorted angrily. ''Waiting for us to weaken for a single moment; then they'll swoop down and do their filthy work. They're not clean fighters.''

Raudbjorn disagreed, naturally, that there was anything unsavory about the profession of thief-taking. ''Like vultures and carcasses,'' he explained, contorting his brow in mighty thought. ''Thief-takers feed on bad things, too. Thief-takers and vultures make Skarpsey cleaner place to live.'' He beamed at the nobility of the idea. ''Scavengers not much liked, but Skarpsey needs plenty vultures and thief-takers.''

Starkad shook his head, huddling under a sheepskin against the resentful blasts of a late spring blizzard. ''I suppose that's true. Wherever you find thief-takers, you'll soon find vultures.''

Leifr could scarcely keep his temper. The place Sorkvir had ordered them to stop was hardly fit for a camping place, with no food or water for the horses and scant protection from the grimly patient Naglissons.

''You speak of vultures and ravens as if our carcasses weren't about to be picked and scattered by them,'' Leifr snarled in ferocious impatience as he unfurled his maps for some painstaking scrutiny, comparing Sorkvir's vellum with the maps Thurid had given him. A plan was gradually forming in his head as he studied the similarities of the maps, and the urgency of his success in this plan rendered him almost intolerable company.

Raudbjorn shrugged his mighty shoulders. "No man knows own fate, Leifr. Can't change threads Norns spin."

Leifr folded up his maps to stride up and down watchfully beside their wretched little fire, coaxed together from twigs and the dung of wild reindeer. He growled, "When Sorkvir gets here tonight, I'm going to attempt some thread-changing. You're going to help me convince him."

Starkad eyed him with alarm, having swiftly learned the lesson that Sorkvir could scarcely tolerate the presence of such a young Alfar as he was, let alone any injudicious words Starkad might inadvisedly address to him.

"Sorkvir will rip my head off," he said. "You're the only one he'll even speak to."

"You don't have to say anything," Leifr replied. "Just stand here and look hungry. I'm going to convince him we need to go to a settlement to barter for provisions."

"That won't be hard," Starkad said. "We're almost starving. I refuse to eat anything Raudbjorn scavenges. He thinks roasted maggots are a great delicacy. But what are you going to do, Leifr? Sorkvir isn't the most patient creature. He's a draug, not a mortal man. He doesn't get hungry or thirsty or tired. You can't reason with him."

"We'll see," Leifr said grimly. "He's desperate to lay his hands on Thurid and Heldur's orb, and we're his only tools for getting Thurid out of the Guildhall. He might listen to any idea that will further his purpose."

"You don't want to help him get to Thurid," Starkad said. "But I suppose you could dump the whole bloody mess in his lap, once we get there, and let Thurid figure out a way to get rid of Sorkvir. I doubt if he would like that much, though."

"You don't need to worry about anything," Leifr retorted. "Just be ready to come with me when Sorkvir appears tonight."

For the past four nights Sorkvir had appeared a few hours after dark, in a great gust of wind and driving hail. Perhaps he was powerful enough to command the elements to carry him where he wished, or else he was making an impressive display to intimidate his captives. As long as it kept the Naglissons at a distance, Leifr did not care what manifestations Sorkvir presented upon his arrival.

Sorkvir appeared on a distant ridgetop, galloping along heedlessly in the dark, trailing a cloud of greenish mist. Halting on a hilltop overlooking the small camp, he extended one hand in a commanding, beckoning gesture and waited for Leifr to approach. Leifr's scalp tightened, anticipating the fiery raking pain of Sorkvir's spell over him. He motioned to Starkad to follow, leaving Raudbjorn standing guard atop a skarp.

Sorkvir sat his horse, waiting impatiently, clutching his spewing staff. In four days, Sorkvir's aspect had taken on a loathsome greenish glow, like the slime covering a rotting log in a bog. Mist seemed to exude from his body in a cloud. As Leifr stood gazing at this horror from Hel, he earnestly hoped that Sorkvir's governing spell was fading away, even as the rest of Djofull's illusions had faded with his death.

Sorkvir's horse danced in a nervous half circle, blowing icy breaths that reeked of barrows and dust.

"Tomorrow, Jugardur-dahl," Sorkvir rasped. "We are very near the end of our journey. The Guildhall is across the river and half a day beyond. Jugardur will be your final stopping place."

"Is there a settlement at Jugardur?" Leifr asked.

"Not unless you count the dead in their graves. Why do you ask? There is no one who can rid you of me."

Leifr glanced at Starkad, who huddled with desperate courage in his flapping cloak. "I ask because we're in need of provisions. Hefillstad is also a day's journey from here, and closer besides to the Guildhall."

"Closer indeed," rasped Sorkvir. "It's right at the foot of the fortress. Hefillstad is full of wizards and acolytes and other leeches who prey upon the favor of the Guildhall. You won't be going there."

"We won't be going anywhere if we don't reprovision soon," Leifr answered. "We're getting weak from surviving on almost nothing. We need some strength if we're going to outwit Fire Wizards. Besides, how can we get ourselves into the Guildhall with no help? What we need is a mentor, known by the wizards."

"Mentor? You're not likely to get one," Sorkvir snorted in contempt. "Unless you have a friend in Hefillstad." His tone was laced with menace, but his gaze was speculative.

"Thurid has a friend in Hefillstad," Leifr went on. "The wizard who trained him for Guild service."

"And failed to train him well enough to get accepted for an apprenticeship," Sorkvir concluded. "What is the name of this wizard?"

"Gradagur."

"Gradagur—yes, I've heard of the name. He's the laughing-stock of the Fire Wizards' Guild. He's completely insane. Is this the friend in Hefillstad you thought you could count upon to get you inside the Guildhall?"

"Yes. Who could be further above suspicion?"

"You're as mad as he is, Scipling. What earthly good do you think he'll do you?" Sorkvir almost chuckled, if such a nasty sound could be construed as mirth.

"He got Thurid into the Guildhall. If he's known for training students, it wouldn't be unusual that he might have a couple more. How else do you propose we get into the strongest, best-protected fortress in the entire Ljosalfar realm? There must be a hundred Fire Wizards there at any given time, all as suspicious and vigilant as adders. Did you think the three of us would boldly attack their front gate, demanding entrance?"

Sorkvir hissed at this disrespect and raised his hand. Leifr winced, bracing himself for the jolt. But Sorkvir only beckoned him to come closer.

"I had a plan," Sorkvir said, his sunken eyes boring into Leifr, searching for deception. "But your plan might be better. I can't see where Gradagur is any threat. He was old when he trained Thurid, and now he is older as well as perfectly mad. You couldn't have worse help if you decide to betray me."

"I won't betray you before I get Thurid out of the Guildhall," Leifr answered. "You forget that we have the same goal. After he's safe, be on your guard. I'll destroy you at the first opportunity."

"You no doubt take great comfort in your idle threats," Sorkvir said. "You'll do nothing as long as I have control of Hroaldsdottir."

"Only as long as she comes to no harm," Leifr replied.

"What do I care for your threats? What can you do to one such as I, with your Rhbu sword buried under the ruins of Djo-fullhol?"

Leifr restrained himself from rising to the bait, swallowing his temper with difficulty. Quarrels with Sorkvir always ended rather badly for him, as long as Sorkvir possessed that cursed little bag with a lock of his hair in it and no telling what other powerful amulets. Besides, he feared to speak where the sword was concerned, lest Sorkvir somehow discern that *Endalaus Daudi* was in its sheath beside the fire.

"We will go to Hefillstad tomorrow," Leifr said curtly. "Will you dare show yourself there?"

"You may count upon it that I will be watching your every move," Sorkvir answered. "When I wish to speak to you, I'll send you the summons you're already familiar with, and you will come at my command." He raised his hand and passed it back and forth, and Leifr felt the needles of pain shooting through his head.

With a harsh growl to his horse, Sorkvir sent the beast charging away, its hooves churning a fast tattoo on the earth, the wind of its passage fanning Leifr with a cold breath that smelled of death and decay. Not for the first time, Leifr shook his head in grim wonder. This was a far worse situation than he had escaped in the Scipling realm, where he had been outlawed for his misdeeds. This time he could not see the impending events coming to a satisfactory resolution for anyone involved. Sorkvir was a disease, contaminating everything that touched him.

And Leifr himself was almost as bad, contaminating everyone with his hideously bad luck. With a groan, he went back and sat by the fire to brood in unfriendly silence.

Chapter 5

✤✦✤✦✤✦✤✦✤✦✤✦✤✦✤✦✤✦✤✦✤✦✤✦✤✦✤✦✤✦✤✦✤✦✤✦✤✤

After seeing Ulfskrittinn and Djofullhol, Leifr had similar expectations for Hefillstad. His surprise was considerable and pleasant when he crossed the river ford and discovered that Hefillstad was a haven from the darkness and terror of Dokkalfar rule. The steep slopes of the fells were green, dotted with flocks of sheep and cattle brought up from the homesteads to graze. Leifr counted seven homesteads visible from their vantage point, in addition to the cluster of houses gathered at the quay, where the fishing and trading folk lived. The river emptied into a narrow, far-roaming fjord, which gave the inhabitants the freedom and power of eventual access to the open sea, as well as the trade from other seacoast settlements.

Overlooking the peaceful settlement was the Guildhall of the Fire Wizards, perched upon the highest neck of land thrusting out into the sea, surrounded by water on three sides and a deep rocky chasm on the landward side. Eagerly Leifr studied it, soon discerning that it consisted of a dismaying number of walls and courtyards and towers and halls built around an ancient black ruin, rising higher and yet more gracefully than any recent structure. Three of four delicate towers were in various stages of crumbling and falling away, but the fourth and last remained intact, a tall, watchful needle presiding over the sea and the land. Leifr called to mind Starkad's statement that magic rather than mortar held the old Rhbu ruins together; seeing such an impossible structure convinced him of the truth of it. No Scipling or Alfar could have built four soaring towers without collapse, particularly in a land so subject to subterranean shakings and rumblings as Skarpsey. Almost as awe-inspiring as the towers was the black maw of the gorge separating the Guildhall on

59

its spit of headland from the common settlement on its other side. No gradual process of nature had carved it. The black heart of Skarpsey lay exposed and steaming, veiling the lower reaches of the headland in mist. Above, black and haughty, the Guildhall perched, unattainable to common men.

Leifr sniffed the familiar fishy smell of salt water, considering the fresh delicacies in the nets of the fishermen, rowing slowly home from their barges tethered in the fishing waters. It reminded him of home, a faraway and haunting memory, buried some time ago.

A grunt and a sinister rattling of arms from Raudbjorn sharpened his attention upon the path below, leading into the settlement. A lone horseman was approaching warily.

"Halloa," he called. "What is your business here, travelers?"

Leifr came forward a short way, stopping before he reached the crucial zone of possible threat. "We're seeking to become acolytes to the Fire Wizards' Guild," he answered.

The sentry nodded toward Raudbjorn. "That one doesn't much look like an acolyte."

"We brought him along for protection." Starkad spoke up. "It's a dangerous journey all the way from Solvorfirth to the Guildhall. My name is Starkad, and this is Leifr, and the Norskur is Raudbjorn."

The sentry lost his vigilant stance and slowly shook his head. "I might have known you'd be acolytes. You have that look of innocent hopefulness. We see at least fifty of your sort here every year. But I suppose you're welcome enough. The Guild seems to use up acolytes like firewood. Myself, I can't see the nobility of it, getting blown up in experiments, or having your shape shifted for the amusement of some old sooty Meistari and his apprentice. But I guess it's the next best thing, when you have no real talent for magic yourself. Sometimes it seems a pity, though. The life of an acolyte to the Guild is not an easy one."

"We know, but we like to suffer for a good cause," Starkad said virtuously. "It's the best way to thwart the rising tide of the evil Dokkalfar. Could you guide us to the lodgings of our wizard mentor? We've heard of the greatness of Gradagur, and we've resolved to be trained by none other. We come from wealthy households, and we're used to nothing but the best.''

The watchman's eyes rounded with astonishment, then his features crinkled up with suppressed mirth. He could barely swallow a great laugh, turning it into a coughing fit at the last moment.

"Gradagur, of course,'' he wheezed, his eyes watering. "Certainly, he's most famous. How did you hear of him?''

Leifr gazed at Starkad fearfully, half admiring his adroitness at telling falsehoods.

"From travelers who had visited the Guildhall,'' Starkad replied loftily. "I demanded to know the name of the most respected of the wizard mentors, and of course it was Gradagur. No price is too high to pay for his training.''

"Oh, indeed, of course,'' the sentry hastened to agree. "I can't take you there myself, because I'm on duty, but you'll find Gradagur in the ruins of Hardurjord. Do you see that rocky fell above the fishing houses and the boat stand? Right on the top of it is Hardurjord. You'd better get there before dark, or you might fall off the cliff, or there's things about that place—'' Suddenly relenting, the sentry interrupted himself. "Now listen, you young fellows. Gradagur isn't the mentor you want. He's as crazy as bot flies in the summertime. Go to someone else. Murari will be glad to take you in and train you. Gradagur is old and crazy, and I doubt if the Guildhall would let you in if he was with you. Someone gave you the wrong information, probably as a nasty joke.''

"You must be the one who is joking,'' Starkad said in a shocked tone.

"We'll have to see him for ourselves,'' Leifr added in a suspicious voice. "It's often this way when someone is trying to keep you from something.''

"Indeed I am,'' the sentry said. "I'm trying to keep you from making a big mistake. But it's your time you'll be wasting. Go up and see Gradagur, if you don't believe me. You'll probably find him trying to make some strange machine fly through the air, or trying to get struck by lightning. I tell you, if he's not actually deliberately dangerous, you could still get hurt around him.''

"We'll go," Leifr said, with genuine misgivings. "We'll have to see for ourselves."

"Don't say I didn't warn you," the sentry said. "When you get back, come looking for me at Finn's gistihus. You can spend the night there and buy some passable food and drink. I'll help you find a decent mentor."

Starkad thanked him solemnly and they watched him ride away back to his sentry duty. With misgivings, Leifr led the way up the rugged trail toward Hardurjord. Before long they all had to dismount and lead their horses. It was twilight by the time they reached the top, where the wind was whistling through the walls of the ruins with a most unwelcoming howl. A storm was piling up over the headland, roiling and churning and promising a good drenching for anyone without shelter that night. The troll-hounds flattened their ears and crouched in the shelter of the jumbled blocks of stone, looking at Leifr through slitted eyes. Raudbjorn and Starkad also gazed at him in silent reproach, their cloaks flapping, their hands blue and stiff on their reins, while the hope of a pleasant supper quickly dissolved.

Leifr saw no signs of life or human occupation in the ruin. A lone squat tower with no top leaned over the edge of the steep drop to the firth, as if a leap were imminent, but at least it would offer some shelter from the wind.

"Maybe he died," Starkad said once they were inside the tower, "and nobody noticed."

Leifr stifled a sigh. The tower was damp and smelled of generations of bird nests and bird droppings. Slowly his eyes traveled upward to the jagged circle of twilight sky visible not far above, where the disturbed seabirds were squalling and screeling. Then a movement of something larger than a bird caught his eye. A human figure in a wildly flapping cloak sidled along the top of the broken wall, crouching over something in his hands and peering upward with rapt intensity. He scuttled a few steps back and forth in evident excitement, still gazing into the sky, where the storm clouds seemed to have lodged over Hardurjord, crackling and rumbling ominously. The nearer the storm and the louder its bolts and blasts, the better the personage on the tower wall seemed to like it. He capered around and in intervals of the wind's howling, Leifr could hear a cracked, elated cackling.

"That must be Gradagur," Starkad said. "Only a crazy person would be up there in a lightning storm!"

Suddenly the storm broke overhead with a brilliant flickering bolt of lightning that turned every illuminated object a livid purple, with a sputtering crackle, followed by a ferocious crash of thunder. Leifr stared upward in horror as the slight figure above was enveloped in a sizzling shower of sparks, and a hissing bolt of fire came zinging straight down toward him and the others. With another sinister burst of crackling it struck a large object standing near the wall, illuminating it with a fizzing and hissing. The horses squealed and snorted and plunged around in terror, threatening to trample anything smaller that got in their way. Raudbjorn quieted them, by main force, gripping a couple of forelocks or ears and growling soothingly. After the lightning bolt, nothing further happened, so Leifr looked up with dazzled eyes at the top of the tower, not expecting to see the wizard alive, but there he was, hopping briskly down the crude stairway as if being struck by lightning was a most invigorating occurrence.

"Halloa!" the wizard exclaimed, stopping short at the sight of his guests. "Company! Let me turn on some lights!"

He swooped down on the fizzing, glowing object, and suddenly a brilliant glow like lightning filled the old tower. Gradagur stood beaming at them beside a nest of finely worked wire coming out of the stone box. His hair stood up in singed wisps, and his beard was almost burnt completely away, framing a rosy, wizened face where blazed a childlike, infectious enthusiasm.

"Isn't it lovely?" he asked in a tone of reverent awe. "Once it was believed that only the sun could make light in dark places, but one day men will make their own light in any place they desire it. The power of lightning will be harnessed. Do you know what it will mean if mankind conquers the dark?" Not waiting for an answer, for which Leifr was at a complete loss anyway, he continued with great significance, "It means that the Dokkalfar will no longer have power over Skarpsey for half the year. Can you imagine every hall, every homestead, illuminated with such glorious light?"

"Will everyone get accustomed to being struck by lightning?" Starkad inquired uneasily, squinting in the brilliant glare of the glowing wires.

"In the future there will be better ways," Gradagur said judiciously. "Oh, my lads, if you could only see the future as I have seen it! There will be no darkness anywhere, and great machines will carry people over and across the face of the earth and through the air at wizard speeds. Every man, woman, and child who lives will have such powers at their fingertips as to make the most powerful of those arrogant fools in the Guildhall weep from sheer envy. We'll have no need of wizards then."

"What is this—this energy called?" Leifr asked, still gazing at the glowing wires in awe.

"I call it rafmagn," Gradagur replied pridefully. "You see that great long pole reaching up into the sky? It carries the lightning down to this device, which stores it until I want to use it. I don't have a name for it yet. In the future, I'm sure it'll have one. Would you like to see some of my other experiments? I'm trying to use rafmagn to turn a grinding wheel. Did you know that one day men won't have to rely upon horses to carry them everywhere? Great machines will do the carrying and the pulling and the plowing and the harvesting. I've seen the wonderful engines that power these machines, but for the life of me I can't find the proper metal, or get it forged into the correct shapes. It may surprise you to know that the people of Hefillstad think I'm slightly cracked because of all my visions." He giggled, shaking his frazzled head in amazement as he led the way toward the door. "And then there's the flying machines, almost as dear a project to me as rafmagn. You can't imagine what it's like to get off the ground at last. Men are intended to soar like birds. If it weren't so dark and windy, I'd show you."

"That's very interesting, but have you got anything to eat?" Starkad asked bluntly. "Or do they eat food in the future?"

Gradagur clapped one hand to his forehead. "These wits are blasted so often they can't remember anything! Of course you're hungry and cold and tired. Forgive me for being carried away on the wings of my dreams. I do so much living in the future that I scarcely see the present. Leave your horses here and follow me. There's a little lad who will look after them, quite gone in the wits, I'm afraid, but he works hard enough. Ten years old and hasn't spoken a word yet, but he's got an observing mind. I shouldn't be at all surprised if he startled the friendly folk of Hefillstad one day. I wasn't much of a specimen myself when I was young.''

Leifr noted silently that a good wind would probably carry Gradagur away. With a snapping and popping of sparks Gradagur disconnected his rafmagn, plunging the tower once more into familiar and comforting darkness. Shaking his singed fingers, he led the way out of the tower, calling for his boy to attend to the horses.

Gradagur's house was a room hollowed out of the fallen ruin, down a short flight of crumbling steps. A large wooden door opened inward on a room that reminded Leifr much of Thurid's old cave back in Dallir. The articles cluttering the tables and shelves were nothing like Leifr had ever seen before, mostly made of polished metals in bizarre shapes, and things of glass and fine wires, where bits of rafmagn glowed in a sinister fashion.

''Did you ever dream,'' Gradagur began in a voice hushed by reverence, ''that one day men's voices will be carried on the wind itself, faster than any arrow can fly? You could be here, in my house, and speak to your father or mother at home in—in— wherever you came from. Even the mighty oceans will be no barrier. And the stars themselves—''

Leifr shook his head, wanting to plug his ears. This was all madness, the most terrifying case he had ever encountered. If he hadn't been so desperate with hunger and exhaustion and worry, he would have turned and gotten straight out of there.

''Gradagur,'' he said gently, feeling sorry for the pitiful creature in spite of himself, ''I'm sure nothing could be more splendid than to fly through the air and talk on the wind, but what we need now is a place to rest and food to eat, if we might beg your hospitality.''

''Of course, of course,'' Gradagur exclaimed, calling himself back to the present with another startled slap on the forehead. Briskly he laid out a large moldy cheese, hard black bread, and a huge sooty pot of turnips, potatoes, rabbit meat, and other savory vegetables and grains. While they ate, Gradagur described a marvelous procedure by which rafmagn could be used to cook food without the use of firewood; when they were finished, he showed them a bucket of peculiar black sticky stuff which he said came out of the earth, and would one day be more precious than gold to everyone on the face of the earth. By then, Leifr knew the old fellow was completely insane, and Starkad could scarcely restrain himself from laughing. Raudbjorn looked on with a total lack of comprehension.

"Future is strange place," he grunted doubtfully, scratching the back of his bristly neck. "Any thief-takers there?"

"I haven't seen any," Gradagur replied. "People then will be very different from now. Thousands and thousands of them will live in great cities, in houses big and tall enough for hundreds of them to live at the same time. I'm sure there will be thief-takers among them. But there will be no wizards. Nobody will need them for anything."

Upon this final bit of lunacy, Leifr found a spot near the hearth and curled up to go to sleep, with his troll-hounds gathered comfortably around him to warn him of any threat, as well as to keep him warm. In the morning, they would find Finn's inn and the sentry. Gradagur might have once been a suitable wizard mentor, if he had given Thurid any degree of instruction at all, but now his mind was in regrettable shambles. Probably he had forgotten the Guildhall even existed, so engrossed was he in his experiments with lightning and all sorts of other undoubtedly forbidden knowledge.

Once during the night he was awakened by the growling of the troll-hounds, and a warning lash of prickling pain inside his head betrayed the presence of Sorkvir somewhere outside. He got up and went quietly to the door, but he felt no compulsion to seek him out, so he lay down again. Sorkvir had merely warned him and gone on.

In the morning, Gradagur could hardly wait to show them his flying machines, fragile structures made into enormous long wings with nothing but strips of wood, cloth, ropes, and wires. Gradagur demonstrated how the machine was harnessed to a person's shoulders, like a giant set of butterfly wings.

"I haven't flown this design yet," he said, "but it could be done, if we pushed it off the cliff by the tower. I don't know how well that rudder design will work, though. There's some lovely updrafts that could carry you along for half the day, like an eagle. Would you believe that I've flown over Hefillstad in this kite?'' He proudly pointed to a thing shaped more like a sail, with a small sling for a seat. ''I sailed right over the Guildhall, and there was nothing they could do to stop me. You should have seen them, staring up at me in my little airship with their mouths open, as if they had never seen anything so wonderful as a man flying unassisted by their primitive superstitious powers. If ever there was a benighted lot of blunderers, fumbling blindly around what they know not, practically stepping on the most wonderful of miracles—and do you know, they don't regard me highly. They're afraid I'll discover something they don't know. They live in dread of me, if the truth were to be told.'' He chuckled delightedly. ''How would you like to go for a ride in this, Leifr? You'd soon get the hang of the controls—''

''No thanks! I prefer to keep my feet upon the earth where they belong,'' Leifr said quickly. ''You may think you're a bird, but I know I'm not. Gradagur, about the Wizards' Guildhall—have you ever been inside?''

''Oh yes, back in the old days when I was trying to be a wizard. Doomed to failure, they said.''

''Do you remember Thurid, a student of yours?''

''Certainly I remember Thurid. A bright youth, but he took himself far too seriously. Plenty of lads fail their First Examinations, and come back to try again and succeed—for all that's worth. I try to be tolerant. No one else has my vision of the future. But Thurid took it to heart and decided he'd been humiliated. And all for nothing, too. He could have been as good as any of them.''

''We're friends of Thurid,'' Leifr said. ''He's done better than anyone could have dreamed—so well that the Guild has him in for an Inquisition.''

''Inquisition! You don't say! I wondered what poor wretch it was. They put up a red flag whenever an Inquisition is on, so nobody will try to disturb them. It's a nasty business. Poor Thurid! I wonder what the lad did to get their backs up against him.''

''Rhbu magic,'' Leifr said.

Gradagur groaned and smote his brow. "Oh no! That dolt. He shouldn't have touched that stuff. Earth magic is even more dangerous than fire magic. It comes from the other worlds, and their positions change its influence. Even I have a very sketchy view of what happens beyond our own world, in the dark reaches of outer space. There are worlds without number out there, Leifr lad. It's grander than you can ever imagine, ever know, in your short and ignorant lifetime."

Leifr shuddered suddenly, and his neck hairs bristled up as if a cold wave had struck him. Gradagur's clear eyes gazed away into the sky as if he did indeed see other worlds besides the one he now walked upon. The only world, as far as Leifr was concerned, was the one around him.

"Gradagur, about Thurid," he began, in an attempt to steer Gradagur's far-flung thoughts back to the matter at hand. The most harmless of statements led to another wild flight of his disordered mind, until one could scarcely talk intelligently with him.

"Yes, Thurid, in the hands of the Guild," Gradagur replied smartly. "And you've come to get him out. The only way you'll do it is to fly over their walls and drop down among them, like a hawk in a chicken yard. Unfortunately, I don't know how you can fly Thurid out again, until somehow we come up with powered flight. We don't have enough time for that, I'm afraid. But there is my lighter-than-air flying ship. I abandoned it when dragon-gas proved too dangerous to work with—as well as rather difficult to obtain. It made a spectacular explosion, one that the people of Hefillstad won't soon forget. But I've been thinking there must be an easier way than dragon-gas—"

Leifr abandoned his hope of enlisting Gradagur's aid. "What we wanted was a wizard mentor to get us into the Guildhall so we could find Thurid," he said in disgust.

"A mentor? You want to become acolytes to that obsolete, moth-eaten, fire-breathing assortment of alchemists and shape-shifters and sorcerers? Leifr, you seriously disappoint me. I thought you were more intelligent than that. In a few thousand years they'll be gone, and people like me will have replaced their mind-powers with real powers of steel and wires and raf-magn."

"I don't care about all that," Leifr snapped. "I'll be dead considerably sooner, and all I care about is getting Thurid out of the Guildhall in the way that I'm best fit for, which is to sneak in and steal him out somehow. I don't want to have to fight the Fire Wizards, but I have a weapon that can stand against them, if I have to use it. You're so caught up in your crazy visions of the future that you've forgotten about the present. Men don't fly. Your rafmagn is nothing but a strange and useless trick—for now. All this talk is getting us nowhere. Can you help us, or should we look for someone else to help us? We don't have much time."

Gradagur turned upon Leifr with a rare shrewd expression, suddenly shedding his dreamer's blindness.

"Being followed, are you?" he asked, and went on after scarcely waiting for Leifr's cautious nod. "Yes, I saw where that draug creature came around Hardurjord last night. You're safe enough with me, behind that good stout door. If it's any consolation to you, in the future they'll very likely find a preventive for the walking dead. It's such an annoyance, isn't it? I wonder if there's not something we could embalm them with—"

"Gradagur, if I don't get Thurid out of the Guildhall, this draug is going to destroy a lot of innocent people, with me among them. Just tell me if you want to mentor us into the Guildhall or not. If you don't, or can't, we'll be on our way to find someone who can."

"You've got a one-track mind, haven't you?" Gradagur looked at him pityingly a moment, then his expression brightened. "In the future, great engines will run upon two tracks, carrying people and sheep and wool and wheat, and huge loads of ore from the bowels of the earth. What a glorious time it will be to live then, although I daresay I won't see it, and neither will you or Thurid. Thurid, Thurid, yes-yes-yes, what to do about Thurid? I can mentor you into the Guildhall, never fear about that. I was once respected as a wizard, until I began receiving my glorious visions of the future. Funny how the most wonderful stroke of fortune can render one so perfectly unacceptable to one's former friends. You might not believe it, but they think I'm mad." He bent over, laughing until the tears came, and clutched his knees to support himself.

"I tell you, lad," he went on, wiping his eyes, "I'm more sane than any of them. I'm just ahead of my own time. It's the curse of greatness, I suppose, to lose the understanding of the average man as well as his friendship. Well, it's no matter to me. We've got to start educating you properly to fill acolyte positions. It won't be easy, I'm afraid. You're about as dense as a fence post when it comes to Alfar powers. It would help, you know, if you had a few skills—and even a tiny grain of a carbuncle."

Leifr's wits whirled under such an onslaught of verbiage, but he managed to pounce upon this slight opening. "Thank you, but I'm not an Alfar. I'm a Scipling."

"Oh well, then that explains it perfectly. I'm afraid it won't do at all for you to go into the Guildhall. They'd smell you out instantly and throw you out of there so fast you wouldn't have a chance to blink twice. They're monstrously particular about their acolytes. They want someone stupid enough to tolerate their experiments, but not so hopelessly inept that there's no power to draw from. You stubborn Sciplings have nothing to give voluntarily, although it can be taken against your will, but that would violate the benevolent codes of the Guild, in theory—"

Gradagur's breath ran out, and Leifr interrupted, "But I do have a carbuncle. It's just not—not fastened in. Yet, anyway. If I ever do decide to adopt it." Nervously he rubbed the carbuncle through the hole he had worn in its leather pouch, and felt an irritated prodding from Fridmarr, telling him as plainly as if a voice were speaking to him, "Now you'll have to do it, if you want to save Thurid!"

Leifr reluctantly produced the pouch and rolled the glittering red stone into the palm of his hand. Gradagur stared at him in great consternation and at the carbuncle, his mouth gaping uselessly, for once seemingly at a loss for something to say.

"Do you know what might happen to you if you attempt to implant a carbuncle of such power under your skin?" Gradagur demanded in a hushed tone.

Leifr nodded impatiently. "Something terrible, but there's nothing else to be done if we're to save Thurid, and it's terribly important that he not be changed in any way by the Guild. I wouldn't mind if he changed them, but I doubt if that will happen."

"So do I," Gradagur said. "But you won't do him any good if you're dead, or completely possessed by whoever was born with that stone. Look at the size of it. Imagine the memories and powers and voices it has absorbed from the past. Your knowledge would be positively ancient."

"Acceptable to the Guild?"

"Highly. Perhaps they would eventually let you become an apprentice. It's very rare that an acolyte is apprenticed. They might be suspicious of someone with such strength appearing on their doorstep, as it were, and they're bound to notice you're a Scipling, or at least an outlander of some sort, but they'll be greedy for that stone and the one who possesses it. Greed is a wonderful cure for suspicion. It might work—indeed, I think it will work. You have that Norskur sent to protect you, as if someone knew you were a very valuable commodity."

"The wizards might like the idea that I'm unknown," Leifr suggested, his voice a bit stiff as he contemplated the inevitable surrender to the stone. Fear nagged at him, as well as his own proud resistance to outside domination. There was also the matter of Sorkvir's holding spell over him. He wondered how Fridmarr would react to it, and if Sorkvir would know that he had joined forces with the carbuncle. For a grim moment, he imagined his own body as a battleground between two such bitter enemies. He might not survive, or, if he did, his sanity might be destroyed by the conflict. Clutching the carbuncle in his fist, he resolved to go ahead with it, and the red stone blazed in response.

Gradagur shook his head. "I never dreamed I'd have to get involved in this primitive knowledge again. It's sometimes hard to remember I still live in a world of magic and spell and uncontrolled currents of power. One day it will not always be thus. Everything will be safe and sure and predictable. Well, I don't much like doing this, but I suppose it's the only choice I've got. I'll have to do a bit of studying to make sure it's done properly. I've made a point of forgetting all my magical, mystical training that I can, but I fear it's bred in the bones, so you needn't fear

I'll bungle it too badly.'' He heaved a sigh, and a grim look replaced his buoyant expression.

As they had stood talking near Gradagur's strange airships, Leifr suddenly became aware of a cat stalking slowly around them, easing suspiciously into a safe place to watch them. Before Ljosa, he had always regarded cats as furtive, slinking characters whenever he had deigned to notice them. Now he eyed the furry little predators more shrewdly, noting that this one was particularly large. It was completely black and bony-looking, with the ragged ears and swollen jowls of a thousand battles. With flattened ears and narrowed green eyes it watched Leifr, its tail twitching as it crouched atop a moss-chinked stone wall. The troll-hounds growled softly, lying down protectively at Leifr's feet with their back fur bristling with menace. Usually they were more than glad to see a cat, greeting one's appearance with wagging tails, lolling tongues, clownish yelps and absurd caracoles, in anticipation of a merry chase. This cat opened its jaws in a virulent hiss, rising onto its toes truculently.

"There's an ugly brute," Gradagur observed. "I haven't seen him around before. Cheeky devil, isn't he? Well, we'd best get on with the preparations. Don't disturb me until sundown. I'd stay close around here today, if I were you, and hope that word doesn't spread as far as the Guildhall that you've arrived. Fodur and those others might be greatly interested to know that you're here. In a few days there's going to be a batch of acolytes taken up to the Guildhall, and we'll slip you and Starkad into the midst of them and hope nobody's the wiser. One acolyte looks much like another. You won't be as well prepared as you ought to be, but then you're not real acolytes, either. By the time somebody notices, it'll be too late and you'll be inside the Guildhall." Gradagur blinked his eyes, a humorous grin suddenly splitting his features. "I should have thought of sabotaging the Wizards' Guild long ago. It's an idea I rather enjoy."

Chapter 6

At sundown, Gradagur came out of his house, looking worn and solemn. He stood and gazed longingly at his tower for a few moments, where a tall pole reached up to snare lightning bolts when they were in season. Clearly he would have preferred to be experimenting with his rafmagn and airships and other strange inventions.

"It is time," he greeted Leifr heavily. "I wish I didn't have to do what I'm about to do. We shall implant this carbuncle beneath your skin, and you'll be forever one of the Ljosalfar. Or completely insane, or dead. I fear I can't promise you any specific result. You're certain you wouldn't rather fly over their walls and drop into the midst of them unexpectedly? No, I didn't suppose you would. It would be hard to tell where you might land, in the middle of the laundry green or the turnip field or into some secret enclave where they would know you had no business. Well, let's begin. I've got a good sharp knife. I recommend that Starkad and Raudbjorn wait outside. We don't know what the results of this union between Scipling and carbuncle are going to be."

"Starkad," Leifr said battling with his own fears and his resolve to help Thurid, "if something should happen to me, I want you to search out Ljosa and get her back to her true form. Raudbjorn, I want you to stay with Starkad and protect him as you've protected me. The troll-hounds will be yours. Starkad, you can have Jolfr. And *Endalaus Daudi* must be hidden somewhere, so neither the Dokkalfar nor the Wizards' Guild can lay their hands on it. Gradagur, I'll leave that burden up to you."

Raudbjorn glowered suspiciously from Leifr to Gradagur.

"Leifr won't die," he growled. "Eh, wizard? Raudbjorn skin wizard like rabbit."

Starkad shook Leifr's hand, swallowed hard, and tried not to look worried. "Raudbjorn isn't quite the inheritance I've always dreamed of," he said. "You'd better not take the worms' way out, Leifr. You're sure this has to be done now?" he added anxiously.

Leifr nodded, not trusting himself to speak, and followed Gradagur into the house, where Gradagur commenced boiling and steaming with elaborate care the tools he thought needful, with his mouth and nose muffled under a kerchief. Watching his strange rituals made Leifr even more uneasy. After all, he was probably entrusting his life to a complete madman. He said nothing, realizing it was all part of some elaborate magical ritual, deeming it best to remain absolutely still, lest he disturb Gradagur's concentration.

Gradagur scrupulously boiled everything he touched, then washed his hands for a long time with soap, a substance Leifr had not seen much of in his lifetime. Then he instructed Leifr to scrub his left arm with the same thoroughness.

"This is the best that I can do under the present conditions," Gradagur said. "In the future, men will discover that everything they touch is covered with countless tiny creatures, so small we can't even see them, and these little creatures cause fevers, wounds to fester, women to die after childbirth, and every sort of illness that can bring about a man's death. It's possible that one of these invisible animals could cause you to die, while the carbuncle does nothing to harm you."

"Gradagur, don't think about the future now!" Leifr exclaimed. "As to invisible animals, I hope you haven't told many people, or one day you'll find yourself chained to a wall, or maybe someone will even burn you in your house. Can't you just forget all this nonsense and get started? The sooner it's begun, the sooner it will be over, and we'll know what's going to happen. Are you certain my arm is the best location?"

Gradagur took up a small knife, honed to utmost sharpness. "If you have to lose something, it would be better to lose your left arm. It will be the only way to get rid of this carbuncle if it tries to possess you."

Leifr winced at the thought. "Fridmarr wouldn't do anything like that," he said.

"Unembodied spirits will do anything to take a body again," Gradagur said. "One day there'll be a cure for them, too, when necromancers no longer call them out of the ground, or wizards' curses can keep them from staying dead. One day all this chaos and wizardry will be gone, forgotten, useless, when there are machines to do all the work that men desire to be done."

"What nonsense," Leifr growled uncomfortably. "There will always be the powers of Ljosalfar and Dokkalfar. Do you mean to say the battles will end one day?"

"My lad, there will be no Ljosalfar and no Dokkalfar," Gradagur answered. "Or if there are, they will have forgotten what their ancestors once were."

"You're mad," Leifr said. "Everything you say is nothing but craziness. It's impossible that men will ever fly like birds. Wizards might do it with their powers, but you can never do it with your machines. I don't think I want to go through with this. I'm going to leave this place and never come back."

Gradagur shrugged his shoulders. "I've told you too much. There's nothing like a taste of the future to frighten a man, which is why it's usually kept so well from us. Perhaps I am mad. Everyone in Hefillstad thinks so. I rather enjoy telling them something startling whenever I go to the market. All that I have foreseen will come to pass without my assistance, so it doesn't matter much what happens to me. I'm nothing but an observer outside the window. I don't know who or what opened the window. I can't see anything as near as tomorrow, or even next year, but I can see centuries down the corridor of time. There are many kinds of sight, Leifr. Do you really believe it so impossible that I should have this kind of sight?"

"I don't know," Leifr growled. "I'm only a Scipling, and we're not troubled much by sights and powers. I suppose such a thing could happen to you, particularly since you are—or were—a wizard. I just can't believe that the future could be so different from what is now. What use is this gift to you? It seems to bring you more grief than anything else, and no one wants to believe what you say."

"It doesn't matter, my lad, if no one can see the same view

that I see. I've climbed a mountain no one else can reach. I wouldn't give up my view for anything."

Leifr sighed and sat down again at the table. "Well, I guess it doesn't matter what you think you see. You aren't going to make many changes in the Dokkalfar, or in the Wizards' Guild. Get your knife and let's do this. Perhaps Fridmarr will make enough trouble that I can forget about you and your insane visions."

"Very well," Gradagur said heavily, and took up his knife. At that moment, Leifr stiffened under a raking blast of pain that nearly blinded him. He clutched the edge of the table to steady himself.

"Stop! Wait! We can't do it!" he gasped. "He's here, somewhere, and he knows! He won't let us do it!"

"Now who's talking mad?" Gradagur demanded. "Who's here? There's no one but us, and your friends outside."

Leifr clutched his temples, whispering hoarsely, "No, you're wrong. Sorkvir is here. The walking draug. He's following me, and he's got a hold over me through a lock of hair. My skull is about to burst. I've got to get away from here." Leifr stood up and staggered toward the door, half blinded with the agony. When he opened it, the black cat was crouched there, glaring at him balefully. With a hiss it glided away and took up a watchful position on the roof.

Anxiously Starkad leaped up and came forward, followed by Raudbjorn, huffing and glaring around for an opponent.

"More sorcery! What a blasted nuisance!" Gradagur muttered. "He's shifted shapes. I'd like to shift him, if I could, all the way to Niflheim. Are you going to give up on the carbuncle, Leifr?"

"Yes," Leifr answered wretchedly, still looking at the cat. At once the pain vanished. "We'll have to find another way to get into the Guildhall, Gradagur."

Gradagur's worried expression brightened instantly. "Of course we shall! I know we can! We'll sail over their walls like eagles and drop onto their roofs, where they least expect an attack to come from."

Starkad's eyes began to gleam with anticipation. "Like eagles!" he murmured. "This is something most wizards can't do. I doubt if anyone has ever gotten into the Guildhall before by stealth. We shall be the first to fly in.''

"Gradagur!" Leifr glowered at him in horror. "We can't fly! We're not birds!"

"No, but we can imitate them," Gradagur replied eagerly. His old enthusiasm took hold of him, as if a bolt of lightning had just illuminated him with rafmagn. "It's much, much better this way! You won't have to risk possession of that carbuncle, or invisible little animals, or the wrath of Sorkvir, and I shall get to taunt some of my old friends in the Guildhall once again.''

"No indeed, you're not going with us!" Leifr protested, but Gradagur was already scuttling toward his collection of airships. "Gradagur! How will we get Thurid out, without one of your great kites for him?"

"Oh, that's the least of our worries!" Gradagur replied impatiently. "He can have mine, and I'll just put myself in some obvious position and allow the wizards to throw me out, as they have done so many times. They'll assume that I've merely come to spout my insane visions to them again. There are advantages to madness, you see. No one ever takes you seriously. But this time—hah, wizards! Be on your guard!''

Leifr allowed Gradagur to drag him along, teaching him and Starkad all the parts of the glider and how they worked, although he couldn't see how a fragile structure that weighed so little could carry his weight through the air without flapping like birdwings. Raudbjorn steadfastly refused even to consider the idea. He took up a watchful position on a wall beside the tower, surrounded by the troll-hounds, and glared at Leifr in bitter betrayal.

"Future no place for Norskur," Raudbjorn growled. "Sky is for the birds, not Raudbjorn. Raudbjorn stay here.''

An aerial attack upon the Guildhall was evidently a long-held and greatly anticipated ambition of Gradagur's. If the day had not been nearly spent, he would have insisted upon demonstrating his aircraft then and there, but the air currents were declining as the earth cooled.

In the morning, however, they were treated to a rare and unbelievable sight as Gradagur fastened the big kite to his shoulders and crept toward the edge of the steep fell. With a few running steps downward, he launched himself into midair, soaring away with a delighted shout. He circled over the ruins of Hardurjord, rising steadily, and soared along the spine of the fell overlooking the entire settlement. Presently he glided to earth like some huge and oddly graceful bird, a short distance from Hardurjord in a grassy space between the thickly sown rocks.

"You see, it's perfectly natural for men to fly," he greeted Leifr and Starkad when they came to help him carry the glider home. "In the future, men will fly to the stars, and beyond to worlds you can't even begin to number—"

"Gradagur!" Leifr admonished him. "I was just beginning to believe you weren't completely mad. Let's see if we can make it from Hardurjord to the Guildhall before you start talking about the stars." The idea would have been laughable, if it weren't so preposterous. No one knew what the stars were, except a force for good or ill to be manipulated by skillful wizardry. The boundaries of the known lands and realms themselves were shadowed in mystery. No man except Gradagur considered the stars as reachable.

Leifr shook his head, which still ached from Sorkvir's punishment of the previous day. If Sorkvir disapproved of Gradagur's methods, he had made no sign of it so far.

By the end of the day, Leifr and Starkad had flown the glider three times each and landed in reasonable proximity to Hardurjord. It was more exhilarating than anything Leifr had ever done, leaving him with a sense of incredulous awe that such a thing was possible and that such a marvelous invention had come from the foggy brain of a person like Gradagur. Great deeds were most often accomplished by men of great stature, ferocity, wealth, or sorcery, but Gradagur was a spindly little old fellow who possessed none of the typical prerequisites.

With Leifr and Starkad to help him, Gradagur finished the half-built glider in four days, which gave them three aircraft. He made a solitary trip to the house of a weaver, and came back staggering under a load of tightly woven cloth made from nettle fiber. Gradagur tested the new glider and, after some adjustments, pronounced it fit to fly. It was larger than the others with a more complicated system for steering, which enabled Gradagur to land it almost anywhere he wanted it.

"We are ready," he announced with a grin. "The Guild is overrun with clumsy new acolytes, and no one will notice three more. Tomorrow at dawn, when the air has begun to rise, we'll set sail for the Guildhall."

In the morning, Raudbjorn moaned and covered his eyes when they were ready to depart. He couldn't bear to look when anyone flew, as if his eyes were seeing something completely impossible, and he doubted his own sanity. Miserably he trailed Leifr to the edge of the fell and leaned upon his halberd, scowling uncomprehendingly. Leifr knew it was sheer courage and loyalty that brought Raudbjorn so far beyond the safe limits of his own understanding to watch his friend and liege fly away through the air, although the thief-taker knew it was impossible, especially with no magic involved. Magic was easy not to understand, because it was intended to be mysterious, but at least it existed as a demonstrable force that a man could recognize.

At first Leifr was uneasy about flying over the firth that separated Hardurjord from the Guildhall, but he soon gained confidence as he followed Gradagur's kite. From one rising plume of air to the next, they soared until they were circling high above the Guildhall. Then Gradagur steered his glider out of the column of warm air and began to spiral downward. Leifr followed, with Starkad bringing up the rear. The bright-green turf roofs of the Guildhall grew larger and larger, making a handsome pattern Leifr had never imagined existed. A freshly turned field, the buildings and walls and paddocks, two-tracked cart roads, and winding footpaths seen from directly above all were rendered with a fresh perspective that took away all Leifr's common notions about those everyday details, until he felt as if he were seeing them for the first time in his life. He was so enchanted by the beauty that he forgot this larger anxiety, until he realized that Gradagur was guiding them in for a landing on the laundry bleaching green behind the thralls' huts and the pigsties and cow byres. These humble structures were part of the Guildhall, but the fastidious wizards wanted them out of view and as far away as possible, so the least desirable facilities were located beyond the main gate of the central fortress.

Gradagur landed neatly in the midst of a washing spread out to bleach in the sun, but Leifr came down in a huge tangle of currant bushes adjoining a pigsty. Starkad had rather better luck, and landed nearby in a garden plot. Swiftly, as they had rehearsed, they dismantled the gliders and concealed them underneath the bushes; then they donned the long gray hooded garments worn by acolytes. Gradagur didn't say how he had managed to obtain them, but Leifr supposed it wasn't honestly.

"Now that we're wearing these," Gradagur said grimly, peering out of the muffling hood, "we're less than humans. We've become the property of the Guild."

The first demonstration of Gradagur's observance came almost immediately. As they rather furtively made their way through the morass of huts and pigpens toward the main gate, it was impossible to escape the notice of the thralls they encountered, who made way for them without speaking or acknowledgment of any sort. The presence of acolytes made thralls uneasy, although curious. A few turned and stared after them when they passed, nudging their companions and whispering. Leifr had seen the same guilty curiosity among a crowd waiting to witness a public hanging.

"One thing I forgot to mention," Gradagur said as they presented themselves at the main gate. "Acolytes are never permitted to speak once they enter this gate. The outer chamber lies beyond where common guests are allowed to enter. Should we become separated, which is likely, we'll try to meet in the outer chamber each day between dawn and noon. It's rather a slack period for experimenting with spells. You'll do most of your work at midnight, dawn, or sundown. Wizards are forced to keep such inconvenient hours, but I hope to turn this to our advantage."

Gradagur reached up and pulled a heavy knotted rope, which resulted in the clanking of a bell on the other side.

At once a suspicious voice demanded, "Who's there, and what do you want?"

"Gradagur! Wait!" Leifr whispered. "How can we get out again, once we get through this door? It's guarded!"

"Don't worry, we can get out. It's forbidden, but it's done all the time," Gradagur answered. "Not even acolytes can go forever without talking and acting like normal people. Wizards might be able to do it, but they aren't normal. Sometimes I wonder if they're even human—''

A small wicket in the gate opened up and a broad red face peered through. "Oh, so it's you? Already? Not a fortnight in the Guildhall and you've got to get out. What a lump of weaklings. Missed your families, I suppose, or maybe you had some important business to see to? Don't you dolts remember that you swore you'd renounced all claims on life outside this gate, and abandoned all claims against you? Come on, come on, get inside here. I hope you get a real hiding when you get back to wherever you belong.''

Bars and bolts slid aside as the porter talked, and the door creaked open, revealing the porter beckoning to them impatiently. Seized by sudden trepidation, Starkad did not step immediately over the threshold, so the porter grabbed him by the front of his hood, as if it were the forelock of a horse, and hauled him inside. The door slammed shut with a final, spirit-smothering thud, and the porter jammed all the bolts and bars and chains back into place and retreated into his tiny cubicle, where a small charcoal fire smoldered on a grate.

Leifr peered around the outer chamber anxiously. It seemed to be the gathering place for unoccupied acolytes, who loitered in silent gray groups. Most of it was an open courtyard, lined with rough benches, bordered on one side by a long low turf building that Leifr assumed was a stable. The acolytes seemed a dispirited lot, sitting with their heads drooping, eyes upon the ground, some of them sleeping and some of them looking definitely ill. Then Leifr noticed a group who were scorched, burned, and blistered. A couple of thralls were bandaging their injuries and replacing their charred gowns with new ones. None of the other acolytes seemed alarmed by such a procedure, as if it were quite commonplace.

"Another experiment gone sour, I'd say," Gradagur muttered inside his hood, without turning his head. He sat down on a bench and leaned against the wall.

Starkad looked around wildly a moment before Leifr pulled him down on a bench, already filled with the cold certainty that he was going to regret coming into this place. In one brilliant flash of revelation he realized that he must have lost his mind to have trusted Gradagur, who was insane by anyone's standards, who had been drummed out of the Guild, and who was obviously blissfully unconcerned about the dangers the unfortunate acolytes faced.

As he was allowing his dread to build, two wizards strode into the courtyard from a nearby doorway, where a pair of copper-bound doors stood open. The wizards' long gowns and cloaks were made of finely spun fabrics dyed brilliant colors Leifr had never seen before in the humble homespun wool and nettle cloths he was accustomed to, and their clothing rustled with a sibilant hiss when they moved. Gold chains and devices clinked softly around their necks, dangling from their belts, and their fingers gleamed with gold and silver wrought into the shapes of animals and birds. They carried tall staffs, wondrously carved, with gold knobs made in the shape of animals' heads, trickling clouds of mist or smoke.

The wizards stopped directly in front of Leifr and stood a moment surveying the courtyard.

"Not much of a choice," one remarked. "All the fresh ones are taken. Except these three. They must be new, or stupid, or they wouldn't sit here by the doors, first in line for the choosing."

"Perhaps that's what they hope we'll think."

"Stand up, you fellows, and let's have a look at you. This one's all right," he said, giving Starkad a few punches and pokes and turning to Gradagur, "but this one's skinny."

"He'll have to do, for a while. The middle one's awfully tall. Must be some mixed blood there."

"Nothing dangerous, I hope."

"It's always dangerous, and it must be in this case or he wouldn't be here. What else can you do with a halfblood except send him out to fight or else to the Guildhall? Who would want such a creature around?"

"Rydgadur, he's completely blank. There's nothing, no spirit, no voices, no past—nothing. He's like a stick of wood. Completely lifeless."

"Nonsense. No one can be totally blank, can he? No one with a drop of Alfar blood, either Ljosalfar or Dokkalfar."

Leifr drew a breath and held it, staring straight ahead, while the wizards both peered into his face and poked him as if he were a questionable piece of merchandise. Suddenly one of them happened to poke the region where the carbuncle hung in his worn leather pouch around his neck. At once there was a spark that jolted Leifr, and the wizard leaped back with a flaming oath, shaking his hand.

The other wizard, Rydgadur, opened his mouth in a bellow of mirth, folded himself in half and leaned on his staff for support, laughing until tears came to his eyes.

"Hygginn, that was not prudent," he chuckled, and went into another paroxysm of laughing.

"It's not polite to make jokes upon the meaning of one's friend's name," Hygginn said with wounded dignity. "I've never mentioned the obvious gibes possible with your name. Rusty by name, rusty in skills!"

"Well, let me say it then. We're both rather rusty or we wouldn't be here to sharpen up our skills under certified Guild instruction. I daresay you've changed your mind about that lifeless stick of wood?"

Hygginn glared at Leifr a moment. "Well, I suppose, but he'd better not do anything like that again. He could ruin a good spell."

"Come on, you fellows," Rydgadur said, beckoning to the three supposed acolytes, "we've got plenty of work for you to do. Which of you has had experience at shape-shifting? No one? Well, I haven't had much myself, so that makes us about equal, I suppose. We'll all learn together."

He laughed as if it were a great joke, but Leifr failed to see the humor of it. He glanced sidewise at Gradagur as they followed the wizards into the Guildhall, down a long corridor of carved wood pillars.

Gradagur was entirely rapt by what he was seeing. The corridor led into a number of lofty halls, where gatherings of wizards were talking, arguing vociferously, or listening intently to the words of the master wizards of the Guild. The very air seemed to crackle with power, flinging a constant bombardment of words and parts of sentences about on gusts of wind. Acolytes, Leifr swiftly learned during the walk through the teaching

halls, were used for purposes of demonstration. Their shapes
were shifted, they vanished and appeared, shrank and grew,
became strong or fell down helpless, and any number of afflic-
tions great and small were practiced upon the hapless acolytes
in the absence of any genuine enemies to scourge. Nor was a
promising wizard to risk himself with a chancy spell if there
was an acolyte handy, so the Guildhall kept a ready supply of
them, rather than waste time retrieving wizards from disasters
of their own making. Acolytes considered it their duty to suffer
for the cause of the Fire Wizards' Guild, much as a warrior had
to suffer injuries and eventual death for the defense of his land
and liege and freedom.

The Guild masters were easily recognized in their black
gowns, black being the color of greatest power and authority, as
well as austerity. Eagerly Leifr looked for Thurid in every room
they passed. Then in a long hall he glimpsed the Inquisitors,
seated around a table with one of the long-bearded masters presiding at the head, but Thurid was not present. Fodur, plain as
day, was reading off a long list, probably of someone's crimes
and aberrations.

Gradagur also noticed the Inquisitors and reached out and
closed his hand over Leifr's wrist warningly, slowing his pace.
A group of about ten young apprentices approached from the
opposite direction, following their black-clad instructors. A knot
of dejected acolytes trailed behind them. Gradagur about-faced
swiftly and joined the acolytes and the apprentices. When they
passed the Inquisitors' hall again, Gradagur nipped into a dark,
winding side passage and shoved Leifr and Starkad into the first
open door he found. It was a long hall intended as the sleeping
place of the apprentices, a stark and barren place with a door at
either end, a hearthstone in the middle, and sleeping platforms
around the sides. This group of apprentices was very young,
only seven or eight years of age, perhaps, judging by the small-
ness of the cloaks hanging on the pegs near the door and the
fleece slippers waiting by each small pallet.

Starkad was almost ready to explode from his long-enforced
silence.

"Gradagur!" he snapped ferociously. "This is madness!

There must be a thousand wizards out there! We can't do this! We've got to get out of here! What if those two recognize us?"

"They won't," Gradagur said. "We're nameless, faceless gray creatures, and there's at least two hundred of us. There are about fifty visiting wizards and guests, maybe a hundred apprentices—they have a rather high failure rate, rather like acolytes. A hundred Guild wizards, and only twenty of the oldest and best are called Meistari, or master. The other eighty are Instructors, Inquisitors, Counselors, Selectors, and Protectors."

"What do the Protectors do?" Leifr asked suspiciously, thinking longingly of his sword back at Hardurjord.

"Their specialty is warfare," Gradagur answered. "They defend the Guildhall in case of attack."

"How many of them are there?" Leifr asked.

"Ten. You'll know them by their staffs. Their symbol is a dragon's head."

"Only ten?" Starkad demanded incredulously. "To defend a fortress the size of the Guildhall?"

Gradagur shrugged. "It's all they need, considering."

"Considering what?" Leifr demanded.

"Considering how dangerous they are. Once a wizard reaches the Protector stage, he can't be allowed outside the Guildhall. Fortunately a Protector can't be created anywhere else but here, so the threat to Skarpsey is small, unless the Guildhall is attacked. You've seen that chasm that separates the fortress from the mainland? Well, that's the work of one Protector. Two hundred Dokkalfar were storming the Guildhall. There used to be two walls and ditches and a huge gate with two watch towers. The Dokkalfar were ramming the gate and nearly had it broken in. One of the Protectors loosed a bolt, and you've seen the result. They have only one bolt like that in a lifetime. Then they die."

"Well, it would tend to discourage any careless bolt-throwing," Starkad observed. "What happens if all ten Protectors are dead?"

"There wouldn't be anybody left to attack the Guildhall. Besides, they still have their conventional powers, which are more than adequate for most purposes. I doubt if we'll have any trouble with the Protectors—unless they become suspicious of intruders within the Guildhall. They don't treat spies kindly, I'm afraid. In fact, we might just as well say they kill them without mercy.''

Gradagur's attention seemed to be straying afield somewhere as he gazed around the dim hall with a peculiar dreamy look dawning upon his rosy countenance. ''It seems just like yesterday!'' he suddenly exclaimed rapturously. ''A small boy came here bearing the burden of all his father's and kinfolk's hopes. Right over there was where he slept.''

''Gradagur,'' Leifr began warningly, wondering if the fool's sanity had slipped a notch.

''I was that small boy,'' Gradagur confided. ''I only lasted a year in the apprentice guild. One of the many failures.''

''Failures have a way of finding their own way,'' Starkad observed, ''often rather spectacularly, for better or worse.''

''Thank you,'' Gradagur replied. ''This time my endeavor will be more successful. At least, I hope so.''

''Where will Thurid be?'' Leifr asked. ''They must have dungeons somewhere.''

''Oh, they do, the most wonderful dungeons you've ever seen,'' Gradagur said. ''The cliff where the Guildhall is built is riddled with dungeons and tunnels dug into the solid rock of Skarpsey by magical means. It's where everyone conducts their experiments.''

''And prisoners are held?'' Leifr asked.

''I never saw any prisoners,'' Gradagur mused. ''But where there are dungeons, there must be prisoners, or must have been in earlier days. It's as good a place to start as any, and not an unusual place to find acolytes wandering around.''

He was ready to go on, but a sudden gonging from the corridor interrupted him. Twelve reverberating gongs followed. Leifr and Starkad gazed at Gradagur, waiting for an explanation.

''The Meistari are being convened,'' Gradagur said. ''It must be something important. Let's go see.''

''It might have something to do with Thurid,'' Leifr said.

''Gracious, I doubt if he's done anything that important,'' Gradagur said in consternation. ''Has he?''

''We believe so,'' Leifr said guardedly.

They slipped out of the apprentices' quarters and back to the main thoroughfare of the fortress in time to see the solemn procession of the Meistari wizards treading slowly toward the central hall, where the tall carven door stood open, waiting to receive the chosen ones. A red-cloaked Protector stood on each side of the door, holding his dragon staff and surveying the scene with scathing interest, as if yearning for something to challenge.

Each master bore his staff and satchel, walking with the regal grandeur of royalty, scarcely deigning to look right or left at the common folk lining the way. A few of the most ancient wizards had to be carried into the hall in chairs, but this only increased their advantage, ensuring that everyone notice and admire their advanced seniority and status. The radiation of powers from such an august body of wizards filled the bystanders with fearful awe and gusted around them like errant spring breezes.

Finally came the Inquisitors, led by Fodur. Beside him walked a hooded figure in a saffron-yellow gown.

"That's him!" Gradagur whispered in great excitement. "It's got to be Thurid! Yellow is for the initiates! Wizards who have been purged wear yellow! Follow me, lads, we've got to get inside that room!"

Chapter 7

◆◆◆◆◆◆◆◆◆◆◆◆◆◆◆◆◆◆◆◆◆◆◆◆◆◆◆◆◆◆◆◆◆◆◆◆◆

"Gradagur, don't be insane!" Leifr urged, trying to catch hold of Gradagur's robe as he scuttled past him, after the procession. "We're liable to be in there as actual prisoners if you're not careful!"

"Exactly! What a good idea, Leifr!" Gradagur beamed with sudden inspiration. From a nearby pony cart, standing neglected in the excitement of seeing the masters going to an Inquisition, Gradagur stole a piece of rope from the pony's harness and looped it loosely around his wrist and held his arms behind his back. The loose sleeves of the acolyte gown concealed the fact that he was not actually bound.

"There now, each of you take an end," Gradagur instructed, "and now we're ready to go to the Inquisition for some heinous crime. Talking, no doubt, or sleeping, both of which are great offenses, along with eating something actually palatable. Come along, follow me."

Gradagur put his head down, like a sullen prisoner, and plowed into a watching group of older apprentices, who obligingly shoved the miscreants along toward the central hall. It was far easier than Leifr had dreamed to appear guilty, and everyone seemed willing to believe that three of their fellows had done something wrong, shoving them along quite gladly toward whatever fate awaited them.

The Protectors closed the doors practically on Leifr's heels, coming inside to stand on either side of the three offending acolytes. Prodding Leifr in the back, one of them ordered the supposed acolytes to sit down on the floor.

The twenty master wizards were still talking and greeting one another with the good humor of old and close associates, neglecting the solemnity of the occasion until Fodur had rasped his throat suggestively three times. Only then did the masters take their places in the half circle of seats on the dais facing the Inquisitors' seats below. Behind those were a few rows of benches for wizards of rank who came to observe. It was an ordinary hall between Inquisitions, with the usual tables and benches arranged for eating and drinking. Now the tables were removed from their trestles and stacked out of the way, leaving a bare region between wizards and Inquisitors where the accused would stand.

The eldest of the masters occupied the largest seat in the center of the half circle, a burly fellow with a bushy beard not yet entirely white, who apparently kept a bountiful table and cellar, judging by his ruddy color and numerous chins. Six acolytes had carried him into the hall in a sedan chair, not without difficulty, and now he reposed in his place of honor, slightly red-faced and breathless, with one foot resting on a small cushioned stool. His big toe was carefully bandaged, sticking tenderly out of a large fleece slipper.

"Well, Fodur," he began jovially, "let's get started with this regrettable business. You've called our attention to another rogue wizard in our midst, spouting all sorts of dissention and perverse magic. It's not to be endured, of course, but it seems to me if you quit searching so diligently, you wouldn't keep finding so much perversion."

The other wizards chuckled benignly, except for the younger ones on the extreme end of the left-hand side, who hadn't yet learned to be amused at their lofty position.

Fodur was not particularly amused, either. "If the Guild had no need of Inquisitors, the office would not exist," he said in a thinly veiled tone of protest. "Meistari Olag, this is the fellow I told you about earlier, who has been experimenting with Rhbu magic. He's gotten himself deeply embroiled with Sorkvir and Djofull and the Dokkur Lavardur because of it. I would not be astonished to learn that he knows something about the recent destruction of Djofullhol and the secret murder of Djofull himself, but I won't make any accusations on those accounts until I know more."

Meistari Olag pulled his hairy nether lip, with a disturbed

wrinkling of his brow. "Indeed, any dispute with the Dokkur Lavardur is a serious business," he said. "I am deeply grieved to say so, but some sort of action is required on the part of the Guild. My friend Thurid, what do you have to say for yourself?"

The yellow-robed figure stepped forward. Thurid uncovered his head, bestowing a glare upon Fodur. The yellow robe was of roughly woven material, a one-piece garment similar to that of an acolyte.

"Respected wizards of the Guild," Thurid began, exuding an aura of dignity and outrage even in his humble garb, "I'm not here to plead my cause before you, as if I were a criminal caught in some supposed misdeed. You have called me a rogue, a dissident, and an aberrant wizard, because I was not trained up in magic by an approved instructor for the Guild, or at least a wizard trained by a Guild instructor. I was forced to find my own way to the sources of secret knowledge, and you question the ways that I have found. Very well, I say, question what you will, but I seek the right to prove that my powers are as safe as any that are espoused by any wizard in this room. Return to me my staff and I will show you that Rhbu magic is not to be scorned, merely because it is misunderstood by wizards who have never dealt with it satisfactorily."

"Hear, hear!" one of the younger masters muttered. His beard was barely streaked with white. Only a wizard of exceptional skill could have advanced so far in the Guild hierarchy at his early age.

"Most inadvisable," Olag said regretfully, over the faint groundswell of approval. "We must be cautious when we are dealing with unknown powers. The entire Guild could be corrupted merely by seeing this wizard performing his unauthorized magic, and all of us would have to be purged, with certain inevitable losses among our membership. We can't take the risk, not with the Dokkur Lavardur involved."

Thurid's eyes gleamed. "But I have the weapon to use against him," he said, "and the man to wield it. We need fear nothing from the Dokkur Lavardur. We could destroy him with the sword of endless death!"

The masters buzzed excitedly among themselves, disagreeing worriedly.

"You are mistaken," Meistari Olag said, shaking his wattles sorrowfully. "No one can destroy the Dokkur Lavardur. You see how far you have been misled by your ambitions, Thurid? The Rhbus destroyed themselves against the Dokkalfar, and you would do the same to the Ljosalfar if you tried to bring this sword to bear against the Dokkur Lavardur. We have become more wise than the Rhbus were. We'll exist alongside the Dokkalfar, ever vigilant, instead of rashly attempting to eradicate them."

"The Ljosalfar are losing ground," Thurid retorted. "How long will the Dokkalfar endure our presence? Are you sure they believe in your policy of peaceful coexistence? Come, Meistari Olag, this isn't the time to lag behind. If we don't get ahead of the Dokkalfar, they'll destroy us. They aren't endowed with your fine moral principles."

From the elder side, the wizard on Olag's right spoke up sharply, a narrow-featured fellow with a goatlike wisp of a beard on his chin. "If we attack the Dokkalfar, we'll become as extinct as the Rhbus! They may have had some fine knowledge in their day, but, thanks to their arrogance, it's all gone now. You don't even know for certain what your powers are, Thurid, whether Rhbu or Dokkalfar, and yet you propose to lead us in the most dangerous of all schemes possible—an attack upon the Dokkur Lavardur himself. It's preposterous!"

From the younger side, the wizard on Olag's left added, "We're here for an Inquisition, are we not? An Inquisition is the examination of a wizard's practices, and the selection and eradication of the perverse and disparate. Why don't we test him, and see how his powers react with ours?"

"Heldur's orb cannot be trusted!" another wizard protested from the elder side.

"But Thurid himself is trustworthy," one of the younger wizards countered.

"How do we know that?" the retort came. "Just because he says so, and seems so? Ljosalfar have turned traitor many times before. Rhbu and Dokkalfar both call upon earth powers for their spells. They're too closely related, in my opinion, for Rhbu powers to safely mix with Ljosalfar. Just because the Rhbus were enemies of the Dokkalfar is no reason that we could trust them, if they were alive today.''

Leifr wanted to charge forward to Thurid's defense. He muttered to Gradagur, "But there are Rhbus alive today. I've seen them and spoken to them!"

The Protector behind Leifr poked him sharply with his staff, glaring at him in furious outrage, making a throat-slitting motion for silence.

Meistari Olag silenced the storm of debate clamoring around him. "I rather like the idea of a test," he said thoughtfully. "It would tell us if an Inquisition and a purge is necessary."

"Not so," one of the younger masters protested. "A test would tell us only that Thurid's powers are different, not whether they are in harmony with ours. Once perceived as different, Thurid's powers would then be held in suspicion by the Guild, and subject to purging."

"A test could show if his skills are compatible with Guild power," Meistari Olag said in a tone of remonstrance. "You seem to forget, brother, that the Guild is not solely devoted to squelching new ideas. When you are as old as I am, you'll realize that most of the new ideas presented to us are merely old idea in new wrappers—old ideas that didn't work dozens of times before."

"Rhbu powers are very old ideas," Thurid said quietly. "Older even than Ljosalfar powers. I will await your tests with eagerness, Meistari, to prove the worthiness of myself and my knowledge."

"Indeed, and I hope you succeed," Meistari Olag said earnestly. "We'll adjourn this Inquisition hearing until tomorrow, when suitable tests will be administered in the round chamber belowstairs. Is there any other business to be brought to our attention?"

Suddenly everyone's eyes were turned toward Leifr and Gradagur and Starkad, kneeling by the door.

"Well, what's the complaint?" Meistari Olag demanded. "Who has brought these acolytes before this council? If someone wants to be heard, he'd better come forward."

No one came forward, and everyone stared in curiosity. One

of the Protectors took a step forward and said, "I'd venture to bet it was talking. I saw one of them whispering to the other."

"You must have managed to lock out the one who was about to complain," Meistari Olag said chidingly.

"There's always such a crowd when there's an Inquisition," the Protector growled. "How am I to know who is supposed to come in, and who stays out? Maybe these acolytes don't even belong in here. I just assumed they had done something wrong, seeing their hands were bound."

The Guildmasters chuckled wryly. Olag waved his hand and said, "Then throw them out of here. Next time you'd better ask some questions, Vitni. They could be spies, for all we know. Maybe we'd better have a look at them."

Leifr's heart stopped beating at that moment. The Protector hauled Gradagur to his feet and stripped back his close-fitting acolyte's hood. There was a moment of shocked silence, then a great howl of laughter filled the chamber. Even the exalted Meistari Olag grinned and chuckled, shaking his head in pitying admiration.

"Gradagur, Gradagur," he said gently. "You'll never give up, will you?"

Gradagur stood as stiff and straight as a poker, radiating a glow of fanatic eagerness, much like his precious rafmagn illuminated a lightning rod. "No, your greatness, I can't give up," he said with lofty dignity. "I have seen the future, and I know what it will be like, and I know there's no place in it for wizards and magical powers. Rafmagn is the power of the future, Meistari—"

Another howl greeted this solemn observation as the wizards and Inquisitors dissolved into laughter again. Olag motioned to the Protector and said, "Put him outside, Vitni, and be gentle with the poor mad fool. There's no harm in him, except a touch of lunacy. The world wouldn't be such a grim place if we had more Gradagurs in it."

"And the other two?" Vitni asked with unpleasant relish, taking a handful of Leifr's hood and drawing him to his feet. His eyes widened with surprise as Leifr loomed over him by a considerable number of inches, gazing down at him with a resentful scowl.

"A pair of your new acolytes," Gradagur said. "It was wrong of me to take them, but I figured there was safety in numbers. I heard you had Thurid here. He was once a pupil of mine, in case you've forgotten. Can I say something in his behalf?" He sidled forward hopefully.

"There's nothing you could say to help him," Olag replied. "Perhaps something in your training has sent him off on the wrong track. He couldn't pass the First Examination."

Thurid suddenly hurled himself forward. "Gradagur? Is that truly you? I can scarcely believe it! My old master!"

The suspicious Inquisitors blocked his way warily, and Fodur ventured to lay a cautious hand on his shoulder, but Thurid instantly twitched it off with an explosive puff of sparks and smoke, and Fodur jumped back a step.

"This is all highly suspicious," Fodur said irritably. "I can't believe it's such a coincidence."

"Bah!" Gradagur snorted. "Did you think I came here to help him escape? What could I do against so many? I just wanted to see him again, and perhaps talk to him. It's been so many years since I saw him, and when I heard what a furor he's caused with that Rhbu magic—"

The Protector thrust him out the door, and the second one shoved Leifr and Starkad out after him, shutting the doors firmly.

"Back to the outer chamber for you two," one of the Protectors said, giving Leifr and Starkad a poke to urge them forward. "I hope you don't get into any more trouble. And you, old fellow, had better scurry back to Hardurjord and stay there." He gave Gradagur's arm a small shake.

"There are no secrets in the Guildhall," the Protector called Vitni observed ruefully to the other guard as they walked along the thoroughfare with Gradagur dangling between them. Leifr noticed how everyone gave them ample space. "I daresay all of Skarpsey knows about Thurid's powers and that Rhbu sword. I wish I knew who it was who spreads all that gossip; I'd put a knot in his gullet. Who told you about Thurid's being at the Guildhall, Gradagur?"

Gradagur pretended to think very hard. "I heard it from so many sources, I can't recall who was the first. I believe it was old Snari, the horse merchant."

"Ha!" Vitni pounced. "Then it was Snari! He was out here not long ago buying and selling nags!"

"That was before," the other said. "If you want to stop people from talking, you'll have to kill them all, and we don't have time for that. I don't want to miss the Meistari's tests tomorrow. I'll wager Thurid proves himself and his Rhbu powers perfectly clean."

"Bah!" Vitni said. "He's doomed! I'll wager my piebald stallion he gets purged and walks out of here less a wizard than mad old Gradagur here."

"Done. I've always coveted that horse."

When they returned to the outer chamber, Leifr and Starkad were directed to sit down and stay out of trouble. Gradagur was taken toward the gate, where the porter waited, scowling ferociously.

"How did the old blighter get in this time?" the porter demanded.

"I flew in," Gradagur answered haughtily. "Like an eagle on silent wings."

"Don't try it again," Vitni said, "or next time we'll clip your wings permanently. Maybe we should keep him for further questioning."

"Let him go," the other said. "He's too addled to be a threat to the Guildhall."

The Protectors came back to the outer chamber and gazed around at the waiting acolytes. Leifr and Starkad had separated and slipped into the ranks of gray, faceless creatures, and Leifr slouched down slightly among the smaller Ljosalfar to conceal himself further.

"One of those acolytes gave me a peculiar feeling," Vitni said uneasily, still scanning the acolytes shrinking under his gaze.

"They're all peculiar creatures," the other said. "No one in his right mind would want to be an acolyte, yet every one of them is here of his own free will to become a martyr for the cause."

"Come on, I want to talk to the Meistari. That sentry at Finn's was full of a tall tale about some strangers, if gossip is to be believed. I wish I'd been there to ask him some questions. I'm going to have him summoned to the Guildhall."

"That should frighten him properly. He'll gladly tell you anything he thinks you want to hear, whether it's the truth or not."

"He told Finn about three strangers coming over Brattur-neck and asking where to find Gradagur."

"There weren't three with Gradagur, only two."

"Indeed. Which causes me to think there's one more outsider roaming around inside the Guildhall right now while we're distracted with Gradagur."

"Or maybe Gradagur came by himself. He couldn't get three men inside that gate."

"Couldn't he? He gets himself in now and again, trying to peddle his visions and inventions."

"If it's any comfort, Vitni, if he's got somebody in, they won't get out again very easily."

"They'll be blasted hard to find, disguised as acolytes. We may have to hold an Inquisition on all the acolytes in the Guildhall until we find them."

"We can do it easily. Do you think one of them is Thurid's Scipling with the Rhbu sword?"

"If it is," Vitni growled, "I can't believe he'd be so foolish as to risk his neck just to free Thurid. We're not dealing with sane, enlightened individuals, Foringi. These are madmen, convinced they can kill the Dokkur Lavardur with a sword and satchel taken from a Rhbu barrow. It's creatures like these that we must ferret out and destroy, for their own good as well as our safety."

Vitni paced up and down, gazing at the acolytes with a wolfish gleam in his eye. None of them moved or spoke, like a flock of gray sheep petrified by a menacing predator.

"I'll wager we find no one who doesn't belong," Foringi said with a shrug.

"Wager your Hestur saddle and I'll bet with you."

The two Protectors moved away, still arguing, leaving Leifr wondering what he was going to do now and silently cursing Gradagur for getting him into such an untenable situation. He couldn't stay where he was, or some wizard was likely to think he wouldn't mind being shape-shifted or subjected to illusions or some other unpleasant occupation, which he might or might not survive, depending upon the skill of the wizard. For a moment he thought about the passive disposition of the acolytes, and wondered what sort of man would permit himself to die for a cause without raising a weapon or a word of protest.

Abruptly he stood up and strode out of the courtyard, back into the passages of the Guildhall. If the acolytes were so indisposed to save their own skins, they very likely wouldn't care what he did with his own. Besides, they weren't permitted to talk, so they could tell no one.

Starkad followed him at such a distance as to appear to be alone. Leifr found his way back to the Inquisitors' hall easily enough, and no one bestowed him a second glance, but the hall was now empty, and a pair of thralls were replacing the tables and benches. A cautious search up one corridor led to a pair of outside doors and a courtyard, where two Guild wizards were expounding to a group of visiting wizards. The other passage was the main thoroughfare winding among the various buildings of the fortress. Presently the lofty halls ceased, giving way to the outdoors, and an open thoroughfare between the humble turf structures of the craftsmen necessary to maintain the fortress, such as millers, masons, carpenters, blacksmiths, laundrywomen, tailors, bakers, and plenty of others who lived upon the exclusive patronage of the Guildhall. In the jumble of carts and bundles and heaps of goods, Leifr felt comfortably inconspicuous, since there were plenty of other acolytes and thralls present. The smells coming from a baker's ovens reminded Leifr how long it had been since he had eaten. By dint of careful loitering, he was able to steal a loaf of bread from a basket of loaves when a dogfight started in the dooryard of the house next door. After sauntering away casually, he and Starkad sat down on the tail of a cart and divided their scanty fare, waiting to speak only when no one was nearby.

Leifr did not turn his head to talk, lest the natural posture betray him to anyone watching. "Don't you wish you were back in Fangelsi now?" he muttered. "At least you had a chance for getting out of there and an honorable share of the food."

"Gradagur won't leave us here," Starkad replied.

"How do you know? He might have forgotten us already. I must have been mad to agree to this scheme."

"It was your idea, if you recall."

"Was it? In this realm, you never know if your ideas are even your own or someone else's manipulation. At least we're safe from Sorkvir inside the walls of the Guildhall. He couldn't get past those Protectors."

"I haven't seen any way leading down to the dungeons," Starkad said. "We must've missed it somewhere."

A sudden angry shout behind them caused them both to twitch nervously.

"Halloa, you lazy good-for-naughts, I told you to get that cart unloaded! Are your ears missing? If they're not, it can be arranged!" From nowhere, a tall, cadaverous-looking wizard in a patched cloak suddenly hove alongside the cart and took a vicious swipe at them with a battered staff exuding pink mist.

Leifr and Starkad leaped up in surprise, hastily surveying the wizard and the cart, which was loaded with bundles of something and covered over with a ragged cloth.

"Surprised, are you? Well, I don't wonder," the wizard growled with another thrust of his staff. "Real work doesn't come naturally to acolytes. Useless lot of maundering idiots, herded around like sheep by incompetents and fools, taken shameless advantage of, and all for what, I don't know. In my day an acolyte was a true follower, instead of a dummy, but I can see you prefer being dummies and fence posts, so you don't ever have to think again. Now get this cart unloaded fast. We've got another load to go back for. It's been a rather bad day belowstairs."

Leifr and Starkad climbed into the cart and immediately learned the nature of the cargo they were unloading like firewood. It was about a dozen hapless acolytes, some stiffly frozen and twisted into grotesque shapes, some apparently limp and lifeless as dolls, and others unable to move for no apparent reason, simply gazing upward like a batch of newly landed mackerel. The whole litter of them reeked of smoke and spells, trickling clouds of mist from leftover magical influences. Leifr and Starkad lifted them out by feet and shoulders and hauled the hapless creatures inside the wizard's hut, placing them in a row against the wall.

"They botch and blunder their spells," the wizard growled angrily, striding up and down, "and they expect me to unravel all their murky ignorance and restore these creatures to a semblance of life so it can be done all over again. Look at this one. Some dolt transmogrified his shape, probably to something clever like a rat or a lizard, and they've lost him somewhere. A cat probably ate him, or a hawk, and so I'm left with a live carcass and no essence to put into it. Fortunately the butcher isn't far from here, and sheep essences or pig essences work well enough, and he doesn't need them, since his business is the destruction of one life for the fattening of others."

Leifr glowered at him in moral outrage, yearning to say what he thought. The wizard glared back—a hunted, oppressed man surrounded by the mistakes of others, which made his temper dangerous. "Do you think I enjoy my job? Did I grow up as a child, longing with all my heart to be a Retriever of lost essences? Hah! No one ever mentions the lowly Retriever, when there's Protectors and Inquisitors and Masters of this and Masters of that. But where would they be without me? Out of acolytes most of the time, that's where. At one time I have ten of these senseless lumps cluttering up my lumber room, and what am I supposed to do with them? Even a necromancer can't bring back life to something whose life is flitting or skulking around somewhere—or eaten by something, and what good is it to put a lizard essence into a man's body? You get a man who wants to eat flies and lie in the sun on a warm rock all day. Or they get vicious, if they're meat-eating lizards. That was a mistake I didn't make more than four or five times. Oh, this is a nice job of work." The wizard uncovered an acolyte bound hand and foot, who bared his teeth and snarled ferociously. "They've made this one into a dog. Somewhere among the hundred-odd dogs of the Guildhall is one who is human. I ask you, how am I supposed to tell the difference, when dogs and acolytes are so very nearly the same order of creature?"

It was a fine, passionate speech, and Leifr hoped the Retriever would be able to deliver it one day to the person he intended it for. As they were carrying the last victim into the hut, the dog man, who was snapping and snarling with every intention of biting someone, a thrall led a horse up to the cart and tied it there.

"He's been switched with something," the thrall said. "Won't eat his grass and wants to follow me around all day."

The Retriever smote his brow in exasperation. "Can't you people ever learn to keep your animals locked up? You know those apprentices will stop short of nothing to cause mischief. They tire of torturing acolytes, you know. They want to do whatever is not allowed. And we mustn't discourage them, because they are the future Masters of the Guild!"

This culminating folly was too much for the Retriever to bear. He stalked away a few paces with his jaws clenching rigidly, with gnashing and growling sounds, like a suppressed cat fight, then turned to the horse, doing something behind it.

Conferring in silence, Leifr and Starkad climbed into the cart and waited for the Retriever. He hitched up the formerly transmogrified horse, which immediately set up a desolate nickering, and climbed into the cart with a weary grunt.

"This is not the life I intended," he said to no one in particular as they rumbled slowly through the tradesmen's street.

The dungeons were reached through a guarded portal, where a couple of Protectors eyed the Retriever suspiciously and poked at the coverings in the cart.

"What's all this?" the Retriever snarled. "I've come and gone here a thousand times. Do you think I'm somebody else, you great dolts? Have you forgotten this face?" He stuck his face out, already rendered ugly enough by years of bitter and thankless toil, and made it even more gruesome with a ferocious grimace.

The Protector stepped back, gripping his dragon-headed staff. "Something's amiss in the Guildhall today," he said. "There may be intruders. Old Gradagur was here. You haven't seen anything strange, have you, Vonbrigdi?"

The Retriever chuckled and flicked the reins. "Nobody questions the Retriever of lost spirits. One day I may have to go in search of yours, my friend."

Chapter 8

❖❖❖❖❖❖❖❖❖❖❖❖❖❖❖❖❖❖❖❖❖❖❖❖❖❖❖❖❖❖❖

The cart rolled through the archway, which was carved with crumbling figures and flanked by two large doors, also carved with devices Leifr recognized as Rhbu. Wondering what the Rhbus had wanted dungeons for, Leifr watched eagerly as the cart rumbled down a long passageway, illuminated only by a few scutcheons thrust into a fissure. Presently the tunnel opened into a large underground courtyard, which reminded Leifr of the huge galleried assembly room of Bjartur, only this was not as large and lacked the tiers of galleries. In the center was a well, once a sacred site, now used for the mundane purpose for which most wells are intended. A water-carrier's cart was loaded up with crocks and bladders of water to haul above for man and beast.

Like the rays of a star, six tunnels branched away from the central court, and plenty of foot traffic was coming and going from all but one of the corridors. Leifr gazed with interest at two Protectors guarding the sixth tunnel, where no lights gleamed down its length to indicate human occupation. He nudged Starkad, nodding slightly in that direction.

The Retriever's cart rolled down another tunnel, one crowded with groups of apprentices and acolytes and black-robed Master Instructors. Along either side were deep pits, where sudden flares and explosions frequently illuminated the craggy rock, accompanied by the shouts of the Instructors and other student observers from above. For the first time, it occurred to Leifr that the business of training young apprentices and teaching new spells to wizards was a dangerous one for the Guildmasters. They stood on the brink of the pits shouting down words of encouragement, assistance, or warning to their students laboring in the sooty depths below. The air was thick with sulfurous smoke, and writhing snakes of spontaneous flame flared intermittently overhead as some aborted spell combined unexpectedly with another in a brief fizzle of energy.

The Retriever seemed in no particular hurry. Craning his neck, he stopped the cart several times and peered into the fire holes to watch an apprentice wrestling with his powers. Some were wreathed in flames, apparently unhurt but obviously not entirely in control; others dodged fire bolts caroming off the walls; yet others stood in the gloom with their staffs clenched determinedly in their hands, endlessly chanting summons to the powers they hoped would make them Fire Wizards.

"No more than one in ten will make it," the Retriever said dolorously, climbing back onto his ramshackle cart. "If you ask me, one in ten is too many." He aimed a few vicious kicks at the students perching impudently on his cart, imitating his hangdog demeanor. They laughed and jeered at each other, as if the Retriever's cart were an object of sardonic mirth, a symbol of the failure of spells.

The cart trundled along the tunnel and back, then entered another tunnel where spells of another sort were being practiced. There was no fire or smoke, but the air was laden with furtive shapes and snatches of spoken spells that somehow lingered among the walls of the cave until they faded away. Leifr supposed it was a precaution against Ljosalfar magic formulae falling into the wrong hands. This was the shape-shifter's tunnel, and there was plenty of work for the Retriever and his acolytes. The most troublesome piece of work was a shape-shifting spell that had gone only halfway, leaving an acolyte half transformed into a dog. Head and shoulders were canine, the rest was human. The abashed student's Instructor was very annoyed, while the rest of the apprentices were stifling derisive laughter.

"Another failure," the Retriever grunted, shepherding the creation into the cart. "Another would-be wizard who will end his days weaving petty spells for the amusement of greasy drovers in dingy inns, or maybe if he's terribly lucky, a healer of diseases in sheep and cattle. But the worst fate of all likely awaits a few of these hapless wretches. Some of them are bound to become Retrievers."

Starkad's mouth opened to voice a dozen questions, but Leifr silenced him with a sharp jab in the ribs. They were yet in the tunnel, where wizards, acolytes, and students were passing by. Silently Leifr and Starkad loaded up the failed spells in the cart, with one unlucky apprentice among the ones frozen between two body forms, neither here nor there, until the Retriever's skill unraveled the clumsy spell that had resulted in such a bolix.

When they had gathered all the mistakes, the Retriever's horse plodded homeward. Leifr stood in the cart behind the driver. When they had passed the two Protectors without incident and started along the road back to the squalid settlement, he whispered, "Retriever! I want to talk to you."

The Retriever looked around uneasily, as if doubting his ears. His dreary eyes rested suspiciously upon Leifr.

"Did you—speak?" he inquired with a note of puzzled indignation in his voice, as if his horse had just addressed him.

"Yes," Leifr said. "I want to ask you a question—"

"Speaking is unheard of for acolytes," the Retriever said firmly. "You must be mistaken. There are serious penalties for an acolyte speaking to a wizard, or somebody of importance."

"We're not acolytes," Leifr said. "Gradagur brought us in, then he got thrown out."

"Well, that explains it. Say no more until we're back at my house."

They returned to the Retriever's shabby house in the approved silence. No one looked twice at the Retriever's cart lumbering along with two acolytes sitting dispiritedly on the tailboard. When the skinny horse was stabled and fed, Leifr and Starkad went into the house, trying not to move with any sign of unseemly haste.

Vonbrigdi sat beside his hearth solemnly puffing at his pipe with his pouch perched on one knee. A sooty pot dangling over the fire was beginning to make reluctant hissing and gurgling sounds.

"What do you want?" he demanded once the door was closed. "To spy, steal spells, murder someone? Or do you have some wonderful invention you'd like to demonstrate before the Guild, which will revolutionize everything we've ever done or thought of, and render wizards and magic totally obsolete?"

"If Gradagur can do it, he probably ought to," Leifr retorted. "But all I want to know is how you can help me retrieve a lost spirit. It's a girl who changed herself into a cat during an escape spell, rather than be destroyed, and she was holding a Rhbu staff—"

"Escape spells are bad enough without being complicated by a Rhbu staff," the Retriever said, his manner suddenly eager and furtive. He glanced from side to side, as if someone could be listening from the shadows. "And you say you've slipped into the Guildhall for the express purpose of asking me for my help?"

"Yes," Leifr lied, "although there is other business related to the girl."

"You've heard of me, then? Vonbrigdi, the Retriever? The greatest of the Retrievers?"

"Vonbrigdi, we don't have much time. The Guildmasters know we're in here somewhere, and they'll find us before long if we don't hurry. Can you help me find Ljosa? Other wizards have said she's trapped in her cat form and can't change herself back. One mentioned something about a person not being able to be in two places at once—"

"That's very true, no matter how many forms you're in. Where is this girl's body? She had to do something with it at the time of her escape spell. Did it vanish? Did it turn into something else? A burr in the cat's fur, perhaps? A grain of wheat? A double shift is only for the most experienced of shape-shifters. Most often the body is wished away to a safe place, until the spirit can return to its abode. Do you know of a place where this girl might have sent her body? If not, then she might have sent it someplace without intending to, and thereby lost track of it, thereby requiring the services of a Retriever. Speak up now, don't be timid. Tell me what I need to know and I shall try to help you."

"I don't know exactly what happened when Ljosa shifted shapes. I think her body is lost somewhere, although it was brought back for a time in Djofullhol by Sorkvir, when he tried to deceive me—"

"Sorkvir!" Vonbrigdi swore. "You were in Djofullhol? Then you must be Djofull's murderer. Begging your pardon, of course,

I don't mean to offend you, but that is the crime you're being sought for, is it not? You're the ones being sought by those disgusting creatures, the Naglissons."

Leifr maintained his silence, knowing that denial of a crime was the surest way to harden suspicion against him.

"Yes, but Leifr didn't do it," Starkad declared. "Not directly, but it was a member of my group who did it—if she was still with us, that is, but she was possessed at the time by a disembodied hand, so if there is a murderer, it might be the hand."

Vonbridgi paused a long moment to digest this complicated information, whistling almost soundlessly through his large teeth. At last he shifted on his seat and said, "Gradagur's got himself messed up in a nasty situation this time. I hope you won't harm the poor old fellow. He's a Guild failure, as I am. Gossip has it that he used to be the instructor of that renegade wizard, Thurid."

"He was," Leifr replied impatiently, "but all that is secondary to Ljosa's predicament. What I want to know is whether or not you can help her."

"Can? Can help her?" The Retriever leaned forward and spoke in a whisper. "The question is not whether I can help; it's whether I dare help. I know who you are, and I've heard your story. You're something of a legend in this realm, Scipling. But legends have complicated lives; their troubles are larger troubles than common men are accustomed to, but the rewards are often far less."

"I'm not asking you to come with me," Leifr said. "All I want is your advice. Carve some spells on rune sticks, or whatever you need to do to tell Thurid how to rescue Ljosa."

"Then you have come for Thurid," Vonbrigdi said. "The Guild oddsmakers were split down the middle whether or not you'd come for Thurid or go after the girl."

"There are circumstances your oddsmakers know nothing about," Leifr said impatiently. "But I am glad to hear the Guild is taking an interest in what's happening. I was afraid they were all indifferent. Now that you know which way to lay your money, are you going to help us?"

Vonbridgi removed his pipe from his mouth and shrugged his

shoulders. "You'd have to bring me the cat form, at least, and I'd have to determine if it is merely a shape-shift, or if the girl's fylgja form is involved. If that were the case, that changes my procedure also."

"Well, I can't get you the cat, or the body. As far as I know, the cat is in the possession of the Dokkur Lavardur, and perhaps the body, too. I did glimpse her when Sorkvir attempted to restore her to human form, and I held her in my arms and she felt warm and alive, but I don't think he was able to hold the spell together permanently. The human form was beginning to fade away, and the cat was returning when I saw her last."

Leifr looked up from his scowling into the fire. Vonbrigdi was frantically making signs against evil influences and juggling a handful of amulets.

"You shouldn't mention such names so casually!" the Retriever gasped indignantly. "There is power in their names alone! Especially his—the Dark Ruler. Perhaps you Sciplings aren't susceptible, or aren't aware of the trouble you can stir up by carelessly dropping a name. I'm afraid there's nothing I can do if the Dark One has got your friend. He takes everything to himself, and once he's got it no one can get it back. Unless it's given, for some reason you are bound to regret later."

"Then there's nothing you can do?"

"Nothing. Except to warn you. Advise you to give up and go back to the Scipling realm, but I suspect that would be futile. A great combination of events has been put into action by your presence in this realm, a chain of consequences and results that possibly has no end, at least in your lifetime."

"I wouldn't leave now. Ljosa helped me once, and saved my life when Sorkvir was hunting me. I can't forget a debt like that. It's like an alog I've laid against myself."

"You're a noble sort, Scipling. I've not heard much good about Sciplings. I hope there's more like you. I only wish I could help you in some way—"

"There is," Leifr said. "You must know where the Guildmasters have imprisoned Thurid and where they have hidden his staff and satchel. Show us the place."

Vonbrigdi turned pale, but his mournful eye began to glitter. "I can't do that," he protested. "Don't you think I possess some grain of loyalty to my Guildmasters? If not for them I'd be out there somewhere struggling to make a living from some meager bit of ground—I'm really quite content here, doing what I'm doing. They were kind enough to leave me what few skills I've got—''

Vonbrigdi stood up and took a few agitated turns back and forth across the room, assuring himself, ''I'm really not as bad off as I could have been. I can't get involved with Rhbu magic—not again, I couldn't bear to get near anyone who is working it. You can't dream—you can't know what I've suffered because of Rhbu magic.''

Starkad said in awe, ''You've been through the purge.''

Vonbridgi nodded. ''Yes, I'm one of the survivors. I was young when I came here, certain I had something that would revolutionize the Fire Wizards' Guild. I was going to lead them out of their benighted ignorance. Instead, they destroyed almost everything I had, and left me this wrecked carcass to drag around, and enough skills to repair the mistakes their worst students made. But I'm not complaining. It could have been a lot worse. I'm lucky to be alive—I suppose.''

Leifr turned the Rhbu ring around and around in his pocket, staring at the ruined face before him. ''Vonbrigdi, who were you?'' he asked softly.

''Who was I?'' Vonbrigdi eyed him warily. ''Why, I was a young fellow with skills—strange and dangerous skills, in the opinion of the Guild Inquisitors, and I was a threat to the Guild and all it represents. I was a stupid young fool to think I could change them. I should have kept out of their way and done what I could. But if you have a gift it's hard to keep it hidden, when it's recognition you crave. At least I have the protection of the Guild now, and work to do, and everyone knows I am the Guild Retriever, and one of the best Retrievers to be found—''

Leifr opened his fist slowly, revealing the ring Vidskipti had given him from the treasure of the warring kings. Vonbrigdi's eyes widened and he raised one trembling hand gently to touch the ring with a single finger, as if he feared it might burn him. Then he virtuously snatched his hand back, as if suddenly reminded to do his utmost to resist temptation, but he was still shaking and pale.

"Where did you get that ring?" he demanded in a fierce whisper. "How did you dare bring it into the Guildhall?"

"You recognize it, do you?" Leifr smiled, knowing he had Vonbrigdi hooked.

"Of course. Every Rhbu would know it. It's the ring of the peddler, the merchant, the vagabond, whatever name you care to afix to him. Where did you come by his ring?"

"He gave it to me. And a name, which shook Djofullhol to the ground when I spoke it. If I am forced to, I shall speak it again to free Thurid from the Guild prison."

Vonbrigdi shook his head. "No need. Thurid isn't in any prison cell. He's not being forcibly held against his will. That's not the way of the Guild. They hold you by the force of your own reason. You know they are right, and indeed they are right to destroy creatures such as myself and Thurid. They must have a pure source of power. The only difficulty is when two pure sources meet, when the powers are so divergent as Rhbu and Ljosalfar."

"Who are you, Vonbrigdi?" Starkad demanded. "Are you one of them? One of the Rhbus?"

Vonbrigdi's wretched face sank into his hands. In a faint voice he said, "I was, once, but no longer. I'm a hollow man now, no one, nothing, from nowhere. Whatever I was, they took away."

"You're—a Rhbu?" Leifr questioned. "I thought there were only three of them left."

"Only three of the great masters are left—Malasteinn, Gullskeggi, and Vidskipti. But there are others, the lesser ones, a very scattered few people left in the highest places where they fled from the Dokkalfar destruction. I came from one of these scattered few, with dreams that my people would be allowed to come down from the mountains and live on the land like anyone else. But I learned that the Guild isn't ready to permit it. My people are still wandering from place to place, avoiding both Dokkalfar and Ljosalfar. The three Masters are not permitted to stand still long, because the Dokkur Lavardur is still searching for them to destroy them. Once they are gone, all our knowledge is destroyed. I was their hope once, but you see what good I'd be to the Rhbus."

"Can't you go back?" Starkad asked.

"No, never. I'm too ashamed of what has happened. I was given a great trust of knowledge, and through my stupidity it was destroyed."

"What about Thurid?" Leifr asked. "He has a great deal of your knowledge."

"Ah, yes, Thurid. He's a problem, especially for himself. How could an ordinary Ljosalfar have been so foolish as to take into himself so much Rhbu magic?"

"Perhaps it wasn't just foolishness," Starkad said. "Perhaps it was guidance from the great Three themselves."

"I don't know, I don't know. And I don't know what to do about him. I don't know that I ought to do anything about him, but yet—yet—" Vonbrigdi shook his head in anguish. "You'd think that a man would give it up and forget, sooner or later, wouldn't you?"

"No, never," Leifr answered. "You can't escape from what you are."

"I owe my loyalty to the Guild," Vonbrigdi sputtered in a last attempt to convince himself.

"The Guild took a Rhbu wizard and made him into a refuse collector," Starkad said. "A scavenger of useless things. In their efforts to protect themselves, they haven't done you any great service. From what I've heard of the purge, it's like being burned at the stake until all your powers are gone—and they don't particularly care if you die."

Vonbrigdi raised one hand to his ravaged, scarred face, speaking as if to himself as he gazed away into the fire. "Sometimes it is necessary to die," he murmured. "Sometimes even preferable. A faint scrap of something could survive the awful effects of the purge—" He sighed and shook his head. "It's past midnight. We'll sleep, and in the morning perhaps—perhaps—"

He left Leifr and Starkad to wonder what would happen in the morning, and pointed out a couple of thin eiders they could curl up in beside the fire. Vonbrigdi briefly examined the unfortunate enchanted acolytes to see if there were any spontaneous cures among them, a not-uncommon occurrence, he explained, but not one the average person would plan upon. There were no cures, but the half-dog apprentice howled like a banshee.

In the morning, Vonbrigdi set about unsnarling the spells over the acolytes. He placed the victim in the center of a five-pointed star and stood in another for protection from whatever influences the fumbling apprentice had disturbed, and used his Retriever's powers to call back the blunders that had left the acolyte's essence lost between forms, or trapped in an unknown shape. The Retriever's job was to discover what shape it was and where it was located, and what powers to appease so he could have it back.

"It makes it so difficult," he grumbled, "when a particular apprentice has sent a particular acolyte to the same place about a dozen times. It makes a track like a wagon rut, so the same stupid apprentice keeps making the same stupid mistakes, and it gets easier each time. But for me it gets harder to bring them back, with the weight of those awkward spells."

When he had salvaged six of the acolytes, he stopped his work and directed Starkad to harness his horse to the cart. "We'll take this many back to the apprentices," he said. "It will give us an excuse for being down there when the tests are performed."

"Can we get in there?" Leifr asked quickly.

"No. You wouldn't want to see your friend suffer. I had those tests once myself. For a Rhbu, it's almost as bad as the purge itself."

"Thurid's not young," Leifr said with growing unease. "He's more bones than flesh. I don't think he can tolerate these tests and purges. He gets upset when his clothes aren't tidy. He's not all that strong."

"No one is, when it's twenty to one."

Starkad scowled. "Then Thurid will fail the tests, and they'll move on to the next step, which is a full purge, and after that, Thurid won't be worth rescuing."

Vonbrigdi shook his head. "You won't have to rescue him. The Guildmasters will be looking for someone to take him away—if he's still alive, that is."

Vonbrigdi did not speak again until the cart was in the central well area of the underground fortress. Then, instead of turning the horse toward the fire pits, he deliberately turned toward the dark tunnel guarded by the two Protectors. They stepped forward to block his path, eyeing him suspiciously.

"The Guildmasters have no need for acolytes here," one said. "Turn around and take them where they belong."

Vonbrigdi hunched his shoulders and heaved a withering sigh. "I was told to bring them here. I don't ask questions, I just do as I'm told. Maybe it's for the tests they're doing. I don't know, and I don't really care, but I'm here, and I'm going to stay here as long as necessary."

"He wouldn't lie," the Protector said, looking dubiously at the cart and the acolytes. "It's different this time, you know. They're dealing with Rhbu powers."

"Nobody told us they'd be bringing in acolytes."

"It doesn't matter, does it?"

With that, the Protectors waved the cart through into the dark corridor, which soon opened into a single chamber at the end, where a large door stood ajar. Light came from beyond, pale silvery skylight instead of the yellow glare of torch or candle. Vonbrigdi motioned to Leifr and Starkad and climbed off the cart, leaving it behind without a backward glance.

Beyond was a room, lit by a beam of light pouring down through a fissure in the far-distant roof of the cave. Smooth pillars supported a gallery all around, looking down into the chamber from above. A dais occupied the far end of the room, and the usual benches and tables were gathered in the center. A slow fire in a brazier burned in the center of the dais, letting the smoke trickle upward to its eventual outlet far above, lending the room a veiled appearance. Small knots of wizards stood talking, or sat at the benches with charts and small devices. Some of the wizards were the Masters of the Guild, and the others were clad in the yellow gowns of the apprentice, with the addition of long-tailed black hoods to indicate that the status of these students was almost fully adept. Here indeed there would be no need for acolytes, Leifr realized. These apprentices didn't make such drastic mistakes any longer.

Vonbrigdi stood still beside the door, while curious but indifferent glances were sent his way. Leifr and Starkad did not dare to move, even to look at him. After a painfully long wait, the Retriever slowly advanced across the room, his very raggedness and awfulness striking such a note of contrast in the refinement of the wizards' inmost chamber as to excite awe in those who gazed upon him. He stopped his slow advance beside a table where a crowd of perhaps a dozen wizards and advanced apprentices were gathered. They moved away from him and his two silent acolytes, too startled by his appearance in such a place to protest the wrongness of it.

In the center of this group was Thurid, still arguing with a minor Meistari in a vain attempt to bring him around to his view of the benefits of inculcating Rhbu magic into the Fire Wizards' Guild. Thurid looked up in annoyance to see what had distracted his audience, and froze at the sight of the Retriever's raddled face gazing down into his own. The blood drained out of his face as the obvious thought struck him that one day he might look as bad as this unfortunate purged creature.

The Retriever spoke in his hoarse voice. "You have need for a Retriever."

"I did not send for one," Thurid said a bit nervously. "What is it that you believe needs retrieval? Have I lost something I'm not aware of?"

"You will soon, and it will be lost beyond any retrieval," Vonbrigdi replied.

The wizards and apprentices seated nearby stirred uneasily, and one of them said, "Come now, Vonbrigdi, what would Thurid want a Retriever for? Your duties are in the other tunnels of the underground. I think you're a bit confused. There's no one here who is lost between realms."

"You are wrong," Vonbrigdi answered, studying Thurid's face intently. "I am lost." He raised his scarred hands in a supplicating gesture.

A nervous chuckle ran through the chamber, and most of the wizards turned away and resumed their conversing and probing for ideas. Behind him, Leifr heard someone whisper, "Poor old Vonbrigdi's making a fool of himself. I always rather thought the Masters scarcely left him his sanity, and precious little of that. Once he gets out of his beaten track he's lost."

A minor Meistari rose from the table. "You're not lost, Vonbrigdi, you've just taken the wrong tunnel, that's all. Poor old lad, you're just a bit confused. How about some ale to settle your wits and wet your tongue?''

Vonbrigdi shook his head and turned away. ''No, I have work to do. I must go.'' In a ponderous, shuffling tread he retreated toward the door, having created a considerable stir in the chamber. Leifr hardly dared move or breathe. It was all he could do to leave Thurid still sitting there, after coming so far and coming so close. Thurid sat immobile, never even realizing how near Leifr had come. Leifr yearned to speak one word to him, but didn't dare, so he moved backward, struggling with all his might to signal silently to him through the power of his thoughts. Thurid should have known he was there, but he sat like a lump, not even looking at him or at Vonbrigdi. Leifr glared at him one last time before turning to follow the Retriever. In the smoky light of the chamber, perhaps only Leifr saw the faint shadow of a bird kiting across the great star on the floor. Looking up, he saw the outline of a small bird of prey circling toward the fissure above.

Altogether too soon, he was again standing in the gloom of the dark tunnel, feeling robbed and cheated.

''Vonbrigdi,'' he said, when he was certain no one was around, ''you failed. We were in arm's length of Thurid, and we could do nothing.''

The Retriever turned to him slowly and held out his fist, motioning Leifr to hold out his hand.

''If you want to see your wizard again, don't lose this,'' he said. ''It was a triple spell. Not many of them in there could do it.''

Leifr looked at the object in his hand in disbelief. It was a smooth piece of bone with a small red stone embedded in it, which glittered with life.

''A carbuncle!'' Leifr whispered. ''Where—whose—'' He stared at Vonbrigdi in stupefaction. ''Thurid's?''

The Retriever nodded slowly and shook the reins, sending the plodding horse and the creaking cart back toward the fire pits. ''A triple shape-shifting,'' he repeated with a touch of pride. ''Right under their noses, and they didn't even see anything happening.''

''The bird was his fylgja,'' Leifr said. ''I've seen the owl before. And this is what you've done with his body. But what was that thing you left sitting at the table?''

Vonbrigdi uttered the ghost of a dark chuckle. "A bit of mud, a bit of spit. I call it a leikfang—a toy. It will move and talk to them for a while, until Thurid's presence fades. It took some of his energy, but it will soon dissolve. When we were children—" His harsh voice softened slightly as he remembered, as if he were smiling to himself in the dark. "We children used to make leikfangur to do our work for us, but they always faded away before the work was finished."

Starkad cleared his throat nervously. "What's going to happen to this one when the Guildmasters start their tests?''

"It's going to melt away, of course."

"They'll know we must have had something to do with it," Leifr said. "We've got to get out of this fortress before they start looking for us."

"What can you do to them?" Vonbrigdi said. "They know their own strength, so they have no need for anger or reprisal. Only the weak have cause to fear."

"Then I'm weak," Starkad said, "because I'm afraid of what they might do to me. Look what they did to you, Vonbrigdi. Somehow I fail to find much comfort in your words. They're going to suspect you. Why don't you try to escape?''

"Escape?" The idea seemed foreign to Vonbrigdi. "No one escapes from the Guildhall. This is the last safe refuge in the Alfar realm. Everyone is safe within its walls."

"You're forgetting, Starkad. We can't go without the staff and satchel," Leifr said. "Vonbrigdi, do you know where they are? Can you help us get them?''

Vonbrigdi heaved a long sigh, as if crushed by a monstrous weight of ingratitude. "The Dark Chamber," he said after a long moment's thought, "where no light can exist, no fire can burn, and no man can find his way. If we go into there, we will certainly die."

Leifr looked at him expectantly. "But a Rhbu must know a way to thwart the darkness."

"No. The Fire Wizards have created the Dark Chamber from the darkness and evils they have purged from themselves and others. The Grand Meistari knows how to fetch the staff and satchel out of there, but anyone else who tries will perish in the dark. Fire won't burn there, so even a Fire Wizard with a blazing staff is helpless. The darkness is invulnerable to man's puny attempts.''

Chapter 9

Leifr expected a hullaballoo when Thurid's escape was discovered, but Vonbrigdi completed his rounds, dropping off restored acolytes and gathering up another eight or ten, and was at home heating their evening meal before any sign was given that anything was amiss with the Guild.

Since Vonbrigdi preferred to dine in solitude, his food was brought to him twice a day from the next-to-last-standard apprentices' hall. Therefore, the food was almost the quality of the Instructors' and last-standard apprentices, who dined together, since many of the apprentices were very nearly Instructors themselves by the time their education was finished. Only the most honored guests and travelers were allowed to dine with the twenty Guildmasters in their grand hall, and the Inquisitors kept a hall with the Protectors and various other wizards involved with the execution of Guild law. Of all these, Vonbrigdi's status was the most humble. He ate and slept and did his work outside the walls of the Guild, whether by choice or not, Leifr had no idea, but he suspected that none of the benevolent wizards wished to see the negative effects of their purging on another human creature. They would prefer to think that they had done him a great service and had even offered him a job afterward as compensation.

As Leifr and Starkad picked the bones of the fowl, Vonbrigdi suddenly raised his head from his half-dozing enjoyment of his smoldering pipe. Silently he motioned Leifr and Starkad toward the other end of the room, where a line of acolytes lay in a limp row awaiting the retrieval of their spirits. Leifr and Starkad pulled up their hoods and lay down in the row as a knock sounded at the shuttered window.

A Protector came inside at Vonbrigdi's summons. He gazed around a moment with a bright, weasel eye while Vonbrigdi sat and gazed into the fire as if no one were there.

"The renegade Thurid escaped today," the Protector said. "You helped him, didn't you, Retriever?"

Vonbrigdi sat as if he hadn't heard, until the Protector was forced to repeat his question, a little louder and more sharply this time. Then the Retriever stirred, tapping out his pipe and putting it fumblingly into his pouch, gazing meditatively all the while at a point above the Protector's hooded head.

"Thurid was retrieved," he said with heavy deliberation. "It was something I was compelled to do."

"By the Scipling, Leifr Thorljotsson?" The Protector leaned forward menacingly.

"No, no. What do Sciplings know of retrieval?" A note of impatience crept into Vonbrigdi's slow speech. "This was a command from someone—something higher."

The Protector shook his head. "I think you're in need of another purging, or else your wits have slipped."

"I suppose it's possible," Vonbrigdi agreed. "I never was very bright, after the first one."

"Why did you betray the Guild, Retriever? Don't you know you've committed treason?"

"No, it wasn't treason. I did what I was told."

"Told by whom, the Scipling? You aren't allowed to follow anyone else's orders except those of the Meistari, and he didn't order you to free Thurid."

"Thurid was no prisoner. The Guild does not hold prisoners, except by their own power of reason. He didn't have to leave, just because I shifted his shape, unless he considered himself a prisoner. Then I suppose he thought he was obliged to escape. It's rather puzzling, is it not? He wasn't a prisoner until after he escaped?"

"I'm afraid I shall have to tell the Meistari that you're deranged, Retriever."

"Thank you, I'm most grateful. Would you care to sit down and share my ale?"

"I think not. It's a grievous thing when a Guild wizard goes awry. You're now forbidden to enter the Guildhall, and that includes the underground passages, until the Guild can make a judgment on what's to be done with you. I'm sorry to bring you this news, and I know you're not entirely to blame, of yourself.''

"Myself? What self was left to me by the Guild?" Vonbrigdi inquired with a raddled scowl. "Vonbrigdi the Rhbu is no longer. What I am now is a Guild creation. If I have done wrong, it is the fault of the Guildmaster. Since the purge, I have no self to command."

"All that will be taken into consideration," the Protector said, again scrutinizing the row of acolytes. "But it would help if you knew where that Scipling is hiding, and that other Alfar who is with him. It's not the great Norskur he's always been seen with, but a Ljosalfar from Hraedsladalur."

"I am incapable of lying," Vonbrigdi said, "but nothing can force me to speak when I don't wish to."

"Unlucky fool," the Protector murmured as he ducked out of the low doorway into the night beyond.

Leifr rolled to his feet when he was sure the Protector was gone. "Vonbrigdi, we've ruined you," he said.

"Ruined me?" A startled expression crossed Vonbrigdi's ravaged face. "I was ruined long ago by the Guild. You're going to be my Retriever—my friend. Now I know where I'm going— what must be done. I shall be retrieved, at last."

"I don't see how that can happen," Starkad grumbled, "when there's no chance that we can get to the staff and satchel in the Dark Chamber. What are we going to do?"

Vonbrigdi slowly took out his pipe and stuffed it again with trembling fingers. Clearly, a second pipeful after supper was a new precedent for him. "It is the Rhbu way to wait and be patient when things seem impossible," he said, his eyes half closed. "The nature of life and events of mankind is endless change. There is no need for haste."

Leifr felt dizzy, inhaling the fumes of his smoke. Moving away from it, he added, "It is also the nature of man to be impatient, especially when a Guild of wizards might be looking for him."

The Retriever made no answer. Possibly the leaves he smoked in his pipe had a soporific effect on him, or else he was such a creature of habit that no physical activity was possible after supper.

In the morning, Vonbrigdi went to work unraveling the spells over the acolytes, as if he had completely forgotten the warnings of the Protector the night before. Indeed, he loaded up the acolytes and took them back to the underground portal, where the way was firmly barred against him by two Protectors. After a long moment of sitting silently on his cart with his shoulders hunched, Vonbrigdi raised his head and turned his horse around, heading for the rear gates of the fortress. Getting rid of the acolytes was the only objective in his mind. He took them through the fortress to the outer courtyard and left them there, while Leifr and Starkad lurked in the corridors, not wanting anyone to make the obvious connection between Vonbrigdi and two acolytes. Instead of turning his cart around and returning home, Vonbrigdi lingered in the outer courtyard until Leifr became so impatient that he crept back to the cart and sat down on a bench near enough to talk to the Retriever.

"Vonbrigdi!" he whispered. "What are you doing? Let's get out of here! There are Guildmasters all over the place!"

"I have nothing to do," Vonbrigdi said in a broken voice. "They've taken away my work. What am I now, if I'm not a Retriever? There is no purpose to my existence. I shall die soon."

"Nonsense. You're a Rhbu," Leifr whispered.

"I was, once, but that was long ago. Much has been taken away and lost. Go now, leave me to my death."

Leifr eyed the double guard on the outer gate and edged back into the safety of the corridor, where Starkad was waiting, seething with questions. He had just started to spew them out when the Retriever's cart started forward again, approaching the gate. After a moment of conferring, the Protectors signaled to the porter to allow him to pass.

"What's he doing?" Starkad sputtered. "He can't go out and leave us in here! First Gradagur abandons us, now him!"

Leifr watched incredulously as the gate was shut and locked. "This is the last time I'll rely on a madman for assistance," he growled in disgust. "You simply can't trust them not to forget all about you and go haring off on the wrong track. It looks as if we're left to our own devices again, Starkad.''

Starkad groaned, ''Just when we thought we were getting somewhere. How long are we going to be able to roam around the Guildhall without—''

A pair of wizards suddenly strode purposefully out of the bathhouse passage behind them, arguing loudly, their staffs trailing puffs of smoke.

The foremost wizard was a portly individual in a florid purple and orange cloak and gown, and the other was tall and thin, with a beaky nose poking out of a drab green hood with a fraying tail. Neither saw the two supposed acolytes until they nearly stepped on them, so involved were they in their discussion.

''I tell you, it will work!'' the florid wizard boomed, coming to a sudden halt. ''Look, here's a couple of stooges, let's grab them and I'll show you! He must have done a triple shift to get Thurid out of that room!''

''You can't do a triple shift, Feitur,'' the other protested, ''no more than you could do a triple somersault. I'm not convinced it was the Retriever at all. I was there, watching the entire event from the gallery, while you were off stuffing your gullet with smoked herring eggs and pickled svid. Those pig's heads you were gnawing on had more brains in them than you have. I tell you, the Retriever is innocent. He did absolutely nothing.''

''He's clever. So clever he pulled off a triple shift right under your nose, Erfidi, and you didn't even see it with both eyes open. Come on, you slugs, this is your lucky day. You're going to help me make a fool of this underfed, undereducated renegade wizard.''

Feitur prodded Leifr and Starkad ahead of him like a jovial shepherd herding a pair of very reluctant sheep. Knowing as they did that the Guildhall no longer possessed a Retriever to go after acolytes lost between bodies by clumsy magicians, neither was at all willing to be experimented upon by such a questionable wizard.

''This is far enough,'' Feitur said unexpectedly, motioning them into a side passage.

''This is the Inquisitors' hall,'' Erdifi objected nervously. ''Experiments are allowed only in the pits.''

"This is only a little one, and won't take long," Feitur retorted, shutting the doors. "And no one's in here, so no one will ever know the difference. Don't be such an old woman, Erfidi."

"There are rules of hospitality, you recall," Erfidi snapped. "The Guildmasters will probably throw you out if they discover you experimenting in here."

"But if I should capture Thurid, I shall be rewarded," Feitur said with a greedy gleam in his eye. "Perhaps they'll offer me what I truly deserve—the title of Meistari. Or at least a seat among the Alternants. I understand the Alternants are very well kept, but what I aspire to is the Guildmasters' table!"

"You'll most likely be there as a crock of pickled pork," Erfidi said, "and tallow for their candles."

Feitur ignored him and began scratching a circle on the floor around Leifr's feet. Leifr tried to step out of it, but discovered that he could not cross the line, as if a well had been built around him. The circle was not yet complete, so he gave Feitur a shove, sending him sprawling, and leaped out of the ring over his back. Starkad read his intentions perfectly, and together they made a rush for the door while Feitur was still trying to get to his feet.

"Stop!" Feitur roared from his knees, throwing out one hand and a string of powerful language, and Leifr and Starkad were halted like flies in honey, unable to move another foot.

Feitur finally heaved himself to his feet, with all the grace of a cow, and slowly circled Leifr and Starkad with his staff held ready, spewing clouds of acrid smoke. Belatedly it occurred to Leifr that this was no indolent, overdressed fool, although years of easy living had made Feitur appear so.

"What have we here?" Feitur mused, still a little breathless, with a slow and unpleasant smile dawning over his beefy features. "Two acolytes behaving rather strangely? Acolytes don't resist their fate. Something unusual is happening in the Guildhall. A current of disturbance, intruders who have gained entry, suspicion, and fear."

Leifr made no move, although he could feel the paralyzing spell fading. Feitur's eyes bored into him, raking his thoughts with a painful crackle, like a red-hot iron stirring the sparks of a forge. Raising one hand, Feitur warily tested the air before him, reaching unerringly toward Leifr's chest where Fridmarr's carbuncle hung inside his acolyte's gown. The carbuncle responded with a fiery retort that sent Feitur back a pace or two, cursing and shaking his fingers. Erfidi leaped back, astonished and consternated, gripping his staff across his chest defensively.

"Most unusual," Feitur said, swiftly recovering his aplomb. Undaunted, he resumed his cautious search, this time hovering over the pocket where Thurid's bone and carbuncle rested. Then he pounced swiftly like a hawk, his hand gripping the bone and dissolving the handful of gray cloth with a puff of fire and smoke. He blew away the charred cloth and held up the bone and the carbuncle.

"Do you know what we've stumbled onto here, Erfidi?" he inquired, keeping his eyes upon Leifr, who was gradually unthawing from the spell that had stopped him. "This is no harmless, brainless acolyte, nor that other one, either, I daresay. And this object is most suspicious—look, a small bit of bone and a carbuncle, small enough to hide in the palm of one's hand. Or a Retriever's hand. Didn't I tell you that the Retriever was guilty? Weren't there two acolytes with him in the Guildmasters' hall? A very tall one and a smaller one? I venture to say that these are the two, and I also venture to say that neither of them is an acolyte. They are spies, Erfidi, strangers in our midst. Who are you, stranger? Speak, for your life depends upon it, and I know you're no silent acolyte."

So saying, he yanked Leifr's hood off his head and summoned a brilliant flare to his staff's knob. Leifr found he was able to raise one hand to shield his eyes from the glare, and he also discovered he was able to speak.

"Give me back that piece of bone," he said hoarsely, reaching out for it, "or I won't answer for the penalties. You're butting your nose in where it's very dangerous for an ignorant nose to butt in."

Feitur closed his hand quickly around the bone, with a wide grin covering his round face. "I knew it was a triple shift," he said with a triumphant, booming laugh that must have graced many a winehall feast. "I now hold control over the renegade wizard Thurid, and my seat at the Guildmasters' table is hereby ensured. All that remains to do is to reverse the shape-shifting spell, and Thurid will return here, safe in the arms of the Guild once more where rebels and atavists belong, and the purge will resume. All your efforts will be as naught, Scipling.'' He added the epithet with a challenging leer, daring Leifr to deny it.

"It can't be done,'' Leifr said. "The Retriever is gone, and you'd better not risk it yourself. If you fail, the entire Guild will be on your neck, and there'll be lean times ahead for a wizard without Guild sanction, as well I should know from Thurid.''

"That's some very sound advice,'' Erfidi said hastily, his eyes darting anxiously. His tone became wheedling, that of a weary parent with a precocious child. "Turn over the bone to the Meistari, Feitur, and take what glory you can from it. Don't get greedy now, you're awfully close to a nice reward. Don't be stupid, Feitur.''

"Two outlaws and a bone is not the same as two outlaws and a wizard,'' Feitur mused, his expression suffused with the same lofty, fanatic gleam that had so often led Thurid into trouble when in pursuit of his ambitions.

"You don't have the wizard yet,'' Erfidi pointed out.

"Nonsense,'' Feitur declared. "I can call him back to his body. It will be as easy as buttering bread. Watch these two outlaws, Erfidi. If my holding spell shows signs of fading, give it a boost for me, won't you? Be careful of the Scipling, though, he's got a very dangerous carbuncle from somewhere. Luckily it's not implanted, or he'd be impossible to hold.''

Feitur took possession of a table, summoning one to come skating over to him like a stiff-legged horse. He placed the bone carefully on the planks, hardly daring to take his eyes off it while he delved in his satchel for an assortment of rune wands and engraved stones. Breathing deeply, he studied two wands several times, obviously laboring in the depths of a quandary. Finally he chose one and thrust the other back into his satchel out of sight. Smoothing his gown and sleeves, he cleared his throat and commenced to read the runes in a loud, authoritarian voice, with his arms outstretched in a magnificent pose. His staff smoked and his cloak flapped in gusts of power.

"Ahrif, hlusta a thessi madkur—madkur?'' Feitur interrupted himself, opening his eyes and seizing the rune wand. "That's maggot. Does it mean madur, which is man? It could be mafur, but I doubt if the spell is for seagulls. I can't quite tell for sure. I'll try it all three ways and see what happens.''

He chanted the man version of the spell three times with no result, so he tried the maggot version. After two repetitions, the room suddenly darkened and became chilly. Feitur uttered a triumphant crow and kept on chanting. Suddenly a burst of wind roared through the room, and the metal weapons hanging on the walls gleamed with a fierce red light, swinging on their pegs as if reliving their hours upon the battlefield. A mighty force shoved its way into the room with a rending sound like wood splitting and cloth tearing. Leifr cringed, feeling as if the room were suddenly too crowded. Then, with a final crack like thunder, the table where the bone rested was riven into splinters, and Thurid stood in the midst of the exploding wood, holding his hands raised at ready, his cloak flying in the wind.

"Hah! I've done it!" Feitur exclaimed in high glee. "Thurid, you're my prisoner, and I command you to surrender to me without resistance!"

Thurid turned to Feitur a moment, then gestured at him with both hands simultaneously, sending him staggering backward in a sharp blast of high wind. Feitur and Erfidi both retreated, unable to see and scarcely able to stand, in the case of the lean Erfidi. Finally both of them lost their footing and rolled across the hall to lodge against the wall. Thurid walked behind a wall of force, urging them onward.

"Unfortunately, I don't know who you are," Thurid said, holding them immobile against the wall. "But I'm sure you won't mind lending me your cloak. I feel so fearfully ill clad in this humble smock."

Feitur made some gasps and croaks of protest, quite unable to move, but his rolling, bulging eyes signified his lack of consent to Thurid's proposal. Thurid crooked one finger, and the hem of Feitur's cloak began to wave around like a curious snake, commencing to slither toward Thurid, and nearly choking Feitur until he was able to pull the pins out of his brooches and let it get away. Thurid wrapped it around himself in a sweeping gesture, eyeing Feitur and Erfidi all the while.

"I truly regret to hasten away and leave you in this spell," Thurid said, "but I've got some pressing business to attend to and people waiting for me. Next time we meet I shan't be so rude, I hope."

Leaving the two wizards helplessly paralyzed, Thurid strode from the room, impatiently motioning Leifr and Starkad to follow him. He thrust his way imperiously through a group of apprentices and acolytes, not halting his jerky stride to speak until they were down the corridor between the Guildmasters' hall and the Instructors' hall and no one else was about.

Turning to Leifr he snarled, "I hope you know you've made a complete mare's nest of this business with the Guild! When I realized you'd followed me here I was so furious I could have bitten a pair of hot tongs in two. Why did you have to come meddling and interfering and spoiling things, you wretched, clumsy Scipling?"

Leifr looked into Thurid's blazing eyes, noted his beard and hair bristling, and the way his nostrils quivered, and realized that Thurid was genuinely angry, which served to ignite his own smoldering temper.

"Would you have rather we left you here?" he demanded. "To let the Guildmasters make a senseless puppet out of you? Perhaps to kill you with one of their so-called purges?"

"I was in no danger whatsoever, except of convincing them that Rhbu magic is nothing to be afraid of and that it is the only way to destroy the Dokkur Lavardur! I had them listening to me, you bumbling oaf! They were ready to accept me! They were practically at my feet, ready to be taught the spells and words that would put an end to the Dokkalfar! Then suspicion reared its ugly head, in the form of one interfering Scipling, and everything I had gained was swept away in the moment that insane Retriever appeared in the Guildmasters' hall. Why oh why, Leifr, couldn't you have left well enough alone, for once in your life? I've never been so happy, or felt as if I belonged, until I came to the Guildhall. All I would ever ask of anyone is to be allowed to stay here as the humblest servant of these great ones. This is the fount of all knowledge, and I could stay here and drown myself forever!"

"Don't be a fool, Thurid," Leifr snapped. "They must have put a hold on you for you to think like that. What about your staff? What about Ljosa? And Sorkvir is loose again—

Fridmarr's killer—and who knows how many more will follow unless we end what we've begun? The Guild will never accept your knowledge, Thurid. You'll lose it all if you stay here, if you survive. The Retriever was purged of his Rhbu knowledge, and there's nothing left of him but a list of commands the Meistari has given him and a hideous emptiness where his own will used to be. He was a Rhbu, Thurid, and they destroyed him. Do you think they'll allow you to survive, if they can't tolerate the real Rhbus?''

Thurid's glazed eyes suddenly focused. "A real Rhbu, you say? How could that be?''

"Some of them survived and fled to the highest places in the mountains. He came here, as you did, to try to sway the Guild to the Rhbu side. They won't change, Thurid. They can't. Rhbu magic must stay away from Guild magic, at least until there are more Rhbu wizards.''

"A real Rhbu, you say!'' Thurid repeated thoughtfully, as a new idea took root within his fertile imagination. "I should be trying to discover the Rhbus, instead of wasting my efforts with a bunch of lump-headed, hidebound Fire Wizards. Why walk when you can soar with the eagles? Where is this Retriever? I've got to talk to him!''

Starkad groaned and shook his head. "He's gone,'' he said exasperatedly. "When they took his duty away from him, he wandered away. He's outside the Guildhall, doing who knows what or how long he's going to survive.''

"And you let him go?'' Thurid demanded, glaring at Leifr accusingly. "Leifr, what have I ever done to deserve this deliberate sabotage of my every harmless dream?''

Leifr fell back, groping for words sufficiently cutting and furious. "Then see how you manage without me!'' he exploded, giving Thurid a shove backward to stalk past him. "Stay here and rot, for all I care! Starkad, get up here or I'll leave you too!''

"You won't last another fortnight without me,'' Thurid snorted fierily, turning his back.

Starkad ventured to grab Leifr's sleeve, which was snatched away with a savage growl. Undaunted, Starkad persisted. "Leifr, what about Sorkvir?'' he asked. "He's out there waiting for you.

You're safer in here as an acolyte, rather than facing Sorkvir without what you promised to bring him.''

Leifr faltered, hesitating and glancing once over his shoulder. "It might be a pleasure to turn him over to Sorkvir," he muttered.

"You won't do that," Starkad said. "He's your friend. His pride is injured just now. No one likes to be rescued from a predicament by someone who is likely to be around for a long time to keep you reminded of your debt of gratitude. As younger sons, we both know how painful it is to be grateful, how difficult to be humble."

Leifr glowered at Thurid, who glowered back. "Well, you may tell him for me that I suppose we can forgive and forget. I don't want his gratitude, and I know it's impossible for him to feel even a grain of humility."

Starkad promptly pattered back to Thurid and whispered, "He begs your forgiveness and entreats you to help him, and says he's really quite helpless in the Alfar realm without you, and there's nothing he values more than your advice and friendship. He's promised Sorkvir to bring you out to him, and Sorkvir's got a hairlock spell over him that you must break. You see what a fix we're in without you. We're both very sorry the Guild is against you, and we want nothing more than to get you out of here as soon as we get our hands on your satchel and staff. Now that we've got your help, we can discover a solution for the Dark Chamber."

Thurid's sagging head came up with a snap and his nostrils flared as he whirled around. In three quick strides he had overtaken Leifr, nearly bowling Starkad over in his abrupt passage.

"The Dark Chamber?" Thurid cried, his eyes alight with battle fever, his lean form exuding waves of excitement. "Is that where they've put my satchel and staff?"

"According to the Retriever," Leifr answered, "but we can't get in there. Fire won't burn, eyes won't see, it's impossible—"

"We'll find a way," Thurid said, pinching his lip in thought. "Come along, we can't stand here arguing, or somebody is bound to see us. Where have you been hiding, Leifr? Is there a fairly safe place where we can get out of sight for a while?"

The Retriever's hut was as they had left it earlier, except that a basket of food and a pot of ale had been delivered by the apprentices' hall, which enabled them to pass the rest of the day and the evening quite comfortably. Thurid strode up and down, thinking, then he carefully outlined his plans for retrieving his staff and satchel from the Dark Chamber.

"It's really quite simple," he said confidently, stretching out his legs beside the fire. "I'll bribe one of the minor Guildmasters. They're a dissatisfied lot, as a general rule, and one of them will be glad to possess some Rhbu spells in exchange for helping us get into the Dark Chamber and make our escape."

"You're going to corrupt a member of the Guild?" Leifr demanded incredulously. "One of the twenty masters?"

"Yes, of course," Thurid said. "It's a distinct possibility. The Guildmasters themselves fear temptation, and are secretly fascinated by it. Taken together, they're strong enough to withstand temptation, but if I corner one of those young conceited upstarts by himself, he won't be able to resist. What a man publicly loathes, he secretly courts. It will be neat and quiet this way, and we'll be gone before the Guildmasters know it. This is the professional way to work, with grace and discretion."

It was near midnight when a horse and cart came to a rattling halt outside the door, accompanied by a loud howling and barking. A chorus of barking responded from every stoop to this uproar, thus augmenting it, which led to some shouting and cursing and throwing of available objects to quell the barking from nearly every doorstep. Lights were lit, and the baker next door and the stonemason came striding over to investigate the arrival of the cart, which was followed by the arrival of a pair of mounted Protectors carrying flaring staffs. Children scuttled out of their beds, and curious housewives stood in doorways, craning their necks to shout at the straying children while they clustered around the source of the uproar. Their upturned faces reflected awe, a little fear, and plenty of frightened delight at the return of the familiar apparition of the Retriever and his dilapidated cart, loaded with a heavy awkward burden, with a single acolyte tethered by a collar to the top of it. The poor fellow had been convinced he was a dog guarding his master's earthly goods. He pranced about on all fours, barking and growling ferociously as the Protectors approached.

Chapter 10

❖❖❖❖❖❖❖❖❖❖❖❖❖❖❖❖❖❖❖❖❖❖❖❖❖❖❖❖❖

"Home again, Vonbrigdi?" one of the Protectors inquired. "It's not such a fine world outside after all, is it? What's this you've got here in the cart?"

Vonbrigdi turned slowly from unharnessing his horse. In his usual ponderous monotone he said, "The remains of an acolyte. Or a dog. He doesn't know which himself."

"And this?" The other Protector prodded at the square object in the cart. "Feels like big cooking pots, big enough to scald a pig in."

"It's rendering pots," Vonbrigdi grunted, bending down to unharness his horse. "The Retriever is now a scavenger of carcasses instead of a scavenger of essences. Old bones, old hides, cows, sheep, horses, dogs, cats, trolls, men, it makes no difference to me."

The Protectors shrugged their shoulders and moved away, no longer interested, and gradually the crowd of observers melted away also, leaving only the acolyte crouching atop the cart. When Vonbrigdi went inside the house, the creature followed at his heels, like a dog intending to slip inside unnoticed to lie by the fire, or to beg for bones under the table.

"It was good of you to return," Thurid said, watching Vonbrigdi filling a pot to set over the coals. "Everyone in the Guildhall should know about it before dawn. I'd thought that you'd be a bit more clever about your return, if you're truly going to help me."

"It's too late for cleverness," Vonbrigdi said. "Only the shortest path will take you to the center of the Dark Chamber."

Starkad was unable to take his eyes off Vonbrigdi.

"You're one of them!" Starkad whispered. "At last, I've seen

133

one, Leifr, so you can stop preening yourself about the grindstone Rhbu!"

"Malasteinn," Vonbrigdi rumbled, turning again to the hearth. "His true name is unknown and never spoken, but we call him Malasteinn."

"You're one of them," Starkad persisted, his eyes probing like needles. "Why do you stay here, so poor and ragged, when you've got powers that could make you rich and free from all want?"

"No longer," Vonbrigdi answered. "The Guildmasters robbed me of all that. Just as they will rob Thurid of his knowledge and skill, in their fear and ignorance. Mistakes are common among the inexperienced."

"Inexperienced?" Thurid snorted. "The Guild has been here on this spot for two thousand years. Don't you think they've learned a few things in that time?"

"Yes, a few," Vonbrigdi replied, turning to gaze upon Thurid with his almost colorless eyes. "But the Rhbus have been here as long as the mists have risen from Ginungagap and Muspell. Perhaps longer. Who can say? You are the new people and impatient. Yet you, Thurid, have reached out and grasped the old powers. In you there is hope for all the remaining Rhbus. It is an honor to share my roof and fire with you." He beckoned for Thurid to sit down in his only chair, drawn up near the small fire.

Thurid sat down, his eyes drawn thoughtfully to the flame. "When Fridmarr came back from Bjartur with that staff and satchel, I never dreamed they would lead me so far away from Dallir and my familiar pathways and friends."

"At the beginning of every road there was a choice," Vonbrigdi said, drawing up a stool to sit upon. "One choice leads you into a deeper net of choices, until there is no return. You don't wish to go back, do you, wizard?"

"As you say, there is no return," Thurid said. "I must retrieve my satchel and staff and continue. I see now that my road is going to be that of the old Rhbus, who took refuge in the high places. When I leave this place, I shall be considered an outlaw for the rest of my natural days."

Vonbrigdi raised his scarred face to the light. "There are

worse things, my friend. It is lucky for you that you have come to my house in your need. I am a Retriever yet, despite what the Guildmaster says, and I can retrieve other things besides lost acolytes. I can retrieve your satchel and staff from its hiding place, and yourselves from the Guildhall."

"You know how to make your way through the Dark Chamber?" Leifr inquired with skepticism.

The dog acolyte who had crept in upon Vonbrigdi's heels suddenly uttered a shrill cackle and threw back his hood. With a gleeful leap he hurled himself into the ring of firelight, making a low bow to the assembled company. It was Gradagur, still singed-looking, still abounding with his never-ending enthusiasm.

"Thurid, my old fellow!" he crowed, grasping Thurid's hand with both his own. "Didn't I once promise you that I'd get you into the Guild? I was right, wasn't I? Here we both are at last, just as I foretold!"

"Gradagur, it's not quite as you once envisioned," Thurid said gently, darting Leifr a worried glance. "I'm an outlaw, and they say you're a madman. Hardly a happy conclusion of our days together as master and pupil."

"Never mind, that doesn't matter," Gradagur said. "To me, you'll always be my best student, no matter how far you fall in public opinion. I cast away all my pride and arrogance long ago, when I cast away my magic. There are better things than spells and secret powers, Thurid. In the future, everyone will have access to such powers, such marvels, as would make this Guildhall of powerful wizards look absolutely foolish. Magic is archaic, Thurid. In the future—"

"We're not in the future," Thurid interrupted, "we're in the present, and magic is the only weapon I've got to defend myself and my beliefs. I hope I can count on your assistance, Gradagur, or at least let me do what I must to retrieve my staff and satchel—"

"It's all settled," Gradagur said. "Vonbrigdi and I have made the plan. You don't have to do anything except watch. Didn't you hear him? He's the Retriever of anything lost. It's a wonderful gift. He told me exactly where to look for a tool I'd lost, and where to dig for the ore I want. He's a valuable creature."

"Wait now, I've got a plan of my own for getting my possessions back," Thurid protested futilely.

"Shh, shh, our plan is better," Gradagur said. "We'll not have to rely upon magic. This will be a triumph of the new power over the old, and you'll see how one day my inventions will drive magic off the face of this earth. Oh, don't look so alarmed, Thurid, I'll do your precious staff and satchel no harm, no harm at all. The time is not ready for my inventions, I know, and I doubt if I'll ever see the day when that time arrives, but I'm going to have some fun while I can."

Not another word could be pried out of him about his plan, and he smirked and gloated gleefully for the rest of the evening.

Before dawn, the Retriever was awake, harnessing his horse to the cart. Gradagur jittered around nervously, as if it were his wedding day.

"Thurid, you're to ride beside the Retriever," he fussed. "Leifr and Starkad, we'll be in the back—acolytes, of course. I'll be there to assist you in case you need me, Thurid, but it's going to be up to you to get us past the Protectors into the fire pits."

Thurid hoisted one eyebrow doubtfully. "Is that all? You don't think they'll be on the alert for interference exactly like this? I'm supposed to do the Dark Chamber alone, without outside help from tainted sources."

"They'll be expecting a clumsy and stupid maneuver such as this," Gradagur replied briskly. "Well, we shan't disappoint them. You can argue that you alone will go into the Dark Chamber, while the rest of us wait outside. What sort of help can they expect from Vonbrigdi, demoted as he is to collecting rubbish and tallow? I'm a madman, so what can I do? And Leifr and Starkad—"

"That's all the encouragement I can take just now," Thurid interrupted testily. "Let's get on with this, since I can't talk you out of it."

Thurid drew his hood over his head and climbed onto the cart. Plenty of activity commenced in the Guildhall in the hours just before dawn, as students and Instructors anticipated the boundary time for the working of their spells. The Retriever's cart passed several groups of apprentices, following their masters toward the gates to the ancient underground fortress.

The Protectors barred the path as Vonbrigdi approached.

"Retriever, you are banned from the experimental and instructional areas," one of them intoned, seething with a red aura in the darkness.

"Nonsense," a strange voice snapped, and Leifr peered around apprehensively. Thurid's lean form in Feitur's cloak shifted and swirled before Leifr's eyes, taking on the appearance of Feitur himself. "I require the services of a Retriever for my spell. I'm going to attempt a triple shape shift upon myself, and I don't want to get lost in case it doesn't work right. Stand aside, you brigands, and let me pass. My reputation is at stake. Now that the harm has been done, what good does it do to punish the poor old Retriever for his misdeeds? It won't help you defeat Thurid. He's quite a splendid fellow, and I don't think the Dark Chamber is going to thwart him in the least. Just passing by him in the corridor, I felt a tremendous wave of power and importance radiating from him. Mark my words, Protector, one day you'll hear his name connected with great deeds and valorous heroes."

"We'll have to search this cart before it goes inside," the other Protector said with scant patience.

"Be very careful," Thurid said. "Touch nothing, or I can't be held responsible for what might happen to you."

The Protectors scarcely glanced at the three acolytes, but they were very curious about the objects in the cart. In addition to the huge pots, there was a senseless tangle of wires and strings and other familiar nonsense. Leifr could have groaned aloud when he recognized it, but he was afraid to.

"It's nothing but great pots of water," one of them muttered, "and a lot of metal scrap and wire. What sort of spell do you intend to work with this junk? It doesn't look like a Guild spell to me."

"It's a bit untidy and awkward," Thurid said stiffly, "but I think it will work. The trick is what to do with the body once one has shifted shapes and left it behind, am I right? Well, I'm going to solve that problem today, I hope, and the Retriever is going to share his secret with us, whether he really wants to or not."

The Retriever shrugged his shoulders and grunted resentfully. The Protectors conferred a moment, then waved the cart through the portal.

The Retriever's cart rolled slowly through the area of the fire pits without being questioned, then he again selected the dark tunnel, where a Protector stood guard. He stepped forward, taking care to hide some gestures behind his back, but nothing could conceal his distaste and fear of the grim figure of the Retriever and his cart. Thurid sat beside him, in his own form once more, with the cloak muffled around him from his eyes to his toes.

"Stop, you may not pass, Retriever. You have been forbidden to these chambers. Who let you pass through?"

"I am not one to be forbidden easily," the Retriever said. "I have been sent for. Someone is lost in the Dark."

The Protector's scrutiny traveled the length and width of the cart, and all those who occupied it.

"No one can be retrieved from the Dark," he said suspiciously. "And I've heard nothing of anyone getting into there, by mistake or by design."

"They aren't there yet." The Retriever turned his raddled face toward the Protector and his tone became chiding. "Alveg, you should know the vagaries of magical practice by now. The Guild ascends to the stars and descends to the depths in search of knowledge. Does not the Guild include practicing futurists?" He nodded slightly toward Thurid, who responded with a baleful stare.

"A nicer word for necromancers, you mean," the Protector said with another uneasy gesture to ward off evil at the mention of this ill-favored clan. "The Guild should not be tampering with the knowledge of the dead."

"Why do you think the Guild created a Retriever?" Vonbrigdi went on. "Merely to repair the mistakes of blundering students? I know the way to Hela's realm, and I have been there many times to bring back a spirit to answer the questions of those who seek."

"I know that, everyone knows what you do." Alveg's face

twisted in a grimace of disgust and fear. "But I must know who is sending for you, and why your banishment has been lifted without my knowledge."

"Beware of questions, Alveg," the Retriever went on inexorably. "You don't know who might be willing to answer them or from what realm they might speak. The Retriever is not compelled to answer anyone's questions, but you may accompany him in his travels to Hela's realm if you wish to hear the answers yourself."

"No, no, that's one journey I hope to make only once, and a long time hence," Alveg said quickly, standing well aside for the cart to pass. "Good luck to you, Vonbrigdi."

Vonbrigdi did not turn his head as he replied, "I don't trust myself or my endeavors to luck, Protector."

At the far end of the tunnel, a stout door stood barred securely, with wards and runes gleaming warningly in the gloom. Starkad held a torch, but its light sputtered and dimmed as wisps of darkness fingered through the passage, suddenly blotting out all light and vision a moment before dispersing. Ignoring the runes, Vonbrigdi dispersed the wards with a sputtering and crackling and heaved the heavy door open. Thurid swiftly extended his arms as a barrier as Leifr and Starkad leaned forward to peer within.

"Stay back!" Thurid commanded. "I don't know how we'd get you out of there if it drew you in. This is nothing but pure chaos. You'd be scattered like chaff."

Beyond Thurid's restraining arm, there was nothing to be seen, as if they were trying to see through a black curtain. The only sensation was unseen movement, as if an entity lurked and breathed and waited where it knew it could not be seen. It was a huge and hungry void, and Leifr could feel it pulling at him, encouraging him to obliterate himself in its faceless, nameless evil.

"What did the Rhbus want with such a place?" he whispered to Thurid, overheard by the Retriever.

"They wanted to keep it away from the Dokkalfar," the Retriever answered. "They were the guardians of this secret, and the Fire Wizards' Guild is their inheritor."

"But what is it?" Starkad asked urgently.

"Simply a remnant of ancient chaos," the Retriever answered. "What was here before everything had names and boundaries, what will be here when we're gone. It's what the wizards wish to banish with their spells. It's where they put their mistakes, when purging isn't enough."

"This is far enough," Gradagur warned, his eyes shining with a fanatic light. "Vonbrigdi, be ready to go ahead with the cart when I give the order. Thurid, Leifr, Starkad, come and help me arrange the equipment."

"Gradagur, don't do this," Leifr said, the awful realization of his own idiotic folly dawning upon him. Once again he had put his trust in a madman, with absurd results. "This is your rafmagn equipment. This isn't going to do us any good underground. How do you think lightning is going to find it beneath earth and rock?"

"Lightning? Who needs lightning?" Gradagur retorted, unraveling a nest of wires. "I carry my own lightning with me, Leifr. You'll see, very soon, you'll see what a glorious invention this is. The clouds of dark ignorance and superstition will be banished."

Leifr went around to the other side of the cart to find Thurid. "Thurid, do you know what he's doing? He's got this ridiculous invention and he thinks it's going to help us see in the dark, but it's going to get us all captured by the Guild. Or worse. We could all get swallowed up in that, beyond there." He motioned toward the terrible darkness surging beyond the doors, lapping at them in black wavelets.

Thurid's eyes glowed, too, almost like rafmagn. "It's going to be splendid, Leifr. He was trying to discover this when I was with him. It's taken him a long time to make the devices he needed, but now it's ready."

The light at the other end of the tunnel was suddenly diminished, obstructed by the arrival of a group of cloaked wizards.

"Stop! The Guild Inquisitors command you!" boomed the voice of Fodur, advancing cautiously with his staff held at ready, oozing clouds of pale smoke. "Thurid, command these madmen to halt what they're doing and surrender themselves to Guild protection! They both require a purging!"

Gradagur glanced up only briefly from his wires, which he

was stretching between the two vats of water. "Stand back!" he commanded. "Don't come any nearer! This device has been know to explode with disastrous results!"

The Inquisitors fanned out in the passageway, moving warily through the seething wisps of darkness. Foremost was the Grand Meistari himself, carried in a sedan chair. He held his lighted staff ahead of him to light the way, and the light battled with the coils of solid darkness, writhing over the ground like angered snakes.

"Thurid! Gradagur! Halt what you're doing!" he commanded. "This is absolute folly! I can't permit you to destroy yourselves! Come back to the Inquisitors' hall and we'll talk. We can come to some sort of agreement, we're not irrational men to deal with. I've no intention of letting you destroy yourselves this way."

Leifr's hands closed around a comfortable-feeling length of wood and he took a few truculent steps forward to face the Inquisitors. "You'd rather do it the Guild way, I suppose," he growled, "which means the destruction of all things Rhbu. You're too late to stop us this time!"

"Too late indeed!" Gradagur chortled, jamming the last of his wires into place. Stepping back, he gazed hopefully at his invention.

With a hissing and sputtering, a red glow suffused the racks of stretched wires, growing to a brilliant white glow that dazzled the eyes. Fireballs hopped hither and thither as some of the wires melted and snapped. The Inquisitors shielded their eyes with their hands, too curious to retreat, too alarmed to come any closer. They cringed in the glare, as if they found it noxious, their faces blanched and startled in the naked brilliance.

Gradagur hopped around the cart, dodging sparks and squinting in the glare. "Magnificent! Amazing!" he yelled. "This is rafmagn, you wizards! This is the power of the future, not your magical mumbling and fumbling! You've never in all your lives conjured such a light as this!"

"Child's play!" Fodur grunted, lifting his staff. "The Guild wizards won't be intimidated by your unnatural powers! They come from nowhere, and I'll send them back." He raised his staff, summoning a fire bolt with a single word. It sputtered and fizzled in the glare of the rafmagn and fell to earth short of its target. Fodur gaped in dismay and growing embarrassment and hastily sketched some signs in the air to avert evil powers. Instead of glowing, the lines were broken and smoky, and the symbol faded immediately, much to the astonishment and consternation of the rest of the Inquisitors and Protectors.

"You see?" Gradagur said. "That won't do you any good. Magic will fail when inventions such as this become common. Leifr! Starkad! Hold on to the cart! We're going inside!"

The cart lurched forward into the Dark Chamber. The jolting of the rough cart caused more of the wires to fuse and sputter and burn, but plenty of light remained to cast glaring beams into the forbidden region. The darkness fled as if dissolved, like smoke dissipating. The cart groaned and lurched, and the horse strained as if drawing it up a steep hill. Leifr's legs would scarcely move, and he felt as if he were climbing a slope, although he could see perfectly well amid the jumping shadows that the chamber was nothing more extraordinary than a round room, in the style favored by the Rhbus, with a crumbling gallery above and many doors leading into it. The retreating darkness revealed a central platform crowned by a squat standing stone, where rested Thurid's satchel and staff. The blue orb glowed with a brilliant light, and Thurid started forward to claim it.

"Be careful!" Gradagur exclaimed. "The forces are still present! I can feel them pulling and pushing at us! This place is a vortex of power, like a maelstrom."

Thurid staggered across the ground as if drunken, seized his staff with a cackle of victory, and turned to face the Inquisitors. A shower of blue sparks rained down around him as he raised his staff, and the lurking powers of the vortex responded with a distant roar, like heavy surf.

"I'm leaving the Guildhall now, Meistari," Thurid said. "I don't wish to use my destructive powers to defend myself, so I beg you not to hinder my departure, or that of my companions. I bear no Guild wizard any ill will, but if I never see any of you again, it will be far too soon. Our agreement will be simple— you will avoid anything Rhbu and I will avoid anything Guild. Fair enough, I trust?"

"Thurid, you don't know what dangers you're toying with,"

the Meistari said, but he motioned to the Inquisitors to retreat. Grudgingly they moved backward, except Fodur.

"You don't know what they are, either," Thurid said with a note of sadness in his voice. "All my life I believed that the Guild was the highest order a wizard could attain, but now I know you have limitations, too. I must renew my search for the last of the Rhbus, Meistari. They are greater than the Fire Wizards' Guild, even with all its knowledge and teaching and apprentices."

"Bah! They're nothing but aimless wanderers!" the Meistari declared. "If you find the Three Rhbus, I'll wager that you'll find nothing but a mass of legend, lies, and exaggeration—all that remains of a once-great people."

"I don't believe you," Thurid said. "I'm going to search for them and their knowledge."

"Then leave the blue orb," Fodur said. "We cannot permit such an object to leave the Guild. No one shall possess this creation who could do us harm."

"I mean the Guild no harm, and I'd gladly leave you this blue abomination," Thurid replied testily, "but my staff is firmly affixed to it, and I can't leave it. My powers would gradually wither away and disappear without my staff. I must take it, as well as Heldur's orb, whether I like it or not."

"So much the worse for you," the Meistari said with a sad, weary note in his voice. "From now on, the Guild regards you as outlawed, with a price upon your head, if you choose to go into rebellion against us."

"I don't," Thurid said bitterly. "And I'm not in rebellion. It is the Guild who has turned against me."

A Protector strode forward, cradling his red-orbed staff. "I'll stop them, Meistari," he said. "Neither rafmagn nor Heldur's abomination shall return in the hands of our enemies to haunt us. This is the last resort. We must destroy them all."

The Meistari pondered a moment, his expression sorrowful. Then he called, "Do you hear, Thurid? Gradagur, you know what force the Protectors wield. Do you still wish to stand in opposition against it?"

Gradagur countered, "Do you wish to risk it against an unknown force, Meistari? It's the vortex you're challenging, not merely me and Thurid's orb. What befalls will be on your head, if you attempt to stop us.''

The Meistari nodded reluctantly to the Protector, who raised his staff. Thurid raised the blue orb and braced himself. The ferocious jolt of invisible powers colliding shook the chamber, dislodging carvings and railings and loose rocks from above. The roar of distant surf filled the room with an ear-splitting bellow, and the wizards were driven back against the walls, pinned like leaves in a strong gale. The Protector who had made the spell struggled to stand against the force, but he was forced backward inexorably, a step at a time, until he was flattened against the wall in the glare of rafmagn, like a pressed insect.

"I surrender!" he croaked. "Kill me or take it away!"

Thurid dropped his stance and the contending forces burst through one of the doors, funneling away down a corridor with a deafening scream, leaving the round chamber suddenly breathless and still. He tapped his staff upon the ground, looking at the blue orb with new respect.

The wizards picked themselves up, much chastened, and helped the Meistari extract himself from the overturned sedan chair.

"That's the way out," Gradagur said, pointing after the screaming winds. "I can smell the sea." He took the reins of the horse and led the cart forward, with another sputtering and flaring of the rafmagn.

"Thurid, don't go," Fodur said. Turning toward the Meistari, he spoke rapidly. "Meistari, hasn't this gone far enough? We'll lose that orb and Thurid both if he escapes now. Not to mention our honor, if word of this cursed invention gets out." He motioned angrily toward Gradagur and his device.

"How can we stop him?" the Meistari demanded indignantly. "This is exactly what I feared would happen. He can't be controlled by ordinary means!"

"Then you'll have to ally the Guild with him," Fodur said. "And maybe Gradagur isn't so mad after all. This invention of his could be used against the Dokkalfar."

"No indeed, letting them in would ruin everything."

"Isn't it already ruined, or very nearly so?"

"Certainly not. Wait and see what happens next. We can get

the upper hand again sometime, if need be. Very likely our troubles will be taken care of, when Thurid and Gradagur destroy themselves with powers they can't control. Yes, I daresay we've little to worry about, since they choose to reject our offer of help."

Thurid turned away without speaking, to preserve his dignity, but Leifr's temper was rising. He tore off the acolyte's confining hood and faced the Meistari and the Inquisitors.

"Your offer of help is nothing but death to Thurid," Leifr said, "and you'd never use rafmagn in the way Gradagur intends. He'd rather die with his secret than see it used for warfare. You're deceiving no one by your supposed good will. You fear that someone else will wield greater powers than yours, and you're jealous and mean with what you'll permit in others. Remember the old example of a handful of sand, Meistari. The tighter you squeeze it, the more of it you lose. You've lost Thurid and Gradagur, and one day you'll regret it."

"Thank you for your advice, Scipling," the Meistari answered with a slight bow. "We've met only briefly, in the Inquisitors' hall, so there's no reason for you to bear me such ill will. Had I wished, I could have swept you under the rug like dirt long ago. Do you think anyone comes into this Guildhall without being permitted? We saw your flying devices, and we watched you almost every moment, waiting to see what you would do. Nothing surprised us, except possibly the Retriever, and Feitur, who is, by the way, recovering from a broken collarbone and severely damaged pride. Since you've been kind enough to advise me, Scipling, I'll return the favor and give you some words to live by. Until that carbuncle is properly implanted, you'll never completely deceive anyone."

"It's not my intent to deceive," Leifr retorted. "All I want to do is survive."

"A man can't survive alone in the Alfar realm," the Meistari replied. "None of you will get far without Guild help. Remember, we're not your enemies."

"I shall try," Leifr answered dryly.

Gradagur ordered over one shoulder to him, "Hurry! The rafmagn is almost used up!"

"Retriever!" The Meistari's voice rang out. "Are you going

outside the walls of the Guild? You know the consequences of leaving!''

Vonbrigdi turned to look back a moment and nodded his head, as if confirming his own dark suspicions.

"I know, Meistari," he said. "But I'll count myself lucky. May the gods of sea and sky help the next Retriever of the Guild!"

The tunnel, barely wide enough for the Retriever's cart, ended abruptly on the face of the mighty gorge, Saknaskill, which cut off the Guild from the Alfar world. The cart could go no further, so the Retriever turned the blind horse around carefully, patted his neck, and spoke to him quietly for a few moments, then sent him back into the tunnel.

"Do you know what you're doing?" Thurid asked him.

"It matters not," the Retriever said with a shrug.

Gradagur added with a sly chuckle, "I'm losing my rafmagn device, but I don't mind. Let the wizards try to figure out how it works, if they dare. I'll build another one, and wait for a good lightning storm. That vortex gave me the strangest notion, a great thing turning and turning, around and around without stopping, and it's got something to do with rafmagn. In the future, great turning wheels will be important. All I see are wheels turning in my dreams, if I can only figure out the connection to the rafmagn."

"Rafmagn!" Thurid snorted, giving the blue orb a cautious polishing with his sleeve before starting down the rough slope to the bottom of the ravine. "A nice trick, Gradagur, but you won't have much use for it, even in the future, as long as there's plenty of candles and whale oil."

When they gained the relative comfort of the visitors' road to the Guildhall, they made good time to the settlement of Hefill-stad, where the sight of unusual travelers coming to and fro on that road was nothing to excite curiosity. Nor did anyone follow them from the Guildhall, as Leifr had expected. All the way back to Hardurjord he kept looking back, and looking at Thurid to see if he had detected anything suspicious by magical means, but Thurid plodded along with his usual complaints and remarks that horses were made for walking, not men.

When they reached Gradagur's citadel on the fell, Raudbjorn and the troll-hounds were waiting, having watched their progress for as long as they were visible below.

Raudbjorn grinned, his small eyes nearly lost in pleased creases, greeting Leifr with a cuff on the side of his head, growling, ''Raudbjorn happy to see you, Scipling,'' which was terribly effusive for a Norskur.

Thurid toured his old domain, delighted to find so little that had changed, although the flying devices failed to please him much, and he was similarly skeptical about the tower and the lightning rod. He and Gradagur retired to the hut to argue loud and long about it.

With the hounds clinging possessively to his side, and Raudbjorn's shadowy hulk lurking nearby, Leifr sat on a broken wall and watched the sun descending. Once again the Rhbu sword was hanging comfortingly at his side. Once again the Guildhall was veiled in clouds of obscuring mist, and he could scarcely believe that he had ever been there.

The troll-hounds suddenly growled and bristled, gazing toward the fell above. Leifr felt the ominous tightening grip of Sorkvir's hairlock spell, reminding him that Sorkvir was nearby, waiting to fulfill the next part of their bargain.

Chapter 11

❖❖❖❖❖❖❖❖❖❖❖❖❖❖❖❖❖❖❖❖❖❖❖❖❖❖❖❖❖❖

Upon their return to Hardurjord, Gradagur and Thurid at once retired to Gradagur's lightning tower, more crowded than before with rafmagn equipment. In high spirits, they stayed inside well into the night, talking and making explosions of sparks and smoke and bluish light. Leifr and Starkad searched Gradagur's larder for something to eat, then fell asleep after a meal of hard cheese and harder bread. Vonbrigdi posted himself beside the hearth, smoking his pipe and gazing into the flames, far away in his own thoughts.

Leifr awakened from a doze suddenly as a familiar warning prickle swept over him, instantly banishing his contented feelings of well-being and satisfaction. Uneasily he got to his feet and peered out the door into the night, knowing Sorkvir was nearby. Raudbjorn grunted suspiciously in his sleep, his hand automatically closing around the haft of his halberd. Before he could stop them, the troll-hounds surged silently around his knees and outside, to stand growling, ears cocked. Leifr closed the door at his back and moved forward a few paces, listening. With scarcely a sound of its hooves and a few dislodged stones, Sorkvir's black horse came leaping down the side of the rough fell to stand in the dooryard prancing and snorting clouds of mist.

Sorkvir dismounted and gazed a moment toward the tower, his face nothing but darkness. Then he chuckled, an evil, rasping sound that bore no resemblance to true amusement.

"So you've succeeded," he said. "Better than I'd expected. You've brought Thurid out of the Guildhall on your first attempt. Has he got that blue orb with him?"

"Of course," Leifr replied. "He wouldn't leave without his staff."

"And he's so grateful to you and trusts you exceedingly and regards you with the highest of esteem," Sorkvir went on, with a sneering note to his speech. "You day-farers get so maudlin about such things. Really, you shouldn't attach so much importance to any person, who may change his mind without notice and decide to stab you in the back one day for reasons beneficial solely to himself. It always happens. One you trust betrays that trust without a second thought."

"Yes, I saw how you turned against Djofull," Leifr answered. "Among Dokkalfar and night-farers that is probably true most of the time, but you've got no one to blame except yourselves."

Sorkvir shifted his spuming staff with an angry gesture, and Leifr felt a spire of shooting pain up the back of his neck.

"Enough of this meaningless chatter. I want that blue orb," Sorkvir snarled. "Bring me that staff. He won't be expecting you to betray him and he won't harm you even after he sees you steal it. He'll be too startled and confused. Just get it as far as the door and throw it into the darkness. I'll be waiting. You have no choice except to do it."

"What will happen afterward?" Leifr asked resentfully, trying to shrug away the pain in his neck and skull.

"That's none of your concern."

"It's not?"

"Concern for the lives and safety of yourself and others is reserved for those with all their free will intact. You are my property, Scipling, as long as I possess this power over you. Now walk to the house and do as I say, and take these idiot growling dogs with you, or I'll start by ridding myself of them first."

Leifr felt an ominous wave thrusting him backward and toward the house, reinforced by barbs of pain. He tried to force his dragging footsteps in the direction of the tower to warn Thurid, but he could not make himself disobey Sorkvir's bidding. Sorkvir retreated, waving Leifr onward impatiently as Gradagur and Thurid emerged from the tower, trooping jovially toward the house, trailing streamers of smoke and the peculiar smell of rafmagn. Vainly Leifr tried to summon the strength of will to call out to Thurid, but his throat and tongue seemed paralyzed. He stumbled into the house and sat down, his wits racing frantically, like rats in a rat catcher's cage.

Gradagur and Thurid came trampling in noisily and busied themselves with eating the remains of the stale bread and cheese as if it were a feast. With their feet propped up to the fire, they stuffed their pipes, although a great deal more reminiscing than smoking was likely to occur. Fully awake, Starkad sat on a stool as near as he could get, his eyes shining with rapture as he listened, every inch of him admiring and yearning for the knowledge possessed by the two wizards. Even the gloomy and cadaverous Retriever appeared softened by the atmosphere of old and thriving friendship renewed.

The staff leaned against the wall behind Thurid, within easy reach. Thurid did not even turn his head as Leifr walked up behind him and reached out to grasp it. Suddenly, inexplicably, Thurid reached around and grabbed the staff without even glancing at Leifr, and laid it across his knees, where the sinister blue orb sparkled with a thousand internal rays as brilliant as lightning.

Leifr stood helpless, unable to will himself to move without Sorkvir's command, and Sorkvir also seemed unable to decide what to do next. Leifr gazed at Thurid in helpless fascination as the wizard crossed the hut casually and flung open the door to inhale a great breath of night air.

"It's dreadfully stuffy in here," Thurid declared, leaning the staff against the wall to stretch his arms as he inhaled the night air.

As Leifr reached out toward the staff, a small dark form suddenly scuttled into the room from the darkness outside and leaped at him with an angry spitting and squalling. It was a gray cat, and it struck him chest-high with its paws before bouncing across the room again and out the door. It sufficed to break his paralysis. With a yell he lurched forward with the intent of hurling Thurid back into the house and flinging himself into Sorkvir's path. Thurid's staff flared with bright light as he gripped Leifr by one shoulder and firmly pulled him out of the way with a strength not to be resisted, as his own strength drained away in Sorkvir's wrath.

"Sorkvir!" Leifr gasped inarticulately, feeling the savage grip of the hairlock spell crushing his skull, destroying his power to warn Thurid, to tell him about the hairlock spell. His final free word was a croak. "Ljosa!" Then he collapsed on the floor, helplessly gripped by Sorkvir's spell.

A dark-cloaked figure loomed suddenly in the doorway, and Sorkvir confronted them from the safety of the threshold, a boundary place that strengthened his powers.

"Deceive me, will you, Scipling?" Sorkvir snarled, squinting in the glare of the orb and making signs with his hand as the occupants of the room rose warily to their feet. "Now that I've got the prize within my grasp, I've no further need for you." He held the hairlock amulet aloft, slowly tightening his grasp upon it.

"Stop!" Thurid commanded. "Let the Scipling go. You'll deal with me if you're any kind of wizard at all, Sorkvir. I won't destroy you until we've talked."

"Then talk away," Sorkvir said. "I've remarkably little to say, except that we must come to terms about that orb. I bespoke it for my own stealing long ago, and I take it much amiss that you've beaten me to it, through the interference of this Scipling." He gestured toward Leifr, who had used the distraction to stagger to his feet. "Surrender that orb to me, Thurid, and I'll allow the two of you to live. Deny me, and everyone here will die, and this mountainside will be nothing but a black hole when I'm done blasting it. I'll even allow you to keep the lady Ljosa, who has chewed her way out of a very stout leather bag to try to warn the Scipling away. I've generously given Leifr the essence he needs to restore her to her true form, am I right, Scipling?"

Leifr was able to nod and raise one hand to clutch the pocket where the small black vial was carefully sewn in his shirt.

Thurid darted a suspicious glance at Leifr. Pondering, he scratched his chin, musing "Well, it's true this blue abomination isn't much good to me. I might not mind getting rid of it, especially in exchange for some favors. If we had Hroaldsdottir back, we might peacefully return to Dallir and forget our quarrels with the Dokkalfar and the Wizards' Guild. Let's talk like reasonable beings, instead of barbarians." His tones were his most mellifluous, his manner most courteous as he added with a wry chuckle, "I was able to reason with the Guild, as you can see, and we parted on equable terms. I'm sure you and I can come to the same understanding."

Leifr struggled to shake his head, aided by a wave of indignation. Fridmarr's carbuncle burned against his chest, reminding him of the sole reason he had been brought to the Alfar realm. He had come to destroy Sorkvir, whom he had learned to hate for his own personal reasons. The cruelty and helplessness of the hairlock spell only enraged him further, whetting his desire for revenge.

Sorkvir gazed at Thurid suspiciously, sweeping his eyes briefly over Leifr, Gradagur, Starkad, and the Retriever. He glared a moment at Raudbjorn and the troll-hounds growling and huffing and snorting and looking to Leifr for a signal to attack.

"It seems your sojourn with the Guild has refined your manners somewhat," Sorkvir observed, his deep-sunken eyes glittering with suspicion. "Often I wondered how they would receive you there."

"Rest assured, no Rhbu magic has polluted the Guild," Thurid replied in his oiliest tones. "Otherwise I was very well treated, but I don't know how long their hospitality was going to last. Guests and fish lose their charms after three days, you know. Unfortunately I was prevented from leaving in time to stop Djofull from resuscitating your ashes. A pity, that; it would have saved me ever so much work, for I fear I'll have to destroy you all over again unless you release Leifr from whatever nasty little spell you're holding over him. And all for this bauble." He rapped his staff on the ground, eliciting a few sparks.

Sorkvir tapped his black fingernails on his staff and his scarred and withered countenance drew into the lines of a dark scowl. From the rafters above, Ljosa's cat form uttered a vicious hiss, and his eyes traveled upward.

"Blast that cat," Sorkvir muttered. "I knew there'd be trouble if she escaped while the Scipling has that vial. Well, through my own misfortune and clumsiness you have the cat and the essence, so in effect you have Hroaldsdottir in your possession, as well as that orb which I so much desire. But there remains the hairlock spell over your Scipling hero. Perhaps we could make an exchange—his freedom for the orb.''

Thurid chuckled indulgently, still exuding all the pleasant charm he could muster. "Come now, a hairlock spell? I daresay I could break it myself, Sorkvir. I'm surprised you used something so primitive and simple.''

"Maybe it is, maybe it isn't," Sorkvir growled. "A hairlock spell for an orb you don't want, it seems a reasonable exchange.''

"But the orb is of great and terrible value to certain people," Thurid said. "I may not want it, but neither do I wish to sell it cheap.''

"You hold the life and freedom of this Scipling as cheap?" Sorkvir queried. "How can you trust him ever, knowing that I hold this power over him, slight though it may be?"

It did not seem slight to Leifr, standing trembling in the grip of a force that could kill him as easily as Sorkvir could crush a beetle with his booted foot. At the moment he would have gladly traded a dozen blue orbs for deliverance from the digging claws of pain that held him immobile.

"Very well," Thurid said, evidently making up his mind. "You may take the orb if you'll free Leifr first." He rested the staff upon the earth with a thump and beckoned for Sorkvir to approach. Gripping the glowing sphere, he twisted at it, grimacing in the glare. "There, it's loose. Now lift the spell from Leifr. I want to see that hairlock burned to ash.''

Sorkvir removed the small pouch from his sleeve pocket and held it up for Thurid's inspection. Thurid extended the tip of his staff and Sorkvir looped the string of the bag over it. Gingerly Thurid took the pouch between two fingers and opened it slightly to peer inside rather dubiously.

"That's it, all right," Sorkvir said impatiently. "Now you've got it, you could use it yourself against him.''

"It could be useful, Sciplings being what they are," Thurid agreed, glancing at Leifr, who turned a furious glare upon him. "But it's not my way of dealing with subordinates.''

In a sudden puff of flame, the pouch burned to ash in the palm of Thurid's hand without so much as blackening his skin. Leifr reeled from the sudden withdrawal of the dark influence, feeling as if he had just been delivered from the jaws of death. He stretched his numbed muscles, feeling his own will flowing back into them. The touch of the Rhbu sword hilt strengthened him even further.

Thurid stirred the ashes in his palm a moment, then pursed his lips and dispersed them with a sharp gust of breath. "I hope that takes care of it," he said.

"Thurid," Leifr began to protest immediately, "you can't give him the orb for such a paltry exchange."

"I shall be the judge of that," Thurid snapped. "Now be silent before I begin to have regrets about destroying that hairlock so precipitately."

"A bargain is a bargain," Sorkvir said, stretching out one clawlike hand toward the orb, his eyes fervid with greed. He paused to ask, "Do you dare stop me, Scipling?"

"I'll fight you for it first," Leifr declared, striding forward with every intention of making a stance and once again challenging Sorkvir's magic with *Endalaus Daudi*.

Thurid extended one arm to bar Leifr's path, but Leifr thrust him aside and stepped up to Sorkvir, eye to eye.

"Don't touch that orb, you corpse carrion, or I'll cut off your arm," Leifr snarled, inhaling the disgusting dead smell of the wizard, mixed with the concoctions he used to preserve himself. Combined with his own berserk, bottled-up rage, it was a heady enough mixture to compel him to almost any heedlessly heroic feat.

Sorkvir moved as if to shrink back in fear, then one claw shot out and seized a handful of Leifr's shirt, exactly where Ljosa's black vial was sewn. Simultaneously Sorkvir blew an icy breath of wind into Leifr's face that blinded him with a cloud of agonizing droplets that burned and stung like snake venom. With a shout, Leifr covered his smarting, watering eyes and staggered back, instantly repenting of his bravado as far as wizards were concerned. Sorkvir ripped away the black vial and bounded away with a triumphant cackle, almost lost in the sound of Raudbjorn's enraged bellow. Still blinded, Leifr heard his huge feet coming, his breath huffing furiously, weapons rattling, armor creaking like some massive engine of destruction, spinning him half around as it passed. Clearing his eyes at last, he saw Raud-

bjorn and Starkad and Gradagur all armed and prancing ferociously around Sorkvir, now on horseback and thrusting at
Raudbjorn with his staff, while Thurid hopped back and forth
trying for a clear shot at Sorkvir with a spell. Raising *Endalaus
Daudi* over his head, Leifr charged forward, bellowing, "Stand
aside! He's mine! I'm going to kill him!"

Wisely the others got out of his way, and Sorkvir spurred his
horse to the top of the roof where he stopped the beast, rearing
aloft and squealing in rage at the troll-hounds swirling and snapping around it.

"I'll see you all die for this!" Sorkvir snarled. "That orb is
mine! The wrath of the Dokkur Lavardur is going to find you!
Hela will have your entrails!"

"Coward!" Leifr spat, climbing after the wizard, every ounce
of common sense gone. "Are you too frightened to fight with
men's weapons? Do you always hide behind a shroud of sorcery
and deceit? I'll make you a shroud with my own hands, after I
carve the life out of you once more!"

Sorkvir held up the black vial. "Scipling! Beware! This holds
the soul of Ljosa Hroaldsdottir! Be careful what you do, or it
will be lost to your forever! You might even be the agent of her
death!"

Leifr snarled, "I don't believe anything you say! You had your
chance to take the orb, but you took something that wasn't even
on offer! Coward, thief, killer! I defy you! I challenge you for
all the Alfar realm to hear, Sorkvir! Fight for your name and
honor, or die like a beggar in a ditch!"

Raising his voice to a furious bellow, Leifr scrambled onto
the roof and made his way across the steep pitch toward the
peak, where Sorkvir's horse danced for its balance. Sorkvir held
the black vial in one hand, his staff in the other, and for the first
time Leifr observed that the horse had no reins to guide it. He
saw the madness in the creature's eyes and understood its pain
and fear from his own torment in the hairlock spell.

"Scipling! Hear me!" Sorkvir commanded, pulling the stopper from the vial, with a sinister grin stretching his lips. "What
happens if I pour this essence upon the ground? The lady dies."

"And I kill you," Leifr added. "Sooner or later, I'll find you and kill you, and this time there's no Djofull to bring you back from Hela's cold embrace.''

"True enough. I don't doubt you. But consider this, Scipling. If you kill me, you kill her.'' After pressing one finger to his opposite nostril, he inhaled the contents of the vial and tossed it away with a derisive laugh.

Leifr froze, staring, as the wizard's features suddenly seemed to melt into mist, and Ljosa's face looked out at him, her eyes large and terrified. Her lips parted in a scream of pure horror that went through him like daggers, turning his knees to water. Her pale hair swirled and she cried out, "Leifr! Help me! I can't bear it! Let me out! Let me out! Leifr!''

The haunting cry faded, and Sorkvir's hideous, warped face returned, gloating like the cat who ate the butter.

"Did you hear, Scipling?'' he gloated. "I have her in the safest place of all now—sharing this carcass, imprisoned where she can't ever get out, except by my doing. What do you think now of wizards' power, you crawling maggot? With a sword in your hand you're a roaring lion, but when you're forced to use the wits and skills of power and thought which you'll never possess, you're as helpless as a new-weaned child. Farewell, Scipling, until we meet again. You may keep that orb awhile longer yet. I charge you to bring it to me at Hringurhol in the Dokkalfar realm, if you wish for the lady to live. If you're wise, you'll take great care to preserve my health, should you ever want to see Hroaldsdottir again.''

With a vile laugh, he sent the horse plunging away wildly up the side of the fell. Before he passed completely out of reach, Leifr heard Ljosa's voice again, calling to him in desperate terror. Leifr half fell down from the roof somehow, staring in the direction Sorkvir had taken, never having felt so utterly defeated.

"You great nitwit!'' Thurid greeted him with a thrust from the staff's end. "If you hadn't goaded him, he wouldn't have done it!''

"If you hadn't offered such an absurd trade, this wouldn't have happened,'' Leifr answered with a smoldering glower over one shoulder at Thurid. "Raudbjorn, are we ready to leave? At dawn and no later. Hringurhol was what he said, Thurid. Get out your maps.''

''Ready to go,'' Raudbjorn replied, grinning with delight. The troll-hounds mirrored his pleasure, crowding around Leifr, licking their chops and yawning and stretching.

''Where's Ljosa's fylgja cat?'' Leifr demanded. ''Did anyone see where she went?''

''After Sorkvir and her own life essence,'' Vonbrigdi said. ''Like a gray streak. You needn't worry about her. Cats are clever creatures.''

Thurid avoided Kraftig's friendly jostling, sidestepped Farlig and Frimodig's advances, and dodged into the house, where Starkad and Gradagur had followed Leifr with a cloud of excited questions. Motioning them aside, Thurid approached Leifr to speak privately and pointed to Gradagur's sleeping platform as a sitting place.

''Sit down,'' Thurid said. ''We must talk before we act.''

''No,'' Leifr said, calm on the exterior, simmering within from the wounds of shame and defeat. ''This time we'll finish him off with no hope of return. Endless Death—it's a blissful thought, is it not? How far is Hringurhol?''

''Leifr, he wasn't about to touch this orb,'' Thurid said. ''He played you right into his trap. He knows you won't kill him as long as he's got Ljosa. And now he's got you to carry the orb for him right to Hringurhol and the Dokkur Lavardur.''

''We'll get her out,'' Leifr said grimly. ''We've got a Retriever. He must know about this sort of thing. We'll take him to Hringurhol to retrieve Ljosa. He can unsort the most complicated of shape-shifting spells.''

''Leifr, Sorkvir will go wherever we push him. If we go back to Dallir, he'll follow the blue orb. If we go in search of the Rhbus, he'll follow. If we go charging into Hringurhol, he'll have us where he can get the advantage over us, don't you see?''

Leifr's gaze was not friendly. ''You're suggesting we do nothing, is that right?''

''No, I'm not suggesting we do nothing,'' Thurid snorted, his eye kindling with suppressed temper. ''It would be impossible to do nothing, when inaction is as sure a method to a future course as fighting it out with all your might.''

"Good. Then we'll fight it out with all our strength," Leifr said. "I'm glad you agree."

Thurid gripped his own wrists, as if preventing himself from committing a crime. "No, that's not entirely what I meant," he said with insufferable patience. "If we chase Sorkvir to Hringurhol, we'll be doing as he expects and he'll lead us where he wants us, which won't be to anyplace pleasant or healthful. Is that what you want—or would you rather meet Sorkvir on our own terms, on our own turf?"

"It makes no difference to me," Leifr said. "What do you think Ljosa would think, if we didn't come after her? I don't think she's anyplace pleasant or healthful. I've been in his grip, Thurid. It's like slow death, wondering when the final stab or twist is going to end it."

Thurid sighed and rose to his feet, leaning upon the staff. His eye came to rest upon the blue orb, clutched in its claw of once-molten gold and silver.

"I wonder why this had to happen," he muttered. "I was happy as I used to be. And do you know what the worst of it is? Fridmarr isn't here to suffer along with us."

"Don't speak ill of the dead," Leifr said. "In this realm, they are capable of hearing every word you say and taking exception to it. As well as taking action on it." He touched the carbuncle hanging inside his shirt, thinking of Fridmarr with a rueful smile. "He knew all along there was more to it than the Pentacle, didn't he?"

"Blast him, he was devious that way. First Skrymir's great ruby heart, and now this blue jewel of Heldur's, both powerful tokens in the game of dominion over Skarpsey. Blast it, Leifr, if only you'd use that wretched carbuncle the way it was meant to be, we'd know what Fridmarr knew!"

"I don't want to know that badly," Leifr said hastily, getting to his feet. "You'd better get some rest, Thurid. We're leaving early in the morning, before the Guild has second thoughts and sends somebody after us. I'm going to stand the first watch tonight, and Starkad can watch the second. Starkad!" He spoke sternly and Starkad looked up eagerly from the pack he was stuffing with provisions.

"I'll stand both watches, if you want," Starkad volunteered.

"I'll never sleep again and I'll eat grass with the horses, only don't tell me I'm not going with you, because you know I'll follow you again, and that's really not fair to Ermingerd and my aunt, because you promised to watch out for me."

Leifr frowned, trying to remember if he had made such a promise or not. "You'd be safer here with Gradagur," he said, with a sharp look at Gradagur. "He's not going. Of that I'm perfectly certain. We'll have no need for his rafmagn and strange inventions. *Endalaus Daudi* is all we need."

Gradagur folded his arms and nodded his head. "I would be most willing to volunteer my services," he said, "but I'd prefer to stay here with my inventions and harry the blind, obsolescent Wizards' Guild from this quarter. Swords and fighting and that sort of rubbish are too uncivilized for me, now that I know how futile it all is. And what a lot of work. Killing in the future will be much easier, too." He heaved a gloomy sigh, his face twisted by a tortured grimace. "Sometimes the future is a place I wouldn't want to live in, not at all," he confessed.

Leifr looked at the Retriever, sitting quietly in his corner, smoking his long pipe, and gazing at the fire, as if he were back in his little house behind the Guildhall.

"Retriever?" Leifr said. "You saw what happened. You can get Ljosa away from Sorkvir by some means, can't you?"

The Retriever thought a moment, then nodded slowly. "If he—they were before me right now, I could do it," he said. "But as time passes and I get farther from the Guildhall, I feel my strength draining away from me." He shrugged his shoulders. "Perhaps the high country will be more agreeable to me, and plenty of high country lies between here and Hringurhol."

"When we catch Sorkvir, he won't be much farther from the Guildhall," Leifr said. "That I can promise you."

In the morning before dawn they were ready to begin, a curiously silent group. Gradagur's humble horse was offered and accepted as the Retriever's mount with no great sacrifice or gratitude on either side, but Gradagur walked a long way beside the Retriever's knee before their ways parted. Then he solemnly shook all their hands and wished them well, as he had done repeatedly already by impoverishing his store of provisions to send them on their way. Last of all he bid Thurid farewell.

"It seems our paths are always doomed to part," he said with an earnest tear trickling down his cheek. "I knew from the beginning that you were better than any apprentice I'd had or ever would have, Thurid. I knew from the start you were cut out for grand things and great events."

"Bah, that's nonsense," Thurid said gently. "And you know it."

"Well, yes. I didn't know you knew it, though. You won't forget me, when all this is over, will you? You'll all come back for a long visit when the dust is all settled?"

"It is rather near to the Guildhall," Thurid suggested a bit uneasily, glancing in the direction of the shrouded towers across the firth.

"They won't bother you," Gradagur promised. "They've had a taste of rafmagn, and they don't like it. We'll all outlive this present quarrel with the Guild and one day we'll all forgive and forget—or at least be able to tolerate each other's existence without too much trouble."

"I hope you're right," Thurid said, "but at the moment it doesn't seem very possible."

"I'm used to the impossible," Gradagur said. "I live much of the time in the future."

They left him at the Hefill crossroads and took the eastern road. Leifr noted with increasing interest that the road followed an ancient ley line, running straight as a die from hill to notch to mound and spring, although the stones that should have been standing to channel the earth's energy were toppled or missing completely. Looking back, he could see that the final point of the ley line was the Guildhall, perching on its black pinnacle. Even if the Fire Wizards had no use for the ley lines, Thurid seemed intent on some plan in his head, which he did not care to divulge. Perhaps his first objective was to put as much distance as possible between himself and the Guildhall, which also seemed like a worthy goal to Leifr.

By the third day of travel, however, he discovered the true nature of the matter. The Retriever rode behind Thurid, apparently slouching indifferently in his saddle as if sunken in his own woebegone thoughts, but at intervals he bestirred himself and looked around half interestedly; at these times Thurid watched him closely. The Retriever sometimes stopped his horse, or rode in an aimless half circle, his head raised almost alertly, his colorless eyes alight with a peculiar curiosity. Sometimes he circled two or three times before coming to a halt, his scarred nose pointed steadily ahead, his manner once more loose and despondent. Then Thurid would cease his officious map-rattling and his pretentious and inconclusive dowsing, and the direction the Retriever pointed was the direction that he chose. The longer the Retriever took to decipher the right way, the louder and more arresting Thurid's behavior.

As for Thurid, his eyes were positively maniacal and he pushed the horses as fast as he dared. After five days, their course had wound higher and higher over the rocky spine of Skarpsey, where the air was thin and cold and scarcely enough grass grew to keep a horse alive. By this time Leifr and Starkad had reformed their old conspiracy, since Thurid and the Retriever were definitely shutting the others out from some secret they shared. Leifr supposed it was their common Rhbu knowledge, but he didn't see why it had to be so exclusive, particularly after the trouble he and Starkad had gone to rescuing Thurid from the Guild.

"When it comes to gratitude," Starkad remarked one night around their miserable little fire, "the memory of the recipient is ungratefully short, while the giver remembers every detail forever."

In the morning they started the way down. In most places nothing marked the way except two or three rocks piled up in an abbreviated cairn. The exposed stone bore no mark of a path, except an infrequent scrape of a shod hoof. In the bottom of steep ravines were the bones of horses that had lost their footing above, and perhaps a few lone riders had met their doom unnoted in the vast, scarcely traveled silence of the mountains.

At noontime the Retriever called a halt. Raising one thin arm, he pointed into the green valley far below, waiting like a wonderful dream after the nightmare of mountain travel. A cloud of lingering smoke promised a settlement, where food and shelter could be obtained, although Leifr could scarcely justify the existence of a settlement so far from the sea. Then he saw the dark track of a good deep river that could carry goods to and from the ships. A faint tracery of trails told him that the settlement was also reached by pony-train over the mountains that entrapped it on all sides.

"That is Laglendi-hlid," Vonbrigdi said. "The lowland gate. What you seek lies beyond there, but I am not the one to take you farther." He dismounted from his horse and offered the reins to Thurid. "Take this steed. I won't be needing him where I'm going."

Thurid blinked in astonishment. "We can't leave you here with no horse. How would you carry your provisions? On your back?"

"I need no provisions, either, Thurid. I'm not going much farther."

"Vonbrigdi, are you mad? Of course you're going farther, much farther, until we overtake Sorkvir. What sort of nonsense is this?"

"I've come as far as I can go," the Retriever said gently. "I wanted only to die in the high country, and I've come to the place I've chosen. Part of the Guild purge was a curse that I would die if I left the influence of the Guild. I'm surprised that I've lasted this long. You'll have to go on, Thurid. Learn to develop your own finding abilities. It's part of the Rhbu heritage, and you have it somewhere in that satchel. Even though you weren't born to it, you're near to becoming a Rhbu. Now go on with your journey, and leave me to mine. As soon as you get to Laglendi-hlid you'll know the way to go, without my advice."

Thurid tore off his hood in exasperation and leaped off his horse to confront Vonbrigdi. "We're not leaving you here to die alone," he said. "I can accept what the wizards have done to you, but only if you pass your last hours in comfort and friendship. If you won't come down with us to the settlement, then we'll stay here with you. At least we can keep off the foxes and ravens."

"You can't, my friend. You mustn't. It's not the Rhbu way to stand in defiance of the advancing curtain of death. We go alone to the high places and wait. Let the foxes and ravens have their due, Thurid. It matters not to me, when I've gone beyond to that bright place where all knowledge waits to be discovered. It's not such a bad thing for a Rhbu to die. The gloomy and awful Hel you talk about is only one fork of the road after the crossroads of life and death. One who knows the proper way can avoid that place."

"Vonbrigdi, there is so much I could learn from you," Thurid implored. "My curiosity is whetted to a painful degree. Tell me more about the crossroads and Hel and the bright place you mentioned."

"There are other teachers waiting for you," Vonbrigdi said. "Teachers who are complete Rhbus, instead of this shattered shell before you. One day you'll understand how little there is that I can give you. Now go, there is knowledge awaiting you in plenty. Don't stumble and hesitate on the bottom step, Thurid, when there are so many stairs ahead for you to climb. Let my dying be the humble and private deed a true Rhbu means it to be."

Leifr dismounted on the narrow path so he could stand eye to eye with Vonbrigdi. A faint smile disrupted the scars and creases of the Retriever's face as he clasped Leifr's hand in farewell.

"You knew it would kill you to leave the Guildhall," Leifr said, almost accusingly. "I never meant to cause your death, Vonbrigdi. Is it too late to take you back there?"

Vonbrigdi shook his head. "Nothing could force me to go back now that you've reminded me of what I once was and that I still have this one last freedom. Is this not a better way than hauling wizard fodder back and forth? Thank you for restoring my pride, Leifr. May the all-powerful and benevolent Rhbus guide you on your journey."

"I don't know how we can rescue Ljosa without you," Leifr said.

Slowly the Retriever unslung his battered old satchel off his thin shoulder and held it out to Thurid. "All the wisdom of my craft lies within. It is now yours, Thurid. I wish I could be there when you challenge Sorkvir for possession of the girl. My work is finished."

Chapter 12

With gnawing reluctance they left him, a lone dark figure in the wasteland of skarp and crag. Resolutely Thurid squared his shoulders and refused to look back. Looking at the marble-like set of his pale features and the distraught twitching of his jaw, Leifr wisely kept back and motioned Starkad and Raudbjorn to stay well away from him. Thurid tended to grieve as a bereaved mother bear would, by tearing the head off the nearest available scapegoat.

Falling back to the rear of the silent party, Leifr led Vonbrigdi's horse. As they descended, the cloud cover seemed to follow them, gradually wreathing the high peaks in banners of gray mist that promised snow.

Starkad dropped back beside Leifr, unable to bear the gloom and loss in silence. In a low voice he said, "If not for us, he wouldn't have had to die. If we hadn't gone into the Guildhall, if we hadn't happened to sit down on his cart—"

"He's not sorry, Starkad, and we're only being sorry for ourselves because we've lost him," Leifr interrupted. "It was his choice to help us, his choice that brought him here. Happy is the man who can choose his own death, when there are so many ways of being found by it. If I weren't willing to die by sword or axe, I'd throw this sword away and go hide somewhere. I choose this eventual end for myself merely by being here, doing what I'm doing, and Vonbrigdi chose his mountaintop. Is that so bad?"

Starkad shrugged his shoulders. "Not when you look at it in your dull Scipling way, as if one day is all a man has to live and his living and dying makes no real difference to the entire web of things. Look at Raudbjorn, for example. He has no more idea of living than an animal. As long as his eyes open up in the morning, he's content, and real happiness is getting enough fame to become a legend, so scops will sing about you in fire halls when you're dead.''

Leifr eyed Starkad in consternation and puzzlement.

"Fame lives on after the body rots," he said. "I don't see what's so terrible about that. It was a lesson I learned at my grandmother's knee. There's not much you can do about anything after you're dead, so you'd better do it all while you're still able. What's gotten into you, Starkad? We've had a lot of fun times since we robbed Slagfid's Ban together. Are you losing your nerve?''

"I'm losing something. I'm not sure what. Maybe the Retriever gave me something else to think about besides fame and danger.''

Leifr rode in silence a moment, considering this new and slightly absurd idea. "Like what?" he finally demanded.

"Like what I'm going to do to make up for Vonbrigdi's dying. He's left a gap in this realm, Leifr, and he never raised a sword in his life. Think of the knowledge he once possessed. His retrieving powers were all that was left. Even the Guild wizards could not retrieve as he did. Think what he must have been or could have been. If Thurid can practice their spells and become a Rhbu, perhaps I can, too, if he'll teach me what he knows.''

"If you do, you'll never see Ermingerd or your family again," Leifr said with a queer shiver of prophecy. "You'll be a fugitive from the Guild, like Thurid. You could end up purged and wrecked, like Vonbrigdi.''

Starkad wasn't thinking of consequences, judging from the way his eyes were shining with fervid zeal and gazing away into the middle distance without seeing much. Leifr glanced back once toward the place where they had left Vonbrigdi and saw that the clouds had covered it.

Laglendi-hlid at once reminded Leifr of Ulfskrittin and the settlement festering around the walls of Djofullhol. Where there was a crossing of several ways, commercial enterprises of any unsavory sort were liable to flourish along with the legitimate trades. Travelers were there in plenty, evident from the number of tents pitched outside the walls of the suspiciously huddled walled houses and stables. They had come from up or down the broad river, which was the color of ink from chewing its way through the black lava of Skarpsey landscape. Several boats stood in the stands, and a ferry barge waited to take them across. A few carts rumbled through the main gate, which looked like part of an ancient, more noble ruin, beyond which a maze of streets, alleys, and buildings had clustered for protection against marauders.

Leifr stopped his horse beside Thurid, who was scowling down at the settlement in lofty distaste.

"Gradagur says that settlements such as this will grow even larger and more numerous in the future," Leifr said. "People will live hundreds to a single house."

Thurid darted him a slanting glare. "Don't you start," he snapped. "One prophet among my acquaintances is more than enough. Besides, I think he's wrong. People don't want to live among one another's animals and midden heaps, eye to elbow. These villages are nothing but a fleeting experiment that certainly won't last long. People will go back to their lords and land when they see that freedom isn't as easy as they'd thought, if they don't kill one another first. Most of these fellows are renegade thralls or outlaws. They'd be better off bound to some heavy-handed earl who'd make them behave, and so would the rest of the innocent world these robbers prey upon, although they do have the nerve to call themselves merchants. What sort of merchants charge you three prices, or even four, because there's nowhere else you can buy the goods? Thieves, that's what. I daresay a lot of their wares come from raided ships and pony-trains. Or murdered travelers. The inns in a place like this are nothing short of deathtraps. Plague holes, that's what these villages are, with every sort of vice and vicious person to be found. What can you expect from a Dokkalfar invention?"

Starkad's eyes shone with anticipation. "Hogni and Horgull always went to do the trading in a settlement such as this, and I went only a few times, always under their eye. There are booths and stalls of every type of food, jewelry, weapons, clothing, cooking pots, and strange, wonderful things brought from lands across the sea. Unknown metals, odd garments and boots, spices, incense, dancers, musicians, slaves, dogs—''

"And you'd better stay away from it all," Thurid interrupted. "I'd bypass this place entirely, if the Retriever hadn't told me we have to come here. We have to hire a guide to take us any nearer Hringurhol."

Leifr's interest sharpened. "Dowsing and maps and ley lines and carbuncles are no longer enough?" he asked. "We've always found our own way before."

"We've lost the Retriever's tracking ability, and we've never gone into the Dokkalfar realm before," Thurid retorted. "The moment we cross this river, we're in their domain, subject to their anarchistic rules. Sorkvir is in this morass somewhere. You see how we've let him lead us directly into his own realm?"

"Better that we follow him to Hel's kettle than let him disappear with Ljosa imprisoned inside that carcass of his," Leifr answered grimly, nudging his horse forward in the direction of the ferry.

The ferryman was a one-eyed, unsavory-looking old dwarf, as short and gnarled as a tree stump. He swept his one eye over the newcomers dispassionately and bent his back to the oar.

Laglendi-hlid was all that Starkad and Thurid had said, and more. Its noise and filth and glorious, tantalizing opportunities assaulted the senses. The crowding of house upon house filled Leifr with a heady sense of danger, considering all those strangers who might be observing him without his knowledge, yet there was a wonderful festive air of tough independence in the manner of the hawkers who shouted and beckoned to him, demanding his appraisal of their wares. Dokkalfar outnumbered any other persuasion, their faces wrapped or masked as they plied their trades in booths or carts or loitered about the drinking and eating booths. Day-farers moved among them in the cautious camaraderie of the equally damned, and the sight of Dokkalfar and Ljosalfar mingling and talking together so casually was such an abrogation of all the rules Leifr had grown accustomed to that he began to feel that there were no rules in Laglendi-hlid, as long as your behavior didn't lead to your own death somehow. Even then, nobody would care.

Thurid selected a small inn at the end of a street of metalsmiths, partly because it was away from the brawling uproar of the central market square, and partly because he was fascinated in spite of himself by the precious and unknown metals he saw on display. After dividing his attention between the booths and anxiously watching Leifr and Starkad, who were growing more restless with each moment, he reluctantly consented to allow them to walk through the town, on the condition that they return before nightfall. With Raudbjorn treading protectively at their heels, they made good use of their time and beheld a lot of interesting sights, most of which involved the antics of hawkers trying to get them to part with their silver. When the sun declined, the noise and the tempo increased as more Dokkalfar tradesmen and travelers crowded the streets. What they had seen during the day was a pale shadow of the delights that occurred at night. Leifr had never heard such music, seen such dancing women, nor tasted such liquor. Before he knew it, a great deal of time had passed and it was long past sundown, when he had promised Thurid they would return.

"He won't be angry," Starkad observed blissfully, full of good food and drink and sublime confidence. "We've come to no harm, and we've had such a good time. He'll understand. He was young once, too, wasn't he?"

"A long time ago, maybe," Leifr answered, peering around at the fetid, crowded streets and trying to remember which one they had come out of. Even the troll-hounds were confused in the crush of trampling feet and mingled smells. They had been stepped on and stumbled over with exasperated curses, but no one objected very strenuously with Raudbjorn glowering and muttering down at him.

Choosing a street that seemed quieter and hardly crowded at all, Leifr led the way in what he hoped was the direction back to the metalsmiths' street. The farther he advanced, however, the more certain he became that he had made a bad choice. The street was too quiet, and he became suspicious of the eyes that watched through cracks and peepholes. Rounding the end of a cart blocking most of the way, they suddenly realized the nature of this region. One cloaked figure was counting out glittering silver into the hand of another, who carried a halberd like Raudbjorn's. In the cart behind him was a heap of corpses. The two businessmen froze a moment while the intruders passed. Raudbjorn grunted and nodded in passing, sharing with those strangers in the brotherhood of blood for money.

"Good catch," he grunted, as would one fisherman to another after a successful day.

"Only middling," the other answered with typical reluctance to boast.

Leifr let out a long breath when they were safely past.

"This must be the street of assassins," he whispered. "It's not a healthy place for a midnight stroll."

"We might find Sorkvir here," Starkad said. "Sorcerers come to places like this to buy corpses after the bounty money has changed hands."

Leifr considered searching for Sorkvir a moment. "No, we might find something a lot worse," he said. "We might even find Thurid, looking for us. We'd better get off this street as soon as we find an alley going across."

They found an alley, with lights showing at the far end, and proceeded to thread their way through tethered horses, carts, sleeping beggars, and refuse they couldn't identify in the dark, except by smell. Their passage was not discreet; they disturbed sheep, pigs, and dogs and raised a few suspicious shouts.

Raudbjorn dropped a heavy hand on Leifr's shoulder, startling him more than he cared to admit.

"Men following, Leifr," the thief-taker rumbled. "Four small ones. Want Raudbjorn to ask questions?" He twanged the edge of his halberd hopefully.

Leifr looked back and saw four shadows lurking suspiciously around a dung cart. Everything in their attitude shouted to Leifr to be on his guard. They were armed and tense, not like casual strollers, and Leifr could feel their eyes upon him, like hawks watching prey.

"Yes, we'll question them," he said to Raudbjorn. Taking a few steps forward, he unsheathed his sword, which glimmered and rippled in the alley gloom.

"Who's there?" Leifr demanded in his most threatening growl. "You'd better not be following us, when there are plenty of other places for you to walk."

One of them stepped forward, spreading out his hands in a

peaceable gesture. A familiar whining voice said, ''Come now, Leifr the Scipling, we're old friends. You should know us by now. We've followed you all the way from Djofullhol.''

''Nagli and the Naglissons!'' Starkad cried. Silently he pointed to the other end of the alley, where another dark form lurked. ''They've got us trapped here!''

''Think they do.'' Raudbjorn chuckled direly. ''Takes more than four fools to trap bear.'' He swung his halberd in a few whistling swipes overhead to loosen up his muscles.

''Nagli,'' Leifr called, ''get out of our way. Remember what happened last time you tried to fight with us.''

''Sorkvir won't stop us this time,'' Nagli replied with his mad hyena's laugh. ''He's the one that told us where to find you. We'll get double wages for this job.''

''The only wages you'll get tonight are the sort that bleed,'' Leifr retorted, waving the sword in a glowing pattern. He took a step forward, and an arrow hissed over one shoulder from behind, burying itself in the dung wagon.

Leifr and Starkad scrambled into the shelter of a heap of building stone, while Nagli and his sons cackled mirthfully. Raudbjorn took to the shadows and began working his way toward the archer at the end of the alley. Arrows continued to hiss and strike deadly near to their mark, and Leifr cursed his optimism in leaving his longbow behind with the rest of his pack, thinking he wouldn't need it as long as he had the sword at his side.

Nagli and his sons crept nearer, taking advantage of the well-cluttered alleyway, scuttling behind carts and wagons and parts of walls and ruins of former houses and outbuildings. Leifr and Starkad waited for their attack, dividing their attention between the Naglissons and Raudbjorn slipping up on the lone archer. In a matter of moments they would be fighting for their lives.

Suddenly a pillar of flame lit up the alley from one end to the other, revealing pale startled faces, stinking pools, and the glint of drawn swords in a bluish glare. Then a bolt of fire roared down the alleyway and exploded the wagonload of firewood where the Naglissons were hiding. They were flung back, stunned, to land in a mucky area behind a pigsty. Flaming fragments rained down amid shouts and curses and cries of alarm from the households surrounding the explosion. At least a hundred dogs began barking and the pigs set up a terrified squealing; in moments the alley was crowded with men and torches. The Naglissons were seized upon immediately as the perpetrators, while they were staggering around dazed and deafened. Leifr and Starkad glided away in the dark toward Raudbjorn, who was disappointed of his intended prey.

They loitered in the street near the end of the alley, and, as Leifr had expected, Thurid came striding out in search of them, with his staff and his temper still smoking.

"It's a lucky thing I was looking for you!" he snapped. "What would you have done in that alley if I hadn't arrived?"

"Something a little less spectacular," Leifr retorted, "but we would've gotten out, never you fear, and the whole town wouldn't have heard about it, either. Sorkvir's going to know we're here, after all that noise and fire gave him ample notice."

"Well, of course he knows!" Thurid snorted. "He's leading us into whatever trap he's got in mind, isn't he? Perhaps you thought you were following discreetly, but you'd just as well have taken an army through where we've gone. If you could have brought yourself to listen to my plan for luring him where we want him, we might have had some help."

"From whom, the old neighbors in Dallir?" Leifr demanded. "Somehow I doubt their willingness."

"No, you dolt. I mean the Rhbus." Thurid's voice dropped to a whisper. "The powerful ones."

"How could we have found them?" Starkad demanded eagerly. "I thought they never stayed long in any one place—to protect themselves from the Dokkalfar."

"The Retriever told me there are ways of finding them," Thurid replied, lofty and elusive. "We could have been doing that instead of playing fox and hunter with Sorkvir."

Leifr shook his head angrily. "Ljosa comes first. Once she's rescued and Sorkvir is completely destroyed, you can search out the Rhbus and spend the rest of your life as you wish. Is that fair enough?"

"Only if we don't all get killed in the process," Thurid snapped. "Blast that Fridmarr! What a mess he's caused by bringing you in here! I wonder if even he could have foreseen what a stubborn, single-minded, pigheaded, reckless, arrogant creature a Scipling is when his personal vanity is on the line! If you could only be cool and calculating, and forget about revenge for a moment—''

''And you'd take the next fifty years to figure out what to do about Sorkvir,'' Leifr replied, ''just as you did in Dallir. Fridmarr did all the work and suffered all the pain, and you just hid your head in a milk bucket on the farm and did nothing to help him. It isn't going to happen that way again, Thurid. He gave you that satchel and staff for a purpose, and it wasn't only to break Sorkvir's hold over the Pentacle and Solvorfirth.''

''Yes, I know,'' Thurid said sarcastically. ''He always wanted to be responsible for my death somehow. Now that we're in the Dokkalfar realm, it looks as if he'll get his wish at any moment, with a great deal of help from you.''

''It's better than the no help we've been getting from the Rhbus,'' Leifr snarled in sudden resentment of the elusive and shadowy Malasteinn, who, with his grindstone, had arbitrarily directed Leifr's path into the direst of circumstances with little evident concern.

Starkad stepped forward between the two combatants. ''There's no sense quarreling over it now,'' he said. ''The actions and consequences have been started, like a rock in a pool making wider and wider rings. Neither of you could leave it now even if you really wanted to.''

Thurid snorted and sputtered, taken off balance for a moment; then he muttered, ''Well, it makes one feel better if he can blame his troubles on somebody else.''

''But it wastes a lot of time in quarreling and frayed tempers,'' Starkad said, ''and we don't have that much time. You've got to teach me spells, Thurid—Rhbu spells.''

''Oh, indeed?'' Thurid almost choked on this new bit of fodder for his outrage. ''Why would I wish to do such a witless thing as that?''

''Because the Rhbus need wizards,'' Starkad said, undiscomfitted. ''Do you want their knowledge to die in the mountaintops, or get purged from the earth, like Vonbrigdi? Their knowledge might be what the Ljosalfar need to save Skarpsey from the Dokkalfar.''

Thurid uttered a groan and shook his head in despair. ''To

think that the future of the Ljosalfar people might depend upon a sword-waving Scipling and a heedless young fool who has barely got his eyes opened yet! Was I chosen and plucked up from my comfortable life as a schoolmaster for torment such as this?''

''Yes, of course,'' Starkad said. ''The Rhbus know what they're doing, and it must have been their plan that I accompany Leifr and come to meet my future teacher.''

Thurid immediately began to protest. Leifr glared at Thurid and Starkad both for a moment, then turned and stalked away with the troll-hounds slinking at his heels, chastened by the tone of the arguing. He had his bearings of the town now and he knew the direction of the inn. With Raudbjorn clumping stolidly at his heels, halberd over shoulder, he felt reassured of the solid truth of swords and axes and using brute force to solve one's problems.

Despite his objections and sneers at town living, Thurid stayed on another day, then another, spending most of his time poking about in the booths of dusty wizard apparati, vended by the scruffiest and most disreputable-looking individuals. Peering over Thurid's shoulder, Leifr thought it looked like a lot of barrow loot, dug up from places where the digger had no business being, and the sellers of the wares themselves appeared to be the lowest sort of failed wizards. Nothing they sold actually worked, it seemed, nor did they even know what the little devices of various shapes were intended for, but they knew they were worth a great deal of money. Thurid selected some few pieces and bartered ferociously until a suitable compromise between the earth and next to nothing was struck upon, and he dropped the devices into his satchel and walked away gloating at his bargain.

''It's all Rhbu stuff!'' he confided to Leifr in a whisper made hoarse by excitement. ''They've stolen it from burial places or dug it up or found it lying about, and they don't know what to do with it!''

''Do you?'' Leifr asked, looking dubiously at a row of strange little devices and thinking of Gradagur. The devices had broken wires coming out of them, much like Gradagur's rafmagn machine. It gave him a very uncomfortable puzzled feeling to look at something for which he had no name or possible purpose.

"Not yet. Nothing works," Thurid admitted. "Or I don't know yet how they work. Look at this, Leifr."

Glancing around on all sides to make sure no one else was watching, Thurid showed him his latest investment. It was a round flat object with a disk of perfectly clear glass covering a white dial marked with lines and strange letters. A shiny needle danced nervously on a spindle, swinging slightly back and forth and always coming to point in the same direction no matter how Thurid turned it about.

"Very pretty," Leifr grunted warily, edging away from it without a grain of understanding. "What does it do?"

"It points north. Always, every time. Imagine how convenient to have a direction-finding device that works day and night. One is no longer required to wait for nightfall to get an accurate reading by the stars, nor does one have to squint at the sun."

"How do you know it works every time?" Leifr queried.

"Because it's something to do with the earth itself. Earth magic never fails." Thurid's reply was curt, his gaze fastening upon something past Leifr, out of his view.

"What about rafmagn?" Leifr asked. "It comes from lightning, so is it earth magic or fire magic?"

Thurid scarcely paid enough notice to be sufficiently contemptuous. "A fool's hobby!" he snorted, dropping the device into his satchel and striding on. "No one's ever going to use rafmagn for anything significant! Poor old Gradagar is more than a trifle mad, I fear."

They left the scavengers' booths behind at last, and Thurid led the way to the hiring fair. Everyone who was searching for a position gathered there, from the lowliest little scullery maid, wanting employment peeling potatoes, to assassins and thief-takers, standing with their weapons thrust into the ground before them, announcing that they were available for murder and the ferreting out of absent enemies; even a few fully adept wizards were there, to find lost treasure, tokens of power, or for challenging rival wizards. Thurid passed them up, after exchanging a few rivalrous glowers, and found the hunters, trackers, and guides lurking next to the winter shepherds. They were a scurrilous lot for the most part, one that Leifr would feel much safer without while traveling through dangerous territory. Roaming for many years in the trackless regions of the Dokkalfar realm had left its mark on most of them—a roving, restless eye, as if the confinement of the town was almost too much to endure, and an air of feral survivability hung about them like a cloak.

Thurid walked up and down, studying them all, and Leifr could tell by his frown that he was perturbed. At last he stalked away to a brewer's tent and sat down on a bench, motioning Leifr to sit nearby. Dokkalfar ale was dark and nutty and strong, and Leifr had learned to sip at it cautiously, after nearly falling under its spell the previous night. Raudbjorn, however, swilled down his horn of it and looked around for more, his eye undimmed.

"Vonbrigdi said I would find something at the hiring fair," Thurid muttered a little self-consciously. "And I don't think it was the compass. He said I'd retrieve something I'd lost. Did he strike you as being in his right mind at the last? Maybe he was a bit obsessed by his retrieving and finding and losing."

Leifr thought about Vonbrigdi, and possibly it was the effects of the ale, but he felt a spreading warm admiration for the Retriever.

"No, he wasn't crazy," Leifr said. "He was stronger than any of us knew. Was it a thing or a person he said you'd find at the hiring fair?"

"I assumed it was a guide to take us to Hringurhol," Thurid said in an undertone, glancing around warily. His eyes narrowed suddenly, fixing upon something behind Leifr. When Leifr turned to look, he saw nothing unusual, except perhaps the familiar form of a wandering beggar who hung about the gates of their inn.

"What's bothering you?" he demanded of Thurid, who merely shrugged his shoulders and signaled for another horn of ale.

"This town makes me nervous," he said. "I imagine I'm being followed."

Leifr again thought of the ragged wanderer he had seen several times loitering about the inn where they were staying. He scarcely heeded the fellow, not perceiving any threat in someone in such helpless straits as his condition implied. However, if he were in league with the Naglissons somehow, his innocuous appearance might be deceiving.

When they had finished with the ale, they went back to the hiring fair, with a good deal of ale sloshing around in Raud-bjorn's insides. Its only effect seemed to be a small pickled smile lingering on his hairy lips. Again Thurid considered the applicants for hunting, tracking, and guiding. This time he approached a few of them, but when they heard where he wanted to go, they invariably shook their heads and said they didn't know how to get there, and moved away to whisper to the others, with dark glances over their shoulders. They all began to disperse, slinking away to lose themselves before Thurid approached them. Thurid glowered after them and shook his head in growing impatience.

"Cowards. They're all lying. Nothing feels right or proper anyway," he said to Leifr. "If I should find something here, I'd know it as surely as if I'd grabbed a hot coal."

A hand descended upon Thurid's shoulder suddenly, startling him into a convulsive leap as he whirled around. A small hooded individual stood behind him, smothered in a ragged hood and cloak from head to toe and carrying a frayed and scanty bundle. It was the same furtive figure that had been lurking about the inn for three days.

"I hear you're going to Hringurhol," a hoarse voice rasped, "and you're in need of a guide. I'll take you there, and very reasonably, too."

Taken aback considerably, Thurid stared at the stranger, breathing in great snorts of air, like a frightened horse scenting danger.

"Who are you?" he demanded, rapping his staff on the ground warningly, and a trickle of smoke crept out from its smothering shroud. "One doesn't creep up behind a wizard and touch his person. I might have transmogrified you first and asked questions later."

"So sorry to have alarmed you." The stranger spread out his hands in a peaceful gesture to show no harm was intended. "Do you wish guide services to Hringurhol? Not everyone will take you there."

"Not anyone wants to go to Hringurhol," Thurid answered testily, surveying the fellow up and down with a critical eye. "It seems they're all a bit too fond of their own hides to risk it. What makes you want to risk it? What makes you think you can take us there? You don't have the look of a wilderness expert."

"Ah, but I am, and remember that I came in search of you. I've been watching you for three days, waiting for you to come to me."

"Yes, I've observed you spying upon us at every opportunity, until I was nearly ready to put a forcible end to it," Thurid replied, still suspicious. "Well, I suppose you're as near to a guide as I'm going to get. You're hired. We wish to leave as soon as possible."

"Fine. Shake hands on it." He held out his hand. It was an unfamiliar gesture, and probably Dokkalfar in origin.

Thurid shifted his staff to his left hand and grasped the stranger's hand. At once he gave a hoarse shout, jerking his head back, and the stranger uttered a mirthful roar of laughter as the hand came away, still clutching Thurid's hand. Then with a bound it leaped to his wrist, scuttled up his forearm, and perched on his shoulder, while Thurid opened his mouth in another great peal of unnatural laughter, not in his own voice. The hand gave a twitch, turning around a glittering red carbuncle ring from its hiding place in its own palm.

"Gedvondur!" Thurid's voice croaked at last, when he could find a space in the laughing.

"Aye, Gedvondur! And Svanlaug!" Thurid answered in Gedvondur's voice. "Reunited at last! I expect you thought you'd left us buried forever under Djofullhol!"

"So you might have hoped," Svanlaug's arrogant voice said, coming incongruently from the form of the small, ragged beggar, "but we got out just before the fortress started to fall. Come, Leifr, don't look so suspicious. That's scarcely a welcome for an old friend."

Chapter 13

✦✦✦✦✦✦✦✦✦✦✦✦✦✦✦✦✦✦✦✦✦✦✦✦✦✦✦✦✦✦✦

"Perhaps you hoped you had gotten rid of us," Svanlaug added caustically, with a characteristic toss of her head, which shook back the ragged hood. She glared back at Leifr in defiance.

"You might have done it far differently," Leifr retorted, "instead of sneaking away, and instead of appearing to have betrayed us again for your own benefit."

"I killed Djofull, didn't I?" she demanded haughtily. "The end justifies the means. Now I can be satisfied."

"Exactly," Thurid answered. "Your crime has been blamed upon us, and you can go your merry way, looking for more people to interfere with and aggravate, and we'll go on with the Naglissons at our heels. It couldn't be better for you."

"I know about the Naglissons and the price on your heads," Svanlaug answered. "It's quite a handsome reward, and you may not know that the Dokkur Lavardur has offered to double it if you are brought to him. More than half of this village would come after you if they knew you were here. A few do, I'm afraid, which is the reason I didn't approach you sooner, until I could find a place I thought was somewhat safe for you. I'm sure they're watching even now. The sooner we're away from Laglendi-hlid, the better."

"It's bad enough to know you're still alive," Thurid said, "Let alone to know you intend to come with us. What is your secret plan this time, Svanlaug? Does that reward of the Dokkur Lavardur's tempt your greedy little heart?"

"You still don't trust me, do you?" Svanlaug glowered at them all. "Would you rather enter the Dokkur Lavardur's domain under the guidance of a total stranger, who may have heard

179

about the reward?" She jerked her head in the direction of the hiring fair. "You didn't find very many who were eager to take you there, did you?"

"Why did you follow us, Svanlaug?" Leifr asked, cutting swiftly through her bluster.

She shrugged her shoulders impatiently. "Gedvondur couldn't very well walk here on his own," she replied. "He made me do it. I think my fate is somehow mingled with that sword and this ridiculous wizard. I know I should escape at the first opportunity, but somehow I can't. A greater force than my own will is driving us together."

Thurid snorted softly. "It must be guilt over the shameful way you've manipulated us at every turn. Don't you know it's rather upsetting when you seem to betray us to our enemies? Can't you trust us with your plans, Svanlaug? I think we have shown a great deal of faith in you and your actions, but you're still as hard and suspicious as a barnacle when it comes to trusting us."

Svanlaug's eyes flashed and her back stiffened as she prepared a stinging reply. Then she reconsidered. "It's not the Dokkalfar way to trust anyone," she said stiffly. "Especially day-farers. But this time I swear I have no secret plans, as I did before. All I could think about was revenge on Djofull and it didn't matter how I got it, but he had to die by my hand. Now I'm free of that, and I feel I owe a debt to you all."

"Bringing back Gedvondur was enough to pay any debt you may feel," Leifr began, but Thurid scowled at him and raised one hand peremptorily for silence.

"Very well, we accept your debt bondage," Thurid said. "You can take us to the stronghold of the Dokkur Lavardur. Assuming, of course, you know how to get us there. None of the other guides seemed to have the least idea."

"They didn't want to get any nearer," Svanlaug answered, "and for very good reasons, one of which is a strong desire not to die. The Ulf-hedin protect the Dokkur Lavardur from attackers such as you. They don't hesitate to destroy anyone they see resisting in any way."

"It's the Ulf-hedin you'll have to challenge if you want to get Ljosa back," the voice of Gedvondur said, speaking through

Thurid. "I knew you'd probably be in a dreadful predicament, once I found you. Amazing how the fate of an innocent girl is leading the ancient forces of Light and Dark into direct confrontation. I feel we're being drawn into a net of Rhbu making, and we're going to be mixed in with some very bad fish before it's done with."

Leifr got to his feet, eyeing the crowded byways around him and the knots of other ale drinkers gathered under the canopy for refreshment. No one seemed to be paying him the slightest heed, or even acknowledging that he existed, but he had the overwhelming feeling that he was being watched by knowing eyes.

"Who are these Ulf-hedin?" he asked. "Why don't they show themselves, if they're so strong and fierce?"

"Hush, or you'll summon them!" Svanlaug glared at him, making some furtive sign with her hand. "They have ears to hear where you least suspect it. Some say they can make themselves invisible and take a man right from the midst of his companions. Once taken, he never returns. They could be watching us at this moment, even standing among us unseen."

Leifr glanced around uneasily, seeing nothing out of the ordinary for Laglendi-hlid. Farlig and Frimodig pressed against his knees and Kraftig looked up at him imploringly, holding up one paw that someone had trod upon. Suddenly they all three turned their heads at the same instant in the same direction, with their hackles bristling and their lips lifting in warning snarls. Leifr looked and saw nothing in the mouth of the alley where they were looking. After a moment the hounds relaxed, as if the threat had disappeared, except for Farlig, who kept glancing toward the alley. Leifr took a step in that direction, but a powerful sense of foreboding swept over him. He touched the carbuncle stone, and it strengthened his feelings of doom.

"It's time to move on," Leifr said uneasily. "We can't stay in one place for long. We could be found. I'm ready to turn my back on Laglendi-hlid, Thurid, since we seem to have all we came here for."

Thurid was saying, "We'll have to provision ourselves before we go. It won't be the best of fare, but we won't be able to rely upon the hospitality of those living in the shadow of the Dokkur

Lavardur. It's going to be cold, too, so we'll have to buy winter garb. And we'll need pack animals and a riding horse—''

''No horses,'' Svanlaug said. ''We'll be going places where no horse could climb, and the mere smell of them would be an invitation to dinner for hundreds of trolls. Leave the transportation to me, Thurid.''

''No horse?'' Raudbjorn rumbled, blinking mournfully. ''Thief-taker not born to walk. Shame and dishonor.''

''You'll have a worthy steed, Raudbjorn, never fear,'' Svanlaug assured him. ''We'll be ready by dawn. Hope for a cold and cloudy day. On the borders of the realm, the weather is an unreliable thing.'' She glanced uneasily at the sky and pulled her hood down a bit at the sight of some blue patches through the gray brume. ''We'll meet tonight, at the place you're staying.''

Thurid nodded distractedly, muttering, ''I wonder where I can find enough black bread on such short notice? And some hard cheese, and stockfish—Raudbjorn, you'll have to come along and carry everything. Once we sell the horses, we'll have more than enough marks for winter cloaks and boots—Starkad, follow me. You're just the sort of sly fellow I want along when I'm selling and buying.''

Leifr started after Thurid and the others, but, as they plunged into the thick of the marketplace, a sound arrested him in midstride, halting him so suddenly that Kraftig collided with the backs of his knees. The carbuncle suddenly felt hot, almost too hot to touch when he felt it with his thumb. His heart began to race as he recognized the protesting sound of metal singing on a grindstone. *Endalaus Daudi* hummed an answering note to the grindstone from inside its sheath.

Turning in his tracks, oblivious of everything around him except the sound, Leifr threaded his way toward it and soon found himself in the street of the sword-makers and smiths. Over all the din of hammering and clanging and the clamor of metal being coaxed into men's designs, for good or ill, Leifr could still hear the thin high sound that drew him like a lodestone. He walked swiftly, peering into each forge and smithy with eager impatience. Then he halted, his eyes locking on the slight figure bent over the whirling grindstone, holding a knife to the stone with its shrill, keening metal cry. It was Malasteinn, the Rhbu who had twice before sharpened his sword, here in the plain view of a thousand of his Dokkalfar enemies.

Malasteinn finished the knife and put it down on a ragged piece of sheep fleece and bent a swift amused glance upon Leifr, a faint smile parting the thin lips beneath his sparse beard. He reached out for Leifr's sword, as would any metalsmith for hire.

"What are you doing here?" Leifr asked softly. "Don't you know it's dangerous for Rhbus? Malasteinn—I know that can't be your true name, but I implore you, hide yourself or something dreadful might happen to you."

Malasteinn's smile broadened and Leifr thought he heard a soft chuckle as the smith pumped his grindstone faster and set the Rhbu metal to the stone with a shower of sparks. A powerful note rang out, causing nearby Dokkalfar and wanderers to look about uneasily and make signs to ward off harmful influences. Others instinctively hurried their steps to leave the smiths' street, glancing around with wary expressions. None seemed to pay Malasteinn any particular heed; he looked much like any other traveling smith, bringing the tools of his trade from one settlement to the next.

Malasteinn paid them no heed, taking his time to sharpen both sides of the Rhbu blade with loving care, frequently testing its sharpness with his calloused black thumb. In the interstices between the grinding, Leifr struggled to ask questions, but somehow his words seemed smothered and unimportant in the serene calm that surrounded Malasteinn and his grindstone. So Leifr gave up and merely watched, entranced, even forgetting the dangerous Dokkalfar world that surged around the edges of the protected zone surrounding Malasteinn.

At last the Rhbu smith was satisfied with his work, and held the sword out to Leifr with a cheerful nod. Leifr found his tongue at last and blurted out, "Wait a minute. Don't go just yet. There are things I've got to know. Can you tell me if Ljosa is all right? What's really going on here? It's not just a matter of saving Ljosa and avoiding the Wizards' Guild any longer, is it? What did Fridmarr discover about the Dokkalfar realm that made Sorkvir and Djofull destroy him?"

Malasteinn lifted one finger and held it to his lips in a silencing gesture, his deeply sunken eyes twinkling beneath their hedges of singed brows. Then he pointed across the street, blocked at present by a train of shaggy ponies laden with packs of raw ore and their shouting, whip-cracking drivers. Leifr discerned a ramshackle cart and a bony-hipped horse, and a familiar ragged form raised one hand to Leifr in a greeting salute.

"Vidskipti!" Leifr gasped, scarcely believing his eyes. "What's he doing here? He's one of you—one of the Three, is he not?"

Turning back to Malasteinn, Leifr found himself standing alone beside a cold forge and silent anvil. Again the Rhbu smith and the grindstone had simply vanished. Leifr supposed he might have hurried away and lost himself among the people and pony-trains, but he doubted it. With a heavy sigh, he picked his way across the street toward Vidskipti and his cart.

The cart was loaded with scavenged metal of several sorts, and Vidskipti was busily hawking his pickings to a sooty Dvergar smith. The dwarf ignored Vidskipti's patter and rummaged among the strange melted lumps and rusted clumps of objects, throwing out the ones he wanted onto a growing heap.

"Two hundred marks in silver," the smith grunted at last with a menacing scowl on his furrowed countenance, "and that's more generous than I ought to be. Bring me your pickings first again and maybe I'll pay you more." A dim and suspicious curiosity dawned in his hard black eyes. "Where do you find so much of the old metals?" he demanded bluntly. "And in such quantities as this? No one else dares to prowl much around Rhbu places."

Vidskipti showed his yellowed teeth in a crafty grin. "That's my secret, Skurdur, and the reason you'll pay me three hundred marks for the next load of old metals I bring you. They're rare, and it's dangerous where I go."

"Three hundred? You're a robber!" Skurdur growled with a menacing clenching of his enormous seamy right fist, bristling with singed hairs.

"But you'll pay it," Vidskipti replied airily, and turned his back upon the glowering Dvergar to greet Leifr with a delighted crow. "Again we meet, old friend! How have you fared since last we broke bread?"

Skurdur eyed Leifr and his sword a moment, rasping his chin with his fist as he darkly deliberated lodging further complaints against Vidskipti's usurious business practices. Leifr glared back at him, thinking of Heldur and how he was coming to distrust Dvergar smiths in general—moody, dark-loving creatures of shifting and unreliable loyalties.

"Three hundred then," Skurdur rumbled, looking away from Leifr's silent challenge to roar suddenly at a couple of his apprentices, "You there! Get this ore loaded up and packed away! It's time we left this useless tinkering and trinket-making and got back to the heart of the mountain for some real forging." He strode away at his lopsided smith's gait, warped and thickened from long years of bracing himself against the twisting force of mighty hammering.

Vidskipti rubbed his hands together avariciously. "Thanks for coming along just then, Leifr," he said. "I always have trouble squeezing more marks out of that fellow. He'd never have agreed to three hundred if you hadn't been here. Do you think you could be here next year, when I ask him for four?"

"Vidskipti!" Leifr shook his head in exasperation and disbelief. Fridmarr's carbuncle still glowed warm against his chest, where his heart was thudding hard. "Malasteinn just sharpened my sword. You know what that means. A journey and a battle. But he never says a word to me. Do you know where I'm supposed to go and who I'm going to fight?"

"Oh, it could be anybody, in this realm," Vidskipti replied, rolling his eyes away evasively. "The Dokkalfar realm offers plenty of opportunities for fighting."

"You know, but you won't tell," Leifr accused, grabbing a shred of Vidskipti's ragged cloak. "This time I'm not going to let you get away until you've answered a few questions, old friend."

"I'd be most glad to share your hospitality for a while," Vidskipti agreed hastily. "It'll be a pleasure to renew my acquaintance with Thurid once more. And look, there he is now and in a frightful hurry."

Thurid strode down the metalworkers' street, looking fiercely right and left until his eye fell upon Leifr and then upon Vidskipti. He checked his pace so abruptly that Raudbjorn nearly trod on him, his view obscured by a large basket slung over one shoulder. Sputtering, Thurid hurried ahead, still darting nervous looks in all directions as he approached.

"Leifr, I heard that sound," he said, sweeping Vidskipti with a disgusted glower. "Was he here? Did you speak to him?"

"I heard it myself," Vidskipti answered jovially. "All Laglendi-hlid should know by now that Rhbu metal was sharpened here today. It sets their teeth on edge, it does, and puts them into a bad temper."

"What are you doing here?" Thurid demanded, his tone becoming sarcastic and needling. "I nearly had my foot crushed because of you and that miserable treasure ghoul. It wasn't real gold, you realize. Old images linger in an old land like this."

"Perhaps a horn or two of ale would refresh my memory," Vidskipti suggested with a hopeful gleam in his crafty eye. "Traveling is a thirsty business. And so is talking."

"Good, we'll talk then," Leifr said. "Thurid just sold our horses, so we've plenty of silver to buy with and plenty of time to talk. Malasteinn won't speak, but perhaps one of his companions can tell us something about the road ahead." He gave Thurid a warning stare that would have penetrated solid stone.

Thurid calmed his indignant swelling and swallowed the fiery retort that was brewing inside him. "Well, I suppose, since we are such old and dear friends and traveling companions," he growled with ill grace.

Noticing Starkad staring at Vidskipti with huge eyes and a rapt expression, Thurid gave him a push, grumbling, "Move along, Starkad, what's the matter with you? You're not taken in by this wandering rogue, are you? If you're going to be a wizard, you're going to have to learn to be an astute judge of character, as I am. Vidskipti is definitely a character and I have judged him a scheming rogue, but I'm still magnanimous enough to buy him a couple of horns of ale."

"Your pupil, is he?" Vidskipti winked at Starkad and grinned. "A fine lad he is, too. You'll learn much with Thurid as your master, my boy, he's an excellent teacher, but you can learn more yet if you'll keep your eyes open to what's around you."

"Don't confuse him," Thurid said jealously. "Starkad, go on ahead and find us a quiet brewer's tent. Make sure no one else is about. I daresay this will be a great waste of time and set us back hours upon our journey.''

Starkad tore his eyes off Vidskipti reluctantly and stared at Thurid. "Thurid, you don't see it?'' he whispered with awe-inspired squeaks in his voice. "He glows!''

"Glows?'' Thurid snorted. "Not yet he doesn't, while he's cold sober. Let him get eight or ten horns over his tongue and then you'll see him glow. Now get going, Starkad, time's a-wasting. And I really think you should learn to call me Master instead of by my familiar name, as if we were equals, which we are not, since you are the apprentice and I am the wizard. A pity we didn't sign your articles up at Fangelsi. We could use the fat fee I would have charged your brothers.''

Starkad glanced incredulously at Leifr, who shrugged slightly and canted his head for Starkad to follow him.

"Why doesn't Thurid see it?'' Starkad demanded as soon as they were out of Thurid's hearing. "There's a circle surrounding Vidskipti, glowing with light and colors. I've never seen anything like it! He's one of them, isn't he?''

"I didn't see it either,'' Leifr replied, "but I know he's one of the Three. It's a sign he's showing you. No one else can see it, either, I'd warrant. He probably doesn't think he has to prove himself to Thurid. Maybe Thurid has to develop the ability to see the Rhbus on his own. He can't see Malasteinn at all, even when he's right before him. It's rather a sensitive matter, so you'd better be quiet about it. Are you sure you want to be Thurid's apprentice, Starkad?'' Leifr heard a wistful note creep into his voice as he recalled all the scrapes he and Starkad had gotten into together. Thurid would keep Starkad far too busy studying and practicing for any more antics. In a rougher tone he added, "He can be a tyrant, and his temper is as short as night on midsummer's eve.''

"How true,'' Starkad replied ruefully. "He's worse than Hogni and Horgull combined, with Syrgja thrown in for good measure. But I don't mind, as long as I learn something. Great wizards can't help but be impatient with the rest of us stumbling around in the dark as we do.''

Vidskipti swilled down four horns of ale with scarcely a breath in between, while Thurid watched him with ill-concealed and mounting choler, which was divided almost equally between Leifr and Vidskipti. Three more horns later and Vidskipti was ready to start singing songs, and three horns after that he suddenly fell sound asleep, in midverse. Leifr shook him in dismay, with no results, while Thurid chuckled in dark triumph.

"The old fake," Thurid growled. "He's gouged us out of a great bellyful of free ale and forgotten about his precious advice, it seems. Leifr, you've been made a fool of by this rambling vagabond. A Rhbu wouldn't guzzle ale like a fish and then pass out in a disgusting heap. I've a mind to leave him here."

Leifr thought of the bag of Skurdur's silver tucked away securely on Vidskipti's ragged person. It wouldn't last an hour with Vidskipti in such a helpless condition. He would at least be robbed, if not beaten or even killed. Leifr had seen enough of the Dokkalfar idea of sport in Laglendi-hlid to make him wary.

"No, we'll take him with us," Leifr said, knowing he was about to precipitate another fiery outburst from Thurid.

Indeed, Thurid raved and ranted, and his eyes bulged, and his nostrils quivered with rage, all the way back to their inn, where Vidskipti was deposited in a safe place.

"You wait," Thurid fumed at Leifr, "you'll regret this. He's nothing but a vulture, and you're nothing but a fool if you believe a word he says. If he has anything to say, that is, which I most sincerely doubt! Starkad!" He raised his voice in a furious shout as he turned to glare around. "Come along, we've got some important purchasing to do, if we're ever to get out of this flea-infested, vulture-ridden pest hole!"

Leifr turned his back on him and went back to watch over Vidskipti as he snored contentedly on the sleeping shelf amid the party's few remaining possessions. The dank interior of the inn was dark and silent, except for the grudging fire on the hearth and some unsavory cooking smells coming from the kitchen annex. Suspicious eyes peered frequently around the hide hanging over the doorway and darted away whenever Leifr moved or looked in that direction. Raudbjorn's services were not required by Thurid, so he hunkered down on his heels nearby with his halberd propped against the wall and watched both Leifr and Vidskipti with a benign, sleepy expression similar to Kraftig's, who was resting his chin on Leifr's knee.

To lighten his spirits, Leifr drew the Rhbu sword, since no curious eyes seemed to be on him at the moment. He laid it across his knees and let the firelight ripple across its silvery blade. He also rolled Fridmarr's carbuncle into his hand and let it sparkle tantalizingly in the light.

Kraftig's golden eyes opened, gazing beyond Leifr with sudden interest. Vidskipti sat up and swung his feet to the ground as if he had never experienced a moment of tipsiness within recent history. The sword hummed in Leifr's hands, and he quickly returned the carbuncle to its worn pouch as Vidskipti approached the low fire. Stretching out his hands, Vidskipti spoke to the fire and at once it burned with the clear, hot flame of a scrub oak fire instead of smoldering peat. Raudbjorn blinked in astonishment and chuckled with pleasure. Then another wave of Vidskipti's hand suddenly put the thief-taker straight to sleep.

"Well then?" Leifr queried reproachfully. "Why is it you dislike Thurid so much? He's suffered a lot because of that Rhbu satchel of spells."

Vidskipti slowly rubbed his hands together, his keen eyes resting upon Leifr. "I don't dislike him, of course. A great deal depends upon Thurid—mule-headed as he is. We have high hopes for him. It's simply not the Rhbu way to force a man's faith in any way."

"Vidskipti, tell me what lies ahead," Leifr said. "I don't much like the way this journey is pointing."

Vidskipti held up one long warning finger, motioning for silence. "Don't question, don't wonder," he said in a low tone. "He who questions begins to doubt, and he who doubts begins to fail. You were doubting me for a few moments, weren't you, Scipling?"

"A wee bit. Did you know Fridmarr, Vidskipti?"

"Ah, Fridmarr. Poor lad, poor lad. But you've got his carbuncle now, and I hope you can learn from his mistakes. He was much like your Svanlaug—a great loner who made his own decisions and paid the price for them in solitude. A man can't always decide for himself only. If only Fridmarr hadn't gone back for revenge, he would be here now and you'd be skulking around in your own realm in your miserable outlaw way. Or perhaps you'd be dead already."

Leifr could see that direct questioning was not the way to get information out of a Rhbu. "Perhaps I shall be dead soon enough as it is," he said. "No one challenges the Dokkur Lavardur and lives to tell about it."

"No, that's true indeed," Vidskipti agreed, taking up a stick and sketching with it in the ash on the floor. "It's the Ulf-hedin you must deal with, and they're all maddened by the spell that binds them. But they will listen to Sorkvir sometimes, as well as their Dark Lord, who leads the Council of Threttan—the Thirteen. They are angry now that Djofull is destroyed. It thwarts the plan of the Dokkur Lavardur when his pawns and Pentacles are destroyed by interfering mortals."

He tapped the ground with his stick, where he had drawn a five-pointed star. Four of the five points had crosses on them, and the empty point was where he tapped his stick.

"You've another Pentacle to destroy, Leifr," Vidskipti went on, his tone soft and earnest, as if he didn't have much time to explain. "The Dokkur Lavardur is too vast and bodiless for you to destroy, even with *Endalaus Daudi*. He's an elemental creature, huge enough to fill the entire sky, or all of Skarpsey, which is what he intends to do. Another name for him is the Fimbul Winter, where land and water and even light itself are locked fast in his grasp. Even you Sciplings know about the Fimbul Winter."

"We didn't know it was a living creature," Leifr said with a shudder of instinctive dread. The carbuncle affirmed Vidskipti's words with a shudder of its own. "How can I—" He cut off his question hastily. "But there must be a way to drive the Dokkur Lavardur back. This pentacle I must destroy—"

"Yes. It's not complete yet. The Dokkur Lavardur has been gathering crystals, one for each point. He wanted part of Skrymir's heart, you recall, from Dokkholur and caused half the mountain to be carved away in his search. You thwarted him nicely in that, I must say, with Fridmarr's help. But the Dokkur Lavardur turned his attention elsewhere, to a blue crystal of power almost as great as the mountain giant's heart."

"Heldur's orb!" Leifr gripped the hilt of his sword, half rising to his feet as he thought of Thurid blithely bartering his way around the Dokkalfar market, oblivious of the dread threat welded to the end of his staff.

Vidskipti stayed him with the light touch of two fingers on his wrist. "Time enough to warn Thurid later. I've only moments in the boundary between midnight and morning. This cursed blue orb will either make or destroy the pentacle of the Dokkur Lavardur, depending upon whether you and Thurid live or die in your attempt. Stay close to that crystal, Leifr, and protect it and Thurid from the Ulf-hedin warriors. They have reason to fear *Endalaus Daudi*. You have my name, Leifr. Use it to good advantage when the right opportunity comes. You won't have a second chance. Perhaps no one in Skarpsey will ever have a second chance when the Dokkur Lavardur rules. Sciplings, Ljosalfar, and Rhbus will all be destroyed in the cold and darkness, and no fire will burn except cold fires of frost and rime. Go north with Svanlaug; she knows the way. We've prepared her to be your guide as far as she is able, but it will be your duty to defend that crystal so Thurid can do his work. We've done almost all any Rhbus can do to help you, so go now and challenge the Council of Threttan, Leifr. You have all the strength and hopes of the remaining Rhbus behind you, and nothing will help us if it isn't enough."

Vidskipti's head sagged, and he slumped forward as if suddenly exhausted by so much intense speech.

"Vidskipti! What about Ljosa?" Leifr demanded. "Tell me something, quickly!"

"The girl—" Vidskipti muttered thickly. "Ulf-hedin have her—waiting for you. Beware—trap—" He sagged even more and would have fallen if Leifr hadn't swiftly reached out to catch him. He was completely limp in Leifr's grasp and already beginning to snore gently.

Raudbjorn's eyes opened with a snap as Leifr carried Vidskipti back to the sleeping shelf. The fire was now a smoking, smoldering heap of peat that cloyed the nostrils with its thick stench and reddened the room with its dim glow. For a moment, Raudbjorn gazed at the fire and at Leifr in puzzled reproach. Then he shook himself and shrugged, a humorous smile cracking his features.

"Funny dream, Leifr," he said. "Raudbjorn get few dreams. Nice fire, no smoke."

Leifr tucked a cloak around Vidskipti's shoulders and returned to his stool by the fire, where Kraftig again rested his chin on his knee and gazed up at him with golden eyes full of pity and sorrow for Leifr's lack of understanding. Stroking the hound's silky ears, Leifr felt his own fears and unworthiness crowding thick around him, like the leering faces of the Naglissons, waiting to destroy him so the dark could prevail.

Thurid came charging in, fresh from the midnight markets of Laglendi-hlid and in a foul temper from the prices the merchants had charged him. Clapping his eyes upon Leifr, he bugled, "So that's what you've been doing all night? Watching over this drunken old sot while the rest of us do all the work? It's a fine life, but it won't do, Leifr. Laglendi-hlid has spoiled you, I'm afraid. Well, tomorrow we're back to hard sledding, and not a moment too soon, from the look of you."

Vidskipti he passed over with an arrogant sniff and went on to direct Starkad on dividing up the load and stuffing everything into packs. In a short while he was finished, and nothing remained but the wait for Svanlaug to return. To calm himself, Thurid dumped out his satchel in the middle of the table and began examining his rune wands.

"Where could she be?" Thurid fumed, notching a stick aggressively with his knife. "Dawn isn't far off. We should be traveling in a few short hours. She could be off negotiating our capture with thief-takers, for all we know. I don't know why you continually insist upon trusting her, Leifr, after all the times she's betrayed us."

"I don't trust her," Leifr said. "You're the one who forgives her each time."

Starkad interjected, "She doesn't mean to betray us. She's just acting upon her own plan, and sometimes we get in her way, is all."

"Ho, and you're her ally now?" Thurid snorted,.

"She talks to me now," Starkad said with barely concealed pride. "She says I'm no threat to her, as the rest of you are. She says she was only pretending to be Djofull's acolyte all along, waiting for the opportunity to kill him. She had to play the part when we were captured. I don't think you're judging her fairly at all.''

"Silence!'' Thurid snarled, his eyes rolling dangerously. "I'll be the best judge of that! I don't want you talking to her on the sly and letting her fill your empty head with her lies and deceptions. If you're to be my student, you're to have no sympathy for the Dark side anywhere in you, or you'll have to go back to the Guild for a purging, and I don't think you'd like that.''

"Bah, you wouldn't do that,'' Starkad muttered to Thurid's backside. "You're too afraid of the Guild yourself.''

"What was that you said?'' Thurid demanded, whirling around to glare at Starkad.

"It was nothing,'' Leifr interrupted, getting to his feet and reaching for his cloak. "We were just deciding to go out and see if we could find Svanlaug. We've been lagging around indoors too long. Come on, Starkad, we'll start looking in the provisioners' street first.''

"See to it you don't cause an uproar this time,'' Thurid said. "I'm sure the Naglissons are still about.''

"And they know we're still about,'' Leifr said. "They'll keep out of our way if they know what's healthy.''

"Where are we going?'' Starkad demanded, once they were well away from the inn. "The ale tents? The woman who dances with snakes? The song maidens? How about one last look at that man who swallows fire?''

Leifr shook his head curtly. "Do you remember where it was we met Svanlaug and Gedvondur today? A booth beside an alley, not far from the hiring market?''

They threaded their way through the metalsmiths' street, glowing luridly in the light and heat of many forges and resounding with the clangor of pounding hammers. By night, the smiths who feared daylight were hard at work at substances that made Leifr wince away in uneasy revulsion. The smiths themselves were dark and mighty creatures clad in leather stained black with sweat, swinging hammers that would have crushed a skull to work their forbidden magic of forge and fire.

They found the ale booth, now crowded with an unsavory lot of drunken drovers who were unwisely picking a fight with a band of mercenary soldiers. A crowd of impartial observers stood around egging them on and taking bets on the side.

Leifr pulled Starkad away from the incipient fight and started down the alleyway where the hounds had signaled the presence of something he hadn't seen. Houses leaned in from either side as the way narrowed, blocking the sky except for a strip overhead. Heavily barred doors opened off the alley, some with a faint gleam of light showing underneath. No roistering voices or music enlivened the fetid atmosphere of the alley; all was as silent as a tomb. The hounds sniffed eagerly, as if scenting a prey, their back fur bristling with apprehension as it would when the prey was a dangerous one.

Leifr let them lead him to the end of the alley, despite Starkad's fearful protests. A doorway stood open at the end, around a corner, with the dim light beckoning wanderers in the dark. On either side of the door lamps burned. Upon nearing the doorway, they saw that the lamps burned in human skulls, whereupon Starkad balked immediately.

"Leifr, we've got to go back," he urged. "I don't like the feel of this place. There's something far more evil inside there than I want to face just now."

Leifr thumbed the carbuncle, feeling its emanating rays of warning and dread.

"Fridmarr has been here, too," Leifr said.

"He shouldn't have been," Starkad growled, shrinking closer to Leifr and the hounds. "Listen, someone's behind us. Following us with their knives out, I'll warrant."

Leifr beckoned Starkad into the shadow of an overhanging archway that formed a shallow cave of darkness. In a moment three men came skulking down the alley, looking all round uneasily and finally coming to a halt not far from the doorway at the end of the passage. They said nothing, but Leifr observed fear in their hunched posture, distrust in their darting eyes, and guilt in their constant looking behind.

Leifr glanced at the hounds, who were crouching quietly at his feet as he had commanded. They watched the loitering men alertly, but more often their sniffing noses were pointed toward the door and its beckoning light.

In another moment, two more men came slinking into the

alley. Hesitating at the sight of the other three, they halted, and both parties stared silently at each other before mutually agreeing to turn all their backs and pretend the others were not there. Two more men joined them and went through the same ritual of not seeing. Five or six others arrived singly, gliding along the walls in the shadows and choosing a spot to stand at a suspicious distance from the others. No one spoke as they waited. Looking at them all standing so tense and still, Leifr felt his neck hairs bristle with a supernatural chill. The hounds, pressing close around his knees, vibrated with deep growls.

The tramping of heavy boots echoed down the alley, not approaching with guilty stealth as the others had. The hounds sniffed and trembled with excitement. Three men passed by their alcove of shadow without a glance right or left, and the men waiting parted from their path without a sound of the protest one heard constantly on the common roadways.

The doorway was suddenly flung open wide, partially blotted by a thick shape. A deep voice rumbled, "Come in, come in, all of you. We're ready to begin."

Leifr and Starkad glided from the shadows when the last man had filed into the room beyond.

"Ho there!" rang out the same guttural voice, and the squat shadow lumbered into their path. "You haven't changed your minds now, have you?"

"No, we have not," Leifr replied warily.

"Then come inside. You won't get another chance for a month and you can't come in once the ceremony begins. You do know what you've come here for, don't you?"

"Of course," Starkad said. "There were others with us and we were about to go back for them."

"There's no time. They've missed out. Come along."

A looming shadow stepped into the doorway, blocking most of the light.

"Trouble, Mordingi?" a deadly soft voice queried.

"None at all. Just a couple of laggards. With dogs."

"Bring them inside. We've uses for them all."

Leifr and Starkad slipped into inconspicuous places in the rear of the hall. The door was shut and barred, and the bearer of the inauspicious name Mordingi folded his arms and braced his back against it. He looked as much a murderer as his epithet stated: short and swarthy, with a scowling square block of a head set on meaty shoulders with almost no neck in between. On a broad studded belt around his waist he wore a short sword, and he clasped a wicked axe lovingly across his chest. Clearly his grim expression stated that no one would leave the hall save by carving a way through him or by stepping over his dead carcass.

In the center of the hall burned a low fire in a brazier and three men sat in tall chairs behind it, their faces barely lit. All eyes were fastened upon them and scarcely a breath was drawn in the motley assemblage. They wore black cloaks, tunics, and breeches, and over their shoulders was flung the pelt of a wolf, complete with the mask and ears, the eye-holes staring emptily over one shoulder or the other. The central figure looked considerably older than the other two, and his wolf cape was nearly white, while theirs were shades of black and gray. A low table stood before them, covered with a wolf pelt and bearing a flask, a bowl, and a small cup.

"To those who have come here willingly tonight, I bid you welcome," the elder one said, rising to his feet to come forward a few steps. He surveyed the audience with a piercing stare. Leifr automatically ducked a little when his eyes raked over him. "You have made the most important decision of your lives—the last decision that will ever matter. I invite you to leave your petty and desperate lives to enter a world of limitless power and freedom from any fear from your fellow man. No Alfar, dwarf, troll, man, or beast will prevail against you ever again. All will shun your path and do your complete bidding. Those who dare defy you will meet with quick and merciless destruction. Tonight, those of you who are judged sufficiently strong and fearless will be welcomed into the growing ranks of the future rulers of the Alfar realm, the loyal servants and protectors of the most high Dokkur Lavardur—the clan of the wolf, the Ulfhedin."

Starkad uttered a faint moan, clearly heard by those nearest in the taut silence of the hall. He darted Leifr a frantic glance and Mordingi a hopeless one.

"Let the bravest among you come forward first to be initiated into our cause."

The first of the applicants was a burly Dokkalfar bearing the same fatal stamp as Mordingi, clad in an assortment of raggedy bits covered with grease and bloodstains. He approached the three Ulf-hedin, swaggering confidently, and commenced a recital of his past heinous deeds. "My name is well known. They call me Eydill the Destroyer. I don't know how many men I've killed for hire, or how many I've killed out of temper. I've lost track long ago. I can be quick, or I can finish them off slow—"

When he was finished, the Ulf-hedin exchanged a glance and nodded their heads.

"That will do," the elder one said, and poured something ruby-dark from the flask into the cup, which was scarcely bigger than a thimble. "Drink this and you will be one of us."

The initiate leered around the hall a moment, then swallowed the drink in one gulp. His grin suddenly faded and he shuddered visibly at the taste of it.

"What is this, poison?" he demanded hoarsely, gripping his throat. "It burns like fire! Is this a trick to kill us?"

"Perhaps the great Eydill is not so brave after all," the Ulf-hedin said mockingly. "It's too late now, my friend. Once you've swallowed the eitur, you either stay with us where you can get more so you can live, or you leave here and die a more miserable death than any you have inflicted."

Eydill glowered at the Ulf-hedin a moment, like a maddened bull, and growled, "I'll stay. I've got too many enemies out there to do otherwise than die. What other torments have you got in store?"

"Only the taking of a few drops of your blood," the Ulf-hedin said, "and a small mark in the palm of your hand to remind you of your loyalty to the Dokkur Lavardur."

Eydill reeled on his legs as the other two Ulf-hedin gripped his arms and half carried his uncooperative carcass toward the altar and the brazier, where they dumped him in a heap. The elder Ulf-hedin produced a small sharp knife from his sleeve and deftly sliced his ear, producing quite a squirt of blood, which was carefully rubbed into a rune wand. A lock of Eydill's greasy hair was snipped off and put into a pouch while he was still trying to get his legs under him to rise.

"What is this?" he sputtered. "Am I not here of my own free will? Rune wands and hairlocks aren't my idea of freedom and power and glory!"

"It's just a simple precautionary measure," the white-maned Ulf-hedin said. "No one else here will object to it, I'm certain, in light of all that we are offering you. Now then, show me your left palm. Approach the altar and kneel."

Unable to rise to his feet, Eydill struggled futilely a moment with arms and legs that were succumbing to irresistible paralysis; then the Ulf-hedin grabbed him none too gently and dragged him forward to the altar. Unsteadily Eydill swung his head back and forth, panting with short breaths, with the sweat rolling off his face.

"I've been poisoned!" he gasped. "All of you are going to die! Fly, fly while you can!"

"So often the most boastful of killers is a coward in his heart," the elder Ulf-hedin said with a derisive sneer. "You shame yourself, Eydill, before many younger and less experienced than yourself. I have seen far less whimpering among captives who are forced to take the oath of the Ulf-hedin against their will."

Reluctantly Eydill unclenched his fist and extended his arm across the table. The Ulf-hedin pressed a silver medallion there briefly, after first wetting it in a bowl of what might have been blood. Eydill gazed at the spiral red mark a moment with an expression of suspicion and dawning horror.

"It's burning!" he declared. "That's not ordinary blood, is it?"

"A brave man asks no questions," the Ulf-hedin retorted, rising to his feet. From a carved chest he took the skin of a wolf, fresh killed, and draped it over Eydill's shoulders, binding the wolf's mask over his head and securing it in place with a thong. A wide belt with a number of buckles was fastened around his thick middle to hold the wolf cape. All this was done while Eydill groaned and snarled and struggled. Then he was hauled to the far side of the room into the dark, where, from the sounds of it, he was chained up for safekeeping. He continued mouthing drunken threats and rattling his chain while the next initiate stepped forward.

"What a coward," someone near Leifr muttered. "I never thought old Eydill was anything but a miserable cur."

Leifr's head reeled with the smell of eitur. It all made horrible sense now, as he remembered the wreck that had been Fridmarr, addicted to eitur and bearing the mark of the Dokkur Lavardur's spiral in his hand. He stole a covert glance at Mordingi guarding the door. No one who came in ever went out a normal mortal again. No doubt Fridmarr had come to spy, as he had, and had gotten more than he had bargained for when he was unable to escape.

Starkad cast him a worried glance. As the number of initiates dwindled, the more reluctant ones shifted gradually to the rear. Most of them were young and lean, Leifr's age and younger. Judging by the way they twitched and trembled, they were as frightened of the step they were taking as they were of whatever threat had driven them to such a desperate resort.

The eitur affected some with convulsions and terrors, while others like Eydill seemed relatively unaffected, except for an unsteady drunken effect. All lost their will to resist and their capability to escape. One unfortunate swallowed the poison, gasped, rolled up his eyes, and collapsed, as limp as a sack of meal.

The Ulf-hedin prodded at him a few moments, then curtly called out, "Who's next?"

"Dead as a hammer," a youth standing near Leifr whispered. "Perhaps he's better off than we are."

"Do you want to escape?" Leifr replied softly.

The youth shook his head. "No, I've got no other life worth living. Even a dog would be better treated by my father than I've been. It will be splendid, being an Ulf-hedin. No one will ever look down his nose at Halmur Otkellsson again. I shall be free at last."

Leifr glanced back at the three Ulf-hedin and was not so certain. The status of the new conscripts seemed rather low to him, as they were dragged away half insensible and fastened to the wall with a chain around their necks.

"There are different sorts of freedom," Starkad said, "and this is not my favorite kind."

"Don't be such a coward," Halmur returned. "I'm not afraid. I'm braver than most of those who have already gone before us. Just watch me, and you'll see."

Halmur's courage failed him again, however, and he did not step forward to volunteer to be initiated any more bravely than the other five or six remaining. He was among the last of them that had to be hauled forward forcibly.

"Leifr! We've got to get out of this," Starkad protested again, when only one recruit stood between them and the three Ulf-hedin. "What are you waiting for?"

"Better odds," Leifr whispered. "When we get rid of the Ulf-hedin, maybe we can help those poor fools."

"We'll be lucky to get out of here alive, let alone rescuing these wretches," Starkad argued. "Most of them are no better than old Eydill. I say let the Ulf-hedin have them and let's get out of here."

"Just stay close and guard my back," Leifr replied. "Mordingi is your responsibility."

Chapter 14

❖❖❖❖❖❖❖❖❖❖❖❖❖❖❖❖❖❖❖❖❖❖❖❖❖

Leifr advanced toward the three Ulf-hedin, with Starkad taking care to keep close, his eyes upon Mordingi.

"I bring you greetings," Leifr said. "From an old friend of mine who is now dead because of you, or someone like you. I know you don't remember him, but I can never forget him as long as I have breath to draw."

"Another vengeance seeker," the elder Ulf-hedin said, shaking his head, with a sneer of scorn twisting his features. "We see such as you very seldom, but the result is always the same. You won't get your revenge. You'll get something much more satisfying."

"I'm not swayed by your lies," Leifr said. "What you've given these scum and murderers is a living death, until they are fortunate enough to die by normal means."

"You will not be permitted to leave here with word of what you have seen," the Ulf-hedin said. "You have the choice—either join us or die. Which do you choose?"

"I choose to fight," Leifr said. "The three of you for Frid-marr is only the beginning of my vengeance."

"As you wish. It won't take long."

The three Ulf-hedin pulled up the wolf skins over their heads, commencing a gruesome transformation into creatures half-man and half animal. The previously lifeless pelts suddenly regained life, as if taking root on human flesh. Wolf hair bristled on their shoulders, covering their arms down to hands that suddenly became huge and powerful, tipped with black claws. Wolf ears pricked upright, and the human countenance was masked by the blunt snout of the wolf, complete with a mouthful of bared fangs. Wolf eyes blazed from the once-empty eye sockets of the pelt, eyes that betrayed no human compassion, only the mindless fury to rend and kill. Crouching slightly, they fanned out around Leifr and Starkad, moving with the slinking grace of the wolf.

A wave of paralyzing cold accompanied the transformation, freezing Leifr motionless with the unspeakable horror of what he had witnessed. He felt as if his heart had stopped from lack of will to survive. Starkad likewise stood and stared.

Unaffected by the spell-casting, the troll-hounds rallied to the cause and sprang forward with a ferocious clamor of barking and snarling. Leifr at once clapped his hand to his sword and drew it with a flourish, right in the faces of the Ulf-hedin. A blue arc of light followed the tip of the sword, sputtering with sparks that hissed and sizzled when they touched wolf fur. The wolf-men leaped back out of the reach of the sword, which filled the air with a network of glowing blue streams that drifted like mist, sputtering as they slowly dispersed. The Ulf-hedin avoided the wafting tendrils of mist, creeping around in an attempt to find a way through to get at Leifr and Starkad.

"I can see you," said Leifr. "You're not invisible to me. I bring another sort of death into your realm—the Endless Death. Who wants to be the first to taste it?"

One of the darker Ulf-hedin suddenly charged forward in an explosive rush, faster than any human figure ever moved. At the last instant, the snapping, foaming jaws clicked shut only inches from Leifr's head as the wolf-man careened past. Leifr made a delayed feint with the sword, too late to touch the creature. The beast veered away from *Endalaus Daudi* with ease. Leifr took another slash at him, feeling like a stupid novice, slow and clumsy, but the blade cut through nothing but air where the wolf-man should have been. Hastily Leifr fanned the Rhbu blade around, making more blue trails of protective influence, which seemed to be his only real defense.

"I didn't come here to play at games," Leifr snapped furiously. "I'll fight you man to man, but don't taunt me with your cowardly magical tricks."

"I know who you are, outlander, and you must learn who you are challenging. Mallaus, osynylegur!"

The Ulf-hedin who had charged at Leifr swaggered forward as if he intended another attack. He crouched, and Leifr braced himself tautly, ready for another lightning rush. The beast crouched and sprang. Leifr raised the sword, but the Ulf-hedin vanished right before his eyes. Feeling like a fool, he glanced around swiftly, but the beast had disappeared, and the door was still barred by Mordingi, who was grinning ingratiatingly and sweating with fear.

"You won't see him," the Ulf-hedin said. " 'Osynylegur' means to become invisible. Only one of the Ulf-hedin powers. He is there, unseen to you, only inches from you."

"You lie!" Leifr retorted.

"I have only to give the word, and you die."

With a sudden snarl, the wolf-man reappeared at Leifr's side, within easy arm's reach. Leifr whirled, but in that instant the Ulf-hedin vanished again and reappeared at his leader's side, well out of danger.

"Let that be a lesson to you," the leader said. "We can kill you at any instant, at any place. We've been warned to watch for the return of this sword, and we are ready to defend the Dokkur Lavardur. Again, we will defeat the bearer of the Rhbu sword. No one can stand against the Dokkur Lavardur and survive."

"We shall," Starkad volunteered pompously, taking a bold half step forward. "We've also got Heldur's blue orb. Even Sorkvir fears it. I can't say what the consequences might be if you attempt to detain us here by force, but I suspect there might be charred wolf-parts from here to Hringurhol."

"It cheers me immensely to know that the orb has indeed arrived safely in Laglendi-hlid," the wolf leader said with a ghastly parody of a grin. "Old prophecies have promised this event for many years, and now they are coming to fruition, and from such an unlikely source. Dismantle, brothers. It is not for us to interfere in the sure and fateful progress of the stone to its final resting place in Hringurhol. For the moment we shall have pity upon these puny mortals, until we have no further use for them."

As he spoke, he muttered a word, and the wolf skin on his shoulders and head at once subsided from its rippling life to nothing but a limp pelt hanging about his shoulders.

"Mordingi! Open the door!" the wolf leader commanded.

"These travelers must be allowed to continue on their way un-molested. But know this, Scipling—the Ulf-hedin are every-where, in places you would not suspect. People you may not suspect keep a wolf skin locked away somewhere, awaiting the call to serve the Dokkur Lavardur. You have rubbed up against a hundred Ulf-hedin without knowing it since you came to Langlendi-hlid. We have watched your every move, and waited, knowing you have no choice but to take the orb where we want it most. It must be bitter gall to you to know you have no way of defeating the all-powerful workings of the Dokkur Lavardur and his servants."

Leifr lowered the sword and halted the fanning of the mist tendrils. "You are mistaken," he said. "We are bringing the blue orb for the purpose of destroying the Dokkur Lavardur."

The Ulf-hedin all grinned nastily or laughed outright.

"It can't be done, at least not by one outlaw wizard and a Scipling," the leader said. "Now go your way, unless you care to continue your pointless search for vengeance. As you can see, it will only end badly for you."

"You're refusing my challenge?" Leifr demanded. "You're taking the cowards' way out?"

"I am only allowing you to live a little while longer," the Ulf-hedin said with a sinister baring of his teeth. "For as long as the Dokkur Lavardur has use for you, you shall not be touched. But the moment you have fulfilled your purpose according to the Council of Threttan, you and I shall meet, Scipling. Mention nothing of this to the wizard, or you shall suffer for it. Believe my words, I will know if you tell him. Now go and don't look back."

Mordingi pulled open the door and stood well aside. Leifr and Starkad edged toward it, with the troll-hounds clinging to their heels, lips curled back in worried snarls.

"We'll meet again," Leifr swore, not taking his eyes off the three Ulf-hedin, "and we'll fight to the finish. This sword was made for killing such as you!"

When they had moved well into the courtyard, Mordingi slammed shut the door. Starkad heaved a sigh, almost a moan.

"It must be nearly dawn," he said. "Thurid will be in a fury, and Svanlaug is probably back by now."

"Come," Leifr snapped. "We'll get back as quick as we can. If they've had to wait for us, they've had to wait. You'll say nothing about this, Starkad."

"Believe me, I won't," Starkad said. "I want to live."

Without looking back, they hurried out of the street back into the busy midnight markets, which showed none of the diminution of energy that usually occurred near dawn.

When they returned, they found Thurid exactly as they had left him, carving runes in a wand, with the contents of his satchel strewn over the table. Vidskipti still snored on the sleeping platform.

"Back so soon? Changed your mind, did you?" Thurid greeted them.

"So soon? How long have we been gone?" Starkad asked.

"You should know," Thurid retorted. "It seemed a short walk, for you two. I didn't think it was a good idea to go haring off, especially on our last night in Laglendi-hlid. I'd recommend a good night's sleep tonight. Besides, I just heard a rumor in the public room that the Ulf-hedin are holding their initiation ceremony tonight. That's one thing you don't want to get mixed up in. Scores of people simply vanish around this time of the moon's phase."

Leifr grunted noncommittally and slipped out of their room for a quick look into the public hall, where the same jolly caravaners and traveling merchants were swilling down ale and quarreling and boasting. All was just as he had left it only moments ago, according to Thurid, except for two dark-clad fellows sitting quietly at the end of the table nearest the door. They wore no wolf capes, but Leifr recognized them instantly as two of the Ulf-hedin he had just seen conducting the initiations. He knew they hadn't been there before. The Ulf-hedin had kept his promise to watch him. Fighting down a swelling tide of unreasoning fear, Leifr looked around the room, wondering how many of the seemingly innocent travelers were actually Ulf-hedin.

Carefully he started edging back into the dark passageway. Suddenly he collided with someone skulking there in the shadows. Already nervous, his reaction was unplanned and lightning-fast. He seized his assailant and flung him against the wall and pressed his knife point to his throat.

"Leifr! It's only me!" Starkad squeaked

"Spying on me?" Leifr snapped, shoving Starkad away down the passage as fast as he could go. "There's Ulf-hedin out there. They've followed us back."

"At least we can't blame Svanlaug for it," Starkad said. "We brought them ourselves. Leifr, we were only gone long enough to walk to the markets and back again—not most of the night as we thought. They've already got us in some spell to make time pass that way. We'd better tell Thurid."

"We daren't. We've got to get out of Laglendi-hlid," Leifr growled. "Curse that Svanlaug! Why is she so slow?"

The night lingered for hours longer in Laglendi-hlid, crouched as it was at the foot of sky-raking mountains, an arrangement that seemed to suit its night-faring occupants entirely. Dawn lurked behind the high peaks until nearly midday, when the sun might finally appear briefly overhead, before falling behind the western mountains in premature twilight. On days when the cloud cover was thick and low, no sun could be seen, and there was little strength to its rays when it did manage to penetrate the gloom. As they waited for Svanlaug to return during those laggard early-dawn hours, the Dokkalfar realm was such a cold and dark place that Leifr wondered if the Fimbul Winter hadn't descended already.

Svanlaug returned at last to the inn, well into the morning hours, after the night-farers had closed their unsavory booths and the disreputable day-faring merchants were beginning to open up.

"It's all arranged," she greeted them, her eyes sparkling as she briefly rubbed her hands over the faint fire and stamped the frost off her boots. "We'll be taken over Skaela-fell this morning, as soon as we can get to the bottom of the trail. It's going to be cold and it will probably snow. That will be enough to put the Naglissons off your trail."

"Let the Naglissons follow if they dare," Thurid snorted, dismissing the thief-takers with a wave of his hand and a significant tap of his staff on the ground. "Now let us be gone from this blighted place. Civilization has taken a distinct turn for the worse in this mercenary, anarchistic arrangement."

The Naglissons were the least of Leifr's worries. As they departed from the inn, Leifr eyed each of the scruffy loiterers standing about, wondering how many of them bore the spiral scar in the palms of their hands. Looking back, he was almost certain he saw the inn's landlord giving someone a cryptic signal, or maybe it was just a peculiar style of greeting. Turning his back upon Laglendi-hlid was not the comfort he had once imagined—not with wondering as he did who might be following.

If anyone was following, he saw no evidence of it. The trail that Svanlaug chose climbed higher into the black and barren crags of Skaela-fell, where it seemed that winter never released its grip on the land. Trees were twisted and stunted, clinging close to the earth for the scant protection it offered from the persistent wind. The wind moaned and howled in the higher crags, its pitch rising to occasional screams of desolate fury.

Because of the endless drying and freezing effects of the wind, no grasses grew among the stones, which might have nourished horses. Ungenerous mosses and lichen gave a few stones a faint nubbly coat of leathery green, like leather that has lain out in the weather for many years.

At last, Svanlaug brought them to a halt at the bottom of a black gorge where an icy freshet chattered down the rock, creating a faint blush of green in its passage. Thurid stood and gazed about with an attitude of disquieting vigilance, his staff spewing tendrils of mist.

"This is a border place," he intoned, his eyes almost lost in a narrow squint upward at the towering rocks. "You never know what you're going to find in a place like this. In the old days, before people traveled about like gypsies with their infernal trading, before the Dokkalfar overspread Skarpsey like an evil blight—" He spared Svanlaug a sidelong glance to see if she was properly goaded by his remark. "—the range of the Skaela-fell was the border between Ljosalfar and Dokkalfar. Few indeed were the travelers between the realms, and their purposes were clouded in secrecy that boded nothing but ill. For all that sorcery and treachery, nothing was so evil and fraught with potential destruction, in my opinion, as this greedy merchandising and city-building. It is a trend that will lead to nothing but chaos and grief for all of us."

Svanlaug curled her lip. "You're merely envious because the Ljosalfar are so backward and benighted as to resist the inevitable merging of the tribes and clans. It was a primitive system, you must admit. Things will get much better, now that the Dokkalfar have come out of the underground world."

"Better indeed, to be overrun and obfuscated as if by rats and trolls and other night-faring vermin," Thurid growled in ill humor, lashing his cloak aside so he could stalk around indignantly. "Where are these guides of yours? We certainly had no luck in finding anyone reputable to take us over Skaela-fell. Everyone knows the danger that lurks up there in those peaks. It wouldn't surprise me if we'd been lured up here just to be robbed and have our throats cut."

"Patience!" Svanlaug snapped, her eyes blazing. "I was told to come this far and to wait."

"It is troll country, you must know," Thurid retorted. "I've seen all manner of signs, warning people back. Like that one there." He pointed into the ravine and the others came around to look. "Don't go near it, you fool!" He grabbed Starkad, who was starting forward. It was the skull of a horse mounted on a short pole, still fluttering with strips of dried hide and hair, its teeth bared in a warning grimace.

"We must wait," Svanlaug said. "I know they are coming. I made the arrangements, and I know we can trust them. Their clan is one that has done business with the Prestur clan for many years."

"And what is the name of this clan of mountain guides and friends of Prestur?" Thurid demanded.

Svanlaug pursed up her lips. "I shan't tell you that. They are people who wish to remain unknown."

Thurid's answer was an eloquent snort. He continued to growl and mutter, striding up and down and casting suspicious glances around at the rocks and clefts where all manner of threatening creatures might hide.

Leifr sat down on a cold rock and watched Thurid and Svanlaug bleakly. Starkad also sat down and leaned his back against him, and the troll-hounds sat down warily on their haunches, sniffing and rumbling softly. Raudbjorn leaned upon the shaft of his halberd, his solitary working eye traveling slowly around the peaks. He, too, sniffed the errant wind and growled softly in his chest.

"Trolls, Leifr," he grumbled.

"Nonsense," Svanlaug snapped. "How could you expect to find trolls this close to Laglendi-hlid? Trolls indeed!"

"Hounds know," Raudbjorn grunted, nodding toward the hounds, who were wrinkling their lips and whining in eager anticipation.

"Keep them quiet," Svanlaug warned, "or we may find ourselves with no guides over Skaela-fell."

She scanned the surrounding cliffs with a nervous combing and tugging at her hair with her fingers, anticipation and dread mingling in her taut expression.

Leifr caught a fleeting movement in the crags. He loosened *Endalaus Daudi* in its sheath, catching Raudbjorn's eye. The thief-taker nodded his head slightly and winked, not missing the movement, either.

"Here they are," Svanlaug said tensely a few moments later. "I've gone to a great deal of trouble arranging for them, so none of you do anything to set them on their guard. I assure you, they're safe and capable guides."

"Very well, we shall see," Thurid said darkly, standing up ahead of them, sternly surveying the two ragged forms that were descending from the rocks with the grace of longtime mountain dwellers. They were bulky fellows, and the large amount of clothing they wore added to their size, giving them an almost awkward, ill-assorted appearance. Leifr supposed that mountain travel was cold enough to justify wearing half a dozen frayed old cloaks and several pairs of greasy trousers, worn with the backs frontwise to cover the holes in the knees, and at least three shirts or tunics, all bound around with strips of cloth and strings and plenty of dangling pouches, swinging from neck or belt. Of their faces, Leifr could catch only a glimpse of wiry beards and deep-set, wary eyes peering from under hedges of bristling eyebrows. They looked so similar and so peculiar that Leifr could only surmise they must be brothers, and both had inherited their odd looks from their parentage.

Svanlaug walked forward to approach them when they halted

and lurked warily around the shoulder of a large rock, as if too abashed to come nearer.

"Eldri, Felag," she greeted them. "We are here, and we're glad to see you. These are my friends I told you about. The wizard, the Scipling—" She waved a hand in faint disgust toward Raudbjorn and Starkad. "—and these others. As I told you, we wish only to get to the far side of the mountains, as quickly as possible, to my homeland."

Eldrin and Felag gazed at the travelers a long moment before remembering to nod their heads in uncertain recognition of what few rules of manners and hospitality they seemed to possess. Their manner was at once ominous and strangely timid, Leifr thought. He glanced at the troll-hounds, who were almost convulsed with snarling and bristling and growling. Kraftig pawed at Leifr repeatedly, gazing up into his face imploringly.

"Down!" Leifr growled sternly, and the hounds crouched at his feet reluctantly, still baring their teeth in awful, silent snarls, rolling their eyes in a menacing fashion.

"We are glad to meet you," Thurid said, striding forward, rapping the ground with his staff. Eldri and Felag lowered their heads suspiciously and took two steps hastily backward. Svanlaug raised one hand warningly to halt Thurid in his tracks.

"They don't like your staff," Svanlaug said. "Keep your flaming and smoking to a minimum, and I strongly advise you to keep a lid on your alf-light. These mountain people don't see much of that sort of thing. Besides, in a border place, you don't know what elementals you might enrage."

"Very true," Thurid said, smothering his smoking at once. "I do apologize."

Eldri and Felag shuffled their great feet and shrugged their thick shoulders, making faint mumbles of additional apology.

"We are in pursuit of one who might have come this way," Thurid said. "One of the dark ones of the two realms. He is heading toward Hringurhol with something stolen from us, something infinitely precious."

Eldri and Felag exchanged a long and ponderous glance.

"There was such a one," Eldri rumbled in a throaty voice. "One we had no wish to interfere with. He went in a great hurry."

"That's the one we seek," Thurid said grimly.

"Well, let's get started," Svanlaug said impatiently. "Leifr, you and those hounds had better keep to the rear. I wish you'd left them in Laglendi-hlid with the horses. They're going to be nothing but a nuisance on this journey."

The hounds continued to growl throughout the day as the expedition climbed into the crags of Skaela-fell. Leifr watched them and Raudbjorn and their two guides, forming his own opinions. At noonday they halted to rest and refresh themselves on the provisions Thurid had brought from Laglendi-hlid. The two silent guides sat down apart and took out their own meal from a pouch and commenced eating it. Leifr eyed them covertly, watching the reactions of Raudbjorn and the troll-hounds. Raudbjorn studied Eldri and Felag, openly puzzled. The three hounds sniffed the air and licked their lips hungrily.

Starkad edged over on his rock until he was near enough to whisper to Leifr, "What would you think of people who ate raw meat?"

Leifr cast a glance at Eldri and Felag, and Starkad nodded his head emphatically.

"Are you sure?" Leifr whispered.

Again Starkad nodded his head. "I saw it. It was oozing a few drops of blood out of the seam of their pouch."

Leifr tried to turn his gaze casually in the direction of Eldri and Felag. "Well, they might just be strange," he said. "And there is a shortage of wood around here."

"And the troll-hounds don't like them," Starkad added. "I've never known Kraftig to make an error in judgment. Remember, he didn't like my brothers much."

"There's nothing we can do about it just now," Leifr said. "And they do seem to be taking us in the proper direction. We'll wait and see if they do anything else suspicious."

"Like kill us and eat us," Starkad said in a dire whisper, his eyes narrowed to mere slits. "Mountain people are strange, you said. But cannibalism is worse than strange, Leifr."

"What makes you think it's human flesh they're eating?" Leifr demanded.

"It's just a feeling I've got," Starkad said, passing his hand through the air in a cryptic gesture, feeling for influences. "Eldri and Felag make my hair stand on end. I know when I've been warned, Leifr. A pity you Sciplings aren't as sensitive as Ljos-alfar to warnings."

"Bah on you and your warnings," Leifr grunted. "As long as I've got a good sword, I don't need your mysterious airs and powers."

Nevertheless, he continued to watch the two brothers, feeling uneasy despite himself. Eldri and Felag seldom raised their heads from their dogged plodding, except to take furtive glances around at the company following them.

Svanlaug expected the journey over Skaela-fell to take three days, which entailed spending two nights with Eldri and Felag, in the terrain known to them, under conditions unfamiliar to Leifr and his party.

The night passed without incident. Eldri and Felag alternated the watch, and so did Leifr and Raudbjorn, covertly, spending just as much time watching Eldri and Felag as they did for any unknown threats. In the morning, Leifr awoke first and began a futile scavenging expedition for a bit of firewood or dried moss to heat a pot of tea. He found nothing to burn, and was bleakly adjusting himself to the idea that it would be a cold start this morning. As he tramped along, leaving black footprints in the night's coating of hoar-frost, he suddenly came upon another set of tracks in the frost, large, three-toed tracks that he would have recognized instantly anywhere. Troll tracks! And they were the biggest he had ever seen. The tracks came out of a cleft in the rock, which Leifr peered into warily, seeing nothing but a dark niche where the creature must have hidden itself, possibly just before his approach had flushed it out. Loosening his sword in its sheath, he started to follow the tracks. They went straight toward their camp. Leifr started to hurry, remaining alert. He heard no sounds of alarm, only the quiet murmur of sleepy voices. Rounding a rock suddenly, he came upon Felag, hunched like a great untidy heap of old clothing as he sat chewing pon-derously on a dried shard of some kind of meat. Leifr halted in his tracks as Felag slowly turned his head and looked at him from beneath his ragged hood. Leifr could see little of his face except hair, but he felt the power of Felag's scrutiny. After a long moment of mutual, suspicious contemplation, Felag slowly extended the blackened bit of meat toward Leifr.

"Have a share," Felag rumbled tentatively.

Leifr crouched down beside him and accepted the proffered gift. He tested it with his teeth. The meat was not raw as Starkad had supposed, but smoked and dried. It was also rather tasty.

"Very good," Leifr said.

"Horsemeat," Felag said with a contented rumble.

Leifr politely ate the meat, secretly repelled at the idea of eating horsemeat. Casually he glanced back at the tracks in the frost, which led right up to the rock where Felag was sitting. He looked at Felag's feet, which were encased in huge and shapeless troll-skin boots, wrapped about with leather strips. A chill passed over Leifr at that moment and his throat became almost too dry to swallow the last of the dried horsemeat.

When he could politely detach himself, he hurried back to camp, bursting to tell Thurid his suspicions. Thurid, however, was occupied in a long consultation with Eldri. The two of them sat apart, their hooded heads almost touching, as they went over a handful of rune sticks from Thurid's satchel. Eldri's long wrinkled hands went over the rune sticks, pointing, gouging notches with a black thumbnail. Leifr heaved a sigh and kept his distance, knowing when not to interrupt Thurid. His outrage increased as the day wore on, and Thurid and Eldri continued their interminable talking and pawing over of the useless trash from the satchel. Worse yet, Leifr had the feeling they were deliberately keeping themselves apart so they could continue their conversation.

On the second night, Eldri and Felag called a halt in a high, narrow valley. One more day of travel, they said, would put them at the edge of the Dokkalfar tribal grounds to the east. Instead of moving away to a distance comfortable to them, Eldri and Felag crouched down in a patient, watchful attitude, while Starkad rattled around among the provisions for some fare that required no cooking.

"Thurid," Leifr said, seizing the opportunity. "Those creatures, Eldri and Felag, aren't what you think they are."

"Oh no?" Thurid queried rather loudly, turning toward their guides. "Eldri, Felag, this Scipling here thinks you are not quite what you seem. Can't you enlighten his benighted mind as to your true natures?''

Leifr glowered at Thurid, but Eldri and Felag seemed undisturbed by Thurid's presumption.

"We are the Gray Ones," said Eldri, and Felag seconded his words with a long and gloomy sigh. "The last of the Elder clans that once ruled Skarpsey. Like the Rhbus, we are only a scant remnant now. There are those who fear us yet, and because of their fear they have given us the name of troll. So they hunt us and kill us, and with us dies our knowledge.''

Leifr's heart nearly stopped beating, but it resumed again at an accelerated rate as Eldri continued talking.

"We are safest in the high places, so we take refuge in the high peaks of Skaela-fell. Only a few of the lowlanders know of us and remember our knowledge. Only those who are seeking come to us, such as the Prestur clan, who are thirsty for our ancient knowledge. Or such as Thurid, who is striving to learn the ways of the Rhbu. You are in no danger from us," he added, his eye falling upon Leifr's stiff and watchful attitude.

"My father Afgang often came to seek out the Gray Ones," Svanlaug said, lifting her head in quiet pride. "And they rewarded him with great gifts of wisdom and power. When I came west, searching for my vengeance, Eldri and Felag guided me across the mountains. Now I have returned with power to complete my revenge upon Sorkvir for my father's death.''

Eldri and Felag nodded slowly. "Vengeance will be had," Felag said, "if you are determined to seek it.''

Eldri added, "And if you are not destroyed by that which you seek. You have great power for good or evil. The blue orb of Heldur is power enough to corrupt any wizard, Thurid. Are you certain you have the strength to resist it, and to give it up when the time comes?''

Thurid's fingers clenched around his staff instinctively. "I have sworn to use what powers I possess only for the working of good," he declared.

"Let me see the orb," Eldri said.

Thurid unwrapped the bag from the end of his staff, letting the rays of the orb throw back the pressing shadows of encroaching night. Eldri and Felag shaded their eyes as they gazed at the orb. Slowly Eldri shook his grizzled head, his eyes still fastened upon it in awe.

"A great injustice was once committed," he murmured. "Now the day of Reikna is coming and the scales will be evened at last. The evil that men do always comes back to them a thousandfold. This orb is coming home to redress ancient wrongs. Always, always beware the homecoming of one who has been wronged, my friends."

He settled himself more comfortably among the rocks and shut his eyes with a long and weary sigh, as if glad to be safe in the tops of his mountains, far from the troubles enmeshing the lowlands. Or perhaps he was exhausted from his prophetic efforts.

It was noonday of the following day when Eldri and Felag called a halt and declared that they would go no farther. Before turning back to the snow-clad peaks, they pointed out the direction the travelers should go. Then they shambled away without a backward glance, turning their backs upon the world below and all its doings. Below lay the lowlands, green and silver-ribboned with rivers and breathing the misty life-giving essences of fertile earth and waters. Leifr was glad to leave behind the barren wasteland of the mountains and descend into hills covered with moss and grass and trees and shrubs, but the words of Eldri niggled at him.

"If the Gray Ones are so wise," he finally blurted out to Thurid, apropos of nothing, "why are they hunted and forced to hide? Why doesn't everyone want to learn what they know?"

Thurid's lips curled in a derisive smile and one brow quirked upward. "Nothing is as frightening as knowledge," he said. "No one wants that kind of wisdom any longer. And what mankind fears, mankind destroys. Hence, these great, wise creatures have become nothing but trolls, hated and hunted into near extinction."

"They do their part to keep people frightened away," Svanlaug said. "The bad reputation of trolls also protects them. Listen to that." She cocked her head to listen to a distant sound, echoing down the corridors of stone. Leifr heard the droning, grumbling sound of troll voices and felt gooseflesh rise on his skin.

Near sundown, they reached the first great road that led into
the settlement of Haeta-fell. Cart wheels had gouged raw, oozing ruts in the earth, and the hooves of horses had churned it to
muck. As they walked, they were passed by pony-trains, laden
with swaying packs bulging with exotic wares from far beyond
the surrounds of Haeta-fell. Lumbering carts and sledges plodded along, carrying things into and away from the market streets
of the settlement.

Thurid walked along with his head held high, snorting and
glowering at the crude drovers and drivers that came flogging
by, dashing mud up from under hooves and wheels as often as
not.

"A fine invention indeed!" Thurid growled. "Before we
know it, the land will be covered with these filthy villages. All
sorts of vermin and disease will be spread throughout the entire
island, thanks to this unnatural commerce!"

The road led them to the ferry landing, where an encampment
of drovers and pony-trains was setting up for the night to await
the return of the ferry in the morning. The ferryman, an ill-
tempered little man with a red scarf tied over his head, was
fending off the advance of a much larger, equally ill-tempered
Dokkalfar with ten ponies.

"The ferry is closed!" roared the ferryman, his eyes protrud-
ing with wrath, brandishing his barge pole. "If you must cross
tonight, do it at the next crossing! Old Smyglari will be glad to
take you across in the dark and dash you to smithereens on the
rocks in the bargain! Now begone, you vagabond, before I
lose my temper!" With a ferocious gnashing of his teeth he took
a savage swipe at the drover, who backed away muttering foul
epithets.

"Batur! Wait a moment!" Svanlaug called, hurrying forward
to the edge of the boat stand and putting one foot upon the ferry
boat. "You've got to go across to get home anyhow, so take us
with you! We haven't got any horses or packs to weigh you
down!"

"The ferry is closed!" Batur answered in a harassed bellow,
raising his barge pole again.

"See here, you ruffian—" Thurid began.

"Haven't you got any ears to hear with?" Batur roared. "No

more fares until tomorrow! You can wait just as easily as the others!"

"That's a fine way to treat a daughter of the Prestur clan," Svanlaug said and held out her hand, palm upward. "Particularly one of the Bergmal sisterhood. Your tribe and mine are the same, Batur, and I implore you for your hospitality."

The ferryman instantly ceased his huffing and shouting and lowered his barge pole. "Why didn't you say so before?" he said irascibly, a cheery grin breaking through a maze of scowling wrinkles. "My house is yours, and I shall be deeply hurt unless I can be of further service to you."

With an arrogant little smile, Svanlaug beckoned to the rest of them.

"Come along," she said. "Batur has agreed to take us across the river now."

Chapter 15

❖❖❖❖❖❖❖❖❖❖❖❖❖❖❖❖❖❖❖❖❖❖❖❖❖❖❖❖❖❖❖❖❖

Leifr soon began to perceive himself at an even greater disadvantage in the realm of the Dokkalfar than he had been with the Ljosalfar. A moment hence, Batur had been willing to crack their heads with his barge pole, but at the mention of tribes and clans and the showing of the mark on Svanlaug's hand, Batur welcomed them all into his house and generously fed them with his food and expected them to stay for a night or two. It was plentiful and good food; Batur's ferry business allowed him to keep fresh meat on the table and the best of ale in his flagon. Astonishingly, he possessed a brace of four handsome young sons, the two elder of whom were large enough to help him with the ferry barge, and the two younger seemed to be around the age of twelve or so.

Batur beamed with inordinate pride as he introduced them. "You wouldn't think an old ferryman would be deserving of such fortune," he said. "There are three girls also, living with their mothers. One is a weaver, one is a woodcarver, and Lise, the youngest, will be a boatbuilder. She's only ten, but she's already built a fine little skip for herself with her little tools."

"Admirable!" Svanlaug said. "You must possess a fine pedigree and lucky stars indeed."

"For a ferryman, yes," he said with dignity. "There has been at least one ferryman in every generation since the Great Alfather scattered his thirteen sons over the face of the earth. Now there's certain to be plenty of room in the trade for all four of my sons, with all this new interest in buying and selling. Their mothers are all coming downriver for a visit at the autumn fairing."

Leifr furrowed up his brow in confusion and vast disapproval.

As he started to open his mouth to ask some questions, Thurid caught his eye and silenced him with a slight shake of his head and a warning scowl. Starkad lifted his shoulders in a resigned shrug, glancing pointedly toward Thurid. He was as curious as Leifr, but obviously he had already been silenced.

The remainder of the day was taken up with welcome resting, more eating and drinking, and listening to Svanlaug and Batur's conversation about friends and relatives they had in common. For the first time it occurred to Leifr that Svanlaug had taken a great risk in leaving her own realm and going among Ljosalfar strangers. Also, she must have been lonely, so far away from her vast extended tribal family. Clan seemed to include her mother, aunts, sisters, and cousins, all in some way related. Tribe and clan were two words she and Batur mentioned a thousand times, and other tribes and clans were discussed with tolerant contempt. Leifr listened with uneasy suspense, hoping to learn more of the peculiar living arrangements of the Dokkalfar, where men and women seemed to live apart in close-knit family clans, instead of pairing off into husbands and wives in the decent Scipling and Ljosalfar manner.

"And are your clan brothers still living in Haeta-fell?" Svanlaug inquired, and Batur shook his head.

"All are scattered now," he said gloomily. "Their hereditary trades did not interest them for long, with such fortunes to be made with pony-trains and trade-goods."

"A great pity," Svanlaug said. "This makes the old ways hard to maintain."

"Are you taking these men with you to Bergmal?" Batur asked, with a nod in Leifr's direction.

"Yes. We keep a tent for male guests." Svanlaug had a way of twitching her shoulders when she was evading a question, and she did it now, Leifr observed; she went on rather quickly to change the subject. "Eldri and Felag mentioned that you would be able to get horses for us. I don't want to show my face much in Haeta-fell, in case someone has brought back the news of my return."

"The killing of Djofull, you mean," Batur said. "We've heard that news, and how it was an outlaw named Leifr Thorljotsson who killed him." He rolled an eye in Leifr's direction and bared his teeth in a grin that showed a few teeth missing from barge fights. "This is one outlaw I don't mind harboring. None of the Ulf-hedin will dare tangle with a ferryman in this life."

"I'm the one who killed Djofull," Svanlaug said indignantly. "It's so like you, Leifr, to take credit when it's due to others!"

"Credit I don't need," Leifr retorted. "I wish I could tell it to the Naglissons."

"Don't worry, it will take them seven or eight days to get upriver from Laglendi-hlid to look for you," Svanlaug said. "Or if they tried to follow us across Skaela-fell you may never be troubled with them again. The great Gray Ones are not man-eaters, but they couldn't refuse five horses. Speaking of which—"

"We'll go immediately," Batur said. "It would be advisable for you to stay hidden, as well as the outlaw Thorljotsson. No one will question my buying horses. They know it's not wise to question a ferryman too closely."

When Batur and his two eldest sons had gone, Leifr sought out Thurid in the bathhouse, where the wizard had just steamed himself like a mussel until every inch of him was a torrid and much-refreshed red. He was putting on his new clothes, acquired in Laglendi-hlid—a blue embroidered gown belted at the waist with a wide studded band, a red and blue short coat thickly stitched and decorated with ermine tails, and a pair of voluminous gray trousers stuffed into new boots trimmed with fleece.

"Quite the red elf, aren't you?" Leifr greeted him, after a moment of pretending to be entirely dazzled.

"The same treatment wouldn't be amiss in your case," Thurid retorted. "That's one advantage of these cursed towns, I'm forced to admit. It's easy to find new clothes. You don't want to look like a ragged pot boy, if we're going to visit a women's clan."

"So. It's the ladies you're thinking of again. No wonder you're dressed up as if you're going to your own wedding feast. Or funeral."

"It never hurts for a man to avail himself of the opportunity to put on a dignified appearance," Thurid answered, throwing a red-lined cloak over his shoulders with an arrogant flourish. "You might as well do the same, while the rocks are still heated. I had the foresight to purchase clean clothes for us all in Laglendi-hlid, knowing we were near the end of our journey. I wonder how long it's been since Raudbjorn had a bath and a good steaming?"

Leifr shook his head in silent wonderment. "I couldn't even begin to calculate such a remote possibility. But how do you know we're close to the end of our journey?"

"Trust me, I know, but this isn't the place to talk about it. Where's Starkad? At the mere mention of bathing, he vanished."

"He went with Batur to the horse market. What's so significant about being a ferryman, Thurid? He's mentioned it more than once, as if it were protection."

"The Dokkalfar believe that a ferryman takes them from Hela's realm of the dead across a river to a more pleasant place, if they've conducted themselves in their lifetime according to the accepted Dokkalfar standards of behavior. So no one wants to antagonize a ferryman, for fear of meeting up with him when one wants to cross the river of death in Hel. A ferryman lives well, what with the gifts and offerings many people make to him now to ensure safe passage when they are dead."

By the time Batur and Starkad had canvassed the horse market, searching for six sound horses and dickering viciously for a reasonable price, the dim daylight had faded ominously into late afternoon. Such a late start was deemed inadvisable by Batur, and Svanlaug reluctantly concurred that a notable number of footpads and outlaws hung around the fringes of the settlement waiting for such predatory opportunities under the cover of darkness.

"Much safer to travel by daylight," Batur advised. "The Ljosalfar have taught us that much. We are becoming a realm that never sleeps."

"Well, I can't just sit here all night," Svanlaug grumbled, pulling up her hood and fastening her cloak around her shoulders. "I'm going to prowl around the taverns and inns and find out what I can. I think I've already seen a few Ulf-hedin around."

"You may have," Batur said, "and I advise you to stay away from them, if you don't want the Council of Threttan coming after you."

"Surely not everyone in Haeta-fell agrees with what the Council of Threttan has done," Svanlaug objected.

"No, but that doesn't give them the strength or courage to resist. Not that anything can be done at this late date. Most Dokkalfar feel that it's best to go about our business as well as we can in spite of the Dokkur Lavardur and the Council, although no one really likes the idea anymore of perpetual winter and darkness. The Council is regarded as rather old-fashioned. Dokkalfar don't want to live underground anymore—not since they've discovered the occupation of trade. We must have our cloud cover to live aboveground, but the Council is becoming ridiculous about the Fimbul Winter. Already some of the larger trading companies are talking about trading with Ljosalfar settlements. They get marvelous things on ships from far places, you know."

Svanlaug shook her head impatiently, causing tendrils of dark hair to escape. "I'll be glad to get back to Bergmal," she said. "I don't like this new mercenary venture of you menfolks. The Council doesn't like it, either, and they're using the Dokkur Lavardur and the Ulf-hedin to squash it."

"Twelve long-bearded old wizards have no right to squash the business of hundreds of traders and sellers," Batur said with a nervous gesture of his hand to indicate listening ears. "Or so the traders say. I keep my opinions to myself these days."

Leifr pulled up his own hood. "I'm going with Svanlaug," he said. "I want to have a look and a listen at this place as well, to see if Sorkvir has passed through. You didn't ferry a revenant wizard across, did you, Batur?"

"Sorkvir, is it now?" Batur's jaw dropped with awe, and he scratched its bristly surface speculatively. "He was here, but I didn't ferry him. I heard talk of him, was all. He wouldn't dare come to me, if he's a revenant, and if he believes the tales they tell about ferrymen. Every profession has its secret powers."

Svanlaug turned to Leifr. "If you're coming with me, you've got to keep quiet and draw no attention. We'll look at the Ulf-hedin and listen quietly for word of Sorkvir, without asking questions."

Batur made some signs to ward off evil influences as he slyly inquired with an ingratiating smile, "Have you come so far in search of Sorkvir, for no other reason?"

Leifr's guard went up suspiciously at the question. "He stole my cat," he retorted shortly in a sinister growl. "And I want it back. You haven't seen a long-furred gray cat around here, have you?" He hadn't much hope; Ljosa would not be seen by anyone unless she wanted to show herself. Most likely she had slipped across on Batur's ferry without his glimpsing her.

Batur's eyes rounded and he swiftly stepped back to a more respectful distance. "A man who comes to the Dokkalfar realm merely to reclaim a cat!" he murmured. "But of course it must be a valuable cat and it is yours, so you have every right to be upset about its theft. May I never do anything to offend you, my friend!"

He anxiously doffed his hat to Leifr, and again to Raudbjorn, whose hackles were raised instantly whenever Leifr was angry, and scuttled away outside on the pretext of looking at something to do with his barge, probably thinking that outlaws were a dangerous and unreasonable lot.

Raudbjorn, of course, accompanied Leifr, leaving a most reluctant Starkad behind to study over some rune sticks with Thurid. Svanlaug strode along eagerly, sniffing at the smells of cooking booths and cocking her head at the sounds of merriment coming from inn and tavern.

"It's as jolly as the spring and autumn fairings, only it never stops," she said. "Traders are always here with their goods, instead of only twice a year."

"But I can see a disadvantage," Leifr said. "A man will always have to carry his money or trade goods around with him, in case he wants to buy something to eat or if he sees something he wants to take home. That's rather awkward, I should think. And convenient for killers and thieves, so a man must arm himself and be on guard continuously, suspicious of everyone."

"So what's different?" Svanlaug demanded. "Dokkalfar have always been armed and suspicious—as well as being killers and thieves, a great share of them. Speaking of eating," she added, stopping still and inhaling the wonderful scent of breads baking, "there's a stall here that makes the most glorious pastry you ever tasted. Light as a cloud, unless you eat too many of them, then your belly feels like a stone. Have you got any money, Leifr?''

''No, not even a smell of a coin,'' Leifr replied with a searing touch of sudden and unaccustomed embarrassment, which even he considered odd in a warrior so capable and well equipped.

''Money,'' Raudbjorn rumbled, inserting one huge paw into his trophy bag, with the gleam of an idea in his eye. After hauling out a string of dried severed ears, he began sorting through them, eliciting some astounded stares from bystanders and passersby. At last he pulled an earring from one and held it up triumphantly. It was a silver coin with a hole drilled through it.

''Money,'' he repeated with a victorious chuckle. ''Now we buy. Buy plenty.''

After some serious bargaining, Svanlaug bought all the pastries in the booth, and the proprietor returned half the coin. Judging from Raudbjorn's blissful expression as he ate his share, the thief-taker obviously considered it one of the best bargains of his lifetime. When they had all finished off their shares, Svanlaug wrapped the remaining pastries in a scarf and they walked on, feeling comfortably anonymous in the throngs of people scurrying about, occupied with buying or selling or offering their services in any number of trades.

A cart with tall wheels, drawn by three piebald ponies, came trotting around a corner at a reckless rate for such a crowded thoroughfare, causing a chorus of shouts and imprecations to follow them. The drivers were three laughing girls decked out in high style, with braided streamers of horsehair trailing from their regional headgear, beaded fringe on their gauntlets, and the feet braced on the splashboard were booted to the knees in soft calfskin, with bright patches of blue and red and yellow stitched on in fancy designs.

''Halloa! It's Svanlaug!'' one girl shouted, and the others added screams of recognition, drawing up the cart suddenly with a rearing and snorting of the the ponies. People everywhere turned to look, and Leifr shot Svanlaug a murderous look.

''Quiet and secret, eh?'' he muttered.

''You must remember us,'' one of the girls said. ''We met at the spring fairing last year. Irina, Alois, and Meris, remember?

We're from the Othalandi clan. My mother is your mother's cousin, but she was traded for a laundrywoman years ago." A certain toss of Irina's head indicated that the slight had not been forgiven or forgotten even yet. "What have you been doing this past year and a half, Svanlaug? Is this your hand-mate with you?" She cast her slanting eyes toward Leifr and smothered her giggling with a mitten.

Svanlaug's chin tilted upward dangerously and Leifr caught a murderous flash in her eye. "No, indeed," she said witheringly. "These are merely my guides from over the mountain. I've been traveling lately on my father's business, instead of sitting around with a bunch of silly girls, waiting for their twentieth birthdays and some misguided matchmaker."

"You are rather beyond that, aren't you, Svanlaug?" Alois added with a sympathetic shake of her head, and the other girls shook with suppressed laughter.

"I'll be twenty in ten months, and the Otholandi matchmaker has a splendid match for me," Meris said coyly. "A horse-breaker from the Hestur clan, and very handsome, they say."

"He's old and gimpy in the legs," Alois said tartly, and all three girls shrieked and laughed.

"Good luck to all of you, I'm sure," Svanlaug said dryly, starting to edge away in discomfiture at the attention they were attracting.

"Yes, I'm sure you're busy on your father's important business," Irina said. "Even though he's been dead quite some time. I didn't know the elder women of the Bergmal clan allowed their young women to gypsy about the countryside. You'd think there would be enough herbs and plants and roots and things to keep you busy at home. What I like about being a weaver is having the excuse to come to Haeta-fell once a month or so to look for new patterns and new fibers to weave. Isn't it frightfully dull, being an herbalist?"

"My father was a wizard, a member of the Council," Svanlaug replied with a haughty toss of her head, "so life is never dull, wherever I go. Good day and good luck to you, Irina—Alois—Meris." She made her escape at last to the shadows between brightly lit doorways and booths, with Leifr and Raudbjorn drifting after her casually.

"She's getting to be a sour old prune, isn't she?" Alois said loudly. "It'll be a miracle if she ever is matched and gets some children."

"Breaking her hereditary trade won't help her, either," Irina rejoined with a spiteful spat with her whip on the rump of the center pony. "Get up there, lazy!"

"That was a foolish mistake," Leifr grumbled. "A hundred people must have recognized you, and most of them were probably your father's enemies."

"Blast those girls," Svanlaug growled between gritted teeth. "Who would have dreamed they'd find me? What a piece of luck! Fortunately we're leaving tomorrow, or I'm certain someone would come looking for me."

"It's a long night in the Dokkalfar realm," Leifr said uneasily. "Who would come looking, if he were?"

"Alfrekar is the chief wizard of the Council," Svanlaug said. "The other ten are his toadies, afraid to hop except when he says hop. He'd send his Ulf-hedin, if he sends anyone after me."

"I don't know why you bothered to return," Leifr growled uneasily, darting looks from side to side. "Don't you know when you're well away from your problems?"

"Eleven wizards," Raudbjorn groaned, plucking disconsolately at the gleaming crescent of his halberd. "Raudbjorn getting bellyful of wizards."

"There might be twelve wizards by now," Svanlaug continued. "Since Djofull and my father Afgang are out of the way, Alfrekar might have chosen two more lackeys for the vacancies. There must be thirteen to represent all the original tribes of Dokkalfar, before Alfrekar can work his will with the Dokkur Lavardur. But we won't have to worry about them until we get to Hringurhol. I visited my father there occasionally."

"You've got your revenge on Djofull," Leifr snapped, peering around suspiciously. "What more do you want? Revenge upon the Council? What do you think you can do?"

Svanlaug gave him a slanting look. "I wouldn't have come back without help from you and Thurid and Gedvondur. Now I see an opportunity beyond my wildest imagining. I never knew Fridmarr, but his dealings with the Council long ago are going to result in its destruction."

It always came back to Fridmarr. Leifr stifled a groan under his breath, feeling certain that Fridmarr had doomed him to a life of endless complications and mysterious enmities.

The street appeared to have forgotten the incident almost immediately, so Svanlaug resumed her cautious promenade, pausing to listen outside the doors of a few inns and taverns. While she was doing this, Leifr stood and watched a street entertainer, whose claim to fame was his ability to swallow unusual objects.

Leifr's first warning was a sudden savage growling of the trollhounds, and Kraftig pawed at his knee worriedly, with his sharp nose pointing back the way they had come. Raudbjorn inhaled a deep angry breath that creaked his body armor as he glowered smolderingly at the two cloaked figures standing in a cleared space on the busy walkway. They stared straight toward Leifr and Raudbjorn with no pretense of stealth.

"Ulf-hedin!" Leifr whispered.

No one wanted to approach them close enough to fall under their scrutiny, so the Ulf-hedin took their privacy with them wherever they went. At the moment, they were plainly illuminated in the light of a bonfire in the yard of an inn. Moments before, a merry company of drovers and traders had been standing around the fire, passing a flagon, but at the approach of the Ulf-hedin they had melted away in silence. The Ulf-hedin were larger than most Dokkalfar, clad in ring armor and leather. Each was armed with two swords at his back, a short sword, a lance, and any quantity of knives and daggers. Their wolf capes were draped casually over their shoulders, with the snarling head forming a grisly helmet, as yet lifeless and limp.

"They're looking for us!" Svanlaug warned, yanking at Leifr's sleeve. "We've got to get out of here as quietly as we can!"

Of a mind to stay and confront these fellows, Leifr hesitated, and Raudbjorn did not budge an inch, until Svanlaug turned and hurried away by herself. Then Leifr followed, with many glances over his shoulder. Whether by chance or from catching a sight of them, the Ulf-hedin chose the same way to follow, strolling along alertly as the walkways cleared before them. Svanlaug began to hurry, and Leifr caught hold of her arm.

"Slow down, or they'll see that someone is running from them," Leifr whispered. "We can't go back to Batur's as long as they're following. We might have to stay out here all night if they don't force a fight.''

Svanlaug nodded her head, drawing some deep breaths. She was genuinely frightened, Leifr realized with astonishment. In all the time he had known her, she had been brave, sly, or deceptive, but never so thoroughly unnerved.

''We'll do what we can,'' she said faintly. ''But when the Ulf-hedin have marked a man for destruction, that man always dies horribly. I fear I've been marked, Leifr. They must know about Djofull and who really killed him.''

''How could they know?'' Leifr asked. ''No one else was there except us to witness his killing.''

''Sorkvir,'' Svanlaug said. ''He must have gotten to Hringur-hol with his news. I thought it was strange that we've been allowed to live this long, with Ulf-hedin everywhere and able to do as they please as far as killing goes.''

''Then why don't they just kill us and take Heldur's orb themselves?'' Leifr asked.

''Ordinary Ulf-hedin would not be able to touch it without disintegrating instantly,'' Svanlaug replied. ''Don't you see how you've been trapped? You've helped bring it right into the grasp of the Council of Threttan. Sorkvir has carefully led you along with Ljosa as bait. Why else would you have rescued Thurid from the Wizards' Guildhall, but for your misguided loyalty to her?''

''Don't try to lay this all at my door,'' Leifr retorted. ''What about Thurid? He's got some lofty scheme in mind himself about the Rhbus and finishing up Fridmarr's business with Sorkvir and Djofull. He'd be here with that crystal, even if I'd never left Dallir when he ran away from the Inquisitors. And just maybe, as long as we're making accusations, things would have been different if you'd stayed home where you belonged, instead of going after Djofull. Revenge is a man's business, not a woman's.''

Svanlaug sighed in exasperation and raked back her tumbled hair from her eyes. ''Exactly what my elder women told me when I told them what I must do,'' she said. ''But my brother had just been killed for trying to avenge Afgang, who was his father. I did what I went to do, didn't I?''

"Yes, you killed him all right, but now you've got to live with the consequences," Leifr said grimly. "Alfrekar would have left you alone otherwise, wouldn't he? Women are usually exempt from feuds, unless they take some action."

Svanlaug's head sank low and she heaved a sigh. "Yes, that's true. Alfrekar would not have come after me. He was an old friend of my father's. As was Djofull. I've known those men all my life, and most of the Council of Threttan. Now they all want to kill me."

"You couldn't be too surprised," Leifr said. "No one likes having his friends killed. Surely you must have known you couldn't ever return. Why didn't you stay dead when Djofullhol was destroyed?"

"Gedvondur didn't find his ashes at Djofullhol. He thinks they're at Hringurhol. We followed you to the Guildhall and laid low, but Sorkvir was lurking around so we didn't dare put our noses out. Then you went over the top of Hefill-fjall, which we couldn't do, so we had to take a boat up the river. It was pure luck we caught you at Laglendi-hlid."

"Bad luck, you mean," Leifr said. "My quarrel is with Sorkvir, not thirteen wizards and hundreds of Ulf-hedin. They could kill us at any time, when they judge we've gotten close enough with the orb. Why did you come back, Svanlaug? Try telling us the truth this time."

Svanlaug replied with a grim smile, "When you seek revenge, you'd better dig two graves—only in this case make it thirteen. Djofull's death wasn't enough, Leifr. I want to see the Council humbled, their plans thwarted, the grip of the Dokkur Lavardur dispersed. You and Thurid can do it. You've got the weapons, and I think the winds of fate are favoring your enterprise this time."

Even as she spoke Raudbjorn uttered a warning grunt.

The Ulf-hedin strolled into view, illuminated by the light of a torch before an uproarious tavern, which suddenly became silent, and a dozen or so hearty drinkers sobered up quickly and decided it was time to go home. They slipped under the walls of the tent and stealthily vanished, perhaps harboring some secret cause for dreading the Ulf-hedin. Almost as if they wished their quarry to see them, the Ulf-hedin stood in the light of the torch, casually looking this way and that like ordinary evening strollers. Or perhaps they were questing the air for traces of their prey, like the wolves they emulated. Then they came on in the direction of Leifr's party, not hurrying in the least, like lordly rulers of death with all the time they required.

Leifr took some deep breaths to dispel the memories of that crowded room in Laglendi-hlid, thick with the smell of fear and eitur.

After crossing the town three times, and what seemed to Leifr hours of casual chase, the Ulf-hedin suddenly vanished. One moment they were standing in the light of a nearby brazier, and the next they were gone. Leifr could easily see the distance between themselves and the brazier, and no Ulf-hedin occupied it. All around, people were again laughing and jostling and quarreling as if there were no Ulf-hedin within miles to strike them into fearful silence or immobility. Just to be certain, Leifr and Svanlaug waited and watched from several positions around the central marketplace, but no Ulf-hedin appeared.

Svanlaug sighed with relief. "We've been warned, that's all," she said. "This time."

"And next time?" Leifr asked and got nothing but a sulky shrug for an answer. "Well, let's go back to Batur's. Thurid will be wild that we've been gone so long."

Indeed Thurid was pacing up and down, spewing furious threats and mutterings when they arrived at the ferryman's hut.

"Where have you been?" he demanded with blazing eyes and hair standing on end from continuous harrowing. "We've had Ulf-hedin prowling around, spying us out, while you've been out seeking frivolous jollification in every fleshpit in Haeta-fell, never giving a thought to the seriousness of the quest before us. What's that you've brought back?"

"Pastries," Svanlaug said, unwrapping the bundle on the table. "Slightly worse for wear, but still delicious."

To the horror of everyone in the room, the bundle she unwrapped was not pastries, but a parcel of bloody entrails from what appeared to be an animal of some kind. Batur fell back with an oath, his eyes bulging with terror. Svanlaug screamed and hurled the mess toward the door.

"They transformed it, right in my own hand!" she gasped, making signs to ward off evil.

"Traded it, more likely," Thurid said, recovering swiftly from an involuntary lurch backward. He prodded the entrails with the end of his staff, and the blue orb sizzled and flared beneath its hood. "Nothing but goose guts, I'd say. They must be chuckling at pulling such a clever trick on you."

"Goose guts," Leifr grunted, now that his heart had stopped racing. It had been a sickening shock, but it was over now. "How appropriate."

"It's no joke," Svanlaug snapped, whirling around to glare at him, her voice still trembling. "You can bet they aren't laughing about it. This is a warning, a sign. Our guts are going to be spilled next."

"Not likely," Leifr retorted, resting his hand on the hilt of *Endalaus Daudi*. "Those Ulf-hedin can die as well as anyone else in this realm, if they're flesh and blood. Flesh can be pierced and blood shed on the ground."

Raudbjorn growled in agreement, scowling ferociously. He was not the sort to appreciate Ulf-hedin humor, if it were such. "Aye, spill Ulf-hedin blood," he rumbled. "Stole pastries. No one steal from Raudbjorn."

"No one knows for certain if they are flesh and blood or not," Svanlaug continued impatiently. "No one knows anything about them, until it's too late, and there's nothing left behind except an empty house or a lot of blood on the ground. You saw them tonight. They're absolutely fearless. They know they have no need even to be cautious. No one would lift a hand against them."

"Then they're in for a surprise," Leifr said in cold anger. "I'm going to lift more than a hand against them if they get in my way."

Batur shook his head in distress. His air of pompous pride over his status as ferryman had dissolved. "It won't do you any good," he whimpered. "They're not ordinary men. They're more like wolves with two legs! You're doomed if you oppose them. Lucky for you they don't think you're dangerous, or it would have been something more swift and deadly than a mere wad of goose guts as a warning."

Raudbjorn and the troll-hounds standing guard outside the door made it easier for Leifr to sleep for the rest of that short night. Nothing could get past those keen ears and noses and eyes, he was certain.

At the first hint of dawn Leifr was awake, ready to depart. He heard Raudbjorn shuffling about outside and the squeaky whines of the hounds stretching and yawning. No one else in the house was stirring yet, so Leifr let himself out quietly onto the porch. The first thing that greeted his sight was the severed head of a pig lying upon the stepping-stone.

Raudbjorn came around the corner at that moment and froze in midstride, his one eye nearly popping from his head. The troll-hounds growled and sniffed, evidently as astonished as he was. Then they shot away in a silent rush, noses to earth, back fur standing stiffly on end.

Raudbjorn raised his stricken gaze to Leifr. Hoarsely he said, "Pig head not here half a moment ago. Raudbjorn watch and see nothing. Hear nothing. Turned back not even half a moment."

Despite himself, Leifr felt the hair raise on his neck as if a cool wind were blowing on him. Gruffly he said, "Just take it and throw it in the river. They're good at fancy tricks and frightening people, it seems. But I'll withhold my judgment until I meet the Ulf-hedin in a real fight. Then we'll see if they're as clever as their tricks, after we count the loose heads and spilled guts."

Chapter 16

❖❖❖❖❖❖❖❖❖❖❖❖❖❖❖❖❖❖❖❖❖❖❖❖❖❖❖❖❖❖❖

Svanlaug could scarcely wait to put Haeta-fell behind her. When it was out of sight, she began to breathe more deeply and let the wind flow through her unconfined hair.

"I'm going home!" she said with greater cheer than Leifr had ever witnessed in her. "What a good feeling it is! I can't wait to see Bergmal again and all my clan sisters. You never know what you'll miss until you leave it behind."

To Leifr's consternation Svanlaug abandoned the road almost immediately and struck off into the gray wilderness of scrubby thickets and skarps of stone.

"We're taking a shortcut," she said, and at those ominous words Leifr's heart contracted and sank. "Now don't scowl like that," she hastened to add. "It's a well-marked trail and I came this way from Bergmal."

"Why isn't there a path then?" Leifr demanded suspiciously. "And what's this place called? Usually one can learn much from the names."

"It's called Ormur-rike," Svanlaug replied. "Certain times of the year there are a lot of snakes, so people have always avoided settling here."

"When is snake season?" Leifr asked, still wary.

Svanlaug waved his question aside with airy contempt. "Oh, the worst of it is in midsummer, when the cloud layer is at its thinnest and things are getting dry. They hang about in the high peaks and skarps sunning themselves, so we don't need to worry about them, especially since it's not midsummer yet. You're not really worried about a few snakes, are you?"

Leifr scanned the landscape. It looked fairly marshy in the low places, the kind of terrain snakes seemed to prefer. "I'd hate to lose one of our horses from snakebite," he said. "We have only one extra, and he's carrying most of the provisions."

Svanlaug smothered a smile behind her hand. "I assure you, these snakes don't bite horses on the fetlocks—if you're a bit careful."

Leifr stared at her back as she rode ahead and wondered why he failed to feel reassured about riding into a place called Ormur-rike. Snake figures were supposed to bring good luck to houses and ships, but he had never cared for the creatures.

By the end of the second day into the flat and virtually featureless Ormur-rike, Leifr still had seen no snakes, so his worries began to abate. His opinion of the Dokkalfar realm and its dark climate did not improve, especially when it began to rain in the night. The following morning was as dank and dreary a day as he had ever seen, with a low ceiling of boiling black clouds crowning the tops of the fells and filling the valleys between with blue mist.

Svanlaug, on the other hand, was exhilarated by the chill wind and the brooding atmosphere. "One of the last fine days before summer, I fear," she said cheerfully, raising her eyes to the sinister black clouds. "Soon you Ljosalfar will get even with us for Fantur's winter rising. Our realm dries out and becomes hot and intolerable, and we have to take refuge from the angry sun."

"At least you have light to see by during your bad season," Starkad retorted, huddling next to the fire in a rumpled and disheveled condition. "I wonder if I'll ever stop shivering."

Thurid held a cup of tea in one hand, with his staff across his knees, glowing and spitting clouds of vapor from the confines of its hood. "This black cloud above us is no ordinary cloud," he said with a scowl. "It's an elemental creature, like the frost giants. The returning strength of the sun is what drives it back to its lair every summer. If it could be persuaded to stay, by means of discouraging the return of the sun to the zenith of the sky, then the Dokkalfar would have perpetual winter—the Fimbul Winter. It is a long and dearly held hope of the Dokkalfar." Turning to Svanlaug, he queried, "This is the objective of your Council of Thirteen, is it not?"

Svanlaug nodded. "And they are too strong to oppose," she said bitterly. "At least by ordinary means. But they have some powerful enemies now. You, Thurid, with that blue crystal, and you, Leifr, with the Rhbu sword—and yes, you too, Gedvondur.''

Gedvondur clambered onto Thurid's shoulder and spoke through Thurid. ''Yes, and as long as I'm here, no one can call us short-handed.'' He added a mirthful guffaw before Thurid plucked him off and tossed him into his satchel.

''Thank you,'' Svanlaug continued. ''My father told me the great secrets of the Council before he died, knowing he was doomed himself, but hoping I could help. Actually, he was hoping that a son of mine might one day come forth to smash the Council and their Pentacle. I saw no sense in waiting that long. It appears that I was guided by a kindly fate to cross your paths.''

''Kindly fate,'' Thurid grumped. ''I doubt there is such a thing. Fate didn't do much for Fridmarr, did it?''

''What great secrets did Afgang tell you before he died, Svanlaug?'' Leifr asked. ''We're not going against the Dokkur Lavardur and the Council without knowing all we can.''

''You shall know, as soon as I get you to a safe place for the telling,'' Svanlaug said. ''At Bergmal.''

Raudbjorn, standing guard atop the small knoll above their encampment, suddenly hooted a soft warning. The troll-hounds came slinking down the knoll to surround Leifr, whining and growling worriedly, gazing toward the southwest. A scrubby copse surrounded a small pool where a spring surfaced. Leifr had wanted to camp near there the previous day, but Svanlaug had criticized the place as too marshy, preying upon Leifr's aversion to snakes.

Suddenly a harsh, braying sound rose from the area around the pool and copse, as if a large horn was being blasted upon very inexpertly. At once Svanlaug leaped to her feet, cursing under her breath as she hastily examined the sky and began smothering the fire.

''Get ready for a quick departure!'' she cried. ''It seems we don't have Ormur-rike all to ourselves after all!''

They saddled the horses, but Svanlaug insisted they lay low in a brushy gully. Leifr was not reconciled to the idea until Raudbjorn grunted and nodded his head.

"Wait and see how many," he rumbled. "Then attack and kill. Good thief-taker way."

Another loud braying blast sounded from the north almost as soon as he had spoken, and Leifr cast him a reproachful glance. "Now we're caught in between. We'll have to change our position before we're cut to ribbons."

"No, don't move," Svanlaug whispered.

An answering honking came from the copse.

"We've got to move," Leifr hissed.

"No, we'll stay right here," Thurid said nervously, wrapping another bag around the blue orb. The first one had charred and crumbled away from the heat. The orb blazed and flickered sullenly, trickling streamers of acrid smoke. "We're in a pretty good position. If we charge out defensively, they may see no option but to attack us."

As he spoke, a roaring of wind began north of them. Leifr crouched down, expecting a sorcerous attack, but the thing that rose up from a neighboring ravine was even more astonishing than any wizard magic Leifr had yet seen. It was like an enormous bird, but more like a snake, with a broad-keeled body exactly like a longboat. A long, sinuous neck was stretched out before, bobbing with each mighty flap of the creature's saillike wings, and a tail with a vicious-looking barb on the end trailed behind.

It passed directly overhead, low enough that its mighty wings kicked up a hurricane of wind. Flattening himself on the ground, Leifr gazed up in fascinated horror at the armor-plated hulk gliding overhead, with the clawed forelegs tucked against the scaly chest, followed by the mighty hind legs, stretched out on either side like outriggers for balance. The creature was so near he thought it was going to land on their hilltop in the midst of them; but, after hovering a moment, perhaps attracted by the plunging and squealing of the horses, it uttered a deafening honk and flapped on, toward the copse.

From Leifr's perspective, it looked exactly like a longboat with the leathery wings of a monstrous bat. It glided to a perch on a rock overlooking the water, holding its wings warily half spread as it bellowed again. Leifr got up from his belly flop in the mud and stared, still half disbelieving what he had seen.

Thurid chuckled dryly. "This is the type of snake most often found in Ormur-rike, am I correct, Svanlaug? No one comes through here because this is the dragons' breeding ground!"

"It's early yet," Svanlaug protested. "In another month when it's hotter, they'll be here in swarms. Then they lay their eggs in the rocky peaks where it's hottest. I'd never dream of coming across here then!"

"But there's a dragon," Thurid snapped. "And from the sounds, there's another in those thickets."

Svanlaug shook her head. "It's dragon hunters. They called this one out of hiding. Dragons get lonely hiding in their solitary caves. It's almost their mating season. This is the time of year when the hunters call them out, one by one, and kill them."

"Kill them!" Starkad exclaimed, his eyes alight with the hope of adventure. "How on earth do they kill a creature the size of a ship?"

"I don't think this is a healthy spot to be in, if they're going to provoke a dragon," Leifr began, but he wasn't able to finish his protest.

The dragon suddenly took to the air with a harsh scream, flapping mightily to gain altitude, coming straight toward their hilltop again. A thunderous report followed, and the dragon's flight skewed suddenly as a gaping rent appeared in one wing. Something thudded into the hill not far from their camp, still smoking after the impact.

The dragon hunters burst from their cover, charging after the wounded dragon. It coasted to the ground awkwardly with its tattered wing and turned to fight with a mighty raking of claws and lashing of its tail, rending the air with a piercing battle cry. Stretching out its long spiked neck, it emitted a blast of fire that seared the soggy ground and set it to steaming balefully.

"They'll never get near enough to kill it," Leifr scoffed. "They'll get roasted alive. No arrow can pierce those scales."

"Watch and see," Svanlaug said. "They have weapons from far places."

The dragon hunters stopped and scurried around, setting up a peculiar piece of equipment, which rolled along on wheels behind a horse with a hood tied over his head to blind him. After a moment the device lurched as it exploded with a roar and a cloud of smoke.

"They've destroyed themselves!" Leifr gasped, but Svanlaug pointed grimly toward the dragon.

The great creature reared onto its hind legs, clawing and uttering a choking cry. A gaping wound in its chest spewed black blood, and the explosion had torn away many of its armored scales. Dying but still fierce, it advanced upon its attackers, snorting gouts of sputtering flame. The dragon hunters retreated, circling their prey until the wounded beast at last collapsed on its side, gasping its last. Then they moved in with a triumphant yell and with axes severed the head from the carcass while two of them stood guard, scanning the sky in case other dragons came to avenge the death of their companion.

Since no assistance seemed forthcoming, two of the dragon hunters commenced chopping a hole in the dragon's skull, while another enlarged the hole in its chest. In a moment he had found the dragon's heart. Bloody to the elbows, he held it up with a speech of some sort before wrapping it up with care.

"What are they doing?" Starkad demanded. "Don't they care about the rest of the meat or anything?"

"Dragons' hearts, if properly cured by the proper person," Thurid said, "are thought by some to assist in foreseeing the future."

Gedvondur scrambled hastily onto Thurid's shoulder, saying "The smallest shred or sliver of cured heart is worth one of your wretched farms and a herd of livestock to go with it and countless yards of cloth. Wouldn't you like to follow those dragon hunters and find out who they sell that raw heart to? We'd have a glimpse of the future!"

"No indeed," Thurid snapped. "I'm as anxious as you are to find your proper carcass, so it's Hringurhol or nothing, my friend."

"How does one get to be a dragon hunter?" Starkad persisted with great interest.

Svanlaug laughed softly. "In this realm you have to be born to the trade, with one or both parents who are dragon hunters. I might add that the dragons don't lose the battle every time. A great many more dragon hunters are lost than dragons. And it's not looked upon as one of the nicer lines of work to be in, although some hunters make a lot of money at it. All they really want is its carbuncle. It's the third eye in a dragon's forehead. You know how valuable carbuncles are. Well, dragon's carbuncles especially are loaded with potent magic, and wizards will pay dearly for even a small one. This one will fetch a nice price. It's a large old dragon, but not one of the largest or oldest. There are bigger stones than this one will yield.'' She cast Thurid an odd, covetous glance, with barely veiled excitement sparkling in her gaze.

Thurid stood immobile as the knowledge dawned upon him. Slowly he unwrapped Heldur's blue orb and looked at it, bound in its claw of gold and silver.

"This is a dragon's carbuncle," he said. "A very large and very old one."

"And very powerful," Gedvondur said, gripping his wrist. "When this carbuncle was obtained from its rightful owner long ago, there were no powerful weapons for blasting a dragon to death from a convenient distance. This one had to be caught and defeated by sorcery. Do you wonder now why the Dokkur Lavardur requires it, why the Council wanted Djofull and Sorkvir to get it, and why I helped you to get it first?"

Thurid pinched his nether lip in profound abstraction, his thoughts obviously scuttling in several directions, all of which seemed distressing to him. His troubled gaze fell upon Leifr. "We're being used," he said.

"I know," Leifr replied. "I told you at Ulfskrittinn not to keep that severed hand, didn't I?"

Thurid snorted indignantly and began, "If you hadn't been so eager to strike up a friendship with Fridmarr in that Scipling barrow field—" but Gedvondur's voice interrupted, "Your troubles began long before that. Long, long before."

The dragon hunters finished up their gory business. One of them held aloft a stone with a greenish flash before wrapping it carefully and putting it away in a pouch. Then they trundled their killing machine away without a backward glance at the fabled creature they had killed.

"Isn't this going to cause a dearth of dragons one day?" Starkad inquired. "They never were plentiful."

"It takes three thousand years for a dragon to grow to the size of this one," Svanlaug replied. "When they mate, they mate for life, returning to find each other every five hundred years in Ormur-rike. A clutch of eggs may contain as many as four, but one is most common. Young dragons also possess small carbuncles, and they have always been easier prey than the big ones. Dragons' eggs are even considered a great delicacy. I predict that within another hundred years, all the dragons will be destroyed, except for perhaps a very few wise old ones who don't ever come out of their caves. There will be no eggs and no nestlings."

Thurid gripped his staff and led the way down the hill to stand beside the massive creature. Starkad skirted it eagerly, venturing to touch its scales and claws, until some long-delayed reaction made its barbed tail twitch.

"Get away from there, Starkad!" Thurid commanded. "There's still enough venom in that barb to kill ten horses!"

After a moment of standing in silent contemplation, Thurid said heavily, "The ancient knowledge and ancient powers of the dragon, or lingorm, has eluded mankind's prying since we were first able to begin coveting them. Who and what the dragons are is a mystery still, and always will be, particularly if they are destroyed before we understand them. A great pity, that."

As they rode away from the site of the battle, Leifr looked back often at the dragon's hulk. He felt a strange sense of loss, as if something greater than its assassins had been senselessly destroyed.

Another two days of traveling revealed no more fresh signs of dragons or their hunters. They did see plenty of bones littering the ground near the high crags where the dragons nested and sunned themselves in the summer, but most of the bones were years old.

By the end of the second day, they were within sight of Bergmal, a towering fell with its head hidden in the cloud cover. As Svanlaug explained, the cloud usually stayed all summer in the higher reaches, which made it pleasant for retreating from the dangerous midyear heat and light. As they rode farther into the rocky defiles of Bergmal, Leifr gazed around uneasily at the hundreds of hiding places for possible foes, and Raudbjorn likewise rode with his head jutting forward at a listening angle. To Leifr's suspicious dismay, Svanlaug hurried along the faint path at an incautious rate and, worse yet, she even halted her horse on a rocky brow of hill and uttered a piercing cry that set all the echoes to repeating themselves a dozen times.

"That should let them know we're coming," she said.

"Who?" Leifr demanded. "It's not as if we don't have enemies in this realm, Svanlaug."

"We're safe here," she assured him smugly and rode on.

They were starting to cross a wide swale of tall brown grass, an open place with scarcely a rock for protection, when Leifr saw trouble approaching. A knot of horsemen came out of a ravine at a gallop, moving with deliberate purpose toward them. From the dull metal flashes of weapons and harness, Leifr knew he was looking at warriors, and there were at least ten of them.

He and Raudbjorn brought their horses to a plunging halt at the same moment, stopping Thurid and Starkad behind them. Svanlaug stopped also to glare back at them, motioning impatiently, as if she had not seen the warriors. Then she turned her back to them and resumed her progress. By this time the riders were almost upon them and burst suddenly over the crest of a small knoll, pouring down the slope to surround their party completely with a ferocious outcry. They were well armed, and kept their small, fast horses in constant motion and themselves obfuscated in swirling cloaks. Leifr glimpsed well-honed weapons, hair worn long in the berserker fashion, and helmets fancifully formed with animal faces, horns, and wings.

Then a different shout rang out. "Halloa! It's Svanlaug!"

The riders halted their weaving and threatening at once and sat still to stare, raising visors of helmets or taking them off completely to see better. Leifr was shocked to realize that they were all women, ranging in age from their gray-haired leader to young girls not even as old as Starkad.

"Girda!" Svanlaug exclaimed. "I'm really home! You're as vigilant as ever! What's gone on since I've been away?"

"A lot of talk about you," Girda replied, a smile brightening her wrinkled countenance, which was permanently creased across her brow from a lifetime of wearing a helmet. "Who are these men with you? Prisoners, I suppose, my lady warrior?"

"Friends," Svanlaug answered, "and our only hope."

"We can always use some hope," Girda said agreeably. "Especially since your leave-taking caused such a furor."

"Are my mother and grandmother still angry?" Svanlaug asked, with a trace of trepidation in her tone.

"Not much anymore. They grieved for a while, thinking you must be dead, but then we heard the word that you had returned to Skaela-fell with some men. Now they're concerned about the future of your unborn children, with a renegade for a mother and who knows what for a father."

"Nonsense!" Svanlaug snorted. "Nothing has changed. I merely went to avenge the death of my father, and now I'm returning, successful in my attempt, and bringing with me the destruction of the Council of Threttan and the defeat of the Dokkur Lavardur. I should think someone would be glad to greet me for those reasons."

"To be sure, they will. But you have damaged your reputation severely by going off as a warrior would to do a warrior's business. I would have gone for you, or any of these others."

"You needn't lecture me, Girda. I'm sure I'll hear plenty of it when I get home."

Leifr glanced at Raudbjorn to see how he was taking it all in. The Norskur sat clutching his halberd, his face drawn up in an incredulous stare that added two new rows of wrinkles above his greatly elevated brow.

"Women?" he muttered to himself. "Warriors?"

Girda and her warriors nodded to their guests politely and rode alongside them in a double row.

"You did do very well," Girda said to Svanlaug, "especially for one who was not born to her task. I don't know where such courage came from in your lines, unless there was some rogue warrior thrown in somewhere that your pedigree is not admitting to."

"I assure you," Svanlaug snapped haughtily, "that my pedigree is a spotless list of healers and physicians and herbalists back to the day of the Alfather's Dispersal of the Thirteen Tribes. My grandmother will tell you the same, as will the Tjaldi, and no one will quarrel with her."

"But someone might quarrel with Thorbjorg," Girda said.

"Bah! What do I care for matchmakers' opinions?"

"One day you might care a great deal, if Thorbjorg can find no match for you because of this adventure of yours. It doesn't look good, child. It looks as if your line must be faulty somewhere, even when it's not. At the very least, a possible mate's brother-kin may think you're just a very slight bit insane."

Svanlaug glared at the older woman riding beside her. "Then perhaps I shall become one of your warriors, if no other life is suitable for me any longer."

"I won't have you," Girda said cheerfully. "How could I? There's not a warrior evident in your entire pedigree."

"What about individual natural propensity?" Svanlaug argued. "Perhaps I'm better suited as a warrior."

"No one has agreed that such a thing as propensity exists," Girda answered. "For centuries we have believed in nothing but heredity. We've had some interesting arguments while you were gone, Svanlaug. Now they'll start again. It will make the summer so much more interesting, if we're stuck indoors when it's too hot out."

Betraying her fear, Svanlaug became as still and pale as marble when they came into view of the encampment of Bergmal. Instead of a permanent settlement such as Leifr was accustomed to, about twenty round tents made of hides were arranged in tidy concentric rings around a large, smoke-blackened central tent. Horses, goats, sheep, and cattle were tethered near the tents of their owners, penned with hurdles in the case of some mottled sheep being sheared, or attended by their herders on the sides of nearby fells. Smoke rising from the tents had tinted them varying shades of brown and gray over the years, but none were as black as the large tent in the center, where a number of women seemed to be waiting to go in.

As the riders approached the village, word of their advent spread before them like ripples in a pool, and more heads appeared in doorways of tents, and more figures hurried back and forth, carrying the news. A dozen small children in short skirts and trollskin boots followed at the heels of the horses, chattering in great excitement. The procession halted at the black tent, where a tall woman dressed in black robes stood waiting. She nodded slightly to Svanlaug, and her eyes rested upon the strangers in a cool stare. Leifr also stared, before he recalled his manners and looked away. As well as being dressed in black, her skin and hair were black as ebony, and even her eyes were solid black, with very little white to them. To Leifr it was strange and beautiful, since the skin of most Dokkalfar was as pale as frog's belly flesh from lack of exposure to light.

"Tjaldi wishes to see you now," the black woman greeted Svanlaug, including the strangers with a slight nod.

"Thank you, Ulfrin," Svanlaug said. "How is our mother's health? I've worried since I left."

"Then you shouldn't have left, if it was such a matter of concern to you," Ulfrin said coldly. "What a blot you've put upon our name!"

Turning quickly, Ulfrin led the way into the tent before Svanlaug could reply.

The hearthstone stood in the center of the tent, and sitting places were arranged on two sides of it. A large chair stood within its circle of light, whereon sat the small upright figure of an aged woman, gazing at the newcomers with the alertness a hawk might bestow upon a mouse. A table stood at her elbow, and it was stacked with small, elaborately carved boxes, each one different, and each worn to glossy black smoothness by much handling.

"So here you are, wayward child," the old woman greeted Svanlaug with snapping eyes. "Your Tjaldi has been very worried about you. How could you go off without a word to me or your mother and grandmother and sister?"

"I'm sorry, Tjaldi, I did wrong," Svanlaug replied with humility heretofore unsuspected. "But I was driven to it by a force I could not withstand."

"Obviously, or you wouldn't have done it," replied the Tjaldi, tapping her yellowed nails on the arm of her chair. "Who are these strange men you're traveling with? That too is forbidden, as well you know."

Thurid took a step forward, executing a courtly bow. "If I may be permitted to introduce myself, I am Thurid, a wizard of Dallir, bent upon business with the Council of Threttan. These warriors are my defenders, Leifr and Raudbjorn, and this unlikely lad will one day be my apprentice, if he's lucky enough to survive and be found fit to continue his studies of powers and practices. We owe a great debt to Svanlaug for helping us out of several very unpleasant situations with mutual enemies, and I might add that we have a benevolent concern for her welfare and are most willing and able to help her in continuing the work her father set her to do before his untimely death at the hands of his trusted associates—assuming of course that we have the generous blessing from your exalted hands, which we naturally require in order to proceed."

The little Tjaldi gazed upon Thurid in his magnificent clothing and listened to his fine speech as if he were putting on a spectacle for her benefit.

"Is this what passes for a wizard nowadays?" she demanded of a woman standing beside her chair. To Thurid she said, "Young man, what tribe do you hail from? Remind me never to allow any marriages with it, whatever it may be."

Thurid stiffened with wounded dignity. "I am proud to say I am from the tribe of Forvitinn the Curious."

The Tjaldi uttered a predatory cry of delight. "Forvitinn, you say? A Ljosalfar, from one of the lost tribes? Thorbjorg, Thorbjorg! This is the opportunity of a lifetime to examine the lines of a Forvitinn! Young man, nothing would delight me more than to hear you recite your lineage, and perhaps one of my scribes might take it down for my collection." She waved one hand toward the table and the boxes. "The history of this clan lies on scrolls in those caskets. It is the pedigree of every woman living here, and many who died without heirs, and many other curious things that I hope to add your history to."

"It would be my extreme pleasure to make myself agreeable in any small way," Thurid replied with another sweeping bow. "But I wish to question your assumption that Forvitinn is one of the lost tribes. Is it not more sensible to assume that the Sciplings comprise the ones who are lost? Leifr here is a Scipling. Inquire of him his pedigree, and I daresay you will see what I mean."

"Scipling!" the Tjaldi cried, her black eyes boring into Leifr. "I am delighted to make your acquaintance! This is a rare day for a genealogist, I assure you. Tell me your lines, my friend. Father and mother."

Leifr drew a deep breath. "My father is Thorljott, his father was Thorgnir, his father was Thorrir, his father was Thorgautr, and beyond that no one can remember."

"What! No one remembers?" The Tjaldi fell back, appalled. "Your ancestors are all lost and forgotten?"

"I fear so," Leifr said, feeling unaccountably guilty, as if all those lost ancestors were accusing him. "There have been fires and wars and shipwrecks, and I doubt if anyone actually wrote the names down. No one knew how."

"Sciplings are a reckless lot," Thurid explained by way of apology. "If there were records, they have been destroyed in constant upheavals. They are so far lost that no one recalls the Alfather or the Dispersal of the Thirteen Sons."

"I am deeply shocked," the Tjaldi said, shaking her head. "But delighted actually to find one of the lost ones. Your tribe is named Rafar, or the Wanderer, and your ancestors have indeed wandered far if they have forgotten who they are."

"Rafar," Leifr repeated, feeling an old thrill of something that might have been recognition. "How can you be so certain about my ancestors?"

"Every man on earth devolves from the Thirteen Tribes," the Tjaldi said with firm conviction. "Even that Norskur. His people are known as the Skortur—the lacking ones. They are one of the lost tribes, too. There's not enough wits among them to keep the proper records, I fear."

"So we are called lost tribes because we don't keep records?" Leifr asked.

"Partly, but mostly because you don't try to keep your lines of profession straight. My tribe is Audur, and my mother's side descends from the third wife of Audur, and she was the genealogist for the tribe. On my father's side, every one of his ancestors was a genealogist for the brother-clans, so you see I am well fitted for my profession, and I have two daughters and a son who are genealogists. Your ancestors, I daresay, are a hodgepodge, brought together by chance or convenience or random choice, so how can you be expected to know who and what you are, with so many different heritages warring in your veins? I sensed your confusion the moment you came into my tent."

"Then Sciplings and Alfar are somehow related?" Leifr

questioned. "We are all descended from the thirteen sons of the Alfather?"

The Tjaldi nodded emphatically. "Of course. Why do you think we appear so similar? Time has wrought changes, of course. The tribes who call themselves Dokkalfar have chosen the night, and the ones who have chosen the day are called Ljosalfar. Little was known of you lost ones—Rafar, Skortur, Thrarr the Stubborn, Bardagi the Fighter. They scattered far and wide, and some of them have come back calling themselves Sciplings. Short-lived, lacking the powers that were your heritage, you see what your ancestors' carelessness has cost you. Had they not strayed and forgotten the old ways, you would have been either Ljosalfar or Dokkalfar, my lad."

"Is there not another lost one that you haven't mentioned?" Thurid inquired. "His name was Rhbu, and he was the eldest son of the Alfather. Audur, his brother next, robbed him of his heritage and drove him out."

"The Rhbus are almost gone," the Tjaldi said in a regretful voice. "They were enemies of the Dokkalfar tribes, but they were still our kin."

"Perhaps one day the Rhbus will return to claim their birthright," Thurid suggested.

"Perhaps indeed, if they get the proper help," the Tjaldi replied, sinking back in the cushions of her chair. "I fear this excitement has worn me out. We'll have to continue this interview tomorrow after I've rested. I'm not finished with you, Svanlaug, so you needn't think I'm letting you off easy—as if I would ever do such a thing to anybody under my leadership."

"Yes, my Tjaldi," Svanlaug said meekly.

As the guests left the Tjaldi's tent, Ulfrin darted Svanlaug a venomous smirk of satisfaction. "I know it must be difficult, being the elder sister of a Sverting," she said in silky tones. "But one day, Svanlaug, you'll simply have to stop competing and admit you're lacking my gifts. You could have destroyed yourself, trying to prove you're better, when you never, ever can be."

Svanlaug turned a cold and hostile stare upon her sister. "I've proved what I wanted to prove, dear sister."

Then she stalked away with a toss of her raven hair, saying

over her shoulder to Leifr, "I'll show you to the guest tent and you can stow your gear. Then we'll go meet my mother. She's nicer than either of her daughters."

Chapter 17

✦✦✦✦✦✦✦✦✦✦✦✦✦✦✦✦✦✦✦✦✦✦✦✦✦✦✦✦

"What was that row about with your sister?" Leifr asked of Svanlaug, after she had shown them the guest tent and was on the way to her mother's tent. "And why is she so black?"

Svanlaug smiled wryly. "You've answered your first question with your second," she said, and added a patient sigh and a twitch of her shoulders. "Once every ten generations or so, a Dokkalfar is born completely black. It's a sign of great favor and power. Ulfrin was intended as a healing physician, and her father is such; but the moment she was born, everyone knew she was sent for much higher things. She will be a sorceress, a black sorceress, which is twice as powerful as an ordinary one, when she reaches her full potential. She's been trained by the best wizards, including all the Council of Threttan, but still it's not enough for Ulfrin. She won't be old and gray when she comes into her powers, like most who study magic as a profession. When she comes of age, all knowledge will be given to her. It's her heritage, as some are born to be weavers and some are born to be genealogists or matchmakers. It makes her quite insufferable, as you can plainly see. Great gifts tend to make the recipient rather too sure of himself—or herself. Especially when you're the favorite of all the family. But I can't blame my mother for that."

Thurid's eyes darted nervously from side to side as Svanlaug halted beside the door flap of a tent. "Don't you wish to greet your mother without us present?" he asked. "Some moments shouldn't be shared by outsiders."

"Don't be ridiculous," Svanlaug said. "I'm hoping that the presence of strangers will force my mother to be somewhat civil. She's going to be angry, you know."

251

"Splendid!" Thurid muttered.

Svanlaug entered her mother's tent, motioning the others to follow. Laekna, whose profession was healing physician, was attending to a small boy-child of about six years who was sporting a virulent-looking rash all over his chest and stomach. His mother looked on with anxious hope while Laekna ground something to a paste with mortar and pestle, releasing a potent aroma into the already pungent atmosphere of the tent.

Laekna looked up, preoccupied, and recognized Svanlaug. "There you are at last," she said with mild reproach, as if Svanlaug had merely taken the day off from her duties, instead of a year and a half. "This little fellow has eaten quite the wrong thing and you can see how it has disagreed with him. I've given him a tea of fjallagross roots and this poultice of eel grass, stonewort, and goose grease will ease the itching. There now, young Bensi, you'll be all right, but I advise you to stay away from those berries, no matter how pretty they look. They disagree with many people this time of year. You must let me know how these spots look in two days, Thryni."

The mother and child departed, and Laekna directed Svanlaug to clean up her tools and wash out her mortar, motioning her guests to sit down. The chairs were low round seats hewn from the stumps of trees and painted with fanciful designs. Laekna gazed at them all, and at the imposing bulk of Raudbjorn blocking the doorway outside, where he attracted quite a ring of curious children and suspicious dogs.

"I never expected to see my eldest daughter again," she greeted them affably. "I thank you for returning her safe to me, although it is rather humiliating for strangers to be forced to retrieve a runaway child. However, her father and older brother are dead, and her two younger brothers are still under the care of their fathers and too young."

Thurid's eyes, darting avariciously around the tent, came back to rest upon Laekna in some surprise. "My lady, I assure you that it is Svanlaug who has brought us here, not we her. She is most capable of defending herself, a very canny and skillful young person indeed."

Svanlaug's eyes flashed, but her voice was mild when she

spoke. "I'm not a child any longer, Modir. I have learned to trust myself, as well as these companions."

"Yes, and while you were learning it, I was left with the burden of the cuts and scratches and fevers and sick livestock," her mother retorted. In a more pleasant voice she addressed Thurid. "You must excuse me for speaking plainly to my daughter, but she's in need of a mother's scolding right now. You may think we're quarreling, but I wouldn't be angry at a person I had no love for. In a settlement of tents, there's no sense in trying to hide your disputes. We are all family, and everyone's business is everyone else's."

"Go right ahead," Thurid advised her in a courtly manner. "I'd do exactly the same thing, were I you."

"I'm sorry about leaving without telling you what I was doing, but I had to go," Svanlaug interjected, with a glare at Thurid. "If I had tried to tell you, you would have locked me up."

"Are you your father's son, or are you my daughter?" Laekna snapped back. "If you were a boy and honor-bound to avenge the deaths and wrongs of our family, I would have put you into trousers and boots when you were eight years old and sent you to Afgang, instead of trying to teach you to be an herbalist and physician. This deed will haunt you forever, child. It may even prevent Thorbjorg from ever finding you any suitable fathers for your children. No respectable man will want to risk possibly breeding a wild streak into his sons and daughters. I don't know who to blame, Afgang's ancestors or mine. I've had the Tjaldi going over both our pedigrees and researching the histories of every name, but none of them have rebelled against their heritage the way you have. I think it is nothing short of bad blood, Svanlaug."

"Bad blood? Am I to be exiled then?" Svanlaug inquired with an arrogant toss of her head and with cool scorn in her voice. "In the old days, infants with bad blood were exposed to die, but I'm rather old for that. Maybe I'll be sold as a thrall, to keep kitchen for some cow herder."

"I don't think you'll be sold," Laekna said. "Perhaps if you spend a few years working hard, you can pass it all off as a temporary delusion, if you're very careful."

"Perhaps I don't want to," Svanlaug retorted. "My father's work is not yet finished. Why do you think I've brought back warriors and a wizard with me, Mother?"

Laekna's eyes dwelt upon Leifr, Thurid, and Starkad speculatively. "Svanlaug, go to the cooking tent and tell Asta I wish to feed four guests. But not the boiled mutton, tell her. She baked today, so there should be some new bread, if that pig Jora didn't take it all."

Svanlaug stood up. "You wish to talk about me while I am gone, don't you, Modir?"

"Of course, Dottir, so hurry yourself. You might also put on a gown and apron for our guests like a proper woman, instead of dressing like a man."

"These are my friends and equals," Svanlaug said indignantly. "Not someone I need to dress up for."

When she was gone, Laekna sighed and spread out her hands in a hopeless gesture of entreaty. "What would you do with a child such as that?" she implored Thurid. "You are a man of age and wisdom. What should I do with her? She's as hard as stone, not the least bit malleable."

"I'm a wizard, not a parent," Thurid said. "I'm sadly unqualified to advise you. But I spent many years as a teacher of young children. I have seen a few headstrong ones who learn only by painful experience. If they are strong enough to endure the constant pain of discovery, they will be excellent leaders one day. But if they can't endure the pain, they turn into paths of weakness and cruelty."

"And which way will my daughter take?" Laekna asked.

Thurid inhaled a deep breath and held it a moment as he considered, his brows drawing together in a scowl. "She has made mistakes," he said finally. "She has a devious nature, I fear. But with the proper instruction, she may learn how to work with people, instead of using them as stepping-stones to take her where she wishes to go. I don't believe you can force her into your mold, Laekna, and the forcing will make her bitter. She has useful work to do, even if she doesn't become a physician."

"You Ljosalfar are kind and wise," Laekna said, nodding her head slowly. "But I can't get accustomed to the idea that you allow your young ones to decide for themselves what they will do with their lives. It's a dangerous business.''

"Yes, freedom usually is risky," Thurid replied. "There's much responsibility, and individuals vary so greatly."

"We don't think about individuals here," Laekna said with a thoughtful frown. "A single clan is about as small a measure of Dokkalfar as you can get. It's hurtful to think that Svanlaug wishes to abandon the claims of clan and tribe and heritage to go off on her own. For a Dokkalfar, true loneliness is to be without one's own kind."

"Yet your realm is changing," Thurid said.

"Yes, the men are destroying many of our most ancient and dearly held traditions," Laekna flared, her eyes kindling at once. "As usual, they are causing all manner of mischief and grief with their lust for plunder and wealth. Soon only the women will maintain the clanships, but if the men don't honor their heritage, soon there will be nothing but confusion. The Council is doing bloody little to put a stop to it. All they can do is quarrel among themselves, which is how Svanlaug's father got himself killed."

"He stood in opposition to what the Council wishes to do?" Thurid queried gently.

"He wanted to dissolve the Council," Laekna retorted. "And I suppose Svanlaug thinks she can do the same, now she's got a wizard and some warriors to help her. The Tjaldi does not find all this the least bit amusing, I can assure you. We haven't heard the last of her concerning Svanlaug's antics, I fear."

Svanlaug returned at this juncture. "Asta is preparing us a worthy feed," she said, sitting down on the same side of the fire as the strangers. "She still uses an appalling amount of grease in everything, though. Thurid, I trust my mother has filled your ears with tales of what an undutiful daughter I am, and I hereby confess that everything she says is likely to be true."

"We were merely chatting pleasantly to pass the time," Thurid said. "It's been long indeed since we were treated to this sort of hospitality."

Starkad opened his mouth and involuntarily added what he

must have been thinking: "Not at all what we expected to find in the Dokkalfar realm."

Laekna chuckled rather darkly. "And you are not what I expected of Ljosalfar. I confess, when I heard that my daughter had returned with three day-farers, and one of them a wizard, I expected the sort of outlaw Ljosalfar who always hang about the village waiting to be hired for some scurrilous purpose."

"Modir, your opinion of my intelligence is apparent," Svanlaug snapped acidly. "These Ljosalfar would have been here even had I never encountered them. They're not mere hirelings. Besides, I have no gold to pay them with."

Laekna's gaze sharpened as she studied her guests. "Then you have business of your own with the Council of Threttan and the Dokkur Lavardur. I don't like the sound of that, particularly where my daughter is concerned."

"I intend to go with them," Svanlaug said. "I must continue in the purpose my father started."

"It's not enough that you've sought out Djofull for your revenge and lived to return?" Laekna demanded. "How long do you think your luck will hold out, child?"

"Long enough," Svanlaug said. "I didn't know you relished the idea of returning to the ice and darkness of the Fimbul Winter, Modir. It would mean the death of all our livestock and returning to the caves underground. The Council of Threttan is a group of old atavists who want to dictate the way all the rest of us will live. I don't want to live underground, nor do I want to be an ice-wanderer above, living off whales and seals."

"Surely the Fimbul Winter wouldn't be as bad as all that," Laekna said, beckoning to a serving woman to bring in the food and drink. "It would merely keep the summer sun covered so we could go out without wrappings, and we'd have plenty of rain to keep the land from drying out. I expect there would be more storms and snow in the high passes, which the traders and sellers wouldn't like, but the Realm has gotten along for centuries without all that business, so we don't really need it. Which reminds me—those are fine and gaudy clothes, daughter. I suppose you got them in Skaela-fell, or Haeta-fell? Couldn't you have chosen something a bit more in keeping with your solemn profession, and the dignity of your sister-clan?"

So the evening passed, with mother and daughter subtly baiting and barbing each other, until a suitable hour for bedtime had arrived, and Svanlaug was glad to make an escape to escort the guests to their tent. Leifr was surprised to observe that most of the encampment was settling down to sleep for the night, except for the warriors who were standing guard.

"Our livestock are not night-farers," Svanlaug explained, "and much of our lives revolves around attending to the wants of cows and sheep and horses; they don't want to graze at night when they can't see what they're eating. Besides, night is the time for predators of all kinds, so we leave the night to them and Girda. Isn't it strange that our respective realms have only seen the worst members of the other? Do you think Ljosalfar and Dokkalfar could ever learn to live in peace, side by side?"

"Not as long as outlaws and renegades from both sides take refuge where they do," Thurid answered grimly.

"Nor do I like the sounds of the Council of Threttan," Leifr said. He had kept his silence most of the evening, not wishing to draw attention to his Sciplingness if he didn't have to, although word of it was certain to spread. "Wizards such as that menace both peoples."

Raudbjorn huffed and growled, settling himself down at the door of the tent as if he intended to do some menacing of his own. Suspiciously he glowered at Girda as she passed by on horseback, bristling with weapons.

"Halloa, thief-taker, how's the fighting in the other realm?" she greeted him.

"Too little for Raudbjorn," he grunted in reply, tweaking the edge of his halberd with a musical note.

"Then stay around here," Girda advised him. "The Ulf-hedin will keep you amused. They haven't bothered us much yet, but I suspect it's going to get worse."

The guest tent was situated on the edge of the encampment, slightly apart from the others, and near the place where the horses were tethered for the night. Raudbjorn lurked about the tent watchfully, with the aid of the troll-hounds, and the warriors signaled to each other with the soft hoots of owls Leifr found reassuring. Once, during the night, the alarm of a hawk rang out, and he heard the watchers moving in preparation for something, but nothing came of it. After standing in the doorway of the tent awhile to listen and watch over Raudbjorn's shoulder, Leifr went back to the luxury of sleep in a heap of fleeces and furs.

In the morning, he was awakened by a startled curse from Raudbjorn. Awake instantly, he leaped to the doorway with the sheathed sword in his hand, ready to draw at an instant's notice. He found Raudbjorn standing and glaring about, and on the foot mat of the tent was the severed head of a goat, still so fresh its ears were warm. The troll-hounds dashed up and down with noses to the ground, searching for a scent without success.

Raudbjorn made a sign to ward off evil and touched one of the amulets hanging around his neck.

"Ulf-hedin," he growled uneasily, his one eye revolving around in angry perplexity, searching the predawn gloom for signs of the enemy. "Come like owls, without sound. Walk like spirits, without scent."

Leifr fought down the feeling that his flesh was creeping and all his hair was bristling. "Well, they're gone now," he said gruffly.

Girda's horse came clopping quietly down the avenue between the tents, where people were beginning to stir about for the early-morning work. With a quick intake of breath she halted and dismounted for a cursory inspection of the goat head. Wonderingly she said, "We had the camp surrounded. Nothing could have gotten in—except of course the Ulf-hedin."

"It's us they're looking for," Leifr said grimly. "They gave us a bit of trouble in Skaela-fell. Once we're gone, they'll leave you alone, won't they?"

Girda shrugged. "Who can say? They mark their prey for reasons known only to themselves, sometimes. You've done something to grieve them seriously. By the time they finally move in to kill you, all your supposed friends will be too terrified to defend you. I've heard tales of Ulf-hedin walking right into a hall crowded with armed warriors to take whomever they please."

"They make themselves invisible," added another warrior ho had joined her leader.

'Bah, I don't believe it," Girda replied. "The others are too frightened to act, so they pretend the Ulf-hedin are invisible. That's how powerful these creatures are. No one wants to see them, so they simply don't.''

"But we'll see them, right enough," Leifr growled, "and they'll see *Endalaus Daudi*.''

"Endless Death!'' Girda murmured. "It would be too good for them! But see here, I'm not going to send the four of you off into the barrens against any number of Ulf-hedin. You're safer here with my warriors at your back.''

The flap of the tent gusted open suddenly as Thurid stepped out onto the mat, fastidiously avoiding the bloodstains. He tossed a pair of severed goat legs on the grounds, his hair swirling around his head and his eyes glaring. The muzzled orb sizzled and smoked, already burning a hole in its bag.

"This is not a joke, I see,'' Thurid snorted, with a glower at Starkad, who came bursting unceremoniously through the tent flap, his eyes bulging with excitement. "I found those legs crossed at the foot of my pallet. It seems these Ulf-hedin are issuing us a challenge.''

"The Tjaldi will have to know about this,'' Girda said, and dispatched the other warrior at a run for the black tent. "Even the Ulf-hedin have left her alone so far. No one is more revered than the keeper of the pedigrees, and next after her the matchmaker. But now you see what a pretty pass we're coming to. If something should happen to the Tjaldi and Thorbjorg, the heritage of the entire Audur tribe would be lost.''

They presented themselves at the Tjaldi's tent and were soon ushered inside. The Tjaldi sat upright at her table surrounded by the little caskets as she perused a heap of scrolls, some of them badly yellowed by age. Thorbjorg sat beside her, also reading the names.

"A match between the Hestur and Bryggja clans seems suitable, on first inspection,'' the Tjaldi was saying. "The Bryggja are seafaring people, not too staid and stolid for the fiery horsemen of the Hestur. A possible conflict must be avoided. A boy-child with no desire for excitement and adventure would have a difficult life with his Hestur father. One would never pair a Hestur and a Skrifari. Peaceful scribes and poets should avoid Hestur.''

"I think it a good pairing," Thorbjorg said. "I'll send a messenger back to Thora with the good news."

"It will be a long ride for you to fetch Vedr and take him to Bryggja," said the Tjaldi. "But your bones are a lot younger than mine. When I was matchmaking, nearly every family clan had a matchmaker. We're suffering a great shortage. A pity you had no daughters, only sons."

"Someone will be found. I don't mind the long ride. There's little to do here at Bergmal, unless Svanlaug or Thjokka make up their minds for a husband, and that's not likely. I'm going to put the word out for a couple of suitable little girls who would be my apprentices. It would be a good way for someone's mother to give their daughters a lift in life."

"And possibly break tradition?" the Tjaldi demanded.

"What else are we to do? The tribe must have a Tjaldi and some matchmakers." She looked up at the disturbance at the doorway, frowning slightly as Girda motioned at her frantically. "What is it, Girda?"

"Ulf-hedin," Girda replied. "They want to frighten us into giving up these Ljosalfar. We found a goat head at the door of their tent this morning, and the legs inside."

"Cheeky devils," the Tjaldi said, her eyes flickering with anger. "The Audur tribe are not so easily frightened."

"We'll go," Leifr said. "We can't stay and endanger you any longer."

"Hush, young one, and listen to your elders," the Tjaldi said to him, raising one withered finger in warning. It was flattened and broad at the tip, from many years of running over pedigrees. "We are not a lot of foolish old women, as you are thinking. For a hundred centuries, the women of the tribes have lived thus, taking care of themselves, and we have grown very wise from it. These Ulf-hedin are under an old curse, as old as the Dokkur Lavardur and the moon itself. This is not the first time we have seen it on the face of the land. I know how this curse is spread. Which leads me to suspect that there are Ulf-hedin among the Bergmal clan."

Girda gasped. "Not here among us! Our own sisters, cousins, and aunts? Impossible!"

"Not impossible," the Tjaldi snapped severely. "Perhaps

some of them have been Ulf-hedin for generations and were too clever to give themselves away. It could be a hereditary curse, or it might be something certain people go looking for, or perhaps it is entrapment. But it is almost a certainty that at least one of them is in our midst.''

"And no one can tell?" Thurid demanded. "Aren't there some signs of it? A fear of light, a distaste for water, a fondness for fresh blood?"

"Would that there were such obvious signs," the Tjaldi said. "Nothing is seen of the Ulf-hedin until they act. And then they execute what passes for judgment, and the obstacle to the will of the Council of Threttan is removed. But not swiftly, not obviously, lest the ire of the Dokkalfar be aroused against the Council. No, they are very careful and devious, leading the doomed one farther and farther from any possible help, until nothing remains between the Ulf-hedin and their prey. You, my friends, are in grave danger. You have been led far from your own kind and your native soil."

Leifr was half mesmerized by her grating, crooning voice. He shook his head to stir himself out of her spell, not liking the thoughts that her words were putting into his head. He didn't want to suspect that Svanlaug had led them all the way from the Ljosalfar realm into a most elaborate trap. It would make him and Thurid appear as trusting fools, to have taken the word of a Dokkalfar—and possibly a Dokkalfar under a hideous curse and an axe to grind for the Council of Threttan besides.

The same thoughts were evidently running through Starkad's mind. He nudged Leifr and muttered, "You and Thurid are the worst of all possible threats to the Dokkur Lavardur and the Council. Quite a few people know that. It makes me wonder if someone has allowed us to come so far just to make sure of trapping us. Sorkvir could have stopped us, or at least tried. But where has he gone?"

At that moment Svanlaug herself burst into the tent, her hair falling down her back in an untidy torrent.

"You're safe!" she greeted them. "I saw the warriors on alert, and no one was in your tent. I was afraid of what might have happened."

The Tjaldi raised one finger to her lips in unmistakable warning. "Nothing has happened, Svanlaug. At least, nothing unforeseen."

"The Ulf-hedin have found us again," Svanlaug said. "It's what I expected also. We'll be on our way today, and we'll take the threat with us."

The Tjaldi pursed her lips and hoisted one eyebrow in an astonished scowl, giving her the expression of a startled and untidy owl. "My child, the situation is more serious than you dream. None of you must leave just yet."

"But we're going to Hringurhol," Svanlaug protested. "To challenge them and drive back the Dokkur Lavardur. Surely you must know we can't allow Alfrekar to complete that Pentacle he's building."

"We have a contagion in our midst," Thorbjorg said with dignity. "You wouldn't want to be the cause of its spreading over the land. You must stay here where you're protected somewhat."

Svanlaug paced up and down with short angry strides. "You mean to say that some measling disease of cattle or sheep is going to stop us, after what we've come through? After fights and fylgjur wolves and jotuns, we're going to be stopped by some miserable pustules and yellow rheum on some wretched cow?"

"I hope you'll be stopped," said the voice of Ulfrin as she glided into the tent. "Your Tjaldi is speaking, and it is she who governs your existence. If she says you must stay, then you must stay. If you have any shreds of regard for your upbringing, that is."

Ulfrin took a seat near Thorbjorg in a familiar manner and smiled with cool, benevolent contempt upon Svanlaug lashing about in her temper.

"The longer we stay, the better a target we make for the Ulf-hedin," Svanlaug said. "If Ulf-hedin are following, more will gather, until there's no escape."

The Tjaldi folded her hands, bowing her head slightly and speaking in a sorrowful voice. "The Ulf-hedin are here already, child, among the Bergmal clan. One of us, or more, has turned traitor, willingly or not. It makes no difference. Whoever it is must be found before the waning of the moon. Once these chosen ones leave us, the cursed one will come and go as usual and we might never know who it is until a tragedy strikes like a lightning bolt from a blue sky. It could be any of us in the clan.''

"Or any of us in this tent," Ulfrin said, looking directly at Svanlaug with a challenging glint in her eyes. "Most likely it is someone who has been straying outside the protection of our warriors and our Tjaldi. It's not a pleasant fate to contemplate, being chained up like a mad dog for the rest of one's life, howling and hideous when the transformation comes upon you.''

"Am I the suspected one?" Svanlaug demanded. "I wish I'd never come back to this place. Nothing has changed. I'm still the much-despised Svanlaug who does everything wrong! I always get the blame whenever something happens!''

"Hush!" the Tjaldi said sharply. "No one is blaming anyone. This is something beyond the scope of everyday blaming and accusing. It will do you no good to go rushing at Alfrekar in Hringur-hol. Bide your time until a plan comes into your minds.''

"The Dokkur Lavardur knows we're here," Svanlaug said. "He knows everything we do and say, so what's the sense of waiting and planning, when everything will be told to Alfrekar? Alfrekar is the true murderer of my father. Djofull would not have done it unless Alfrekar told him. None of them move without Alfrekar.''

Ulfrin cut in, "And Alfrekar does what the Dokkur Lavardur tells him. It's quite comical to think that you're attempting to strike out at the Dokkur Lavardur, sister. A puny little woman and these outlanders won't stop him. Nor will the Fire Wizards' Guild with its ridiculous challenge.''

The Tjaldi's weary eyes narrowed, and Thorbjorg's brows knit together in an incredulous frown. The matchmaker demanded, "What challenge? How do you know of such a thing?''

Ulfrin smiled. "It's simply the privilege of the Sverting to know things from afar. I see things that have not yet happened. I know the future, sometimes. Not all of it, of course, only the smallest of glimpses. But one day perhaps I shall be a foreseer— the first prophetess the Bergmal clan has ever boasted.''

"Nothing will be denied you because of your birth," the Tjaldi said in a stern tone, "but the Bergmal clan does not boast over anything, not even the birth of a girl Sverting. And since you have not yet taken your final training in any trade, I beg to remind you that you yet lack professional status, and thus your predictions of the future may not be what you think they are. Until you are a full prophetess or diviner of the future, you must keep these glimpses, if that's what they are, entirely to yourself. Things such as this can cause irreparable harm, no matter how well you intend them.''

Ulfrin subsided with a stricken expression of contrition. ''Yes, of course, Tjaldi. I was foolish,'' she said humbly.

''It isn't easy for anyone to learn, not even you,'' the Tjaldi added in a kinder tone. ''Now I wish to be left alone to think, except for you, Thorbjorg, and you, Thurid. Your wisdom comforts me. Something about you seems so strong and aged, like the wood that becomes stronger and blacker with passing time. It pleases me to think that one of the Lost Ones yet retains so much wisdom. There yet may be hope, instead of all this warring and hatred.''

Outside the tent, where Raudbjorn and the dogs waited suspiciously, Svanlaug and her sister confronted each other with a silent glare of age-old fury born of the earliest childhood memories, both good and bad.

''The Tjaldi told you what your foreseeing is worth,'' Svanlaug said with an insolent sneer. ''It always caused nothing but trouble—mostly for me. Why don't you go finish your training, instead of hiding here with the clan? Are you afraid to leave and become something, as I did?''

Ulfrin tossed her black mane in a manner identical to Svanlaug's. ''Why should I be afraid of anything? And what is it exactly that you have become? You've got nothing more that I can see, except a huge blot upon your reputation, and our names and all the clan by way of association. And now the Tjaldi suspects you of being an Ulf-hedin.''

''She doesn't, and I'm not!'' Svanlaug flared furiously. ''She knows I'm not! I've been too far away from Svert-strom. There are no Ulf-hedin in the Ljosalfar realm. And if what I've done has ruined my reputation in the tribe, I'd do it a hundred times over. At least now I know I'm not going to spend the rest of my life attending sick babies and old women with digestive complaints. I am my father's child, and I'm going to follow his profession."

"You, a sorceress?" Ulfrin snorted. "You're only jealous of me, because I'm going to be a black sorceress!"

Svanlaug whirled and strode away, leaving Leifr and Starkad gazing dubiously at Ulfrin and wishing they were miles away in any direction. Leifr felt her power, waves of it, surrounding her like ocean waves. But he also sensed that it was lacking in purpose as it nudged at him, and he was able to fend it off much more easily than Thurid's deadly darts questing at his thoughts.

"Forgive her," Ulfrin said graciously. "If you've been traveling with her long, you must know by now what a temper she's got. We don't really mean the things we say. It's just that we're sisters. Now since Svanlaug seems to have forgotten her manners again, I propose to take you on a tour of our village and introduce you around. It seems you'll be here for a while, so you should become acquainted."

Leifr dutifully admired it all, his mind seething with unanswered questions throughout the inspection of the Bergmal horses, the sheep, and introductions to a host of Bergmal women of all ages. A crowd of gaping children followed at his heels, and young girls watched and giggled from behind tent flaps. Altogether, it was a peculiar experience. Starkad was enjoying all the attention tremendously, so Leifr left most of the social amenities to him and allowed himself to remain surlily silent.

When they had managed to leave behind their young admirers to climb the fell behind the camp for a better look at the long-fleeced sheep, Leifr bluntly interrupted Ulfrin and Starkad's conversation regarding the peculiar marriage arrangements of the Dokkalfar sister-clans.

"Is it true that the Wizards' Guild has challenged the Council of Threttan?" he demanded in a low voice.

Ulfrin tensed and her eyes darted around nervously. "Yes, it's true," she whispered. "But you mustn't wait for help from that quarter. You've got to get to Hringurhol ahead of them. Trust me, what I say is true, even if the Tjaldi doesn't believe I have the gift of foresight. I'm going to help you, but no one must know it. Time is shorter than anyone thinks, Leifr Thorljotsson!"

Chapter 18

❖❖❖❖❖❖❖❖❖❖❖❖❖❖❖❖❖❖❖❖❖❖❖❖❖❖❖❖❖

Nothing could have been more objectionable to Leifr than merely standing and waiting. It wasn't so bad for Thurid; he spent most of two days visiting in the Tjaldi's tent and being treated like an honored visitor, with dainty meals and all he wanted to drink and long chatty talks with the Tjaldi and Thorbjorg. Such civilized conduct was not expected of a mere warrior like Leifr, and particularly not Raudbjorn, who was regarded as a species of trained bear by the Bergmal clan and a great source of awe by the children.

Starkad dogged Leifr's heels, as restless as he, and after nightfall when Thurid came humming cheerfully into the guest tent, they were both waiting for him.

"When are we leaving, Thurid?" Leifr demanded. "We've lost two days of travel now, thanks to Svanlaug's clan and the fears of this old woman. We know you're quite comfortable here, but we've spent two days sitting out on the fell in the wind and the rain so we won't have to sit in this tent looking soft."

"I can't be blamed if you're getting wet," Thurid snorted. "The Tjaldi is merely being cautious. All this while she's been searching for evidence of the traitor in her camp. There's a wolf cape here somewhere, and she's clever enough to find it."

"That's not our concern," Leifr grumbled.

"It might be, if Svanlaug's the Ulf-hedin," Thurid said in a low tone of voice, glancing toward the hide walls of the tent. "Her behavior is strange, for a Dokkalfar woman."

"If it were Svanlaug," Starkad said, "she's had plenty of opportunities to kill us before now."

"Silence, you upstart," Thurid retorted. "It's never safe to make generalities like that."

"You suspect Svanlaug, then?" Leifr said, finding himself in the unexpected position of rising to her defense. "She seemed frightened enough that night in Haeta-fell when those Ulf-hedin were following us. You only suspect her because she's running counter to her clan's expectations of what she should be doing."

"In this realm, that's an excellent basis for suspicion," Thurid said. "It is how the Dokkalfar make their lives predictable in a world of mysterious powers and primordial chaos. No one must rebel against the system, or it lets in the factors of doubt and disarray. A good deal too much of that has been going on in the Dokkalfar realm, since buying and selling and trading has become the new way of life for so many."

Leifr heaved an angry sigh and sat down on a stool beside the central hearth. "How much longer before the Tjaldi will let us go?" he demanded.

"A few more days yet," Thurid replied with no great cheer in his aspect.

Starkad added, "Long enough for us to remember what comfort was, then we'll be off again."

"As an apprentice, you'd better forget that such a thing exists," Thurid retorted. "The Tjaldi is waiting for the Ulf-hedin to strike again. Svanlaug is being watched closely, without knowing it."

Leifr posted himself as guard over their tent that night, leaving Raudbjorn at the front while he watched the back. All night he listened to the soft sounds of the penned livestock, hearing occasional movements in the tents nearby, but nothing that could not be explained as perfectly normal. Kraftig sat alertly at Leifr's side, ears cocked and eyes expectant, but not the least suspicion rewarded his vigilance. When the earliest risers of the settlement had commenced their livestock feeding and driving to water, Leifr decided that he had watched long enough and walked around to the front to confer with Raudbjorn.

Surrounded by his weapons and Farlig and Frimodig, the thief-taker sat squarely on the mat in a seemingly indolent heap, but Leifr knew a dozen pairs of eyes could not be more watchful than Raudbjorn's one squinting into the dark.

"No Ulf-hedin last night," Raudbjorn greeted him.

Leifr stopped dead in his tracks, unable to believe his eyes.

Kraftig growled, alerting the other two dogs into suspicious growling and whining as they scented the air and sniffed over the ground intently. Raudbjorn stiffened suddenly, his nostrils twitching as he sniffed. Twisting around, he gazed a moment at the lurid spiral symbol painting on the tent flap with fresh blood. Drops of it had fallen over Raudbjorn's head and shoulders and arms where he sat, while the unknown enemy had done his—or her—work. Even the troll-hounds had been sprinkled with red drops. By some remote chance, Raudbjorn might have fallen asleep, but the troll-hounds would not sleep so soundly that someone could drizzle fresh blood over them without their smelling it at once.

Raudbjorn gritted his teeth in a hideous grimace and smote himself between the eyes with one fist, a blow that would have staggered a horse.

"Raudbjorn fell asleep!" he moaned in an agony of self-accusation. "Great dung-heap! Useless Villimadur! Couldn't keep one eye open for Leifr!" He pawed at the offending eye as if he would claw it out.

"No, Raudbjorn," Leifr hastened. "You didn't fall asleep at your post. It simply couldn't happen. Look at the troll-hounds. They wouldn't sleep so soundly."

Raudbjorn pondered over the spatters of blood on the dogs, which they were speedily licking off each other. His forehead drew into great corrugated wrinkles as he labored with the effort of thinking.

"Spell?" Raudbjorn rumbled dubiously, as if he didn't trust his own abilities.

"What else could explain it?" Leifr answered, and at once Raudbjorn tried to think about it again, since Leifr had asked him to.

By this time, the Ulf-hedin sign had been noticed by some of the Bergmal shepherd women, who sped silently for the Tjaldi's tent with the news. Although there was no overt disturbance, Thurid thrust his head out of the tent and immediately apprised himself of the situation by getting a bloody smear on his hand.

"The spiral again," he muttered, hastily wiping it off. "A favorite device of Sorkvir's, borrowed no doubt from the Council of Threttan for the purpose of frightening people into submission. How did you manage to sleep through this, Raudbjorn? A little too much to drink last night?''

Raudbjorn drew himself up pridefully, huffing and snorting with indignation and presenting a picture of blood-spattered righteous wrath.

"Raudbjorn's eye never closed,'' he said in an angry rumble, his knuckles whitening on the haft of his halberd.

"Perhaps,'' Leifr mused, "the Ulf-hedin really can make themselves invisible, Thurid.''

"Bah! It can't be done, except by trickery,'' Thurid declared. "True invisibility is a much-sought-after spell, and no one has ever truly succeeded at it. There's the legendary Tarnkappe, the cloak that is supposed to make you invisible, but I've never heard of anyone who had one. Except for King Elbegast, perhaps. It wouldn't surprise me if he had one. And perhaps the Rhbus at one time—''

All Thurid's blather was nothing but a screen for his own anxiety as he traced up and down the tent flap with his sensitive fingertips, testing for lingering influences. He ran his hands softly over the ground where the unknown artist must have stood to smear the spiral on the tent. Needing more light than the sickly yellow glow on the eastern horizon that passed for dawn in the Dokkalfar realm, Thurid jammed his staff into the ground and unveiled the glaring blue orb to cast its gleam over the scene.

By this time several of Girda's warriors had arrived and were also searching for clues; several serving women on their way to the spring with water jars and a few wide-eyed tousled children who had escaped from their beds had also come.

"There's nothing,'' Thurid said at last, amazed. "Not a shred of anyone's influence. Except old bits and tatters, and Raudbjorn's, of course, but I don't think he did this.''

Girda had followed Thurid's investigations with a worried frown. "It's Ulf-hedin magic,'' she said quietly. "It's the only explanation. Perhaps they can make themselves invisible. If they really do, it explains how they get their victims.''

"I refuse to believe they can do it,'' Thurid said, his lips pinched up in white envy. "Ljosalfar wizards and sorcerers have sought that spell for generations with no success. It can't fall into evil hands now.''

Thorbjorg touched his sleeve. "The Tjaldi wishes to speak with you," she said. "And with the Norskur and the Thorljotsson."

Svanlaug was in the Tjaldi's tent ahead of them. The Tjaldi sat in her tall chair with her hands folded, a robe across her knees.

"Where were you last night, child?" the Tjaldi asked. "You weren't in your mother's tent this morning when this sign was discovered."

"I was walking," Svanlaug said. "I've always been a night-farer, more so than anyone in the clan. The moon is full now, and its rays are sustenance for some thread of energy within me."

"Ah yes, that would be the influence of your ancestress Ogvalda, nine generations back," the Tjaldi said, casting her eyes thoughtfully toward the ceiling and tapping her chin with one finger. "She was a chieftain in the Tungl cult—worshippers of the moon and its influences. I'm not pleased that her blood has lasted for nine generations. I shall have to make a note of that in your history."

"Another blot, I suppose," Svanlaug said with a resentful sigh.

"A minor one, I assure you," the Tjaldi replied.

"Minor indeed, if you suspect that I am the Ulf-hedin," Svanlaug said bitterly. "But I'm not sorry I avenged my father's death. The price is getting higher and higher, however, if I'm to be exiled from my sister-clan because of it. I think it is time that we departed for Hringurhol, since my return has aroused such ill feeling."

"It is because of your sister that we have such fears," the Tjaldi said. "The Ulf-hedin would like to possess her, and if they could get near her through you, they would do it. Perhaps you've been stricken by this curse and you have no recollection of the commands they give you and what you do to act upon them."

"There's no such mark upon me anywhere," Svanlaug said.

"The Ulf-hedin will let us see only what they want us to see," the Tjaldi said. "Such is their power. I fear what must be done is the calling together of a Clan Council of Inquisition. Then if you are found guilty, you'll have to go before the Audur Tribe Inquisition. I regret to do this, Svanlaug, but we must think of the good of our clan, as well as yours and your sister's."

Svanlaug sat a moment, stunned. Then her shoulders sagged and she said, "It's always Ulfrin who gets me into trouble," she said. "Clans should be advised that if a Sverting is born among them to give away or sell the rest of the mother's brood. What is to be done with me now? Am I to be locked up?"

"There is no other way to be sure," the Tjaldi said. "I'm not happy to do this, my child. It is an unfair burden for you, being the sister of the Sverting. It makes you vulnerable to many dread things."

"There is another way," Thurid said. "If Svanlaug were willing to undergo the purging of her powers, it would remove all traces of Ulf-hedin influence."

"I'd rather be exiled," Svanlaug replied. "At least then I'd have the memories of Bergmal and the knowledge of who I am and my ancestors. Take away my carbuncle and I'd become nothing. I'd just as well be dead."

Leifr listened and scowled, darting angry glances at Thurid, listening to the proceedings. Raudbjorn eyed Leifr worriedly, scarcely daring to breathe for fear of making something creak objectionably.

"How long will your Council of Inquisition take?" Leifr queried. "We need Svanlaug to take us where we're going. I don't care if she's an Ulf-hedin or not, as long as she takes us there. We'll deal with her when we have to, if what you suspect is true."

"And it's not," Svanlaug added firmly, turning hopeful eyes upon the Tjaldi. "If it were, I'd have much more to fear from *Endalaus Daudi* than from the Council of Inquisition of either clan or tribe."

"No, the Council must rule," the Tjaldi said. "We will draw the lots tonight, and in three days, we'll be ready to consider your situation."

"Three days!" Leifr muttered involuntarily.

The Tjaldi nodded her head. "Three days of fasting and ritual are essential for the Council to be convinced that Svanlaug is innocent or guilty. During this time, you are instructed to stay away from Bergmal. Your tent will be removed to a safe distance on the other side of the sheepfolds, and you must approach no closer. Asta will send your food and you may wander about in the fells surrounding us, but you must not set foot within our boundaries. Poles will be set up as a warning to others who are not permitted—servants and children and not-clan guests and men or anyone who sheds blood of man or beast are to be kept out until the end of the third day. We're not being inhospitable; this is simply what the Inquisition ritual demands. I summoned you here to tell you this. Your tent is being moved even now. One of Girda's warriors will take you to it.''

Outside the Tjaldi's tent they found Girda's sister Borgun waiting for them. Leifr glanced back once at Svanlaug, who sat with her back proudly straight and stiff, bestowing a savage glower upon him as if she disdained anyone's pity.

They found the tent had been moved in their absence, along with a startled Starkad, to a location on the far side of the sheepfold, out of sight of the village. Poles with colored strips of cloth were pushed into the earth to warn away those who were not welcome, and a couple of Girda's warriors loitered about in case anyone needed reminding of his status.

Leifr perceived at once that Thurid was uneasy by the manner with which he bundled them all out of the tent and told them not to disturb him before sundown on the pain of death or something much worse. From the distracted way he was heaving things out of his satchel and raking up his hair with his fingers, Thurid intended serious labors. Leifr eyed Gedvondur's hand suspiciously where it rested upon a warm rock, looking fat and lazy and seemingly innocent.

"I daresay I can pick up some of their influences from here," Thurid muttered half to himself, striding to the doorway of the tent to test the breeze with a wetted finger.

"What are they going to do, torture her?" Starkad asked interestedly.

"I don't know," Thurid snapped.

"What are you going to do if they do decide to do something drastic to Svanlaug?" Leifr asked.

"I don't know!" Thurid retorted. "Nothing must happen to Svanlaug right now. We need her to get at the Council. Why did she ever want to come back here to these old vipers? Their power is older and mustier than anything you can imagine. Now get out and let me get to work. Don't worry. I'll know more when you get back.''

The calling of the Inquisition caused an excited bustle among the Bergmal women, who busily removed the tents of the ineligible members beyond the perimeters of the warning poles. Leifr, Starkad, and Raudbjorn lent themselves gladly to the moving effort, hauling bundles, herding livestock, and helping reestablish the tents.

When that was all done, Girda invited the three of them to spend the remainder of the day quite comfortably in her lodge, which was a large one to shelter her twenty-odd warrior women. It was the most austere of accommodations; the warriors did not encumber themselves with an excess of possessions or comforts, only their weapons, armor, tools, clothing, and a pallet for sleeping, all of which belongings could easily be tied behind the cantle of a saddle. A fire burned in the center of the tent, with the smoke mostly trickling out the blackened hole above. A quantity of scattered fleeces offered a comfortable place to lounge in the fire's warmth and listen to Girda's chat. Raudbjorn felt so much at ease that he buried his chins on his chest and went to sleep, propped up from three sides by the luxuriating hounds.

''What are they doing?'' Leifr finally inquired, nodding in the direction of the Tjaldi's tent.

Girda tested the edge of the knife she was honing by slicing at a lock of her straggling gray hair.

''I can't say,'' she said with a shrug. ''I don't know much more than you do. We're not permitted to come near or ask questions, so we don't waste our time thinking about it. If Svanlaug's an Ulf-hedin, the Tjaldi will find out.''

''And then what will they do about it?'' Starkad asked.

''What do you suppose, lad? She'll be killed, of course. That sort of deceit can't be allowed. Svanlaug will serve as an example of anyone else who might be thinking that a wolf cape is a good way to get power. If she's guilty, she must die. I don't know if she is or not, but the signs of rebellion are there, and that won't go well for her. I can take you to Hringurhol, if that's what you're worrying about. It's a well-known road, even to those who have never traveled it. Illraemdur, it's called—the Road of Infamy.''

''But Svanlaug knows Hringurhol from visiting her father there,'' Leifr said. ''If I'm going to find what I'm seeking, I need her knowledge.''

''I could take you within eye-view of it and point out its towers,'' Girda said with a sigh, ''but that's the most I would do. Too many Ulf-hedin in Hringurhol.''

Leifr scowled, his thoughts revolving hopelessly over the question of whether or not Svanlaug was an Ulf-hedin. If she were, she would lead them straight into a trap, one that they wouldn't escape from this time. Yet she had killed Djofull, and he had seen it with his own eyes. But, he reminded himself, a group of power-greedy wizards such as the Council of Thirteen would be a bloodthirsty assortment and murder an acceptable method for succession.

When it was nearly sundown, Leifr stirred Raudbjorn, and they approached Thurid's tent. A blue gleam seeped out around the door flap, hanging like mist in the air and surrounding the tent in an unearthly nimbus that Leifr was loath to touch.

''Thurid?'' Leifr called after a moment of hesitation.

From inside Thurid replied irascibly, ''Stay away, unless you want to be throttled! I'm doing important work!''

Girda kept well away from it, making signs to ward off evil influences. ''You'd better spend the night in the warriors' lodge,'' she said. ''I wouldn't disturb that wizard if I valued my throat.''

They tramped back toward the warriors' lodge, but instead of going inside, Girda swept one arm toward the surrounding fells.

''Let's go for a tramp,'' she said. ''I've got a ring of sisters around both camps and I'd like to speak to them. The Council of Inquisition causes everyone to worry.''

Leifr was glad to get some exercise, and Raudbjorn huffed along at his heels good-naturedly, pleased at the company of other warriors, once he had gotten used to the idea that they were women instead of men.

It was nearly dark when they reached the highest viewpoint over Bergmal, and the long silvery twilight bathed the place in eerie gleamings on the wet rocks and shadows of impenetrable blackness. From afar came the cautious grunts of trolls, scenting the sheep of Bergmal safely folded below. The Bergmal clan also boasted a round dozen hunters, and Leifr had seen them returning at dawn with troll hides slung over their horses' withers, their hunting dogs slinking behind them with bloodstained jaws. They also hunted the wild reindeer and the hairy wild ox with its deadly span of curving horns, valued as much for its long hair as it was for its gamy meat. Thus it was that the trolls were very shy around Bergmal when the clan was in residence, a circumstance for which Leifr was grateful.

Girda halooed to her sisters, who answered from a dark chimney of rock above, and she started across the saddle of the ridge to speak with them. She halted suddenly, clapping her hand to her sword. Raudbjorn grunted suspiciously, and Leifr heard the sudden churning of hooves charging up from the dark ravine below. Horseless and disadvantaged, Girda led a charge to take a stand on a knoll of higher ground, turning to face the horsemen as they rushed to the attack. In the cold sky-gleam of twilight, Leifr saw glowing eyes, teeth, and fur mixed in with flashing weapons and shields and armor. In a fanatic charge, their assailants plunged up onto the knoll, six silent Ulf-hedin with their wolf capes pulled over their heads, thus bringing the wolf-spell alive. They appeared as wolves with men's bodies, with the greater intelligence of men and the ferocity of wolves.

Endalaus Daudi came out of its sheath with a shrill ringing note and Leifr swept one of the attackers out of his saddle, mortally wounded and howling a death cry that chilled the blood. Glancing down at the dying creature, Leifr glimpsed the wolf mask of the Ulf-hedin mingled horribly with human features in a dissolving miasma. Leifr stepped over the convulsed form, waving the sword in defiance at the rest of the Ulf-hedin skirmishing around the defenders of the knoll.

"Who's next to die?" Leifr roared. "This is the metal of Endless Death! Who wants to taste its edge?"

The Ulf-hedin clustered together at a whistle from their leader, perhaps somewhat chastened by the death of their companion. Wolf ears pricking and twitching with nervous life were nothing like the lifeless capes Leifr had seen in Haeta-fell, and the snarling snouts and glaring eyes of wolves had replaced the features of men. From the shoulders up they were wolves, and men from the shoulders down, a sight that sickened Leifr with disgust at such an unnatural transformation. A sensation of fear surrounded these creatures like a cloud.

Their leader moved forward and drove a lance into the earth. "So you are the outlaw Leifr Thorljotsson," the voice of a woman said, gutturally altered by the effects of the spell. "You have come a long way just to perish now."

"If someone perishes, it'll be the ones in wolf capes," Leifr replied ominously, once he had recovered from the astonishment of speaking to a female in wolf-guise.

"You won't be allowed to continue further with your hopeless quest," the leader continued. "The Council of Threttan has heard word of you from your dealings with Sorkvir and Djofull. You've been unwise to pursue this matter so far."

"Allow me to speak," said another voice, this one familiar to Leifr, and much hated. Sorkvir separated his horse from the pack of Ulf-hedin and rode closer than the Ulf-hedin female had approached.

"Leifr, you've passed far beyond the bounds of common sense," the wizard snarled, his eyes gleaming with a feral light. "You're more obstinate than Fridmarr ever was. You should have taken warning from his fate. You might have escaped, had you given me that orb at Fangelsi-hofn. I have given you every chance to extricate yourself from the dealings of the Council, but you've got more courage than common sense, it seems."

"I might have backed away from it," Leifr retorted furiously, "if you had let Ljosa go. That one thing has kept me angry enough to come after you into the jaws of death itself. She matters nothing in all this. You could have let her go at any time with no consequences."

"Aye, that may be so," Sorkvir agreed. "It's merely an unimportant detail I overlooked. But the results have not been unsatisfactory. Now your illogical quest for justice has led you to your destruction. You must be cursing Fridmarr's interference at this moment. If only he'd left you in your own Scipling realm, you might have lived a long life, by Scipling standards, and made something of yourself, instead of dying on a lonely mountain in the Dokkalfar realm. No one will even know where your bones lie.''

Sorkvir motioned with one hand, and the Ulf-hedin leader drew her sword with a swift motion, nudging her horse forward purposefully. Leifr took up a ready stance.

"I'm surprised you don't recognize her, Leifr," Sorkvir chuckled hoarsely. "Look again, and see if there's not something familiar about her."

"It's true, you know who I am," the Ulf-hedin said, swinging her sword in an arc. "Does it comfort you to know you'll die at the hand of a friend?"

"Not particularly," Leifr said coolly, straining to discern the true voice behind the spell. "I don't have that many people to call friend, and those that I do are standing behind me, not facing me over swords' ends. You're nothing but a puppet in Sorkvir's hand, so you're no friend of mine, whoever you are."

He spared a glance behind him at that moment to corroborate his statement about his friends standing at his back, expecting to see Raudbjorn crouching there with his teeth bared, halberd held aloft, Starkad prancing about with some old sword, thirsting for blood, and Girda and her sisters ready with their weapons. What he did see compelled a second and longer look. They stood there as if frozen, in the attitude of suspenseful waiting, unblinking eyes trained upon the place where the Ulf-hedin had burst into view a few moments ago.

Sorkvir chuckled. "You'll be getting no help from that quarter, I fear. They'll remember nothing except the initial charge, and when they come to themselves, all they'll see is the Ulf-hedin retreating. And you, inexplicably dead, in true Ulf-hedin fashion. Their speed and invisibility is legendary, and now you know the secret. But not for long, I'm pleased to say."

"And you think this trick is enough to defeat *Endalaus Daudi*?" Leifr queried haughtily. "A wound from this sword will send your Ulf-hedin to Niflheim, and you as well, now there's no Djofull to bring you back. Are you more cautious of yourself these days, Sorkvir, being mortal again?"

"The Council of Threttan will have the knowledge I once shared with Djofull," Sorkvir replied. "As soon as we retrieve

Heldur's orb from Thurid, there is no knowledge that will be denied us.''

"You'll never get that orb as long as I'm here to defend it," Leifr answered.

"Now you understand why I must get rid of you," Sorkvir said, baring his teeth in a vicious grin as he raised his arm, signaling to the Ulf-hedin.

The female leader rode forward alone, touching her horse into a swift gallop as she charged, leveling a lance at Leifr's chest. One swift stroke from the sword parried the lance with a burst of light and shattered its gleaming tip as the horse plunged past, staggered from the jolt of contrary powers.

Sorkvir waved his hand again, bringing the horse and rider around for another rush. Leifr concentrated on the wolf's head, forgetting the human body beneath. The warrior made another charge at him with the broken lance, which he sent spinning away with another fiery jolting of colliding powers. The horse reared aloft, snorting and squealing in protest, waving its hooves over Leifr's head while the warrior whirled a deadly skull-crushing mace. The horse dropped to all fours again, and Leifr was ready to dodge the mace, not trusting the metal of *Endalaus Daudi* not to shatter under such a blow. The Ulf-hedin charged by him with a furious shriek, striking at him in passing with the haft end of the mace. Turning sharply, she rushed back, again compelled by Sorkvir's gesturing hand.

With the idea in mind of evening up the battle, Leifr raised *Endalaus Daudi* as the horse came charging at him and hit it as hard as he could with the butt of the sword, right between the eyes. As he expected, the horse was knocked senseless, plowed to a halt on its knees, and somersaulted, throwing off its rider. She landed on her feet with astonishing skill and speedily advanced on him, drawing a sword. Leifr could see nothing human in the hairy face baring teeth in snarling jaws, and felt only waves of deadly menace striving to paralyze him with fear. They clashed swords, filling the night with blinding flashes and showers of sparks. Leifr had no doubt he was not fighting merely one warrior, but all the strength and evil of Sorkvir combined against him. The fury of desperation drove him to greater heights of daring and speed, but the female Ulf-hedin was just as fast and strong at parrying his thrusts and retaliating with her own dangerous attacks. One vicious thrust went through his cloak as he twisted away, slashing a long rent in the fabric, but she was out and nimbly gone with Ulf-hedin quickness before he could seize the advantage.

Winded and sweating, he was beginning to consider the unfair advantage that his opponent had over him. Sorkvir would never tire, and his pawn would fight until she achieved Sorkvir's intention of killing Leifr. Leifr, however, had only the protection of *Endalaus Daudi*, and it would do its work only when he managed to wound his opponent. So far, the Ulf-hedin had not only kept out of harm's way, but she was beginning to press Leifr's skill and strength, always circling, always pushing forward, instead of drawing back for the occasional breather.

Then something large and black moved into the tail of Leifr's vision. It was his opponent's horse, recovered from its concussion and moving away to join its fellows. Swiftly Leifr turned and bounded after it in three quick strides, and caught hold of its mane and lofted himself into the saddle. The moment he drove his heels into its sides, it knew what was expected of it and charged at its former rider without hesitation.

Swinging around the Ulf-hedin, Leifr ducked down behind the horse's neck as he almost sideswiped Sorkvir's horse, and hauled his steed around to retreat to the other side of the battleground. Sorkvir uttered a furious shout, a warning perhaps. The Ulf-hedin dodged and retreated from his return rush. Leifr brought the horse around and halted to catch his breath and watch his enemies for a moment, suspecting that Sorkvir would soon tire of this tedious honorable combat and send the rest of his wolves in to finish the job.

In this brief interval, he threw aside his cloak and shifted it to one side to give his sword arm more freedom. As he did so, his attention was arrested by a slight lump in the tail pocket of his hood, dangling down the back of his cloak. With his left hand he reached inside and fished out the ring the traveling trader Vidskipti had given him in the treasure vault of the Dokkalfar kings. Without even pausing to consider possible consequences, he slipped it over his right forefinger and tightened his grip on his sword. It all took only a second, while Sorkvir was controlling the shying of his horse from Leifr's impetuous charge.

At once Leifr knew he had the upper hand in the battle as the Rhbu strength flowed into his arm. Something about him must have looked different to Sorkvir; the wizard started to curse, jerking his hand furiously to signal his fighters to come forward. They rode up even with him and stopped, growling uneasily and muttering protests or suggestions in their half-human voices.

"Cowards, all of you!" the female warrior's voice rang out as she cast a red-eyed glance of withering scorn over them. With a catlike rush she came at Leifr, sword drawn. With one hand she gripped the horse's forelock, vaulting over the beast's neck with a wild yell, driving straight at Leifr with her feet and gleaming sword. It was a maneuver he had never seen before, and he didn't relish close contact with any Ulf-hedin. He rolled off over the horse's croup to escape, landing on his feet. Then he tripped and rolled. The Ulf-hedin landed a second later, vicious and determined as ever, seeing her opportunity to impale her foe on the ground. Leifr twisted to one side as she lunged at him, wolf face foaming and snarling with blood lust. He grabbed the guard of her sword as she thrust, pulling as hard as he could and raising both feet as she fell toward him, off balance. Between his kick and her momentum, she flew overhead and landed hard. Leifr leaped up, sword in hand, even as the creature quickly gathered herself for a spring. Her reddened eyes blazed at him with such an excess of hatred that he felt the waves of it crashing over him, filling him with blind, hopeless fury. Raising his sword, he swung at the hideous wolf's head with its lips wrinkled back in a savage snarl, smiting it off clean in a single stroke. The head rolled away toward Sorkvir and the other watching Ulf-hedin, who backed their horses away as Leifr's attention turned to them.

Sorkvir alone stood firm, although his horse was snorting and dancing nervously at the smell of blood.

"Well done," Sorkvir said. "Just as I expected. Now perhaps you'd care to see who it is you've killed."

Leifr prodded at the wolf's head with one toe. "Whoever it is, I've done her a kindness," he said. "Death is better than living under your spell."

"So you say," Sorkvir answered.

The wolf's white fur was now hair, light-colored where it wasn't dyed with blood. Leifr blinked, not knowing whether a misty substance surrounded the head, or if his eyes were blurred. The face rolled around, revealed in the silvery half-gloom of the northern sky, staring sightlessly at nothing. Leifr shut his eyes to clear them, but when he looked again, the face was still the same, and it was Ljosa's dead face staring back at him.

Sorkvir chuckled dryly. "Now you're free to go back to your own realm, are you not? As you said yourself, you would have gone back except for this girl. What's holding you now, Scipling?"

Chapter 19

◆◆◆◆◆◆◆◆◆◆◆◆◆◆◆◆◆◆◆◆◆◆◆◆◆◆◆◆◆◆◆

The moment lost reality. Leifr swayed slightly on his feet, seeing it all as if through someone else's eyes. He even felt a distant, hollow admiration for his own self-control as he stepped back and wiped the blood from his sword with a fold of the Ulf-hedin cloak. Sparing a moment, he took a last glance at the poor body that had once been Ljosa, tossed about like the token in some grisly game between two monstrously stupid entities and now finally at peace. He drew in a deep, hurtful breath, and another as his sustaining anger slowly came trickling back to him. Gripping his sword, he raised his eyes to Sorkvir.

"Revenge is keeping me here now," he answered in a voice of deceptive calm. "I cut you to pieces once, Sorkvir, and I won't rest until you're finished for good."

"Then let's get on with it," Sorkvir said, motioning his Ulf-hedin to ride forward. "If you can last longer than these warriors."

"Coward. It's you I'm challenging," Leifr snarled, ready nonetheless to dispatch as many Ulf-hedin as it took for him to get to Sorkvir. His entire body ached, but his ache for vengeance caused mere physical pain to diminish into insignificance. The small kernel of self-preservation instinct that remained to him whispered anxiously that eight Ulf-hedin was too much even for the Rhbu ring and sword to cope with at once; advice that was sternly rejected and warned not to surface again.

The Ulf-hedin raised their eerie war cry, milling about, clashing weapons with each other, snarling, howling, and generating the essential, mindless fury required for battle. Their ritual gave him time enough to capture Ljosa's horse again and step into the saddle, giving him that much more defensive advantage in the coming attack.

Leifr swung his sword around to keep his arm from stiffening. As the Ulf-hedin gathered themselves for a berserk charge, a blue bolt of flame suddenly hissed along the ground and burst beneath the feet of the lead horse. The beast was flung over backward to pin its rider's legs beneath its lifeless bulk. Undaunted now that their fury had been worked into a fever pitch, the Ulf-hedin came ranting and flogging toward Leifr, a forest of bristling lances and swords bearing down upon him.

Another searing blue bolt ignited the foremost of the Ulf-hedin like a torch, followed almost instantly by a thunderous explosion. Black shreds and soot choked the air as man and horse vanished. Sensibly, the astonished Ulf-hedin pulled their horses to an abrupt halt, half strangled in the soot and grease created by their late companion's unfortunate demise. For a wild moment, they crouched in their saddles, looking right and left. Before Leifr's eyes, the Ulf-hedin spell came off them as they hastily unfastened the wide black belts they wore around their waists. They tossed back the wolf capes and peered around a moment in wild surmise.

"It's him!" one of them declared. "And he's using that dragon's eye!"

"Out of here, then!" another offered.

"Stay, you fools!" Sorkvir commanded. "I'll deal with Thurid when he gets here! You destroy the Scipling!"

As they hesitated, a bolt came screaming up the fell and burst among them into a thousand hissing, darting blue embers. With howls of terror, they slapped at them, while the coals burned holes into their cloaks, leggings, boots, body armor, or bare flesh. The horses were also burned, and they erupted into rearing, bucking, plunging pandemonium, some dashing away with their riders clinging to their backs, and some falling on their knees to roll in an attempt to quench the burning.

Leifr's horse was not burned, but the terror was infectious. The beast reared aloft with a terrified whinny, and when it came down it broke away in a determined gallop. Leifr guided it straight toward Sorkvir, holding his sword out before him like a lance. Sorkvir whirled his horse around and fled, shedding curls of greenish mist as he cursed and shouted. Several times he held his staff aloft, shouting the words of spells, but each time the staff's orb sputtered and flared uselessly. The bath of dragon power had done his powers harm, but Leifr had no way of guessing how long the countereffect would last. He dug his heels into his horse's ribs and charged on. Sorkvir's pale countenance flashed backward over his shoulder repeatedly. Leifr's horse ran with a good will, perhaps familiar with the terrain he was racing over.

"It's a good place to die, Sorkvir!" Leifr raged into the tearing wind. "No one to call life back into your rotten carcass! No one to fight your fight for you! No one's going to call you back from Hel this time! Die for Ljosa, you filth, you disease! Die for Fridmarr, as well! You'll wish for your precious eitur before I'm done cutting your vile heart out!"

Sorkvir's horse bore his rider to the crest of a fell, where the sharp black rocks dropped away in steep cliffs below. There was a path of sorts, twisting among the shoulders of rock with steep bends and sudden drops. Leifr flogged his horse after, heedless of the shadowy death lurking below if his horse stumbled or fell, his eyes upon the dark flapping figure ahead. He had gained on Sorkvir. A few more lengths and he would be within striking range.

The path bent suddenly to the right, and Leifr's horse skidded to a jolting halt before plunging onward. From the tail of his eye Leifr caught a floating movement below him, over the edge of the cliff, as if some large bird had been disturbed from its roost and had taken flight at their noisy passage. Swiftly Leifr scanned the path ahead in the dim light. There was no sign of Sorkvir, and no sound of pounding hooves. He brought his horse to a noisy, blowing halt and tried to listen. He heard absolutely nothing. After retracing his footsteps to the sharp bend, he stopped and looked down, hoping to see Sorkvir's carcass impaled on one of the sharp peaks below, but there was nothing he could discern among the shadows. Dismounting, he studied the hoofprints. As he had suspected, a set of tracks went off the path and straight over the edge, without skidding or attempting to halt.

Leifr remounted and rode to the best vantage point. Below,

the bottom of the rocky ravine was nothing but shadow. The exhaustion of the past battle suddenly overwhelmed him, and he sagged in miserable weariness. He waited for dawn light, which was a scant few hours away, passing the night locked in the grip of remorse and revengeful thoughts. If Sorkvir had thought he would be discouraged by Ljosa's death, he had sadly mistaken him, underestimating the wrath of a wronged Scipling. If need be, Leifr would spend the rest of his life seeking only to bury his sword in Sorkvir's corrupted carcass, heaving his eitur-preserved entrails in all directions and breaking his bones one by one.

When it was light enough, Leifr looked down into the deep ravine, still hoping to see that Sorkvir had come to his downfall at last. But there was nothing to confirm his hopes, not a shred of cloth or flesh clinging to a pinnacle. Disgustedly Leifr decided that Sorkvir had at last shaken free of the dragon-fire and summoned a spell that had shifted his shape and carried him and his horse away.

Wearily he debated the upward path, leading to the stronghold of the Ulf-hedin and the Council of Threttan, which had sponsored this cruel trick upon him. It was now daylight and his misery was getting the upper hand of his fury; he almost wondered if it weren't enough. Now that Ljosa was dead, he had failed in his driving resolve to repay her for sacrificing herself for his liberty. Numbly he tried to think about the Dokkur Lavardur spreading ice and darkness over the Ljosalfar realm, and how Fridmarr had battled against Sorkvir to his last broken breath. Leifr sighed, more tired than he had ever been after a battle. Perhaps he had been fighting both sides of a worthless conflict, and now he had finally lost. He didn't care which way he went now. Perhaps even over the edge of the cliff was better than going on, or going back.

For the first time he remembered Starkad and Raudbjorn. Once the Ulf-hedin spell left them, they would begin looking for him. While he was deciding what to do about them, a cold drizzle began weeping from the lowering dark ceiling of cloud; the wetter he became, the more reconciled he became to going back to Bergmal. Steeling himself, he turned his horse back toward the site of his battle.

He arrived there and found the place deserted except for a pair of unseen guards who were signaling warily to each other with the hoots of owls. Ignoring them, he looked at the place where Ljosa had died. There was no sign of a body, and no longer any blood, since the rain had washed it away into the rocky earth. Nourished on so much blood, the Dokkalfar land would undoubtedly flourish with wars, feuds, and more bloodletting. Perhaps the blanketing dark and cold of the Dokkur Lavardur was the only way to bring peace to such a world.

A shout summoned him from his dark thoughts, and he turned to see Starkad flogging a horse up the side of the fell, with Raudbjorn churning along in the rear on a horse much too small for him, judging from its rolling eyes and desperate gasps of air. Behind him came Thurid, and Girda and a search party of eight hunters and warriors.

"Where have you been?" Starkad gasped, bringing his horse alongside Leifr and staring at him as if he were a marvelous and frightening oddity. "You disappeared! We thought the Ulf-hedin had taken you! One moment you were there, and the next you had vanished! Thurid was beside himself, let me tell you. What was it like, being vanished? Were you invisible, too?"

"Don't be absurd," Leifr snapped. "I wasn't disappeared or invisible. You were all asleep."

"We were not!" Starkad retorted hotly. "We were right at your back, ready to defend you against the Ulf-hedin! Asleep! What an accusation!"

"Sorkvir was there," Leifr said. "He was controlling the Ulf-hedin, and he put a spell on you."

Thurid came up in time to hear the mention of Sorkvir, and his face darkened in a cunning scowl.

"I knew it was some such threat," he said. "I stepped out of the tent to look around for you, and I had the orb in my hand. I looked into it and saw you as plain as if it were noonday, facing down a pack of Ulf-hedin. I thought it was time to see if that cursed orb was good for anything, so I concentrated on the scene in the crystal and sent up a bolt. A bit low, so I aimed higher the next time, and poof! I blew an Ulf-hedin to shreds from a mile away. It opened my eyes, I assure you."

"What about Ljosa?" Leifr asked. "Did you find her?"

They all looked at him oddly, their pleased and relieved expressions suddenly becoming strained.

"What's wrong?" Leifr demanded, his temper rising at their stupidity. "She was here. Sorkvir had her disguised as one of his filthy Ulf-hedin. And I killed her. She was lying right here. They didn't carry away the body, so I'm asking, who did? And where did they put her?"

"Ljosa!" Starkad whispered to Thurid. "He's daft. I'll swear I didn't see her."

Thurid handed the staff and orb to a reluctant Starkad and knelt down. Swiftly he ran his hands along the earth where Leifr had indicated, his head cocked, his expression pinched and intent. After rising to his feet, he snatched the staff from Starkad, who was gazing into the hypnotic blue depths of the orb in deep fascination.

"Something was here," he said, "although I can't say for certain if it was Ljosa. It happened hours ago and it's raining, which makes it almost impossible to make any sort of identification of the lingering influences."

"Then Sorkvir must have picked her up," Leifr said broodingly. "I almost had him. He's rather more afraid of me now that he's lost Djofull's retrieving powers. He went off a cliff and shifted shapes."

"But how did all this happen?" Starkad demanded, still puzzled. "You were here, then you weren't, so we went down to meet Thurid. We didn't dare search for you last night, for fear of more Ulf-hedin. And Girda said there was no use of it. Once the Ulf-hedin take a man, he's gone."

Girda was nodding in agreement. "Except this time," she said in a wondering tone. "You were lucky. You say we were all asleep, like statues?"

Leifr nodded wearily. "It must be how they smeared blood on our tent and delivered heads of goats and pigs so quietly to our doorsteps."

"The truth is more difficult to believe than the myth of the Ulf-hedin," Girda said doubtfully.

Leifr turned away from the dismal spot and gazed back the way he had come. "We've got at least a half day's travel, if we get started immediately," he said. "Svanlaug can catch up to us, once her Inquisition is over."

"If she's allowed," Girda said. "Those who know have told the rest of us that half the Councilwomen already are convinced she's guilty. Ulfrin is among them, and everyone knows that the Sverting doesn't make mistakes."

Thurid fell into step beside Leifr. "Tomorrow would be as good for starting as today," he said. "I'm most reluctant to leave Bergmal just now. The blue sphere reveals distant events, if you catch my meaning."

"You're spying upon the Inquisition?" Leifr asked.

Thurid nodded, with a sly smile. "I don't know what they'd do to me if they suspected. Their methods of divination are quite interesting, but I fear it's going badly for Svanlaug. Ulfrin sits in the seidr seat and goes into a trance, revealing Svanlaug in a very bad light as an Ulf-hedin."

"If she is one, she'd better not come around me again," Leifr said, so tired and surly that he could scarcely keep from wobbling as he walked.

"That's just the point of it," Thurid said. "Ulfrin's faking it all. I'm sure of it."

"I'm not," Leifr growled. "I hate everyone and everything in this cursed realm. I wouldn't be at all surprised if Svanlaug were one of those beastly creatures. If she was, I'd be more than pleased to kill her and end her misery."

"The Ulf-hedin don't relish their job?" Thurid asked.

Leifr pondered his own remark a moment, remembering the furious desperation and anger of the Ulf-hedin.

"No," he said at last in a voice of complete dejection and fatigue. "They're unwilling captives, most of them. At least Ljosa was. Sorkvir controls them. We've got to destroy Sorkvir and all the rest of that wretched Council of Threttan."

"Some rest will do you good," Thurid said. "There's no difference between going after them today or tomorrow. What's that ring on your finger? I don't remember seeing that before. Where did you get it?"

"Vidskipti, remember? He gave it to me in the treasure vault at that ruin. I lifted that slab off your foot when it closed on you."

"I remember, I remember. Take that thing off. Can't you see

it's draining your strength? You used its power, now it's taking yours. The next time you use it will be the last time it will work for you, so save it in case you need it later. We're going to need all the strength we've got to go against this Council, if they're all equal to Sorkvir.''

Leifr did not remember returning to the tent and flinging himself on his pallet, but when he awakened nearly a full twenty-four hours later, he remembered the dreams. Bad as they were, nothing could compare with the reality of the nightmare of what had happened to Ljosa. He awakened as an older, grimmer person, with one objective only for the rest of his life, however long that might be, and his objective was the destruction of Sorkvir and the Council of Threttan. It would be his monument to Ljosa's memory.

When he awakened, his first sight was Thurid sitting cross-legged on a heap of fleeces and furs with Gedvondur roosting on his shoulder, basking in the glow of the dragon's orb. The staff rested on one of Thurid's knees and Thurid was gazing into the orb with his lean face drawn up into haggard lines of utmost concentration.

''Thurid—'' Leifr began, but the wizard peremptorily hissed him into silence, keeping his eyes fixed upon the orb.

''He's spying upon the women again,'' Starkad said. ''The Inquisition is over and a majority of that council of old crones believes that Svanlaug is guilty. They're trying to decide what to do with her now. Some of them think she ought to be burned at the stake.''

Leifr shivered in the chill and yawned, tentatively stretching his sore and stiff muscles. ''They're going to burn her at the stake?'' he grunted hoarsely, lifting an edge of the tent to see what hour of the night or day it was. Since it was not completely black outside, he deemed it was either twilight or early dawn.

''In a few hours,'' Starkad replied. ''At midnight. Leifr, you've got to do something to stop it. We can't just stand by and let it happen, not after all we've been through together. And she did kill Djofull.''

''Svanlaug's going to be burned?'' Leifr's eyes felt a little less gritty and he was beginning to take a faint interest in the conversation.

"Aye, unless somebody helps her. We could cut a hole in the Tjaldi's tent," Starkad replied hopefully.

"It would only prove their suspicions," Leifr said, shuffling to his feet. "They would think it was the Ulf-hedin. Besides, I'm not so sure she isn't an Ulf-hedin."

"Unless you save her, she'll be nothing but a melted puddle," Starkad said. "Guilty or not."

"I can't believe they'd burn her with no better proof than we've seen," Leifr said, his indignation beginning to simmer in a tiny corner of his ice-cold heart. It was a good feeling, when it seemed before that he could never feel compassion for another human being again.

"We can't let them get away with it, if they really try it," Starkad said earnestly. "Thurid, have they decided yet if they're going to burn her?"

His answer was another impatient hiss and a virulent glare. Gedvondur scuttled down from his perch on Thurid's shoulder and tumbled across the thick fleeces with difficulty to climb onto Leifr's knee.

"I'd like a look at that Rhbu ring sometime, if you don't mind," Gedvondur said, creeping close enough to touch his hand. "I would have looked at it while you were asleep, but you were lying on it."

"Good," Leifr growled, snatching the hand and ring away and trying to tumble Gedvondur off onto the ground. The hand rode out the attempt by clinging to his sleeve. "You can keep your fingers off that ring. Now why don't you get off my shoulder? I don't like the feeling I'm talking to myself."

"Never mind then, if you're going to be selfish about it. I don't need to see the ring to know that it's a double-bind spell. How like a Rhbu to give a gift that can kill you if you use it."

"I used it to help Thurid with no ill effects," Leifr retorted. "I'm not afraid of it."

"It came from a cursed treasure," Gedvondur pursued. "I urge you not to use it again."

"Why should you give me any advice?" Leifr asked in a surly fashion. "I tried to throw you in the fire, and I'm still sorry you didn't burn up."

"I know it, but I'm magnanimous enough to forgive you for your foolish behavior," Gedvondur replied. "We must talk, Leifr."

"So talk," Leifr grunted with ill grace.

Gedvondur began, "Now that you're no longer preoccupied with trying to help Ljosa, maybe you'll listen to reason and we can clean out this nest of vipers called by some the Council of Threttan."

Leifr winced a little at the mention of Ljosa, but his thoughts were clearing admirably.

"Anxious to get back, are you?" he asked. "You were Djofull's right hand, weren't you? You must know a great deal about Hringurhol and the workings of the Council."

"You forget I spent most of my time there locked up in a box where I couldn't see or hear anything. It was Svanlaug's father Afgang who did me in when I got rather too close to the Council. But I did get out after Afgang was murdered, and it's true I do know a few things about where we're going."

"I'll bet you do," Leifr muttered, trying to twitch Gedvondur off his shoulder as he flung on his cloak, but the hand hung on fast. "You and Svanlaug had a good long time to lay your plans while I was getting Thurid away from the Wizards' Guild. You're one of the reasons she went after Djofull, besides the trifling business of killing him if she could manage it. You're deeply involved in all this, aren't you, Gedvondur?"

"Certainly. Svanlaug and Afgang were daughter and father, and they were fond of each other. I don't wonder that Svanlaug gave up her status and reputation to avenge his murder. But you must also remember that it was Afgang's opposition to the Council that got him killed."

"But he was a member of the Council, wasn't he?" Leifr demanded. "Therefore he was as corrupt as the rest of them. He killed you, didn't he?"

"I don't regard myself as dead, it may surprise you to know— only temporarily inconvenienced, or condensed. Who do you think it was that convinced him, finally, to revolt against the Council?"

"You, of course, so it's your fault he got killed by Djofull and Sorkvir," Leifr retorted.

"He knew the risks and he lost the wager."

"Now you're wagering with my life, and Thurid's, Starkad's, and Raudbjorn's," Leifr rejoindered. "For nothing but a hand and a carbuncle, you're truly amazing, Gedvondur, in the way you manipulate everyone to your purpose."

"Thank you, but I can't take all the credit. This duel between the Council of Threttan and the Guild has been a long time in coming. Which is why you've got to save your strength, Leifr."

"You weren't thinking about Thurid's strength at Fangelsi-hofn. You nearly killed him, feasting on his flesh the way you did."

"It was for the orb, Leifr. We had to get it."

"You knew about the orb before he did?"

"Certainly. The Dokkur Lavardur requires it before the rule of ice and darkness can be complete. The enemies of the Dokkur Lavardur must have it to prevent the Fimbul Winter, and we've got it."

"I wonder if we shouldn't have left it with the Wizards' Guild," Leifr mused darkly. "It's their duel, not ours. If it weren't for Ljosa—and Svanlaug's avenging Afgang—none of us would be here. But you had to go blundering into Hringurhol, didn't you? I think this entire mess is your fault, Gedvondur."

"Mine and Fridmarr's," Gedvondur admitted blithely. "Although we didn't plan it this way. It should cheer you up to think about the consequences we suffered for our knowledge. Fridmarr was slowly devoured by Sorkvir's poison, and nothing is left of me but a hand and a stone."

"Yes, I feel enormously cheered by the thoughts of what that Council will do to the rest of us if they get half a chance." Leifr grunted. "They've got imaginative methods of destroying their enemies, I must say."

"They've decided," Thurid said suddenly. "The verdict is guilty, and they're going to burn her at the stake in a few hours at midnight."

"Unless someone does something to prevent it," Starkad added worriedly, his eyes upon Leifr.

"Many times I've yearned to get rid of Svanlaug," Leifr said. "Do you think she's guilty, Thurid?"

"She knows Hringurhol inside out, doesn't she?" Starkad

countered before Thurid could do more than open his mouth. "If we let them burn her, how are we going to get inside? I don't know if she's innocent—she's probably not entirely—"

"But we don't know for certain she's not Ulf-hedin, either," Leifr said. "We know she's clever at deceiving anyone she comes up against."

Thurid gave Starkad a shove toward the doorway. "You've always made calf's eyes at Svanlaug," he said. "We're not going to reach a decision with you interrupting us every second. We've got some time to think about it. Nothing will happen before midnight. I'm famished right now; let's pay a visit to Svanlaug's mother. She keeps the best table in the clan, I think."

"Go ahead, I'm not hungry," Leifr said.

Firmly he shook Gedvondur off his arm, still protesting, onto a heap of fleeces, and strode outside to draw some deep breaths and clear his head of the ache Gedvondur had caused. Or maybe it was the headache a snared rabbit felt with the wire tightening around its neck.

Raudbjorn glided into place at his heels, along with the troll-hounds.

"No Ulf-hedins last night, Leifr," Raudbjorn rumbled in grim joy. "Frightened off by *Endalaus Daudi*. And dragon eye. And Raudbjorn."

Leifr stopped to gaze down at the tent village, still dimly visible in the lingering twilight. Small fires winked through open doorways and more people than usual moved from tent to tent. Spreading the word of Svanlaug's guilt, Leifr thought grimly. A lot of the bustling activity centered on the Tjaldi's tent, with people going in and out. Already a pile of wood was gathering in the clearing before the tent in grim preparation for the execution.

"Are we being guarded, Raudbjorn?" Leifr asked in a low voice, scanning the surrounding cliffs behind the tent.

Raudbjorn hoisted his shoulders in a creaking shrug. "No guards, Leifr."

"Where's Starkad, Raudbjorn?"

The thief-taker shrugged, then brightened. "Up on fell. Goat-keepers killing some goats. Plenty of blood."

Leifr sat down on a stone with the troll-hounds lying around his feet, lifting their ears and sniffing the wind with no real suspicion. Raudbjorn squatted on his heels, making company as content and uncomplicated as the troll-hounds, for which Leifr was grateful. He could be as silent and gloomy as he wished, without anyone pestering him with comforting words that failed to cheer and meaningless platitudes that he found irritating. Ljosa was dead, and he wished to brood about it undisturbed.

The hounds had fallen asleep, Kraftig with his chin and paw hooked protectively over Leifr's foot, and Raudbjorn had not moved nor made a sound. The goat slaughterers trooped by with their carcasses lashed to staffs. A pair of Girda's watchmen rode past and the ones they replaced soon came trotting down the mountainside. The twilight darkened to the last stage of deep purple before nightfall rendered everything black, and the night-flying birds skimmed along barely above the surface of the ground, hunting insects.

Slowly Raudbjorn raised one arm to point at something in the ravine below, voicing a grunt to get Leifr's attention. Someone was walking along slowly, leading two horses. The troll-hounds raised their heads, sniffed the air, and wagged their tails in recognition.

"Starkad," Raudbjorn rumbled with a worried note of premonition in his tone.

Leifr cursed under his breath and leaped to his feet.

"Starkad!" he called softly. "Idiot! He doesn't hear me! He's going to rescue Svanlaug!"

The shadowy form of Starkad slunk away toward the Tjaldi's tent, skirting the rings of firelight surrounding the nearest tents. Leifr went after him, with the troll-hounds sniffing interestedly at the ground. In a rocky interval, Leifr touched a dark spot and found it wet. A quick touch of his tongue told him it was blood.

"That fool!" he muttered to Raudbjorn, hurrying on.

Chapter 20

❖◆❖◆❖◆❖◆❖◆❖◆❖◆❖◆❖◆❖◆❖◆❖◆❖◆❖◆❖◆❖◆❖◆❖

Svanlaug's prison was the bathhouse, a stout little building of stone and turf with a heavy door, now barred and locked from the outside. Starkad was prying ineffectually at the bar with his old sword when he heard the approach of the troll-hounds, who bounded around him gladly.

"What are you doing?" Leifr demanded furiously. "Do you have any idea what could happen if we get caught here behind their flags? Do you think Girda and her lot would hesitate to cut your throat if they thought it necessary?"

"I don't care," Starkad said, "I'm not going to let them burn her!"

"Leifr!" the voice of Svanlaug called from behind the mossy planks. "Did they truly decide I was guilty? You don't believe it, do you? You should know I'm not an Ulf-hedin! Please help me get out, Leifr."

Leifr put his hand on the stout door. It looked heavy enough to keep a raging Ulf-hedin confined. On the doorstep sat the head of a freshly killed goat. To Starkad he said, "Get rid of that thing. It only supports their suspicion that the Ulf-hedin are her allies. Which they might be, for all we know. She's certainly done a clever job of leading us right into the jaws of the Council of Threttan, if she is one of them."

"She's not!" Starkad spat. "How can you say that, after all she's done to help us?"

"Leifr," Raudbjorn rumbled warningly, pointing with his chin toward the clearing where the wood was heaped up. "People coming. Almost midnight."

"We've got to hurry," Starkad pleaded. "Once that flame touches her, she'll perish."

297

"Leifr!" Raudbjorn rumbled, plucking at his halberd with his callused thumb.

Something fluttered and flapped noisily around on the roof of the bathhouse. A small owl with a prey of some sort hopped to the edge of the turves and uttered a shrill protesting screech. Its eyes gleamed in the faint light as it glared at them. Gripping its prey in one foot, it opened its beak and hissed at them with a menacing ruffling of its feathers. Then with another piercing screech, it launched itself off the roof and flew away on silent wings.

"A warning!" Raudbjorn growled.

"A spy, you mean," Leifr answered. "I'll bet it was Thurid, keeping his eye on us."

"It was just a screech owl," Starkad said. "There's hundreds of them everywhere. Listen, we can open this door if we find something to pry with."

The flap of the Tjaldi's tent opened, spilling a wedge of ruddy light into the dark. A cloaked figure stepped into the light warily. Behind, a group of women pressed forward, peering into the darkness.

"Who is out there?" an imperious voice called. "No one is allowed to approach the prisoner!"

Raudbjorn stepped forward into the light with a threatening growl, and the women retreated a step with an excited murmur among themselves like the hiss of wind preceding a storm.

"The outlanders!" they murmured angrily.

"You are wrong in your condemnation of Svanlaug," Leifr said. "She's not the Ulf-hedin among you, and we don't intend to let her die for it."

A torch flared with a greenish light, revealing the face of Ulfrin, holding up a staff.

"Your loyalty is commendable," she said coolly, "and I would have been rather astonished if you had given her up without a quarrel. It's so human of you to make this pitiful attempt—but useless. I fear my sister must die to be purged of the Ulf-hedin stain. Once the eitur has been drunk, there is no returning."

"You have no real proof," Starkad said. "Show us her wolf skin and belt. Let us see her transformed. And she must have eitur to survive once she has tasted it. Have you seen a bottle of it about her?''

"All that is variable," Ulfrin said. "She may not be a fully committed Ulf-hedin. She may have teachers who are showing her the way to power gradually. Do you think that the highest leaders of the Ulf-hedin are mindless addicts to eitur? How could that possibly be?''

"We wish to speak with the Tjaldi," Leifr said. "Even a condemned person has the right to an appeal.''

"The Tjaldi is in seclusion," one of the women behind Ulfrin said. "Mourning the death of one of the clan's daughters. The decision went against her, and she must not show her face until her shame is over. For the next three days, Ulfrin is the one we recognize as Tjaldi.''

Ulfrin inclined her head slightly. "To show my generosity and compassion, I shall forgive you outlanders your breach of propriety. Return to your tent beyond the poles and nothing more will be said.''

"Compassion?'' Leifr repeated. "Svanlaug is your own sister. How can you burn your own flesh and blood?''

"I am pure," said Ulfrin. "My vision is completely unobstructed by the ties of loyalty, vanity, ignorance, and all the other encumbrances the rest of you are subject to. I see what must be done to protect my clan, no matter how personally painful it might be. Do you think this is not a sacrifice for me? Of course it is, but the clan will be much better for it. You may go now and trust to my superior wisdom in this matter.''

"Where is the old Tjaldi?'' Starkad demanded. "I want to speak to her. She'll listen to reason.''

"She has no authority for three days," Ulfrin said. "She argued mightily for Svanlaug, but the clanswomen have ruled her down. Svanlaug must die.''

"You're her sister!'' Starkad flared. "Don't you feel any loyalty for her, any feeling at all?''

"I am grieving also for my sister's folly," Ulfrin said. "As young Tjaldi, I cannot permit my true feelings to show. I can admire your blind, human friendship, but as I told you, I am completely pure of any taint of prejudice. Though at times the burden of it is nearly unendurable, I am very nearly a perfect being. For that reason alone, I will forgive you your human folly if you'll oblige and take yourselves again beyond the poles. I am really being very kind to you in your ignorance. Normally, you should be killed for this presumption.''

Leifr met the steely stare of the clanswomen standing behind Svanlaug and did not doubt Ulfrin's words.

"Very well, we will retreat,'' he said quietly. "Come on, Starkad.''

He had to grip Starkad's arm and half drag him away, protesting furiously. Raudbjorn clumped after them with an unhappy moan rumbling deep in his chest. Leifr did not speak until they were well beyond the forbidden line drawn by the warning poles.

"How could you just let her die?'' Starkad demanded passionately, yanking his arm free of Leifr's grasp. "She came alone all the way from Djofullhol to find us! Are you afraid she's going to take some of your glory? She—''

"Hush,'' Leifr said impatiently. "There's no time for all your squalling. Can't you see there's no reasoning with a person who thinks she can't do anything wrong?''

"Ulfrin's worse than Thurid,'' Starkad admitted. "What are we going to do, Leifr? It's almost midnight.''

"Saddle the rest of our horses,'' Leifr said. "And don't breathe a word to Thurid yet. Come to the tent as soon as you're ready.''

Leifr returned to the guest tent and found it empty. He stationed himself where he had a good view of the Tjaldi's tent, the bathhouse, and the heap of wood growing around the stake. He also had a good view of Thurid when he came puffing up the hill to the tent, with the blue orb casting a lighted trail before him.

Thurid halted before Leifr and thrust the point of his staff into the ground. His eyes blazed with a fanatic gleam and his sparse beard and hair were bristling with rage.

"How could you have interfered so blatantly in something you don't understand?'' Thurid demanded furiously, keeping his voice to a low sputtering hiss.

"I understand it perfectly,'' Leifr returned, keeping his temper in hand with difficulty. "They're going to burn Svanlaug, and she's innocent. I won't permit that to happen."

"I suppose you've got some mad scheme for rescuing her?" Thurid demanded.

"It's better than doing nothing," Leifr said, "which is what you intend, if I'm seeing correctly."

"You must not interfere," Thurid said. "I have the situation under control."

"What are you going to do?" Leifr demanded.

"It's already done," Thurid said. "If you allow it to work. Swear to me you'll remain in this tent and not attempt to interfere with what the clanswomen will do."

"I won't swear," said Leifr. "The time for talking is over, Thurid. The old Tjaldi is powerless for three days, and you can't reason with Ulfrin."

"You have no idea what I can accomplish," Thurid said. "I'm going to go talk to her, and you mustn't stir outside this tent. Where's that buffoon Starkad? You must keep him out of the way also, as well as Raudbjorn."

"You can't go down there alone, Thurid," Leifr said. "Those women with Ulfrin were angry enough when we trespassed. When it comes to anything to do with their clan, they get completely savage."

"Nonsense," said Thurid. "They'll listen to the voice of reason."

"They won't. They might listen to force, if we go down there together, you with the orb and I with the sword, and take Svanlaug whether they like it or not."

"You may stay here and watch," Thurid said, placing the staff and the orb across a low table. "Don't touch it, just watch the images inside." Then he divested his satchel of a small black vole, eyes shut, with its little pink paws clasped over its breast, apparently dead. He stroked it a moment with one small finger and placed it beside the staff.

"This little creature is also highly valuable. Guard it with your life, Leifr. I shall now go down there and prove to you that the voice of reason will be heard no matter how thick the opposition. Force does not always carry the day, Leifr. That's one lesson you've never been able to learn, but being a Scipling, you can't expect yourself to be otherwise and neither can I." He swept his cloak around him and turned toward the tent below, now brilliantly lit by torches. "If that idiot Starkad returns, keep him out of my way."

"Thurid, it won't work," Leifr protested, following Thurid a few paces.

Thurid whirled around and pointed back to the tent, as if Leifr were an unwanted hound. "Stay!" he commanded. "Dvelja!"

Leifr halted, his feet rooted to the spot at the utterance of the Rhbu word, but the rest of him blazed with fury at Thurid's presumptuous treatment. He cursed and swore as Thurid strode away jauntily toward the tent.

As he had predicted, Thurid was met with considerable opposition. The moment he passed the warning poles, six large women came out of the tent to confront him. Leifr could not understand their words, but their voices were unmistakably quarreling. To do him credit, Thurid did not lose his confident stance until four more women came out of the tent and overwhelmed him with a large fishing net and unceremoniously bundled him away into the Tjaldi's tent.

Leifr strained desperately at the invisible bonds Thurid had imposed upon him. He found he could edge backward into the tent, where the orb and the little dead animal lay side by side on the table. He prodded the vole warily and found it still quite flexible for a dead thing. Suspiciously he gazed into the smoky depths of the orb, seeing faces swirling past in a giddy fashion that made him back away from it hastily. Fuming inwardly, he paced around the tent like a caged wolf and returned to peer out the flap toward the scene below.

The yard before the Tjaldi's tent was filled with clanswomen, carrying torches or lanterns, gathered in a silent ring around the stake and the encircling wood. A slow procession was winding its way from the bathhouse, with Svanlaug in the midst of two files of shrouded women. She walked steadily straight ahead, without so much as turning her head or speaking a word.

Leifr paced about the tent with increasing energy. Each time he reached the spot where Thurid had spoken the word "dvelja," he found he could not take a step past it. Passing the orb again, he glanced down and saw the image of Thurid, still trussed up like a goose in the net.

"So much for the voice of reason!" Leifr muttered. "Ho, Thurid, can you hear me? Can you see me?"

Thurid was looking straight at Leifr, his face distorted by the glassy ripples of the stone. His lips were moving and he looked dreadfully earnest, but Leifr could hear nothing. Nor could he see what words Thurid's lips were forming. Desperate and disgusted, he picked up the black vole and hefted its negligible weight in the palm of his hand. It was the inconvenient sort of thing Thurid would be hauling around as part of his magical apparatus, and now he was expected to be responsible for it. He shoved it into his belt pouch with a snort of revulsion.

Tentatively he picked up the staff with his other hand, feeling a shiver of temerity tingling in his scalp. Gingerly he rested the tip on the earth, feeling sudden uneasy spurts of power crackling within him like short flickers of summer lightning until he removed it from contact with the earth. Holding the staff, he stood rooted to the same spot again, still cursing and watching helplessly as Svanlaug's executioners bound her to the stake. Like a fly in honey, he struggled vainly to lift his feet.

They all gathered solemnly around, and Ulfrin stood before them reciting a long litany of Svanlaug's supposed crimes, with the others chiming in at regular intervals as if it were a ritual chant. When it was done, they looked at Svanlaug, waiting in silence for her to speak, but she stared straight ahead and made no sound. The first stack of wood and brush was put to the torch, and the flames climbed skyward. Lashed to the stake, Svanlaug made no move. Other piles were lit, and as the heat increased, the circle of clanswomen retreated.

With a sudden crashing of underbrush, Starkad rode out of a ravine behind the tent, coming to a sliding halt. Raudbjorn followed closely, leading three horses tied together in a train.

"Leifr, it's going to be too late!" Starkad said. "Come on, we've got to save her!"

"I can't move!" Leifr growled furiously. "Thurid's put a binding on me! He thought he could reason with them!"

Starkad flung himself off his horse. "A binding! Can't you get out of it somehow?"

"No, you fool!" Leifr retorted. "That's why it's a binding! Of my own will, I can't move from this spot unless Thurid releases me! You'll have to save Svanlaug yourself! You've also got to rescue Thurid. Those women have got him tied up in the tent!"

"I can't!" Starkad shrilled in desperation. "You've got the Rhbu sword! You're the one who takes the risks!"

Leifr dug the point of the staff into the earth and glowered into the blue orb, where Thurid's face was swimming around like a trapped fish.

"Thurid!" he bellowed at it in a voice that could have carried to Thurid's actual ears inside the tent. "Let me out of this!"

Thurid's face looked directly at him, fishily distorted by the crystal's curved surface and clearly displeased. His lips moved in a single word, and Leifr stumbled forward and nearly fell on his face. He tossed the staff to Starkad and in a fluid rush hurled himself into the saddle of the nearest horse. Over one shoulder he shouted, "You get to Thurid! Meet us in the meadow straight above!"

He charged down the hillside with the troll-hounds in hot pursuit, gaining speed with every stride until the horse felt as if it would somersault at any moment, and burst into the clearing around the Tjaldi's tent with a warning yell. The clanswomen scattered before the barking rush of the hounds, clearing his approach to the fires burning in a circle around Svanlaug. After drawing the sword, he leaned out and scattered the blazing branches and sticks to clear a path, sending his horse plunging wildly into the center of the fires. Gasping for breath in the heated air, he reined the horse around tightly in a circle as he slashed at the cords binding Svanlaug to the stake. Almost choking, he hauled her limp body across the pommel of the saddle and plunged away into the cool darkness beyond the fire where he could breathe. In true warrior style, he stopped and turned around to offer the enemy one last taunt. Starkad and Raudbjorn were clear of the tent, with Thurid thrown over the back of his horse, still enmeshed in the net and sputtering furiously at such undignified treatment.

The clanswomen recovered from their fright swiftly, and one

of them was sounding an alarm on a horn to summon Girda and her warriors.

"Away, Kraftig!" Leifr pointed, and the hounds sped away after Starkad and Raudbjorn. The most protection must accompany the orb, even if it meant leaving him to face the Bergmal clan.

They swept toward him with an angry outcry, but a sharp command from Ulfrin halted them.

She leaned upon her staff and smiled grimly. "Don't waste your time in pursuit, sisters," she said. "The fire has done its work."

The clanswomen stared at Leifr in stony silence. A few whispered and pointed.

Leifr steadied the limp weight of Svanlaug, glancing down at her uneasily. To his horror, her face was dissolving like melted wax, perhaps exposed too long to the heat of the fire. Her entire body felt soft and boneless. A pale mass was sliding down the horse's shoulder and dripping onto the ground. Even her clothing was crumbling away like flakes of soot, and the long strands of her black hair were rapidly turning the crisp brown of corpse hair.

Leifr quickly dismounted and laid the disintegrating body on the ground, horrified but unable to stop watching the Dokkalfar death process. The clanswomen also gathered around, their quarrel forgotten now, many of them openly sorrowing. The body very soon lost its human configuration and dissolved into a shapeless puddle of something that looked like tallow rendering over a slow fire, with patches of fabric and hair mixed in. A sigh of relief rippled through the watching women.

"There, it's over," Ulfrin said in a solemn, heavy tone. "The threat to our clan and our posterity is finished."

Leifr turned away and got onto his horse. No one moved to stop him; very few even turned their heads to look at him as he rode slowly away. One old woman on the fringe of the crowd reached out and patted his knee consolingly and whispered, "It was a good attempt, young man, but you were too slow."

Ahead in the darkness, already beginning to thin somewhat, he heard the mournful baying of the troll-hounds coming from the direction of the meadow where Ljosa had died. With a feeling like lead in his chest, Leifr jog-trotted his horse in that direction and found the others waiting for him in the same clearing where he had fought the Ulf-hedin. Thurid held up his flaring staff as a beacon. In a rare show of compassion, he said nothing about Svanlaug's fate.

"I don't think they'll come after us," he said. "I don't relish the idea of picking our way over these crags and fissures by night, so I suggest we stay right where we are until we get a bit more daylight."

"What about Girda?" Starkad questioned uneasily.

"There's no sign of her," Thurid said. "I have a feeling they won't come up here to bother us, after what happened to those Ulf-hedin."

"As you wish," Leifr grunted, dismounting and wrapping himself up in his cloak to spend the rest of the night watching and listening and thinking his own dissatisfied thoughts about himself and the life that had found him.

In a few hours there was sufficient light for traveling. Looking back at the cliffs of Bergmal receding behind them, Leifr saw a string of riders slowly traversing a high ridge, looking down upon them as they descended into the valley. Girda and her warriors, he thought, but they did not offer to pursue.

Riding ahead, Leifr filled his lungs with a great draft of air and expelled it in a cloud of vapor. It was good to be on the move again. Traveling put an edge on one's sensibilities, and his forced inactivity had made him feel the loss of Ljosa all the more keenly. The lust for adventure was as habit-forming as eitur, and just as dangerous, but it kept him from thinking about painful subjects.

They traveled the entire day without sighting another human creature, crossing the valley and again ascending into the high country where the season had scarcely advanced beyond late winter. At twilight they stopped for the night in a rocky place where a tall skarp sheltered them somewhat from the wind and the occasional blast of snow particles. The ground was almost dry, and the horses were able to forage for early-spring tuffets of grass among the rocks and melting snowbanks. The rivers of runoff kept up a hopeful gurgling until late at night, when they froze over again and were silenced.

Thurid sat beside the fire, hands laced together, and dozed comfortably while Starkad picketed the horses and Leifr and Raudbjorn divided up the watches for the night. The blue orb was safely muzzled beneath a bag, and Gedvondur was basking on a warm rock like a complacent toad.

"Leifr, have you still got that little vole I left you?" Thurid inquired suddenly as Leifr crouched down to huddle near the meager fire.

Leifr removed the thing from his belt pouch. "A good thing it didn't start smelling in there," he grumbled.

"A very good thing," Thurid agreed, placing the vole on a flat rock and unwrapping the orb.

Leifr glared with scant approval. "Every time you unwrap that thing, it causes trouble," he said.

"I fear you're going to prove yourself a prophet," Thurid said, evidently basking in some unnatural glow of affability. He spat upon one hand and pulled a rune wand out of his sleeve pocket. "Now be perfectly silent," he admonished Starkad, who sat down and watched with hollow-eyed disinterest as Thurid began reciting the runes on the stick and sketching images in the air with the orb.

To Leifr's disconcertment, the dead vole began seething and smoking as if it were being cooked. He glanced at Thurid, puzzled and disgusted, and thus missed gazing directly into the explosion that suddenly flared only inches away from him. He leaped up, eyes full of dust, wildly disheveled by the blast of released wind. The troll-hounds leaped away with a startled salvo of barking and snarling.

Thurid was cackling and prancing around through the clouds of dust and mist in exultation. In a total excess of good spirits he cuffed Starkad on both ears and tweaked Raudbjorn's nose.

"I did it, I did it!" he declared. "Bless that old fox Vonbrigdi! A triple shape shift, and I did it myself!"

He stooped over to inspect his work. Leifr sneezed and rubbed the grit out of one eye, not believing what he was seeing. A human form lay on the ground, not a stunned Starkad as he had first suspected. It was Svanlaug, rolled into a protective ball with her hood drawn up over her head. She flung back the hood and sat up, her freed hair catching the wind like a horse's tail.

"Svanlaug, how did you feel during the spell?" asked Thurid. "Were you asleep or awake? Could you hear voices?"

"It's about time," she said hoarsely, getting stiffly to her feet. She stretched and yawned, shivering in the chill wind. "I feel I've been asleep for a long time. I wouldn't have let you talk me into this, wizard, except that I didn't want to get burned."

Leifr gaped at her and at Thurid. Starkad rubbed one of his cuffed ears and grinned in ridiculous delight, much like the hounds who were wagging around Svanlaug and trying to lick her hands and face in welcome.

"The leikfang spell," Leifr said in a sudden burst of revelation. "Like what Vonbrigdi did. You tried it, too?"

"Tried and succeeded," Thurid said haughtily.

"You've me to thank for your rescue," Starkad said. "I couldn't get anyone else to do it."

"Bah!" Thurid said. "I was planning it the entire time, in spite of all your interference. If you'd listened to me, it would have been slick and clean, instead of that ridiculous and daring rescue of Leifr's."

"You might have told us what you were doing," Leifr snapped. "I could have been attacked and killed."

"Tut-tut," Thurid said. "You could have gotten away somehow. I'll admit, I didn't expect to be seized. Some women do find my charm irresistible, it seems."

"Like those slimy nisses of Kerling-tjorn and Alof the half troll?" Leifr asked with a sly grin. "They would have liked to keep you around forever. Especially Finna."

"You needn't have mentioned them in particular," Thurid snapped, stalking away in a huff, but the effect of his departure was spoiled by Gedvondur swinging on the end of his sleeve and scuttling up his arm like a spider.

"I liked the fires best about Bergmal," Gedvondur said from Thurid's shoulder. "It was good to get warm again, wasn't it? Of course, Svanlaug, you missed your greatest opportunity to get good and toasty."

Svanlaug glowered at him. "It's not something to joke about!" she snapped. "They would have burned me alive, thanks to the lies of my dear sister! Now I've got something she's jealous about, and she won't hear of my outshining her in the least way.

Sverting though she may be, she's been spoiled by too much indulgence and not enough discipline. If I had the training of her, I'd send her on a journey such as the one I'm on. That would teach her.''

"Teach her to stay home where it's comfortable and safe, perhaps," Leifr added. "The world doesn't need any more of her ilk running around and causing trouble. She would have killed her own sister.''

"Ulfrin always was insufferable," Svanlaug said, "but now she's intolerable. I'm going to teach her a lesson she won't ever forget, as soon as I'm done with the Council of Threttan. I may now be an outlaw, but I'll never forget my duties to my clan, and one of them will be the humbling of Ulfrin. If she is to be a Sverting and a Tjaldi, she must learn to use her head and her heart together, like our old Tjaldi does. There was never a woman so wise and kind. If she had sentenced me to die, I would have died gladly, knowing she had knowledge beyond mine.''

"Speaking of your Tjaldi," Thurid said, feeling in his sleeve pockets among a handful of miscellaneous trash and producing a small scroll, "she sent you this, signing you over to your father's clan to study sorcery. I hope they appreciate it. You'll be a dreadful student, I fear.''

Svanlaug's eyes widened and she seized the scroll from his fingers. "I'm free! She released me! I'm no longer tied by heredity to something I hate! From this day on, I have begun a new life!''

"A better one, I hope," Leifr said, a trifle bitterly as he thought of Ljosa's life, spent so uselessly. "We risked our lives for it, and it probably won't be the last time.''

Svanlaug tucked away the precious scroll in her belt pouch, too pleased to rise to his baiting. "Thank you," she said. "All of you, for everything. You are true friends.''

"Bah!" Thurid grunted, blinking in embarrassment. "That's enough blather. We're not done yet, so there's no use congratulating ourselves. Hringurhol lies before us, and the Council of Threttan.''

"How much farther to Hringurhol?" Starkad asked.

Svanlaug pointed due east. "Two more days and we shall be out of the mountains and into the valley where the Svart-strom

River cuts off any casual contact with this side of the mountains. You don't get across the river except by merchant barge from Laglendi-hlid, or unless you're sent for by the Council. As Afgangsdottir, I came this way many times.''

Svanlaug paced about restlessly, stretching her stiff limbs and inhaling deep breaths of air. Leifr huddled by the fire and watched her narrowly, wondering if she were hearing some sort of secret Ulf-hedin call, and if there were a wolf cape stowed away someplace where she could get to it. Gedvondur perched on a warm rock near Thurid's foot, where he could communicate, but not too near the blue orb. Gedvondur and Svanlaug and Afgang—Leifr shook his head, not liking to think about such a combination, especially when he added Fridmarr to the list.

On the next day they reached the crest of the mountains that overlooked the valley of the Svart-strom, winding like a giant black snake, carving a chasm through the emerald green of Skarpsey to its black heart beneath. Two tributaries cascaded down the craggy mountains on the far side, forming natural barriers on the north and south of a large plateau overlooking the river.

Svanlaug pointed to the plateau. ''There is Hringurhol, on the edge. It was the fortress of a powerful warlord, Hringur Gold-Giver. A thousand men owed him allegiance, and he gave gold to anyone who swore fealty. He kept the peace for many years. But the Council conquered him, the gold ceased, and so did the peace.''

Leifr surveyed the river, the cliffs, and the walls of Hringurhol rising above it. Behind the fortress walls, settlements and roadways dotted the green plain.

''How do we get across the river and into the fortress?'' he asked.

''They are expecting us,'' Svanlaug said. ''They want nothing more than they want Heldur's orb safely across the water.''

Thurid snorted softly and patted the muzzled orb, which was smoking noxiously in its confining bag. ''They only think that's what they want. They'll soon change their minds.''

They turned their horses' heads toward the faint downward path leading them toward Hringurhol, Thurid leading the way with the staff held in the crook of one arm, followed by Starkad and Svanlaug. Leifr rode behind Svanlaug, where he could watch her, and behind them all rode Raudbjorn, benevolently scanning their backtrail for signs of their enemies. The halberd riding on his shoulder did not bode well for those enemies, were they audacious enough to mount an attack. Soon the throaty roar of the river rose to their ears, and they felt its clammy mist on their faces and smelled its ancient mossy breath.

Heldur's orb burned away its muffling bag and blazed with an intense light.

"You'd better cover it up," Svanlaug said nervously. "No sense in giving them so much forewarning we're coming."

"No, leave it uncovered," Thurid said. "As the great and wise Gray One Eldri said, this carbuncle is coming home."

Here ends *The Dragon's Carbuncle*.
In *The Lord of Chaos*, to be published soon, Leifr, Thurid, Starkad, and Svanlaug face Sorkvir again and find far more—both evil and good—than they ever expected.

ABOUT THE AUTHOR

Elizabeth Boyer began planning her writing career during junior high school in her rural Idaho hometown. She read almost anything the Bookmobile brought, and learned a great love for Nature and wilderness. Science fiction in large quantities led her to Tolkien's writings, which developed a great curiosity about Scandinavian folklore. Ms. Boyer is Scandinavian by descent and hopes to visit the homeland of her ancestors. She has a B.A. from Brigham Young University, at Provo, Utah, in English literature.

After spending several years in the Rocky Mountain wilderness of central Utah, she and her husband now live in a log home in Utah's Oquirrh mountains. Sharing their home are two daughters and an assortment of animals. Ms. Boyer enjoys horseback riding, cross-country skiing, and classical music.

Enjoy the Wonder and Wizardry of
Elizabeth H. Boyer